W9-CAL-752

WOOD SPRITES

BAEN BOOKS by WEN SPENCER

THE ELFHOME SERIES

Tinker

Wolf Who Rules

Elfhome

Wood Sprites

ALSO BY WEN SPENCER

Eight Million Gods

Endless Blue

WOOD SPRITES

WEN SPENCER

WOOD SPRITES

This is a work of fiction. All the characters and events portrayed in this book are fictional, and any resemblance to real people or incidents is purely coincidental.

A Baen Books Original

Baen Publishing Enterprises
P.O. Box 1403
Riverdale, NY 10471
www.baen.com

ISBN: 978-1-4767-3671-6

Cover art by Stephen Hickman

First Baen printing, September 2014

Distributed by Simon & Schuster
1230 Avenue of the Americas
New York, NY 10020

Library of Congress Cataloging-in-Publication Data

Spencer, Wen.
  Wood sprites / Wen Spencer.
      pages cm — (Elfhome ; 4)
   ISBN 978-1-4767-3671-6 (hardback)
1. Twin sisters—Fiction. 2. Gifted persons—Fiction. 3. Imaginary places—Fiction.
4. Families—Fiction. 5. Imaginary wars and battles—Fiction. I. Title.
  PS3619.P4665W88 2014
  813'.6—dc23

                                                  2014020008

10 9 8 7 6 5 4 3 2 1

Pages by Joy Freeman (www.pagesbyjoy.com)
Printed in the United States of America

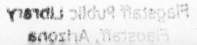

Acknowledgments

Books are not the effort of just one person.
Many thanks to the people who gave me a
helping hand during the course of this book.

Dan Kosak
Brian Chee
Andy Bradford
Bonnie Funk
Kevin Geiselman
Ruth L. Heller, DVM
Nancy Janda
Laurel Jamieson Lohrey
Sue Petroulas
Hope Erica Ring, M.D.
June Drexler Robertson
David Stein
N. A. Young

Aaron, Becky, Katie, and Josh Wollerton for being
willing subjects of science experiments for fiction.

The Barflies at Baen's Bar who were willing to
figure out exactly what I said thirteen years ago.

And especially Traci Scroggins, who fought the good fight.

To my sister, Kathy Sue Flower

Who is eighteen months older and yet has always been shorter than me. She wore dresses that matched mine. She shared long summers of secret forts and rambling adventures. She slept in the top bunk of our bed year in and year out. Because of her, I have an inkling of what it is to be a twin.

1: WHAT'S IN YOUR EASTER BASKET?

Louise Georgina Mayer learned many important life lessons the week before her ninth birthday. The first was that flour was indeed explosive. The second was not to experiment with explosives indoors—or at least not in a small wooden playhouse that doubled as a film studio. The third was that adults—firemen, EMTs, policemen, her parents—liked to state the obvious when trying to make a point. Yes, she realized that they'd miscalculated while still airborne—thank you very much. The fourth was that her twin sister rocked—Jillian sat there with blood streaming down her face and managed a wide-eyed story of innocence that pinned the entire event on their Barbie dolls. Fifth was that people believed the stupidest things if you delivered the story while bleeding.

Sixth was that her parents were liars.

"That can't be right," she told the emergency room nurse who was applying the bracelet to her wrist that claimed she was blood-type AB. The man blithely ignored her, so she said it louder and clearer. "That's not right."

"Hm? What isn't right, sweetie?" the nurse asked although by his tone he still wasn't paying attention.

"I'm blood-type O," Louise stated firmly. She was going to be a geneticist someday. Maybe. A geneticist or an animal trainer or a circus performer. Unlike Jillian, Louise couldn't decide what she wanted to do with her life. Jillian wanted to write, act, and

1

direct big-budget action movies, hence the entire flour explosion. According to their alibi, Barbie was merely pinned under her pink convertible in a blizzard. In truth, the planned small explosion was special effects for Soulful Ember, queen of the elves, using magic to defeat an army of man-eating black-willow trees. It was supposed to be the climax of episode twenty-four in their partially accurate series chronicling the history of Earth's twin sister, Elfhome.

"Type O?" The nurse became focused. He picked up a tester, and there was a sudden sharp pain in her finger. The machine beeped, and he shook his head. "No, you're AB positive. See. Here, let's do your sister."

He made Jillian wince, and the machine beeped again. The display said: AB+.

Which was completely impossible. Both of her parents were blood-type O, which was amazing because they were such different people. Their father was tall, weedy thin, Nordic pale, and hopelessly nerdy looking. Their mother was an equally tall African-American warrior queen who struggled daily not to be anything but solid built. Two type-O people made a boring genetic grid: O across the board with the only possible outcome being O. Louise and Jillian weren't identical twins, which made it even more impossible.

"I always said that we were adopted," Jillian said once the nurse left them alone. While their dusky skin could be a blending of their two parents, the twins' silky straight brown hair was too well behaved to be from either of their parents, and it was becoming apparent that they were never going to be tall.

"We can't be adopted," Louise said. "There's that icky video of us being born. All that screaming and blood and everything. That was Mom saying the S and F words."

Jillian giggled. Their parents had planned to watch the birth videos—again—on their birthday until Jillian reminded them how many times their mother cursed while giving birth. Luckily their parents hadn't mastered video editing to the point that they could simply erase out the swear words.

"Maybe we got it wrong on how blood type works," Jillian said.

"It's not that complicated." Louise sketched out the four boxes on the sheet of the bed with her fingernail. "At least—it didn't seem that complicated."

"Their donor cards are wrong?" Jillian suggested.

Louise shook her head. "They're universal donors. The blood bank wouldn't get that wrong. It would be bad."

However they considered it, the facts just didn't seem to add up.

Eventually their parents swept in, smelling of smoke and radiating concern.

"What were you doing in your playhouse that made it explode?" their mother asked. She cupped Jillian's chin with her elegant dark hands and made a sound of dismay over the stitches at the edge of her scalp.

"Honey," their father said in the tone that said he thought their mother was being silly. As they got older, they were realizing that their father was child-naïve at times.

"George, don't baby them. They're too intelligent to be babied."

Jillian got all wide-eyed innocent again, which didn't work nearly as well without the streaming blood, but the stitches helped. "All we were doing was playing with our dolls. Barbie had spun out in the driving snow—"

"The flour and the sifter and the fan?" their mother asked.

"It was a blizzard," Louise explained since Jillian was losing ground. "The flour was snow."

"What you did was very dangerous." Their father fell back to truth number three: stating the obvious.

"We had no idea—" Louise started

Jillian kicked her and gave her a look that said that it was the wrong thing to do. Jillian was much better at lying, so Louise shut up. "We have no idea what happened. Why did our playhouse blow up?"

"Flour can explode when it fills up the air like that," their father explained patiently. "Don't ever play with flour like that again."

Their mother knew them better. "Or anything like flour. Baby powder. Corn starch. Sawdust."

"Where would they get sawdust?" their father asked. He might not know them, but he knew their neighborhood. Sawdust had proved impossible to find within an easy walk of their house.

"Non-dairy creamer. Baking soda. Sugar." Obviously their mother had spent time researching dust explosions before this conversation. "Anything like flour. Understand?"

They nodded meekly while Jillian bit down on a "darn it."

"Mom." Louise held out her wrist with the plastic bracelet on it. "Why are we AB positive when both you and Dad are O? Isn't that impossible?"

Both of their parents flinched as if struck.

"Baby, that's very complicated," their father started.

"If we don't tell them," their mother murmured, "they'll only guess—and they'll probably guess wrong."

Their parents gazed at each other as if having a long, silent discussion. Finally their father sighed. "Okay, we'll tell them. Babies, we wanted to have children very, very much, but no matter how hard we tried, for a long time, we couldn't. We started to look into adoption when I was offered my position at Cryobank. It's an embryo bank—umm—where—where people who—umm..."

"It's like an adoption service." Their mother took up the explanation. "But instead of babies that have already been born, it's babies that haven't been born yet."

They frowned at their parents until their father added, "It's like Easter, but instead of chicken eggs in your basket, you get—umm—fertilized human eggs."

Their mother covered her face, which meant they weren't to listen to anything their father said. It also meant that they probably weren't going to get a better explanation.

"Soooo, Mommy put these Easter eggs into her tummy and had us," Louise said.

"But they weren't Mommy's Easter eggs. They were someone else's," Jillian said.

"Yes, exactly," their father said.

"Close enough," their mother mumbled into her hands still covering her face.

Louise sighed. They were going to have to research this when they got home.

The seventh life lesson of the day was that when you're nine years old (minus one week) and you blow up your playhouse while you're in it, every adult in the world thinks a night at the hospital is a good idea. Thus they weren't able to investigate their conception until the next morning.

"Embryo bank" turned out to be the keywords. Apparently, when couples went through in vitro fertilization, multiple embryos were created but not used. It came from the fact that they were working at the cellular level with human reproductive systems already not operating properly. More eggs than needed were released, and then flooded with sperm. Because the failure rate was high, it made sense to invite everyone to the party and hope for the best.

While the information answered one question—that of their blood type—it raised dozens of others. They took a carton of chicken eggs out of the refrigerator and set it on the counter. There were eight eggs in the package, as their mother had made four soft-boiled eggs yesterday morning.

"We're the leftovers." Jillian poked at the remaining eggs.

So far they hadn't been able to determine how many eggs were fertilized at once, only that normally up to four were recommended per each implantation.

Louise took out a marker and put eyes and mouth on one egg and then the letter L underneath. "L for Louise. J for Jillian." She went to draw on a second egg, but Jillian snatched the pen out of her hand.

"I want to do mine." Jillian cradled the egg in her hand and carefully wrote out her name and not only did a face but hair.

"According to Wikipedia, they do four embryos per implantation because they expect a high failure rate." Louise found another marker and put Xs for eyes and a squiggle mouth on two of the eggs to indicate that they were failed embryos. "That means there's another four embryos."

"Do you really think they made twelve just like a carton of chicken eggs?"

"Well . . . they keep them in freezers just like chicken eggs."

Jillian put the Jillian-egg back into the carton beside the Louise-egg. "That proves nothing." She tapped the remaining eggs. "These eggs might have never existed. These ones, though . . ." She pointed at the empty cups. "Those eggs existed and were used and were successful—otherwise we wouldn't be leftovers."

Louise rolled the idea around in her head. Their "genetic parents" created a random number of fertilized eggs because they wanted babies. Once they had one or two babies, they didn't want more, so they gave the rest to someone that did: their real parents. Jillian was right; for them to be leftovers, their genetic parents got the babies that they wanted.

"We have sisters," Louise whispered. The possibilities were breathtaking. Two more Louise and Jillian? Did the other Jillian want to create epic movies? Did the other Louise love animals as much as she did? Did she have pets?

"Or brothers," Jillian said. "They could be boys. It's not like we've been cloned."

That was true. Brothers wouldn't be bad; just different. She and Jillian were often mistaken for identical twins because their hair was the same shade of brown and had been the same length prior to the explosion. The fire had singed Louise's ponytail to a short brittle stump that their mother had trimmed even shorter to get rid of the burnt ends. She looked like a boy now.

Louise peered at her reflection in the mirrored side of the toaster. Would their brothers look like her? Were they nine years old, too? Or ten?

"How long to you think we sat in the fridge?" Jillian said. "We are leftovers, after all."

"I don't know." There were reports of pregnancies of embryos that had been stored up to sixteen years. Their sisters could have been teenagers before she and Jillian were born. They could be really old by now—like twenty-one or twenty-two!

Louise decided she liked thinking that their siblings were two girls, exactly their age. What of the other leftovers? Louise took out an egg, pure white, perfectly formed, and considered the possibilities. The others would probably be younger. "I think I would want at least one brother. A baby brother, just learning to talk."

"That would be boring." Jillian picked up one of the unmarked eggs. "I'd rather have a baby sister but one that could talk and walk and act."

Assuming that any other leftovers had actually been used. Louise eyed the egg with slight unease. She knew that she couldn't remember that time between conception and implantation. Despite that, it seemed awful somehow to be stuck frozen at the brink of being alive.

"Do you think they're still in the fridge?" Jillian marked closed eyes on the egg as if it were asleep. A chain of little Zs came from a tiny slack mouth. "Still-unused leftovers?"

"Maybe." How many people wanted other people's Easter eggs, left in the grass after the hunt? Would they stay lost in the darkness, forgotten, until they spoiled?

Louise cradled the egg in her hands. Every Wednesday night their mother would sift through the contents of their refrigerator, sniffing at the suspicious packages, throwing out anything that looked too old. How much time did the unused eggs have left?

Jillian squeaked with alarm and made a wild grab at the egg that had slipped out of her hand. She missed, and it dropped to the floor with a wet splat. Her lip trembled as she fought not to cry.

"Maybe we should ask Mom and Dad to make us baby sisters."

The most important lesson Louise learned a week before her ninth birthday was the hardest one to keep in mind. Sometimes what sounded like a good plan wasn't.

2: THE BEST-LAID PLANS

Their parents had insisted on calling the building in the backyard the girls' "playhouse" despite the fact it was actually a storage shed. Made of dried lumber and asphalt shingles, it had proved to be quite flammable. All that was left was a skeleton of blackened studs. Their father was dismantling it with a reciprocating saw.

"We want to know more," Jillian called to him over the growl of the blade.

"More?" their father echoed. He had soot smeared across his pale cheeks like war paint. On another father, it would probably look cool, but it only made him look silly. The strap on his safety glasses worked his straw-blond hair into spikes, standing up at every conceivable angle. His eyebrows were cocked into an extremely puzzled look. Their mother liked to use his expressions as proof that it was possible to get your face stuck in silly-looking poses. He looked like a startled hedgehog.

"We want to know about our siblings," Louise said.

"Your what?" His mystified look changed to slight panic. He narrowly avoided cutting his left hand with the saw blade and had to turn off the power tool for his own safety.

"Our sisters!" Jillian cried, still at the volume to be heard over the now silent saw.

"And our brother." Odds were that at least one of their siblings would a boy. "We read up on in vitro fertilization. We know that we probably have two or three siblings, if not more."

"We could have dozens!" Jillian cried.

Their father was shaking his head while trying to wave off their questions. "No. No. What are you doing back here? It's dangerous. Go back in the house. You could have been killed in this shed. You were lucky that you weren't trapped in here."

They hadn't been because they'd used an old coffee table as a blast shield. They had stood it on end, its legs against the double doors that opened outward. The explosion had smashed the table through the doorway. They were lucky that the thick legs kept them from being squashed between the two pieces of heavy wood. So far, no one had realized the significance of the heavily charred coffee table out in the middle of the yard.

"Daddy!" Jillian used the ultimate cute attack. "If you had a brother or a sister, wouldn't you want to know?"

Their father melted visibly but remained steadfast. "Yes, I would. I always wanted a brother or sister. But those records are kept confidential. They're secret."

"Why?" Jillian was actually asking why he'd let anything like policy stand in his way. Since he worked at the clinic, it should be easy for him to get the information.

He misunderstood. "It's for our protection. This way, no one can come and... and..."

"And?"

"Get visitation rights for you."

They understood custody battles; several of their classmates had had their lives implode via a divorce. Their situation didn't seem to fit that scenario.

"Why would anyone do that?" Louise asked.

"You and Mom aren't getting divorced, are you?" Jillian asked and did a lip quiver that may or may not have been real.

"No. No. Your mother and I are happy. It's just when people can't have other children, or they have children and lose them in some way, they're desperate enough to use the law to take what really isn't theirs in the first place."

Louise exchanged a glance with Jillian. They hadn't considered "other parents," only "other siblings." "And the law would actually allow that?"

"Yes, honey. The law tries to be fair to everyone, but in trying to cover all the bases, it ends up being grossly unfair to some people. It is possible, even though your mother carried you for nine months and you've been our daughters for nine years, that the court may think the little bit of genetic material we ... we used is enough to warrant someone else rights to you."

The truly frightening thing was that their father always sugar-coated everything. Somehow he never understood that they were constantly growing up; in his mind they were stuck somewhere between the ages of three and four. That he was admitting this much meant there was much more that he wasn't telling them.

Their mother was in full African warrior-queen mode in the laundry room, dealing with her smoke-laden cardigan while she growled at someone on her headset.

"The only exploding car in my backyard is a Barbie Glam Convertible." She shoved the cardigan deeper into the wash water as if thinking about holding someone's head under the suds. It made Louise edge slightly back. Now probably wasn't the best time to talk to their mother.

"I do think that while the demonstrations against the E.I.A. zone expansion are going on that checking for car bombs at the dinner is perfectly reasonable. Anna Desmarais is a complete loon, though, if she thinks my nine-year-olds are terrorists. You tell Taliaferro that if she goes after my girls, I will come down there and set her—" Their mother noticed them standing at the door and winced. "Short hairs on fire."

With a flick of the wrist and a jangle of gold bracelets, she tried to banish them away so she could use real harsh language. They edged back so that they weren't in the room proper but they could still see her rinsing out her cardigan.

She knew that they were still in earshot; she gave a long angry hiss instead of swearing. "She is not a nice little old lady, she is a hedge-fund manager and one of the best. She's a shark; if she smiled a little wider, you'd see how sharp her teeth are. Oh, she hates me just as much as I hate her; we're just both very good at smiling and pretending that everything is just peachy."

Their mother worked in events planning for charities. In some ways, it was a glamorous job as it involved throwing bright and glittering parties for the city's richest. It meant, however, that their mother was constantly faced with drop-dead deadlines and unexpected emergencies. She was quite good at it since, as an

African warrior queen, she was forceful and unbending while extremely polite.

"Jillian needed three stitches." Their mother sniffed the cardigan to see if she had gotten out the smell of smoke from the fine wool. "Louise had half of her hair burnt off. Other than that, they only have minor scrapes and bruises from head to toe. They spent the night at Morgan Stanley Children's Hospital." She paused as the other side asked a question that made her glare at them in the doorway. "It was a dust explosion! Look it up; I had to." She huffed with impatience. "Flour, when airborne in high concentrations, can explode. Flour. The white stuff in cookies and cakes. Tell Taliaferro to tell Desmarais that the fire department already has ruled it was an accident." Another huff of impatience. "My girls videoed the whole thing, and the footage cleared them of everything but stupidity. Yes, the joy of raising children. Said children want their mother, I have to go."

She laid her sweater on the drying rack and pulled off her gloves. Their mother held up her elegant hand as if giving benediction. "I love you two dearly," she said calmly. "I would kill anyone that tried to harm you. I would lay down my life to protect you. But—this—is—not—a good time to push me."

Louise swallowed hard. Jillian held out her hand, and they laced their fingers tightly together.

"No, no, no." Their mother waved her finger at them. "Don't do that *The Shining* twin dead girls on me."

Louise squeezed Jillian's hand tight and then reluctantly let it go. "Mom, we wanted to know. Could you and Dad go back to the embryo bank and use what's still in storage so we can have little sisters and brothers?"

Their mother took a deep breath and sighed it out. She didn't like to give them her knee-jerk reactions, but it sometimes took her a few minutes before she could find safe answers. This took longer than usual, and it was simply, "No."

"Why?" Jillian pushed when she shouldn't have.

Their mother caught hold of them to grip them both fiercely. "Having a child is not just getting knocked up and spitting it out into the world! You are responsible for every moment of that child's life until it can take legal accountability for itself—which with some poor souls is never. Besides adequate food, clothing, and schooling, you must lavish it with love and affection tempered with discipline. Your father and I made that commitment to you two. We do not have the resources to reasonably extend that to other children, no matter how much we would love to have more. So the answer is no."

They nodded and escaped up the stairs. At the top of the steps, though, Jillian paused to look back with her mouth rounded into a silent "Oh" of surprise.

"What?" Louise whispered.

"Lou, they thought about having more. That means there's other leftovers still waiting to be born."

Late that night, they lay in their beds as gleaming stars slowly crawled across their ceiling. The holographic, completely accurate, star field was one of the many expensive birthday gifts that their parents had surprised them with over the years. It had a "lullaby" mode where an AI with Carl Sagan's voice gave astronomy lessons as constellations rose in the east. Louise couldn't understand why their parents hadn't saved their money and gotten more children instead.

"If there are leftovers, we need to do something." Jillian was waving her arms in the darkness. Louise could only see them moving, though, as they rapidly eclipsed the stars. "Big things. Maybe illegal things. They're our little sisters."

"And baby brother." Because odds were that at least one was a boy. "But we don't know for sure if they're still at Dad's work."

"Where would they go? They're popsicles!"

"They might have been born to someone else," Louise pointed out the obvious.

"You heard Mom..."

"They thought about having more and decided to pass on the others. The reason Dad talked about confidentiality might mean someone used the embryos and they're someone else's kids now."

"But they're still going to be like us," Jillian said. "Short and brown and smart..."

"And weird."

"We are not weird. We just think outside the box."

"Way outside."

"So if they've been born, we can watch over them from a distance. And if they haven't been born, make sure they're safe."

Louise blew her breath out in irritation. "If they're not safe at

Dad's work, what are we going to do? It's not like we can stick them in our fridge behind the ice cream. If for some reason they're not 'safe' at Dad's work, the only thing we could do is to implant them into someone. I don't know 'who,' and I'm not totally sure 'how.' I've read all those links about implantation, but those pictures just don't make total sense to me. Really there's nothing between my legs that looks like that and certainly nothing down there is big enough for a baby to come out of."

"It's because we're nine. That's where puberty comes in. We change."

Louise wasn't totally sure about that. She really wished their father hadn't passed out while filming their birth; the video would have been more instructive without the ten minutes of video of the birthing room's floor. Their father missed the whole "come out" part of their birth. "And what are we going to do with the babies afterwards? We can't just show up with them and say we found them. We tried that with the kittens and it didn't work."

A pillow came sailing across from Jillian's bed and hit Louise in the face. "Ow!"

"Don't be a stupid ass." Jillian's voice was muffled by the pillow over Louise's head. "We didn't know Daddy was allergic."

Louise tossed the pillow back. "Don't say 'ass.' This is just like the kittens times a zillion."

"Don't be a stupid butt. Before we start getting all worked up about anything, we need to figure out first if there's anything to go all emo about."

Jillian had a point. If someone else had claimed the embryos, then they wouldn't have to deal with figuring out how to get their siblings born. Louise slipped quietly out of bed, got her tablet off her desk, and climbed under her blankets before turning it on.

"What are you doing?" Jillian whispered.

"Checking Mom and Dad's computers. They probably have some kind of records on this."

A moment later, Jillian climbed into bed with her. "Any records they have are probably going to be dated from before we're born."

With the sheets tented over them, they hacked into their parents' personal files. On their mother's computer they found medical records listing doctor visits and seemingly endless tests on both their parents. The terminology slowed them down, requiring detours to look up words and procedures. The records did prove that their parents had tried for years to have babies without success.

The only information they could find on their conception was the genetic profiles of their donors. The man was listed as white, nonreligious, no known hereditary diseases, father alive, mother killed in a car accident, master level of education obtained. The woman was also listed as white, Jewish, no known hereditary disease, mother alive, father murdered, doctorate level of education obtained.

"Well, that explains why we do the Hanukah lights at Christmas." Jillian sighed with disappointment. "But I thought for sure we were at least a little African-American. Why are we so brown?"

"I don't know." Louise double-checked everything they'd searched for. "There are no names or even lot numbers on this information. We're going to have to hack Dad's company."

Hacking their father's computer wasn't as hard as it sounded since their father was a dangerously predictable man. Most of his passwords were something of sentimental value and the date associated with them. The work password was Paris16, their parents' honeymoon.

Once they were in, though, it was difficult to figure out what exactly they were looking for. There were thousands of frozen embryos stored, all cross-referenced with client numbers. Their parents weren't on the client database.

"Why aren't they on the list?" Jillian asked.

"Maybe because they didn't put anything into storage, they just took stuff out."

They found information on people who paid for implanting embryos that had been donated, but their parents weren't on that list, either.

"Maybe they lied about all this," Louise said.

"Or it wasn't us they were lying to," Jillian whispered.

"What do you mean?"

"What if they stole the embryos? It could be why Dad is all worried about confidentiality."

"If they stole our embryos..." Louise stared at the maze of interlocking databases, all feeding information from one to another. They weren't looking for a reported incident, but the lack of one. "Here. This database shows the date that the embryos are stored and the dates they were accessed. If we count nine months back from our birthday, we have a date range when our parents would have taken us."

Jillian counted back on her fingers. "We were born in April. March. February. January. December. November. October. September. August. July?"

"Let's check from June to August, the year before we were born, just to be sure," Louise said. "I don't know how exact that nine-month thing is. People are always talking about premature babies."

There were only a dozen possible batches.

"I would have thought there would be more," Jillian said. "How are they staying in business?"

"The success rate of the first implant is high for Dad's clinic. It's at seventy percent. The leftovers are stored and used only if the first implant fails, or basically just thirty percent of the clients."

Jillian scanned the dozen listings. "It only shows which embryos were accessed. It doesn't give who pulled them and how they were used."

"Just give me a minute." Louise checked through the other databases. "Billing includes embryo batch numbers. That way the company can keep track of who gets what without worrying about confidentiality. Since our parents didn't pay, our batch number will be the only one that doesn't have a matching invoice. There."

"First, who are our genetic donors?" Jillian chased the information through the databases. "They're the ones we have to be careful around since they probably think we're their kids and we're most definitely not! Huh. What does 'the estate of' mean?"

"How should I know?" Louise was digging through the storage records, trying to find out how many embryos had been stored, what had been taken out, and what remained.

"Ah!" Jillian made the sound of discovery. "Estate means it belongs to dead people."

"Our donors are dead?"

"It looks like it."

"Maybe that's what Dad meant by 'they have children and lose them in some way.' It's not our donors that Mom and Dad are worried about, but our donors' parents."

"Oh my God! Lou! Our sperm donor was Leonardo DaVinci Dufae."

"You're kidding!" Louise leaned over to stare at Jillian's screen.

Dufae was the most well-known inventor of their time. He invented a hyperphase gate that the Chinese built in orbit. They intended to use it to jump colonists to a planet around another star. If it had worked as expected, Dufae probably would have remained obscure. What made him famous was the fact that the gate malfunctioned in a spectacular fashion.

Every time the gate was turned on, Pittsburgh disappeared off Earth and traveled to Elfhome, the world of elves. Luckily, every time the gate was turned off, Pittsburgh returned. Basically, the Chinese had turned a major American city into a giant interdimensional yo-yo.

Earth was nearly plunged into global warfare over whether or not the gate should continue to operate. The biggest problem was that Dufae had died before the gate's first activation. Other scientists couldn't figure out how his gate worked, so they couldn't simply tweak his design to something less inconvenient. No one really wanted to break contact with Elfhome completely. After a great deal of heated negotiations, an awkward schedule of turning the gate on and off, or Startups and Shutdowns, was established.

"That is so cool!" Louise whispered. "But he's been dead for forever. Maybe before Mom and Dad were even born!"

"Lou," Jillian whispered. "Leonardo DaVinci Dufae is *our* father."

"He was just a sperm donor and he's dead," Louise pointed out again. "Who donated the egg? His wife?"

The egg donor was Esme Shenske. They didn't recognize the name, but the Internet did. She was the captain of the third colony ship, the *Dahe Hao*. The holographic star-field ceiling, complete with astronomy lessons, suddenly made sense.

"Wow. Our donors are famous," Jillian said.

"Were famous. He's dead and she's at Alpha Centauri or someplace like that. What the hell happened to our older sisters? Did they go to Alpha Centauri with her?"

After some digging they found that the first batch of embryos had been inserted into April Geiselman of Pittsburgh exactly nine months prior to Esme Shenske leaving the Solar System.

"That means our older sisters are eighteen next month," Louise said. "But where are they? Did Esme take them with her? Or did they stay in Pittsburgh with Geiselman?"

"I'm looking," Jillian said. "What about our baby sisters?"

Louise checked and found that there were indeed more embryos in storage. There was a recent date on their records. She frowned and checked the code for it. "Oh no, they've been flagged for disposal. The company sent out a letter last month to inform the estate that if they didn't respond, the embryos would be thrown away. No one has responded to the letter. We have six months to save them."

3: MUNDANE MONDAY

"I think we're lucky that our male genetic donor is dead," Jillian whispered in art class the next day.

Louise glanced automatically to Jillian's tablet to see what had triggered the comment. Her twin had multiple newspaper web pages up, all featuring a Boston murder case. According to the headlines, the killer's name was John Wright, who had beaten his wife, Ada, to death. "What?"

"Leonardo DaVinci Dufae had one sister. Ada Lovelace Dufae. She married John Wright and had one son, Orville Wright."

Louise snickered at the names. "Wow, the Dufaes have a twisted sense of humor when naming children." DaVinci had been a scientist as well as an artist. Ada Lovelace had worked with Charles Babbage on the prototype of the computer. Orville Wright had invented airplanes with his brother, Wilbur.

"Yes, obviously our grandfather hated being Tim No Middle Name Dufae."

"I wonder what they would have called us."

Jillian squinted a moment. "The mind boggles. The Wright brothers are the only sibling pair of inventors that leap to mind. But Orville is our cousin, not our brother."

"You can be Wilbur. I'll be Jane Goodall."

"I'll be Marie Curie, *merci beaucoup*. You should be Maria Goeppert Mayer, since we're already Mayers."

"Marie? Maria? We have a hard enough time with people telling us apart. I'd rather be Jane Goodall."

18

"Okay, monkey girl."

"Okay, *Wil-burr.*" Louise giggled.

She winced as Miss Gray raised her voice. Gage was causing problems again. He really needed to be on some kind of ADHD medicine.

Jillian sighed. "I can't find out what happened to Orville after his mother was killed."

"Oh." The headlines made sense now; their Aunt Ada had been murdered by her husband. "How old is he?"

"He was ten when his mother died." Jillian pulled up a picture of a boy that looked eerily like Louise now that her hair was boy-short. His dark eyes were haunted; they spoke to her of unimaginable horrors. "He saw it happen. He's twenty-two now. Wherever he is. Trying to find out anything about him is getting me spammed with hits on the airplane inventor. Our stupid grandfather!"

Jillian fell silent, focused on creating a more accurate genetic family tree than the one that hung over their fireplace at home. Ironically both were equally bare. Orville was their only cousin by blood or birth. Their "Aunt Kitty" was a girl that their Grandma Johnson took under her wing but never formally adopted.

Louise tapped the icon in the corner of her tablet to check on their art teacher Miss Gray, who liked to roam while her students sketched. Making eye contact would warn her that the twins weren't working on the assignment. Normally not a good thing, but since they were hacking various computer systems, it could be catastrophic if they were caught. Louise had a monitoring application that tracked the tablet that Miss Gray usually carried during class, but sometimes she put it down. The program showed that Miss Gray was in motion on the other side of the art classroom.

Louise minimized the window and went back to chasing down leads on their older sisters' surrogate mother, April Geiselman. She had three leads so far: one in Hawaii, one in Arizona, and one in New York. She needed to dig into their past to see if any of them had lived in Pittsburgh at some point.

The morning had been surreal agony as they went through the motions of pretending to be normal nine-year-olds. Almost everything covered in class, they'd learned before enrolling in kindergarten as four-year-olds. After a series of tests showed that they read at college level and could do advanced algebra equations, the public school system had tried to push the twins straight into middle school. Their parents resisted the move, stating life was more than just grades. Instead of calculus and chemistry, the twins were enrolled in first grade to learn a more complicated subject: socializing with their peers.

Unfortunately, "peers" was a very imperfect fit.

In theory their school was for the gifted. Yes, all their fellow students tested higher than the typical fifth-grader, but they were also dropped off by nannies in BMWs. At times it seemed that the parents' net worth was more important than their children's IQ. It meant that otherwise fascinating subjects were dumbed down to the class average. Art, for instance; their assignment was to draw a two-dimensional still life of what the teacher arranged on the center table. How interesting could a flat representation of a bouquet of sunflowers, a collection of stoneware bowls, and a length of red velvet be?

Luckily the teacher was letting them use their tablets instead of forcing them to use actual pencils and paper. It meant that for the first time all morning they could work on saving their siblings. According to Cryobank, there were four embryos still in storage. While the sex of the embryos wasn't given, Jillian decided that it would be best if they were three girls and one boy. Louise had considered the matter and had to agree. More than one boy and they would gang up together and be totally annoying. Case in point—the whole reason they weren't using pencil and paper was because Kelsey and Gage had stabbed each other repeatedly during their last freehand drawing lesson. At least the boys kept Miss Gray's attention off Louise and Jillian.

Louise grinned as she hit pay dirt on the April Geiselman in New York. "Look," she whispered, tilting her screen. "Her records show that she was born in Pittsburgh! She's the one! And she lives in the Upper East Side!"

Their datapads suddenly enlarged their drawing window. Louise controlled the urge to glance up to double-check that their teacher had actually moved into viewing range. If their teacher realized that they were using her tablet to track her movements through the classroom, she would probably hover over them, and they would have to actually pay attention to the assignments. Louise's sketch was just a rushed collection of yellow pen swipes to place-hold the sunflowers. Louise winced, picked a red that roughly matched the velvet, and added in the draped fabric in the same quick lines.

"Is that all you have done?" Miss Gray said above her head.

"I had more." Louise made a show of pausing and considering her drawing. "I didn't like how it was going, so I erased it. It seemed too—too real."

"Too real?"

"Well, if we wanted the picture to look real, wouldn't we just take a photograph of the flowers?" Out the corner of her eye, Louise could see Jillian frantically drawing on her blank tablet. Louise held up her picture to keep Miss Gray's attention; she at least had something to show and had already started into a reasonable excuse. "Art is translating what we feel into a visual medium. Obviously, the flowers can't look like a photograph or otherwise I wouldn't be putting my emotions into the picture. To me sunflowers are like...like..."

"Flowing sunlight," Jillian prompted in a whisper.

"Flowing sunlight." Louise babbled on to give Jillian more time. "Like the sun dripped down onto the flower and will flow away again. It's all bright and sunny and temporary. At any moment, poof, it will be gone. What I had before just seemed too permanent. It didn't have that 'life is fleeting' kind feeling."

Miss Gray was getting that slightly panicky look she had often with the twins—like she realized she was in over her head. Jillian's theory was that this was because it was Miss Gray's first year of teaching and she hadn't firmly latched on to the idea that she was an adult. Louise leaned more toward the notion that Miss Gray was smart enough to know that they were pulling something over on her, but not smart enough to figure out what or how.

"I see. Well. Then. Jillian, what do you have?"

Jillian held up her sketch. She'd gone to extreme cartoon to cover her lack of details. The sunflowers had eyes, huge sharp mouths, and were holding wriggling students in their leaves. One student was crying "Help me" as she was being dropped headfirst into a gaping mouth. "These are carnivorous sunflowers from Elfhome. Like strangle vines and black-willow trees, they're distant cousins to Venus flytraps and the waterwheel plant. Those are both snap-trap plants as opposed to flypaper traps or pitfall traps that you have in butterworts and pitcher plants. Did you know that the black-willow trees on Elfhome can walk close to two miles per hour and can swallow a man whole?"

Miss Gray gave a tiny whimper, and her eyes went wider.

Louise ducked her head and pressed her lips tight together to keep from laughing.

Jillian frowned at her datapad as if she was totally unaware of the effect she was having on Miss Gray. "Luckily all Elfhome plants need some magic to thrive, and magic doesn't exist on Earth, so these are most likely harmless."

Miss Gray whimpered again.

Elle Pondwater unintentionally rescued them by waving her hand and calling, "Miss Gray, I've finished!" Elle and her friends were on the other side of the room; all dressed in their Girl Scout uniforms. The distance illustrated that the twins were currently failing at socializing with their peers. "Can I put my picture up on the wall display?"

"That would be good, Elle." Miss Gray fled their table while Elle uploaded her drawing onto the wall display. "Oh, Elle, that is wonderful!"

While reasonably intelligent, Elle was not one to think outside the box. Add in her need to please adults, and it came as no surprise that Elle had done exactly what Miss Gray asked. Her picture looked like a bad photograph of the objects on the center table. Elle beamed with imagined triumph. "My mother set up art classes at the Children's Museum of Art for our Junior Legacy National Proficiency Artist Badges. It was eight sessions of private lessons, all in drawing."

Elle showed off her badge and explained that they were having a meeting after school to coordinate their cookie drive with the Daisies, Brownies, Cadettes, and Seniors. "We donate half the money so that underprivileged girls can go to camp."

Jillian was moving her mouth in silent mimicry of Elle, getting the tilt of her shoulders and toss of her head down perfectly but adding in a dramatic roll of the eyes.

Louise shook her head. She really didn't know why Elle bothered Jillian so much. It could have been because Elle was one of the few people who never believed a word coming out of Jillian's mouth. Or maybe it was because the reason that Elle didn't believe Jillian had nothing to do with the level of truthfulness of her statements. She could say that the sun was hot and Elle wouldn't believe her.

Nor did it help that Elle's mother had been a Miss Universe before becoming a trophy wife. Elle got "classic American Beauty" in bucketloads. She was freakishly tall and had stunningly pale skin that seemingly had never seen the light of day. Despite being blond-haired, blue-eyed, and beautiful, she was also unexpectedly smart, although not in the same league as the twins. Her mother dressed her in impeccable fashion and had taught her stage presence when she was still a toddler. It surprised no one that Elle got all the lead roles for the class plays, from Cinderella to Snow White.

Jillian had wanted those roles, but because the twins were short and brown, she was always cast as the evil stepmother or witch. She tried her hardest to steal the spotlight from Elle by going big and chewing on the scenery. She had taken the news hard when they learned that their father, Leonardo, had only been five foot seven. Their Aunt Ada had never even cleared five foot; she was only four foot and eleven inches when she was killed. While Esme Shenske was five foot six, chances were not good for them getting much taller.

Louise didn't mind being short, but she didn't plan a career in Hollywood.

"I liked your sunflowers," Louise said after the bell rang. Everyone swept out of the art room because recess was next. The twins followed slowly since they planned to continue working on their tablets.

"I can draw better than her when I put any effort into it," Jillian complained.

The twins used their Barbie dolls to do motion capture, painstakingly moving them one step at a time in front of a green screen. Even with their computers doing the bulk of the processing, the twins spent countless hours drawing in finer details on their videos. Their Summer Court Palace of Soulful Ember, Queen of the elves, would put Elle's still life to shame.

"We both know you can, so why let it bug you?" Louise poked at Jillian, trying to push her out of her mood. "I bet Elle only spent so much time learning how to draw well because her mother wanted her to be good at it. She only does things to get praise. She doesn't know what she likes when she's alone."

Jillian snorted. "She likes being popular."

"She doesn't know how to be anything else. You've seen how Mrs. Pondwater treats her like a little puppet." Louise pretended to have a sock puppet on her hand. "Stand straight. Say 'how nice it is to see you' and smile." She had the pretend puppet straighten and mouth the words. "How nice it is to see you." She clawed her fingers so that the "smile" was a showing of fangs.

Jillian snickered and then sobered. "I suppose that's true. I think why I get annoyed by her is because she could be such a cool friend if she wasn't so . . . so . . . her! Everything is a competition, and she has to win."

Louise shrugged. "She's been in beauty pageants since she was three. What do you expect?"

"But she doesn't win because she's smarter or wiser or more creative. She wins because her father is rich and bought himself a beauty queen as a wife. She wins because her mother doesn't need to work and set up endless little bribes to make sure her daughter is the most popular girl in class. She wins because she's tall and blond—and I'm not."

"So basically you're pissed off at her because she's not as smart or creative as we are and needs her mommy to fight her battles?"

"Shush you, monkey girl." Jillian paused at the playground door. On the other side of the asphalt, Elle and the other Girl Scouts were playing jump rope. Elle's loose blond hair waved like a banner in the weak spring sunlight as she skipped through the doubled ropes. They stood a moment, watching enviously, as Double Dutch was one of those things the two of them couldn't do alone. "I just wish sometimes Elle could be our friend without one of us having to be the loser. It's not like with you—I don't ever have to worry about which one of us is the winner."

Said the twin that everyone said was the cutest and the most creative. Louise blinked quickly to keep tears from showing in her eyes and lifted up her tablet to distract Jillian. "So, Wilbur, now that we found April Geiselman, what do we do?"

"We go and see her!" Jillian glanced back at Elle and smirked. "And I think I know how we're going to do it."

Jillian decided that they'd go disguised as Girl Scouts selling cookies.

Louise wasn't sure they needed disguises. And she was fairly positive that they hadn't needed to actually join the Girl Scouts in order to obtain the uniforms. She suspected that Jillian secretly just wanted to join but wouldn't admit it. Elle had been so stunned when they showed up at the after-school meeting that she just stood there, mouth open, with a confused look on her face. Mrs. Pondwater was much better at covering her emotions. She ran on autopilot, welcoming them to the troop with only flashes of horror going through her eyes when she happened to look at Louise's blast-shortened hair. Jillian had told everyone in class that Louise's new hairstyle was because of an accident with bubblegum so there were no embarrassing questions about explosions, leveled playhouses, or emergency-room visits. Mrs. Pondwater apparently knew the truth, which indicated that the woman obsessively tracked everyone who touched upon her daughter's life. She obviously didn't want to take responsibility for anyone who had already managed to blow themselves up once. The spirit of Girl Scouts—as Jillian pointed out—was to accept any girl no matter her ethnic and social group.

So they would have the uniforms, cookie order forms, and a creditable alibi for all of Saturday.

Neither one of them remembered that Saturday was their birthday.

"The Girl Scouts?" their mother said for the third time after they told her. She was in her power business suit, her briefcase on the counter, and dinner from the supermarket's hot deli still in its insulated bag on the kitchen table. The evening news was on but muted.

"Is there something wrong with the Girl Scouts?" Louise got out four plates and four forks.

"You said we should try to play with the other girls more." Jillian investigated the bag. "Oh, good, rotisserie chicken!" She pulled out a small full chicken and then other containers that held steamed brown rice, salad makings, and fresh fruit.

"There's nothing wrong with Girl Scouts." Their mother took off her heels with a sigh of relief. "I thought—oh, what's her name...?"

"Elle Pondwater." Louise supplied the name and four glasses.

"Yes, that Elle's mother ran the Girl Scouts here and you thought she was materialistic and extremely controlling. What's changed?"

Since it was true, Louise let Jillian field the question.

"By ignoring the Girl Scouts, we were allowing Elle to control that power base. By infiltrating that clique, we could disrupt her monopoly on it."

Their mother pursed her lips, studying Jillian with eyes narrowed. "I am never sure whether to be dismayed or proud when you talk that way."

Louise tried to soften the statement. "The other girls don't seem to be aware of what Elle is doing, but she is using the group to exclude us. Today in Art she did a 'Let's all sit together' and then picked the other side of the classroom."

Their mother hummed something that sounded like "Oh, that sneaky bitch." She tried not to say negative things aloud, wanting them to make up their own minds about people. She couldn't, however, keep completely silent when she was angry for their sake.

"She's never mean to our faces." Louise supplied serving forks and spoons for the chicken and the side dishes.

"God forbid people realize what a backstabber she is." Jillian poured milk for herself and Louise. "All the other girls probably think she's always nice."

"Pause!" their mother suddenly cried to the TV, which had frozen the picture at her command. "Go back a story. Unmute."

The screen switched to the Waldorf Astoria's famous façade in Manhattan. The reporter was standing across Park Avenue while people with signs marched in front of the hotel's entrance. "Demonstrators gathered today in front of the Waldorf Astoria to protest the UN's plan to enlarge the quarantine zone controlled by the Earth Interdimensional Agency in southwestern Pennsylvania."

Keywords appeared at the edges of the screen indicating linked stories. In the top left was a mini-window showing the original story that had spawned the current events. The United Nations had set up only a one-mile-wide band around Pittsburgh. When the Earth city shifted to Elfhome, a virgin forest of towering ironwood trees took its place. The lack of magic kept invasive species from taking hold in Pennsylvania, but it hadn't stopped humans from wreaking havoc. A few weeks earlier, someone had managed to illegally log part of the forest, triggering a call from the United Nations to increase the zone to ten miles wide. It would, however, cut deep into several towns that had grown up at the edge of the zone.

The reported continued, "The Waldorf Astoria serves as the embassy for the representatives of the Royal Court of Elfhome when they're on Earth. Currently, however, there are no elves in residence."

"Exactly!" their mother cried. "So why are they there?"

"The famous landmark hotel will be the site of a black-tie event on Saturday evening for the Forest Forever, an United Nations Foundation charity that advocates against deforestation worldwide. Celebrity supporter Lady Lavender of Teal is scheduled to arrive sometime today."

Their mother cried out as if stabbed.

"Isn't that one of your events?" Jillian asked.

"Yes."

The garage door opened and closed as their father arrived.

He came padding in the basement door, dressed in scrubs. "Sorry I'm late." He gestured toward the TV, which was offering more stories about the protests. "Apparently the protests screwed up all the traffic in Manhattan."

"You took the car?" Jillian asked.

Their father found this funny for some reason. "Yes, Detective, I took the car."

"You only take the car when you have stuff to pick up," Louise said.

He took his chair, canting his head toward their mother and spreading his hands in a plea for help.

She sat beside him. "Our daughters have decided to join the Girl Scouts, and on Saturday they will be selling cookies."

"This Saturday? On their birthday?"

Louise winced and glanced at Jillian. They'd forgotten in the flood of information on their genetic donors and siblings, both born and unborn. "We weren't doing anything special on Saturday. You had your event."

"I had that covered." Their mother used "had" instead of "have" to indicate that the news report meant she might have to work after all. "And you didn't want a party, but that doesn't mean we can't plan something special for just the family sometime on Saturday."

Louise exchanged another wince with Jillian. They'd turned down a party because they weren't really friends with any of the kids in class. "Sunday is just as good as Saturday."

Their mother nodded in agreement, probably because she had no way to foresee her work schedule.

"What do we do about their present?" their father asked.

"What present?" the twins cried.

"We can give it to them early," their mother said. "But dinner first. Our food is getting cool."

They ate with Louise wondering what their parents might have gotten them. She could almost hear the capital *P* in "present" that indicated that it was expensive. Her father had taken the car out and picked it up today, so it was something too large to carry home on the subway. Her father obviously thought it was a wonderful gift and that they would love it. Her mother was more reserved; the twins might not like it as much as their father expected them to. Which parent was right? What could they possibly have gotten the girls? What did they want? Jillian would want a camera to replace the one they'd blown up. A camera wouldn't have required the car. Louise would want a dog or a pony or a monkey, but those were all impossible since their father was allergic to animal dander.

Judging by the looks that Jillian was giving her, Jillian couldn't guess, either.

Finally the meal was judged over and their father went back down into the basement garage. Soon he was back, empty-handed.

"Where is . . ." And then Louise saw it and squealed in pure excitement. It was a dog! A pony-sized dog! For a moment she was filled with shimmering, bright, pure joy, and in her delight, missed the first clues.

Then Jillian said quietly, "Oh, Lou." And Louise knew that something was horribly wrong with the gift, and as her excitement drained away, she saw that the dog wasn't real.

"It's beautiful, isn't it?" Their dad had missed her crash and burn. "You really have to look closely at it to see that it's a robot."

"Yes." She forced herself to agree. It was a big, square dog, nearly as tall as the twins, with pure white legs and belly. A creamy gray poured over its back. Its tail, face, and ears were black, with just a little white around its nose and muzzle. Its tail curled tight into a loop of gray that ended with a tip of white. If it had been real, it would have been the most beautiful thing she'd ever seen.

Jillian was watching her closely, bottom lip quivering in sympathy for her disappointment.

"What kind is it?" She pushed the words out, glad that she managed to sound happy. "I don't recognize the breed."

It stood waiting, more impassive than a real dog would ever be. That was the problem with robots. They were either too hyper or too still. Apparently the programmers had decided that with such a big facsimile, they would err toward still.

"It's an American Akita," their father said.

Because her mother was watching her closely, Louise went and petted the dog. The fur was a little too soft. Its tail wagged in perfect imitation but it didn't sniff at her hands or lean against her touch or look about the new room with curiosity.

"It's so big," Louise said.

"But why a dog?" Jillian joined her in petting the robot.

"We've never been comfortable with how much time you spend alone," their mother said. "The explosion really made us rethink your safety."

"It's a nanny-bot?" Jillian looked pained. "We're nine."

"Going on twenty," their mother said. "And Seda Demirjian let us know that she and her husband are getting divorced and they're putting their house up for sale."

"Oh," Louise said as understanding dawned on her. "Vosgi won't be going with us on the subway anymore?"

"No."

Vosgi was sixteen and had acted as their transportation babysitter for the last year. Before that it had been Carl Steinmetz, but he'd graduated. None of their other neighbors attended school in Manhattan.

"We're going to be commuting alone?" Jillian said.

Their parents shared unhappy looks. "Until we can think of a better solution than a nanny-bot, yes," their mother said.

"So, what do we call her?" their dad asked.

Louise didn't want to call the nanny-bot anything.

"What was the name of the cat?" he asked.

They looked at him with confusion. Because of his allergies, they'd never had a cat.

He made a motion of something drifting up and away. "The toy cat?"

"Popoki?" Jillian cried. "No, we're not calling it Popoki."

Once upon a time that was now growing to be a dim memory, they had a small robotic cat, Popoki. It had met an untimely end involving a pair of large helium balloons and their lack of understanding how much lift said balloons could generate versus the weight of the small toy. Louise's last memory of Popoki was it floating up over the Steinmetz's house. It went higher and higher, its electronic meows growing fainter, until the balloons were a tiny dot drifting toward the ocean. Jillian had been inconsolable for days.

"George." Their mother scolded their father with his name. "What was the dog in *Peter Pan*? This one looks like it."

From the perked-up ears to its curled tail, the robot looked nothing like the nanny dog of *Peter Pan*. The only similarity was its size and the pattern of its markings—but then everyone always thought the twins were identical.

"Nana," Louise said. "She was a Newfoundland in the original story, but Disney made her a Saint Bernard. They're the same size dog, only Newfoundlands are usually all black."

"Saint Bernards are easier to illustrate facial emotions, because of their markings," Jillian said.

"It doesn't feel like a girl to me," Louise said. "It feels like a boy dog."

"A boy dog?" their father said.

"Something like..." Louise thought for a moment, but the only male names that were coming to her were Orville and Wilbur. What was another famous inventor? "Tesla."

Jillian giggled, recognizing the path that Louise took to get to the name. "Okay, Tesla!"

"Very cool name." Their father crouched down beside Louise. "Do you like it, honey?"

She wanted to say no. It probably cost a lot of money that could have been spent on things she and Jillian would have liked more. It was, however, a practical gift considering the situation. If they couldn't safely commute to school, their parents would probably take them out of Perelman School for the Gifted and enroll them someplace else. It wasn't that she loved Perelman, but "someplace else" could be anything from a local high school with kids four years older than them to a boarding school. "It's a wonderful present. Thank you, Daddy."

With the magical words, he melted, hugging her tightly. "Oh, I love you two so much. I want to give you the world."

Jillian waited until they were safe in their room.

"*Merde!*" Jillian cursed in French. "*C'est des conneries. Fait chier! Fait chier! Fait chier!*"

Louise shook her head as she pulled up the website of the robot's manufacturer. "If they hear you, they'll ground you," Louise warned, keeping to French until she knew if Tesla had an eavesdropping application or not. They had initiated the robot's setup program in the kitchen by registering his name and that the twins were his primary owners. The big dog robot was slowly working its way around the room, mapping it.

"They wouldn't understand what we're saying even if they heard us." Jillian growled in French and flung herself onto the bed. "It's the whole point of using another language."

"*Merde!*" Louise hissed her own curse and kept to French. "Yes, it has an eavesdropping application and GPS. Not only can they keep track of it via a phone app, they can ask it questions. It can answer in thirty-two languages!" She dialed Tesla's number on her cell phone and he answered with a deep male voice. "*Konnichiwa.*"

She cycled through the various breed voices. German Shepard said "*Guten Tag*" in a slightly more tenor male and Shih Tzu said "*Nĭ hǎo*" in a bright and chipper female voice. She groaned and cycled quickly through the voices, looking for one that didn't set her teeth on edge. The Welsh corgi had a British boy's voice that reminded her of Christopher Robin.

She changed the default and sent a command to the robot.

Tesla shook his head and murmured, "Silly old bear."

Jillian grabbed a pillow and screamed into it.

Louise groaned as she read on. "They can download video from his eyes."

Jillian screamed into the pillow again.

Louise read further and laughed.

"There is nothing funny about this!" Jillian's shout was muffled by the pillow still over her face.

"Tesla has a nano nonstick-coating on its feet. It micro-vibrates each foot before entering a home."

"That's not funny."

"What Tesla doesn't have is the optional gecko feet that lets the robot dog scale walls and ceilings."

"What?" Jillian sat up.

"Look." Louise played the video of a robotic corgi walking up a wall.

"Why would you want your dog to do that?" Jillian cried.

"Spider dog, spider dog, does whatever a spider dog does," Louise sang.

They giggled, playing the video over and over. Tesla continued to work his way around the room, ignoring their laughter. They had slipped out of French with "spider dog," but Jillian carefully returned to it to carry on a serious discussion. Luckily the auto-translate option wasn't the default and their parents hadn't turned it on.

"Seriously, what we are going to do?" Jillian asked, curled beside Louise on her bed. "How are we going to go see April Geiselman with a spy dog in tow? The whole point of doing the Girl Scout thing was so everyone would think that after a short subway ride, we'd be with adults."

Their parents would insist that they take Tesla. The protests against the proposed expansion of the Earth Interdimensional Agency-controlled strip of land around Pittsburgh were spreading across the city to include the United Nations building and the Chinese embassy, as well as the Waldorf Astoria Hotel.

If they took Tesla with them, though, their parents would know about their detour to the Upper East Side to see April Geiselman.

"*Merde.*" Jillian sighed out the curse and continued in French. "So the problem is three part. First is that it reports our position via GPS. Second is that our parents can ask it questions about what we're doing. Third is that they can download video of what it has seen during the course of the day."

"*Oui,*" Louise agreed. "It records video, so the entire day is accessible."

"It's a camera," Jillian said slowly. "We can control what it sees and edit the video like any other camera. So really, it's not a problem."

Louise considered a moment and nodded. "*Oui.*" She flipped to the specs on Tesla's GPS system. "At least we have four days to come up with a plan and test it."

"It's going to be so embarrassing to take it to school." Jillian sighed deeply. "You know how it's going to go down. Everyone is going to say we're too poor for a real nanny. Just like the Darlings."

"*C'est la vie,*" Louise murmured. "They already know we're poor. I don't care. Ah ha!"

"That sounds good."

"*Magnifique!*" Louise said. She'd discovered the weakness of the spy application. It lay not with the robot but with their parents' phones. She reached over and lifted up what was left of their camera that she'd been attempting to fix. Jillian had clung to it until the EMT pried it out of her hand, so it had escaped the fire. The lens, however, had been smashed. It had all the same GPS and communication software that Tesla had. They could simply rig it so that their parents picked up the camera's output when attempting to check on Tesla. "Meet mini-Tesla."

"Ooohhhh!" Jillian grasped the concept instantly. *"C'est magnifique!"*

4: GIRL SCOUT CAMOUFLAGE GREEN

Saturday morning, after taking their hour turn at the cookie-selling event in Queens, they planted mini-Tesla on Elle and took the 7 train into Midtown Manhattan. The Grand Central–42nd Street Station was a kicked beehive of police. Jillian led, smiling innocently at the policemen. Louise followed, leading Tesla by his leash, trying not to look like they were deceiving every adult who crossed their path. They caught the 6 local to the Upper East Side.

"Is she home yet?" Jillian swung her legs, watching the city flash by. Tesla was parked beside her, his camera eyes hacked and currently not recording. Just to be sure, they had his head carefully locked onto the back of their seat.

Louise took out her phone and checked what the GPS on April Geiselman's phone had to say. They had hacked April's phone and had been tracking her for two days. The woman was making steady progress toward her apartment from some mystery address that had kept her out all night. "She's heading home—I think. What do we do if she doesn't go home?"

"We sell cookies until she does."

April lived in a high-rise on the Upper East Side. The Girl Scout uniforms got them past the doorman with a promise of free cookies. According to her phone, April was now home, so they went straight to her apartment.

They rang the doorbell and listened intently as soft footsteps came to the door. There was a long silence as they were examined through the spyhole. After a full minute, the locks were thrown and the door opened.

April was surprisingly young and pretty. She was wearing a tight black dress and last night's makeup. "Wow, I didn't think Girl Scouts went door-to-door anymore. Are you sure you're allowed to do this? It's not really safe, even with a dog that big."

"Hi," Jillian said. "Can we ask you some questions?"

"I'll buy a box or two. I love Thin Mints. Let me get my purse." She started to close the door, but Louise put her foot in the door. "Wait! We want to know what happened to your babies."

Jillian glared at her for going off-script.

"My what?" April said.

"Eighteen years ago, you visited the Cryobank fertility clinic in Manhattan and were implanted with four embryos—but you live in a one-bedroom apartment. What happened to your babies?"

April glanced down the hallway and lowered her voice. "How do you know about that? Who told you that?"

"Your babies are our sisters," Louise said. "We're the embryos that weren't implanted in you."

"Oh, Jesus," April whispered. "Come in."

The apartment was cluttered but clean. The floor was swept, but every surface was crowded with interesting stuff. Books. Art. Toys. They parked Tesla in the corner, staring at the door. April disappeared into the kitchen to make tea.

"I always thought that there might be a day when the doorbell would ring and it would be her wanting to know who the hell I thought I was, having a baby for money and walking away, leaving her there, on that world."

A baby. "You only had one? A girl?" the twins cried.

There was silence in the kitchen. April came to lean on the doorway. "Yeah. A little girl. Her name is Alexander. You know, you can only leave Pittsburgh once a month, and she was born the day after Startup, so I was there with her for thirty days, knowing that she wasn't really mine. It was so hard to walk away. To stay away. But as they say—you make your bed, you have to sleep in it.

"I wanted off of Elfhome. I was seven when Startup took Pittsburgh to Elfhome. It woke us up in the middle of the night. The power off. The phones not working. Giant trees where our backyard had been, pressed right up against our house. A saurus attacked our neighbor's house the next morning. We could hear them screaming. My dad told us to lock ourselves in the bathroom, and he went down the street with his hunting rifle and shot it.

"Here." She went across the living room to a bookcase and got down a picture frame. "This is him with it."

Her father looked like an African explorer with a thick mustache and tan hunting jacket. He beamed with pride at the camera behind the saurus' massive head, its mouth propped open to show off hundreds of long, sharp teeth.

"One day it's the twenty-first century, the next you're living in the Stone Age, complete with dinosaurs. My parents loved it, but it scared me. Strangle vines ate our dog. A tree ate my favorite teacher. A fish ate one of my friends. There was a bunch of us standing on the riverbank looking at this strange big fish. *It was a fish.* We thought as long as we didn't go into the water, we'd be safe. And then all of the sudden..." She made a fast snatching motion with her hand. "And the girl standing right next to me was gone. There was just one of her shoes..."

She shook her head. "I shouldn't be telling little kids like you things like this. It will give you guys nightmares. It will give me nightmares. Do you want something to drink? I have some Diet Coke and tea."

Their parents didn't let them have either, saying that it would stunt their growth. Personally Louise thought it was because their parents were afraid that caffeine would make them even harder to manage.

"I'd like tea," Louise said.

It turned out tea was more complicated than soda because April had what seemed to be an infinite variety of teas. Louise picked a coconut mango oolong. Jillian chose fusion honey, ginseng and white tea. April took a bottle out of the cabinet and added scotch to her Earl Grey.

"So they paid you to have our sister?" Jillian asked while Louise tried to get the tea sweet enough to drink.

"Yes." April sighed. "It sounds so horrible, doesn't it? It felt good and right until it was time to walk away." She opened the fridge, took out a carton of milk, and poured a generous tablespoon into her mug. Her cup read "I ♥ New York."

"My family moved to Neville Island, thinking it would be safer. Mr. Bell lived down the street. He was a sweet, little old man.

He could fix anything and he was always willing to help out. He saved my life once when I was little; I'd gotten too close to some strangle vine, and he cut me free. I felt like I owed him. And it wasn't like he was going to have sex with me—it would all be neat and medical."

"Mr. Bell?" The name on the records had been Leonardo Dufae, the famous inventor. "He was our real father?"

"No, no, it was his son. Um. Gosh, I've forgotten his name. I never met him. He'd been killed on Earth. He had donated some..." She paused, blushing slightly. Apparently she'd just remembered that they were just kids.

"Sperm." Louise provided the proper word.

"Yes." The blush deepened. "Genetic material. It was all that Mr. Bell had left of his son. He just wanted a grandchild. The baby, though, had to be born in Pittsburgh if it was going to grow up on Elfhome with Mr. Bell. The elves limited immigration to a handful of people a year. The EIA—the Earth Interdimensional Agency—preapproves the applicants. They want scientists and researchers, not babies. There weren't any fertility clinics in Pittsburgh, not after the first Startup, and he couldn't have gotten any surrogate mother from Earth into Pittsburgh for more than a month. Since in vitro babies are often premature, it would have been hit or miss whether his granddaughter would be born on Earth or Elfhome. He didn't want to risk having the EIA declare she didn't qualify for the family immigration rule."

"So the surrogate had to be a Pittsburgher," Louise said.

April nodded. "I could come to New York City, have the...the procedure, and go back to Pittsburgh until it was time for her to be born. I would get money to move to Earth. Go to college. We would all live happily ever after. It seemed so simple."

"So Alexander is still in Pittsburgh?" Jillian asked.

"Oh, yes." April got down a leather book from the bookcase. "Mr. Bell sends me a photo every year or so. At least he used to; last time he did, he wrote that the lack of technology on Elfhome frustrates her. I think he's afraid that if she finds out about me, she'll use me as an excuse to come to Earth. This is Alexander."

The first few pictures looked like their own baby pictures where their parents squinted and said "Is this Jillian or Louise?" and their mother would mutter how she should have tagged their photos. At three, though, their sister became wholly herself. Her hair was boy-short. She sported a bandage in nearly every photo. In one she had a black eye, looking extremely pleased. Alexander wore bright T-shirts and blue jeans and often was barefoot. There wasn't a doll or stuffed animal in any of the pictures, but wheeled vehicles that grew larger and larger as she did. When she was nine, she had a go-kart. Louise felt a stab of jealousy.

The last photo held another big surprise; it showed Orville and Alexander together, looking like brother and sister instead of cousins. Orville seemed only a year or two older than the photo taken of him after his mother's murder. In this photo, he beamed with joy, arms wrapped around Alexander as she leaned comfortably back on him.

"Is that Orville?" Jillian asked.

April seemed surprised by the question and then laughed. "Of course you know about him. Yes, it is Orville. He's living with his grandfather. He and Alexander bonded; they're inseparable. Last time Mr. Bell wrote me, they were building go-karts and racing them all over Neville Island."

So it was possible for family to be close as twins even if they were years apart, raised on separate worlds. Louise touched fingers reverently to the photo—proof that they were right in believing that saving their baby brother and sisters would be a wonderful thing.

"Is it really that bad? Living in Pittsburgh?" Jillian asked. "It seems so...fantastical. With magic. Dinosaurs. Elves. Dragons."

April laughed. "We didn't have any dragons in Pittsburgh, thank God. The elves are gorgeous. But magic? It was really just an annoyance. It made machines not work right. Most humans were clueless how to deal with it. Mr. Bell was an exception. He picked it up somehow."

Obviously the Dufaes were all clever, including their sister.

"How did Esme get involved in all this?" They found that most puzzling since Leo had died when Esme was still in middle school.

"Oh, it was all her idea at first. I was there the day she first showed up. She was staying the month with her sister up at the observatory. I think she scared Mr. Bell, talking about his son being killed and everything. He kept saying 'I'm not who you think I am.' Finally she said something like 'The bloodline of his unbounded brilliance must go on. Without his light, darkness will take everything.'"

Louise felt shivers go down her back, and her teacup rattled on the saucer. She fought to still her hand. She felt like she had just heard the most true thing in her life, and it scared her.

Jillian hadn't noticed; she was leaning forward, eyes wide. "Ooohhh, that is so cool."

"What darkness?" Louise asked.

April shrugged and eyed her empty teacup. "I'd grown up in Pittsburgh, which was fast becoming a ghost town compared to what it had been. I'd never met anyone like Esme before. In New York, you meet them here and there, the big fish in a big pond. The movers. The shakers. Forces of nature. She scared me. I started to edge away, saying good-bye. I don't think she had noticed I was in the room until I tried to escape. She turned and saw me by the door and went 'You!'" April pointed forcibly at the door, nearly shouting the word, making Louise jump. "'You're going to help! How would you like to make a million dollars?'"

"A million dollars?" Louise asked.

"She paid you a million dollars to have our sister?" Jillian clarified.

April laughed. "Crazy, right? I didn't believe her at first, but then she gave me some jewelry as a down payment. This amazing tennis bracelet." She held up her right wrist to show off the glitter of large diamonds and blue gemstones. "And a Rolex woman's wristwatch. Her family is rich, and she had this crazy plan of going into space and never coming back, so she was blowing it all on this baby."

"A million dollars for our sister?" Jillian's tone had changed slightly. And Louise understood completely: a million dollars for their older sister and nothing for their siblings still frozen in the lab.

"She had a ton of rules. I wasn't allowed to drink or smoke or do drugs or even date—the last wasn't that hard considering all the decent boys had left Pittsburgh. She swore me to secrecy—I wasn't allowed to tell anyone about the baby. Not my parents. Not her parents. Not even her sister. It would have been impossible to do in the summer, but we had a hard winter and spring was late. I could hide the fact I was pregnant under layers of clothes."

"You're telling us," Louise pointed out.

"Oh, yinz are the exception to the rule." April got up to start poking among her bookcase. "She said that if any of her kids were to show up at my door, I was to tell them everything. Answer every question. And—where is it—oh, here." April pulled out a square wooden box. "And to give you this."

"This" was a Chinese puzzle box, lacquered with a beautiful pattern. April held it out to them and, when neither took it, set it down on the coffee table between them.

"Are you sure she meant us and not our older sister?" Louise asked.

"She said 'any kid.' I think she even added something like 'one or two, together or alone, boy or girl.'" April frowned for a moment. "Where exactly did you come from?"

Louise glanced at Jillian. They hadn't come up with a cover story for that.

"We'd rather not say," Jillian said.

"Our parents stole us," Louise said.

April rubbed at the ridge of her nose. "It's like your whole family has been cursed to live weird and bizarre lives."

"We are not weird," Louise said.

"Oh, so it's perfectly normal for kids your age to disguise themselves as Girl Scouts and ambush people at their front door?"

"We are not disguised as Girl Scouts," Louise snapped. "We *are* Girl Scouts. There's a difference. Do you want to order cookies or not?"

"Yeah, I'll take two boxes of Thin Mints."

They managed to talk April into two boxes of Thin Mints, a box of Samoas, and a box of Trefoils. Then they copied all the pictures of their sister onto their tablets and collected all the personal data on "Mr. Bell," including his phone number and address and his granddaughter's full name, Alexander Graham Bell. Despite being out all night, April insisted on walking them back to the subway station. They barely kept her from escorting them the entire way home, escaping her protection only by promising to go straight home.

"Alexander Graham Bell." Louise rolled the name around, trying to get used to the idea that they had an older sister, nearly eighteen. "Do you think she goes by Alex or Al or Alexi or Xander?"

"Xander?"

"I would," Louise said. "Don't you think it's cool? Xander Bell."

"Alexander Graham Bell is a stupid name. The acting guild

would make you change it. The inventor would spam all hits on your name."

"It would be a way no one could find you. If the first thousand hits were the inventor, people would give up looking for you. I think it's ingenious."

Jillian glared at her and then kicked at the seat in front of them. "It should be Dufae. Tim Bell is obviously Timothy Dufae, Leonardo's father. Why is he going by the name Bell?"

"He's hiding."

"From whom?"

"Whoever killed Leonardo?"

They had just boarded the last train, switching off the feed from mini-Tesla and reactivating Tesla's link with their parents, when Louise's phone rang. She squeaked with alarm: had their parents caught them?

"Hello?" she said tentatively.

Jillian scowled at her; apparently she sounded guilty. Why had her mom picked her to call? Because she knew Jillian lied better?

"Are you still at work?" Louise added to explain her tone. Jillian leaned against her to hear the full conversation. "I thought you'd be at the Forest Forever event until late."

"Louise! Is Jillian with you?" their mother asked, voice full of concern. "Are you two okay?"

"Yes." They answered the first question in unison.

"We're fine," Jillian said as Louise examined the question for traps. They hadn't done anything to warrant a phone call, so something must have happened elsewhere.

"Where are you?" their mother asked with sirens blaring near her.

Louise was glad she could stick to the truth since they were on the correct train to take them to Astoria. "We're on the N train, heading home. We just left Queensboro Plaza. Are you okay?"

"I'm fine." And then hesitantly, she added, "There was an idiot protester with a car bomb, but the police took care of it. It pushed our schedule back nearly two hours. I probably won't be home until tomorrow. The company is paying for a room for me to sleep here tonight."

"Okay," Louise said. "But why are you asking if we're okay?"

"According to a linked story, some of the protestors attacked a nine-year-old at Grand Central–42nd Street Station. Reports are conflicting. Some of them are saying it was a boy who was taken to a hospital, and others are saying it was a girl and she wasn't hurt. I know you were nowhere near there, but I got worried and had to call to check on you."

Louise winced. Since they'd taken the 7 train into the city from the cookie sales in Queens, they'd been at Grand Central–42nd Street Station earlier. It had been full of police, but Louise had been so focused on their mission that she hadn't considered why. The N train connected to 6 local at Lexington Avenue, so they avoided Grand Central on their return. "We're fine. We're almost home."

"I'll call your father and have him meet you at the Astoria-Ditmars station."

"Okay. 'Bye." She hung up and stuffed the Chinese puzzle box into the small storage bin in Tesla's torso. "Oh, God, that was close."

Jillian was doing a little victory dance. "But we weren't caught! We did it! We know all about our older sister, and we got something from our genetic donor."

But they hadn't gotten any closer to saving their baby brother and sisters. Maybe something in Esme's mystery box would help them.

5: PUZZLE BOX

The Chinese puzzle box took them the rest of the day to unlock.

"Esme's lucky we're smart," Jillian complained.

"Maybe if we weren't smart, she didn't want us to open it." Louise spread out the contents.

There were six old-fashioned 2D photographs within the box and an odd rectangle of metal slightly bigger than their pinkies.

"What's this?" Jillian picked up the mystery item and eyed it closely.

"I don't know." Louise watched as Jillian carefully pulled the object into two parts. One piece was a cap that fit over some type of socket at the end.

"I think it plugs into something." Jillian eyed the pronged ending.

Louise picked up the box and examined it closely for hidden connectors. "This doesn't have any place to plug anything into it."

Jillian shook her head. "If I was going to leave something for my kids before getting into a spaceship and leaving Earth forever, I'd leave a hell of lot more. Like pictures of you and our parents, and copies of my movies and Fritz."

Fritz was Jillian's toddler-sized handmade quilt. Their Grandmother Mayer had made both of them one before she died. Louise abandoned her blanket in some long-forgotten period of time, but Jillian's became a fifth member of the family. For years, Jillian never went anywhere without carrying Fritz. It was how everyone told them apart—a fact they used to their advantage

43

often. By the time they were five and starting first grade, Fritz was tattered. Their mother sewed him inside a pillowcase. While they hadn't actually seen Fritz for years, Jillian still slept every night hugging him close.

"Who are you," Louise asked, "and what have you done with my sister?"

Jillian stuck out her tongue. "I know that Esme is still alive out there someplace, but it's like she's dead. She's gone and never coming back, and that's a lot like dead and buried. Taking Fritz would be like destroying him, too."

"I would take him. I would want the company. My kid can get her own blanket."

Jillian laughed and waved the odd piece of metal. "Well, that explains this box then. She took all the cool stuff and only left us this garbage."

Louise held out her hand, and Jillian gave her the mystery item. "I think it's an old computer part. They used to have all sorts of cables and plugs and things." She took out her phone and took several photos of it. "I'll run it through Whatsit."

Jillian spread the 2D photographs out onto the bedspread. They were portraits of three men, two boys, and a woman whose eyes had been masked by black Magic Marker. Between the glossy photos was a folded scrap of paper. Jillian unfolded the note and read it. "Beware the Empire of Evil. They will destroy everything you love to get ahold of you."

Louise shivered. "That is seriously creepy." She picked up the photo of a man in a space suit, patches identifying him as one of the NASA astronauts, apparently from before the Chinese took dominance in space. The patches were too small to read no matter how hard she squinted at them. "Wow, these are old. There are no digital tags to identify these people. What you see is all you get."

"There's writing on the back," Jillian said.

Louise flipped the photo over. "How low tech. She went into space when?"

"Eighteen years ago. What does it say?"

"'The King of Denmark, Neil Shenske.' I think this is Esme's father. Her bio said that her father was an astronaut. This is our grandfather."

"We're Danish princesses?" Jillian was obviously wavering

between fantastical possibility and the logic that princesses weren't born from abandoned embryos. Louise was riding the same emotional rollercoaster.

"Nothing on Esme said anything about her being a princess." Louise forced herself to point out the most logical evidence they had.

They both did searches, racing to find more information.

"American astronaut, inspired by Apollo Moon shots, flew two space-shuttle missions."

"Born in Ohio. Went to MIT. Married Anna Cohan. Had two daughters, Lain and Esme."

"He was killed in a drive-by shooting at a science fair at an inner-city school. Esme was four when he died."

"I'm not finding any reference to him being the king of Denmark."

"He's not even Danish."

Louise flipped the photo and frowned at the words. "Maybe it's some kind of code."

"What do the others say?" Jillian picked up the photo of a dark-haired young man who looked like a movie star caught in a candid moment, his focus intently on something off-camera. Jillian read the back and giggled.

"What does it say?"

"'Crown Prince Kiss Butt of the Evil Empire.'" Jillian giggled more. "It also says, 'Yes, you're smarter, but he's sadistic and short-tempered. Don't get snarky with him.' Esme must have thought we'd be snarky as well as clever. We're not snarky."

"Elle Pondwater thinks we're snarky."

"Elle is rarely right about anything. Besides, snarky is not genetic."

Louise rather thought it might be but didn't want to argue the point. The two blond boys were more average looking. There was, however, a strong family resemblance with the crown prince. "Flying Monkey Four and Five. Where are one, two, and three?"

Jillian shrugged, and they made sure there were no other photos, either still in the box or somehow stuck to the others. Esme had drawn black Magic Marker across the eyes of the woman and trailed it off so the line nearly looked like cloth ribbon blindfolding her. Louise studied the photo, trying to understand their mother. What was the point of a photo if they couldn't see all of the woman's face? The black line did emphasize the woman's

elegance. Her mouth was flawlessly defined by lipstick into a perfect bow that nature hadn't blessed her with. She had a strong,
determined chin. Every hair of her pale blond bob was in place.
She wore a black silk blouse and an amber teardrop necklace.
The back of her photo read: "Queen Gertrude of Denmark, blind
to her husband's crimes led to Hamlet's death. Careful, lest her
blindness lead to your capture."

"Hamlet?" Louise said. "Like the play? Do you think she's an
actress?"

"I think you're right. It's some kind of code."

"Some code. Hi, I went off to space and left you in the fridge,
here's a nice puzzle to hurt your brain."

Jillian giggled and then sobered. "She probably left the box for
Alexander, not us." She pulled up the digital photos of Alexander.
The one of her labeled "nine years old" could have been Louise
with her blast-shortened hair. "We really don't look like Esme
or her father at all."

"Crown Prince Kiss Butt and the flying monkeys look like
brothers. They have the same cheekbones, and their eyes look
vaguely Asian."

Jillian nodded in agreement. "There's no flying monkeys in
Hamlet, though. At least none that I remember." She struck a
dramatic pose. "To be or not to be, that is the question: whether
'tis nobler in the mind to suffer the slings and arrows of out-
rageous fortune or to take arms against a sea of troubles and
by opposing end them." Jillian paused in mid-dramatic gesture.
"Oh! I wonder. Hamlet's story is about him trying to deal with
the murder of his father—the King of Denmark. The odds are
so stacked against him that he pretends to be insane for a part
of the play."

"It ends badly for Hamlet?"

"Very badly. But there's no monkeys—flying or otherwise."

Louise trusted Jillian to know any trivia connected to *Hamlet*.
She tried searching the other direction. "Most of the hits for 'flying monkey' are for *The Wonderful Wizard of Oz*. It's about a
young girl who is swept up by a storm and deposited on another
world filled with magical creatures."

"Maybe that's a reference to Elfhome."

"You know what's odd?" Jillian studied Anna's photo and then
the boys who might be brothers. "Neil and Anna are the only

ones that are looking at the camera. The rest of these seem to be taken without the person aware that they're being photographed."

Louise checked the last photo. The man was sitting at a table in a large sunroom, reading a paper, steam curling up from a cup in front of him. He was striking to look at, with unnaturally white skin and odd amber eyes. His coloring made him seem unreal, like he was a vampire or something. His hair was white, as if he was old, but his face was unlined, making it impossible to guess his age. He was reading an old-fashioned newspaper and seemed unaware of the camera. "I think you're right. They're like stalker pictures."

"What does that one say?"

Louise flipped over the picture of the man with the newspaper. "This one says: 'Ming the Merciless of the Empire of Evil.'"

"It's another literature reference." Jillian frowned at the screen of her tablet. "Ming is an evil emperor from a movie series called *Flash Gordon* filmed in the mid-1900s. Ming has a large army with everything from death rays to robots poised to take over Earth. But he doesn't look anything like this guy."

Louise stared at the photos. "Our genetic donor was weird."

Whatsit identified the item in the box as a "flash drive" with a "USB connector" and had diagrams on how it used to plug into the side of the clunky computers which were common at the turn of the century.

"It could have anything on it." Louise read through the description of the technology's development. Assuming that Esme used the most advanced one she could buy at the time, it could represent a large amount of data. "Photographs. A video blog."

"But we don't have anything to plug it into!" Jillian growled.

"We could buy an old computer . . . or something," Louise murmured. They couldn't be the only people who had had this problem. It turned out that it had been a common difficulty shortly after computers started to use wireless connections exclusively. Adapters had been made so the flash drives could be plugged in to a transmitter and accessed. They would need to download emulators so their tablets could run the decades-old software, but it was just juggling data once a connection was made.

She found several places still selling adapters and whimpered at the price. It wasn't expensive, but it still was a lot more than she had left in her mobile payment account. Louise checked Jillian's account to see if they could pool their money. "We don't have enough money."

Jillian winced. "It's going to take weeks to have enough with our allowance."

"If Mom and Dad don't dock us for the cost of the playhouse."

"Shh!" Jillian whispered. "Don't give them ideas."

"Maybe we can sell something."

"No," Jillian said. "All we have left after the fire is our video-processing equipment, and we're not selling that. We don't know what's on the flash drive, and it might be useless crap." She glared at the photos, the flash drive, and the scrap of paper with the cryptic warning. "Our stupid genetic donor."

6: MERMAID GAMBIT

They had an older sister. Better yet, she wasn't some beauty-pageant poser like Elle Pondwater; she was a super-cool gear-head. She lived on Elfhome. She probably knew Elvish. And their grandfather understood magic, so she might even know some real spells. She couldn't get more perfect unless she also had all sorts of interesting pets. She could own an elfhound. Or a horse! According to April and old satellite maps of Pittsburgh prior to first Shutdown, the hotel where Alexander lived could house an entire zoo.

It was at once terrifying and intoxicating to think that they could actually call their older sister and talk to her. Maybe she could figure out a solution to how to save their baby siblings.

Every thirty days, the Chinese turned off the hyperphase gate (invented by their male genetic donor) and Pittsburgh returned to Earth. Initially Shutdown had been the first of the month. While the thirty-day cycle had worked for September, April, June, and November, all the other months and a half dozen leap years pushed Shutdown to some illogical date currently falling in the middle of the month.

They maintained a website for their production company, Lemon-Lime JEl-Lo. Since their parents forbid them from using the website for any true advertising or promotion, they simply had a counter counting down to the next Shutdown. They used it for an interesting, self-imposed deadline for their videos. Louise sighed at the ticking numbers. While it would only be a few days until they could contact Alexander, it seemed like forever.

And there was the niggling problem that they didn't have a phone number for Alexander. Apparently at some point Tim Bell had changed his phone number, and April had taken it as a sign that she was not to call his house. Trying to find any information out about Pittsburgh was much like being a jewel thief. Even the most mundane of information was locked away. They had to routinely hack into secure databases to get what they needed for their videos. They usually copied anything they could get away with, but up to this point they hadn't needed a telephone list.

Louise glanced at her alarm clock. She had ten minutes until their mother expected them to be eating breakfast. She might have time to find a copy, especially if she got lucky and it was on one of their favorite sites. A band of anonymous hackers ran a data haven, posting information on Pittsburgh they'd "found" in undisclosed locations. As always, she made sure that she couldn't be traced before dropping into the forum.

The first post made her heart jump. The heading was "Looking for Lemon-Lime JEl-Lo." She sat staring at it with fear. Should she read the post? Who in the world even knew that they visited this forum?

Taking a breath, she opened the post. It was breezy in tone, meandering in points, and signed with a name that made her squeak in surprise.

"What?" Jillian called from their bathroom.

"Nigel Reid wants to talk to us."

"Nigel Reid? You mean 'I just love Nigel' Nigel Reid?"

"I never said that!" She respected the filmmaker. He was her favorite naturalist. "But yes, that one."

Jillian squeaked, too. "Seriously? Talk to us?"

"Yes. Well. Lemon-Lime JEl-Lo. He's seen *The Queen's Pantaloons* and wants to know if the gossamer call is real. He's coming to New York to do the *Today Show,* and he wants to know if he can meet us."

"Meet him? Like in person?"

"Generally that's what 'meet' means."

"Are you nuts? You know that Mom and Dad would just freak if they found out that we were going to meet some old guy from the Internet. They'll get him arrested as a pedophile!"

"He wants to meet with a film-production company!" Louise cried in defense. "He doesn't know Lemon-Lime is just two kids. If he did think we were kids, he probably thinks we're in high school or college."

"Pfft, high school is just as bad. Besides, we don't know if this is really Nigel Reid posting this. It could be anyone. We list him as one of our influences. By posing as him, anyone could hope to lure us out."

"It would be so cool if it was." Louise went to Nigel Reid's official personal site. How could they tell if he was actually the person contacting them and not a pervert using his name? "Nigel is going to be on the *Today Show* in like three weeks. We could go see the show." Although "seeing the show" would really be standing on the sidewalk at the corner of 49th and Rockefeller Center with the crowd that gathered daily at the break of dawn.

Jillian considered it. "I don't know. Feels like a trap to me. How is he going to know we're really us? A big sign that says 'Nigel, we're Lemon-Lime'? And if it's not him that posted that? Whoever is trying to lure us out would have us cornered."

Jillian was right. They'd be out in the open for hours, with Nigel probably camping out in a green room. If someone was just using his name to lure them out, they could be in lots of danger. Although, no one knew they were two nine-year-olds. Lemon-Lime could be the group name for fifteen muscle-bound men—who liked Barbie dolls.

But why would someone like Nigel Reid want to meet them? While no one else seemed to realize how the elves were controlling the great living airships, the clues were there if anyone started to look in the right place. All the research they'd done, anyone else could do. They'd sketched out a mock-up of a gossamer call along the lines of a dog whistle, but they had no way of knowing if it would actually work. They agreed that they were probably missing something important in the design. Magic existed, flowed, pooled, and was depleted. The elves harnessed it in countless ways but guarded many of their secrets carefully. Humans still didn't understand magic well enough to quantify it or even determine its source. If the elves were combining an ultrasonic whistle with magic, then no, the twins' call had no hope of actually working.

Did Nigel think they had a working gossamer call?

And why would he think that? The only time they mentioned it in their videos had been a throwaway line in a comedic sketch about frilly underwear. Who in their right mind would use that as evidence of a working prototype? It made no sense.

Still, it was Nigel Reid! And yes, maybe she did love him. He seemed really, really nice, and he was always so gentle and kind to the animals he filmed. If there was a chance to talk to him face-to-face, she wanted it to happen.

What they needed was a two-part recognition process. The *Today Show* would serve to establish that Nigel Reid was the person who posted on the forum. After that they could pick someplace safe to meet.

Like maybe invite him to dinner at their house.

Even though she knew that was impossible, it made her insides go all fluttery with nerves. With trembling fingers, she double-checked that the forum only had an anonymous e-mail account that wasn't linked to them in any way. Once she was sure that a reply couldn't be traced to them, she created a private message and typed in, "This is Lemon-Lime. Say 'hi' to us on the *Today Show* so we know this post is really from you and then check back here. We'll private-message contact information after the show."

"What did you do?" Jillian asked.

Louise showed her the post.

Jillian squeaked in surprise. "You didn't!"

"I did."

Jillian flung arms around Louise and hugged her tight. "That is so awesome! I can't wait to meet him!"

"No," their mother said simply.

"Neither one of us could take the morning off to go with you," their father elaborated. "People start showing up for that at like five-thirty in the morning and stand around in Rockefeller Center until nearly noon."

"We could go alone. We have Tesla."

"No!" their mother said. "Tesla can walk you from point A to point B, but for standing there for over six hours, you need an adult. And don't go calling your Aunt Kitty and asking her—she's got a deadline she's behind on."

"Nigel Reid is the guest," Louise said.

"I know he's your favorite," their mother said.

"And he always brings animals," Louise plowed on.

Their mother laughed as if this was a joke. "Of course he does. He's a naturalist. That's what people like him do when they're on TV shows: bring animals that misbehave in funny ways and scare the daylights out of the hosts."

"It's not like he brings dangerous animals." Louise felt the need to point it out, just in case this was part of their objection.

Their parents exchanged a look.

"Not everyone likes all animals, honey," their father said. "Some people are scared of snakes and, and—"

"Spiders." Their mother added what mildly scared her. "And creepy-looking lizards."

"That's just stupid," Louise muttered quietly.

"Don't pass judgment on people," their mother said. "And no, you can't go, and don't you two dare sneak off by yourselves to see it, or there will be a world of hurt for both of you."

"World of hurt" translated to them losing everything from Internet access to having to surrender their video equipment. In Louise's opinion, corporal punishment would be over faster and thus less painful in the long run—which was probably why their mother opted for her way.

Louise was so disappointed that she forgot why she'd been on the Pittsburgh forum in the first place until they reached school. The day got worse as she searched through the forums and discovered no one had a telephone directory for Pittsburgh.

"This day sucks." Louise explained what she'd found out and why she'd been looking.

"We have Alexander's street address." Jillian pushed Tesla into their shared locker. "He's not going to fit in this when winter comes and we have two coats and snow boots to store in here."

Louise really hoped that by winter they'd have worked something else out, although Tesla was making it so they had a great deal of freedom to move through the city. "Anything we mail has to hit Cranberry days before Shutdown to make it across to the border. If we miss the window, it will sit at the post office for a month until the next Shutdown."

"So?" Jillian leaned against the wall and watched the ebb and flow of fifth-graders in the hallway. "It's not going to go bad unless we send something like cookies. Real homemade cookies, not the

Girl Scout cookies. We can only call during the twenty-four hours of Shutdown. The first five hours are while we're asleep. Then we're here at school. And if we make a call at home, Mom and Dad are going to want to know who the heck we're talking to." Because they never talked to people other than Aunt Kitty on the phone.

"I'd rather talk to Alexander instead of mailing her a letter." Louise started to check sites that might have a Pittsburgh phone book. They were places like the universities and government offices, so she needed to actually hack the sites to search them. At least she could bounce through the café next to the school, so she didn't have to worry about being traced. "Just dropping a letter into the mail feels a little like writing a letter to Santa Claus. In September! If she answers back, it could take months for her letter to get to us."

"Her answering would be Christmas?"

"Duh!"

"Shoot! Well, the day just got worse," Jillian warned. "Incoming."

Louise looked up from her tablet. "Huh?"

Jillian nodded down the hall, where Elle stood surrounded by the girls from the other fifth-grade class, taught by Mr. Howe. "Elle is passing out invitations to the girls."

"Already? I thought her birthday was next month." Elle's elaborate birthday parties were a yearly ritual. Pride and etiquette demanded that Elle invite all the girls in their grade; thus, they were always included. It had taken them two disasters to realize that they were invited only in form, not in spirit. They hadn't attended in third or fourth grade.

"I only did one invitation." Elle handed it over like it should have been on a silver platter. "But it's for both of you. That's why I just put 'Mayer' on it."

"And this is yours." Elle handed Jillian their broken camera that had been standing in as mini-Tesla. "I have no idea how it ended up in my bag, or why you'd want something so broken, but my mother said I had to make sure you got it."

"Thank you." Louise knew her mother would ask later if she'd thanked Elle for the invitation or not. She also knew that because there was only one invitation, Jillian figured that they were both covered by Louise's thanks.

Invitation delivered, Elle turned on her heel and wove down the hallway, skillfully avoiding the curious boys to intercept Zahara. The beautiful African-American girl was in Mr. Howe's class. She was always late to the fifth-grade floor because she had to deliver her younger brother to his classroom downstairs.

Jillian tore open the envelope and muttered a dark curse at the invitation. "Little Mermaid."

"You're kidding me." Louise had never understood the appeal of *The Little Mermaid.* "I thought she would have grown out of that."

Jillian kept cursing.

"We don't have to go," Louise said.

"This isn't about Elle's birthday, it's about the class play. She wants to do the play *The Little Mermaid,* and she's going to be Princess Ariel. I'll end up as the Sea Witch."

"Oh shoot," Louise hissed.

"It wouldn't be so bad if we did the original Hans Christian Andersen story where the mermaid dies after the prince marries another woman. At least that mermaid was a soulless creature made of water who was really after immortality by exchanging a three-hundred-year lifespan for a soul. The husband was just icing on the cake. No, no, we'll be doing the story where she gives every-thing up for a boy, including everyone that she loves dear, screws the world to hell and back and then needs him to kill the villain while she's helpless someplace else. Oh, God, I'm so sick of these wussy princesses and evil women. We've done the evil witches of Sleeping Beauty and Rapunzel, the evil queen of Snow White and the evil stepmother of Cinderella. Is this some kind of campaign against femininity? Our choices are the evil and usually ugly pow-erful female or the helpless princess, desired just for her beauty? And what the heck is this shit about evil stepmothers anyway?"

"Well, it's following a biological imperative that a female devotes all her attention to the children that carry her DNA as opposed to the DNA of another female."

"Oh, shut up, monkey girl, we are not cuckoo birds, tossing eggs out of nests and getting someone else to raise our chicks. We're humans!"

"Okay, Wilbur. What are we going to do about Elle and these damn mermaid zombie chicks?"

Jillian giggled. "Oh, it would be worth it if I could rewrite it to zombies." She grinned. "The boys would love it if it was a zombie play."

"They're never going to let us do a major rewrite of a play again."

Jillian nodded, thinking. "Too bad there are more girls than boys. That way, if we found a play that the boys liked, they could just outvote the girls. Something cool. Like *Macbeth*."

"Like *Macbeth* but in plain English."

"It should have sword fights," Jillian said firmly.

"Robots. Dinosaurs."

"Elves."

"At least try to think like a boy," Louise said.

"It has to be a real play, not something we write, that boys will like."

"Do you think they made *Lord of the Flies* into a play?"

"All the characters in that are boys. There has to be at least one or two girl parts, just so we can sway the girls that don't fall under Elle's spell. If we can get a couple of the girls on our side, it would work."

They thought for a moment. Louise found herself eyeing Tesla sitting statuelike inside their locker. Their mother had thought he looked liked Nana, the Darling's Saint Bernard nanny.

"What about *Peter Pan*? Pirates. Sword fights. Indians."

"Native Americans," Jillian muttered, frowning as she thought through the casting. "Elle would want to be Wendy. That would leave Mrs. Darling or Tinker Bell for me."

"You'd be Peter. He's usually played by a girl."

Jillian's face lit up. "Oh, God, that's perfect. Elle wouldn't want to be a boy, and I would have the lead!"

They had Library as their first-period class, so they spent the hour digging through what had been produced for *Peter Pan*.

"God, I'm starting to understand why Mom never showed us the cartoon. What the hell happened? You take the most manly of boys—he runs around naked except for some leaves, and he fights pirates—and you turn his story into this." Jillian turned her tablet to show off the big-busted blond Tinker Bell. "In the novel, Tinker Bell dies a year after Wendy goes back to London, and Peter forgets all about her."

Louise had forgotten that twist. "Ignore her. She's poison to the boys having any interest in *Peter Pan*."

Jillian nodded. "We stick to the original play and focus on Hook and the pirates and the ticking crocodile."

"But what format are we going to use for the pitch? Boys don't like to read. And most of the movie versions are girly."

Jillian flopped back from her tablet. "How about a music video? We do all things that are cool with Peter Pan and this 'I'm a tough guy, don't mess with me' fight song with a heavy bass beat."

"Let the bodies hit the floor. Let the bodies hit the floor." Louise sung the first song that same to mind.

"Exactly." Jillian opened up a file on her tablet and started to take notes. "Or at least something like that."

"So the Lost Boys, the tree houses, the island, the pirates, sword fights..."

"Yes, a swordfight on the pirate ship!" Jillian called up her storyboard app. "Start with Peter and the Lost Boys at the tree houses, run to the beach, look at the uber cool pirate ship in the moonlight. Then the Lost Boys board the ship and there's a big swordfight."

"In two weeks?"

"We can—could crank out a full episode of *The Adventures of Queen Soulful Ember* in a month, and those have a lot more to storyboard, full original animation, dialogue to dub, sound effects, and a music score."

"We blew up our studio with all our sets and all our models."

"We'll work around that. I can act in front of a green screen for Peter's part. We can base Hook off of... hm." Jillian considered the boys in their classroom with narrowed eyes. The plays were a combined effort of both classes of their grade. With the exception of "the Prince," the boys usually had minor roles like dwarves and mice. Reed normally played the Prince for the same reason Elle got to be the Princess. He was tall, blond and handsome. Unfortunately, he was clumsy and as much a social wallflower as the twins.

If they needed all the boys, though, they should win over the boys' leader.

"Iggy," Louise said. "Iggy should be Hook."

Iggy's real name was Ignatius Martin Chen. He was apparently named after a baby of a movie star. His first-generation Chinese parents obviously didn't realize how uncommon the name was. He was in Mr. Howe's classroom across the hall, only sharing lunch, recess, and class play with them. He was the acknowledged leader of the boys, perhaps because he was also the tallest boy in the fifth grade and naturally athletic.

Jillian tilted her head, thinking. "Iggy does like to be in front of an audience, and he remembers his lines when he actually gets something to say."

"We should use all the boys in the video. It wouldn't be too hard to model their pictures onto CGI skin. We can do half for the Lost Boys and the other half as pirates."

Jillian was nodding. "We can put the Lost Boys in war paint. Make them look cool. We'll have to take pictures of all the boys without them noticing us."

"Or we could tell them we want to cast them for a music video. They'll be more vested in the end product."

Jillian winced. "Actually talk to them?"

"If we're going to highjack the play completely, we'll have to talk to them a lot," Louise pointed out. "We work for almost three months on the play. Half of April and all of May and June." The play represented a massive amount of work, all in the name of learning how to cooperate as a class. Everything was a joint effort, from voting on what play to do, to designing and building sets, to the actual performance. "Either we talk to them or devote all that time to *The Little Mermaid*."

"Ick! Okay, let's talk to the boys at recess about this."

"Today?"

Jillian waved the party invite. "Elle's party is in two weeks. We vote on the play the week after. We have to get this up and running quickly if we're going to head off Elle."

Any time on the video would take time away from their research on finding a way to save their little brother and sisters. If they were going to do it, then they should do it as fast as possible. "Okay, we'll do it this recess."

Perelman School for the Gifted had a rooftop playground with tall perforated metal screens creating a protective enclosure and shade. Through the orange-painted mesh, they had a clear view of all the skyscrapers of New York rising up to loom over the school. Heat of the sunbaked roof battled with the cold April wind off the bay.

The boys played four square at the edge of the playground, taking turns at rotating through the grid as players fouled out of the game. Iggy tended to hold the King's square for long periods, controlling the large red ball with ease. For some reason, today he was sitting in the shade, just watching the game.

While Jillian was fearless around adults, she tended to be shy of other kids, especially boys. Louise suspected it was because "cute" didn't work on kids their own age. Or maybe it did, and they only thought it didn't because when they were younger, what melted adults to helpless puddles utterly failed to impress other toddlers and preschoolers.

Louise marched up to Iggy and asked quickly, "Can we take pictures of you?" before she lost her nerve.

Iggy lifted his head to glare up at her. His left eye was swollen nearly shut and bruised dark purple. "Why do you want my picture?"

"What happened to you?" Louise asked.

"Doh. What does it look like? Some guy hit me."

"A guy? Like an adult? Why?"

"Yeah, he's twenty-four. He was one of those protesters that are pissed at the Chinese over the Elfhome thing. The whole 'China is stealing the heartland of the United States' bullshit. Like I have anything to do with that!"

"Why would he even hit you? You're just a kid."

"All Chinese are short even when they're full grown!" Iggy obviously was imitating someone older than him. "I think the jerk just hit the first Asian-looking person that was shorter than him. There's several billion Chinese on the planet, and most of them don't give a shit about Pittsburgh or Elfhome. My dad says the protesters are a bunch of redneck idiots. The United States makes a hundred times more off the elves than China does, and China is still paying back the loans it took out to cover their original remuneration."

The Saturday newscast that panicked their mother suddenly took on new meaning. The nine-year-old boy attacked on the subway was Iggy. His three older sisters also attended Perelman School for the Gifted.

Louise realized that the reason he was sitting out of the game was that two of the fingers on his left hand were splinted. "Are you okay?"

He followed her gaze to his fingers. "Oh, yeah." He blushed and looked away. "My sister tasered him. We all ended up at the police department. They're calling it a hate crime and throwing the book at him."

"Good," Louise said.

Iggy squinted up at her as if she was a miniature puzzle. "You know, I don't think we've ever talked before."

She wasn't sure what that meant. "You don't know our names?"

He laughed. "We've been in school together for five years. I know who you are. It's just that you don't talk to anyone. It's kind of freaking me out."

"We just want to take pictures of you."

"Yeah, yeah, that's part of the weirdness. Why?"

"We're making a music video."

"If anyone else said that, I'd figure that they were setting me up for a viral-meme joke. I think, though, that you two would only do that if I'd done something epic to really piss you off, and I'm fairly sure I haven't. Have I?"

"No." Louise cut Jillian off because she saw her starting to consider making up a lie. "Elle is talking the girls into doing *The Little Mermaid* for this year's play."

"Oh, gross, another kissy-face play?" Iggy groaned.

Jillian frowned at Louise for telling Iggy the truth. As long as Elle didn't know what they were doing, she couldn't counter-attack the twins. Jillian glanced pointedly at Elle playing jump rope with all the other girls from fifth grade. "What will end up happening is the same thing that happened all the other years. Elle and her friends will all vote together and everyone else will split the rest of their votes on a couple different plays and Elle wins by default. If we get everyone to agree on the same play, then Elle can't win."

"Girls outnumber the boys." Iggy pointed out the flaw to the plan.

"We're not going to vote with Elle. We just need one or two of the other girls to go along with us. Elle doesn't control them all." Just most of them.

"What play do you guys want to do?" Iggy asked.

"One with pirates and swordfights," Jillian said.

"*Peter Pan.*" Louise got another glare from Jillian. She felt, though, if they misled Iggy and he turned against them, they'd lose all the boys. "Mr. Howe and Miss Hamilton aren't going to let us do something like *Hamlet* or *Macbeth*. We need a play with at least twenty-five parts for both girls and boys that the school considers 'a classic' and thus safe. There aren't a lot of those."

"Do you want to be dressed as a hermit crab and sing 'Kiss de Girl' or be a pirate captain?" Jillian said.

"Sing with me now." Iggy raised his hand and snapped his fingers together like a crab's claw. "Sha-la-la-la, my oh my, looks like de boy's too shy." He burst into laughter at their shocked looks. "I have three sisters. The entire soundtrack has been burned into my brain. We've even been to the Broadway version twice."

"You want to do *The Little Mermaid*?" Jillian cried with horror.

"No!" Iggy cried back. "Captain Hook, eh?" He laughed and held out his splinted fingers. "Look, I'm halfway there."

"So, we can take pictures of you for Hook?"

He considered it while making funny thinking faces. "Hook is this weird mix of scary badass and just campy silly. He'd be fun to play. Okay, I'm in."

They moved against the white wall of the gymnasium to shoot the headshots.

Iggy struck a pose. "I want to look more like Captain Jack Sparrow."

"We're not doing poufy Hook." Jillian had gone into director mode. "Peter is coming with the Lost Boys. It's all games to him, but you seriously want to kick his butt."

"Who is going to be Peter?"

"Me," Jillian admitted cautiously.

Iggy broke into surprised laughter.

"Don't smile!" Jillian snapped. "You're a badass pirate. Tell Peter he's a little girly boy in French."

Iggy laughed again. "Why French?"

"Because you'll need to think."

He frowned in concentration. *"Vous... etes... une petite... fille. Un singe. Mange... des... toilettes."*

"Yes, good," Jillian said, even though the sentences made little or no sense.

"Stupide... cul... fromage... singe." He started to giggle.

"What?" Louise couldn't help asking since it sounded like he'd said "Stupid ass cheese monkey."

"I'm only pulling a B in French," Iggy said. "My parents are ready to beat me for it."

Jillian glared at them both, which only made Iggy laugh harder.

"Captain Hook cannot *giggle*," Jillian stated firmly.

"Okay, okay, I got this." Iggy forced himself to be serious. Surprisingly, he managed to look very fierce and determined despite having been giggling a moment before. *"Excusez-moi, je peux vous aider? Vous avez des cartes postales?"*

It was the practice dialogue from last fall with a customer buying postcards in a shop.

After they'd gotten a full set of headshots of him being serious and menacing, he called over the boys standing in line, waiting for their turn at four square. He told them simply that they were doing a music video and reassured them, "It will be awesome." He also suggested that they cast all the Lost Boys from "Peter's" class and the pirates from "Hook's" class.

They managed to get photos of all the boys before the bell rang, ending recess. Iggy walked with them down to their floor.

"You know," he said before they split up to their own classrooms. "You two should talk more to people. You're really cool, but no one knows that."

7: MUCH TO DO ABOUT NOTHING

The twins fought boredom every waking moment. Trapped in the classroom eight hours, endlessly "taught" subjects they already knew, they had to invent ways to quietly keep themselves amused, or run the risk of going insane. It was odd but exhilarating to suddenly be overwhelmed by dozens of projects.

For the first time in Louise's life, she found herself needing a to-do list. She opened a document on her home desktop and started one as she painted backgrounds for the Lost Boys music video.

She still needed to find a Pittsburgh phone directory. If they were really going to contact Alexander for help with the babies, she wanted to hear her older sister's voice. Besides, it was much the same problem they were having with Nigel; how could they be sure that the person they reached was Alexander if they stuck to letters? Since Shutdown was several days away, though, they had plenty of time to track down Alexander's phone number.

They needed to save money to buy an adaptor for Esme's mystery flash drive. With their allowance, it might take weeks, and it meant they would have to delay replacing their broken camera. They still had to identify the people in Esme's photographs, but that was low priority since the pictures were over eighteen years old. Some of the people might be dead.

They were going to miss their deadline on posting their newest Lemon-Lime video. The raw footage was done. Editing on the music video for school, though, took precedence if they wanted to outmaneuver Elle. It might be good, though, to post a filler video. Louise made a note to do something quick and simple. Maybe just a fake title page that erupted into flames and then Queen Soulful Ember announcing, "Blast it all! That was too silly! Try again!"

Giggling, Louise made notes and moved to the next project. She wanted to do more research on the gossamer call, just in case it turned out to be really Nigel Reid posting on the Pittsburgh forum. She marked the date he was supposed to appear on the *Today Show*. She added "Rockefeller Center, 5:30" in the hope that they could figure a way around their mother's edict. What they needed was an adult that they could bully into taking them into the city.

"Do you think we could do a Girl Scout field trip to the *Today Show*?" she asked.

Jillian shook her head, not looking up from the animating that she was doing on her tablet. "It's after the vote on the play. If things go the way we want, I don't think Mrs. Pondwater will be willing to take us anywhere."

"If it's already all set up, she might not be able to back out gracefully."

"We can try."

Louise added it to her list. And on that note, she added that they needed to deliver cookies to April and her doorman. She considered the possibility of talking April into taking them to the *Today Show* and then realized they'd have to explain to their parents how they knew the woman. Nope, that wouldn't work.

The most important thing on her to-do list was the one thing she couldn't move forward on: saving the babies. They had searched out the trust that had paid for the storage over the last eighteen years. Esme had set up the account, but the funds had run out last year. To take over the payments would require thousands of dollars.

The most maddening thing was that they technically had the money in their college fund. Their parents had been saving the money since the twins were born. It was doubtful that the twins would ever need it; between their parents' low income and their placement tests, they were guaranteed full scholarships. They couldn't touch the money until they were eighteen.

"If we could just use our college fund," she growled.

"Never happen." Jillian blew out her breath in disgust. "Stupid waste of money." Their parents saw Jillian's fascination in movies as a phase that she'd outgrow. Louise doubted it; Jillian had planned from the age of four on being the youngest movie director ever to win an Oscar. "They want us to be lawyers or bankers or something stupid and boring like that. The only way they'll let us use our college fund for anything other than school is if we were already out of college and making buckets of money."

It kept coming back to the fact that they had no way of making money as nine-year-olds. It wasn't that they couldn't figure out a way to earn money. Every scheme they'd come up with, though, required a bank account to collect their earnings. Without their parents' consent, and more importantly, their Social Security numbers, the twins couldn't legally apply for one. Louise was sure that if they were normal kids, their parents would have been happy that their kids were taking responsibility and learning how to manage money. Their mother knew them too well; she saw a bank account as a too easily exploitable venture.

"With the money they're making now, Mom and Dad couldn't take on four more kids." Louise had checked into the costs involved in a standard pregnancy. "I had no idea how much time and money goes into having a baby born. You have to go to the doctors constantly. There's blood tests, urine tests, sonograms, ultrasounds. And that's not even what it costs for the delivery. It's a massive amount of time and money if everything goes right. It's a whole other ballgame if things go wrong.

"Then there's food and clothing, and where would the babies sleep? We couldn't have six of us in this bedroom."

"This would be so much easier if we were almost eighteen like Alexander."

Louise nodded in agreement. "What we need most is time."

"We need to be old enough that we can have good jobs. We have to be able to pay for a surrogate mother like April, a place we all can live comfortably, and still be able to buy them stuff like socks and boots and winter coats."

Jillian obviously was thinking of the homeless men they saw on the street sometimes, nearly freezing in the snow.

"And they need their own college fund." Jillian continued. "So if one of them wants to be a lawyer or a doctor, they can."

"We need time and money," Louise said.

"With time, we can get money. It's just time we need."

8: BIRTHDAY GREETINGS

On Thursday, Jillian made the mistake of leaving Elle's invitation out on her desk in their bedroom where their mother saw it during one of her spot-checks on how clean they were keeping their bathroom. They were deeply engrossed in video editing at that moment, so she managed to read it before they even realized she had picked it up off Jillian's desk.

Their mother made a little sound of impatience. "Why didn't you tell me about this? I need to R.S.V.P. by tomorrow."

Louise and Jillian exchanged glances. They shared the responsibility of telling her by both saying, "We're not going."

"It's Elle," Louise added. "We really aren't friends with her."

Their mother pursed her lips, considering. They waited, barely breathing. "She invited all the girls?" she asked finally.

"Yes, but it's just a power maneuver to get control of the play!" Jillian cried. "She's a Gemini, Mom, which means her birthday really is after May twenty-first. She's having her birthday early so she can have it before the joint-class play meeting at the end of this month. She wants to do *The Little Mermaid* and we don't."

Louise winced. Jillian was an amazing liar, but when she stuck to the truth she seemed to have no idea what would be the result of her words.

"What happened to invade and conquer?" their mother asked.

"This is not Iraq," Jillian said. "It's a birthday party."

"It's diplomacy. You need to learn it."

"But we don't want to go," Jillian cried, digging them in deeper.

"Honey, this is going to seem callous and awful, and I hate that I sound like my mother, but life is full of things you don't really want to do that you should do. Everything from going to the dentist to giving blood. I really don't like taking time out of my schedule to let someone jab me with a needle and screw up the rest of my day by sucking blood out of my arm. The only reason, though, that I'm alive today is because some stranger donated blood for my mother before I was born and again when I was a teenager and was in a car accident."

"That's different. That's saving a life."

"We're sending you to school with kids your age so you can learn this, and it's been five years and you haven't learned it. You need people. Yes, it would be great and wonderful if all the people in your life were like Aunt Kitty." They had always called Mom's best friend "aunt" even though she wasn't related by blood; she'd been informally "adopted" by their grandmother when the two friends were in high school. "Those are rare and wonderful treasures when you find them, but you need all the people."

"Are you saying we should suck up to Elle?" Jillian asked because she knew the answer would be "no."

"Obviously you haven't learned the difference between 'sucking up' and 'taking advantage of your opportunities.' It's time you learn. You're going."

"Mom!" Jillian and Louise both cried.

"Let me make myself clear." She raised her right hand up, meaning that she would not tolerate them trying to weasel out. "You are going. You will be nice. You will do your best to have fun. You will be polite to Mrs. Pondwater and Elle. You will do nothing to submarine the party. You will use this opportunity to be friends not with Elle but with Elle's friends, because one of them might be a girl you've discounted and held at arm's length merely because Elle claimed her first. The only way you will ever find a friend like Aunt Kitty is to open yourself up to friendship. You will never find other people to love while sitting in your bedroom, talking only to each other."

She finished giving a slow benediction with her upraised hand by pointing to each of them. "Have I made myself clear?"

"Yes," they both whispered.

She sighed and lowered her hand. "You need to learn how to play the game of diplomacy. Right now you're just fighting for a play. In the future, it could be for getting a job you love or a raise you deserve, or to win support for a law that will save people's lives, or ... or I don't know. You two have the power to change the world. You're letting shallow, self-serving people like the Pondwaters win because they understand the game and you don't."

That Saturday they went into Manhattan to find a present for Elle. They stopped first at FAO Schwarz and wandered through the vast toy store, trying to find something that Elle might want and didn't already have, and that they could afford.

"This is hopeless," Jillian kept muttering darkly. "She probably has everything in this store."

"Live and learn," their mother said. "The trick to giving a woman a gift is to give her something beautiful that she didn't think to buy for herself. Flowers and jewelry are often a good fallback. Here." She stopped in front of a display case of snow globes. "Maybe one of these."

"They're pretty," Louise admitted.

"Here's one with Princess Ariel." Jillian pointed to it.

They gazed at the pink globe with Ariel as a human peering upwards. There seemed to be something vaguely wrong about it.

"It's like she's trapped," Louise said.

"Maybe not that one," their mother said. "Maybe a mermaid Ariel." Their mother pointed to an Ariel with a big rounded head and huge eyes done by a popular statue maker.

"That's a little creepy," Louise said.

Jillian caught Louise's hand and pointed silently at a snow globe on a nearby shelf. It was of Pittsburgh deep in the forest of Elfhome. It wasn't accurate—a lot more of the city was shifted than the small wedge of downtown that they showed. The reason for the inconsistency became apparent when Jillian carefully flipped the globe upside down and righted it. The forest became Earth suburbs surrounding downtown Pittsburgh. Another flip and the city was once again surrounded by forest.

"Oh, that is so cool," Louise whispered.

Unfortunately, their mother noticed their fascination. "You like that one?"

"Elle would hate it," Jillian said quickly. It would be horrible to have to hand it over to Elle.

Their mother laughed. "I meant for you two."

"Us?" Louise cried with surprise.

"We didn't get you anything you *wanted* for your birthday. This could be a late birthday present. Do you want it?"

"Yes!" they both cried.

Their mother signaled over a clerk. "We'll be taking two domes. This one here is the first. We think the other one should have a mermaid in it. Can you point out all the ones you have?"

Within a few minutes, a dozen globes were gathered together for them to choose from. One had a stunning crystal mermaid with a delicate silver tail with coral filaments waving in the invisible currents and detailed fish swimming around her.

"It's so pretty!" Louise said. "She'll love it."

"And it's not that expensive," Jillian said.

"It feels very grown up to me," their mother stated, and they had to agree. It seemed like something anyone would like, not just a little girl. "Do you know—has anyone bought one of these in the last few days?"

"This is the only one we had in stock," the sales clerk said. "It's been discontinued."

"It can be exchanged? It's going to be a gift."

"Yes, I can give you a gift receipt."

As the clerk rang up their purchases, their mother said, "After you buy a nice item, you wrap it as elegantly as possible, along with a sophisticated card. So next stop, a card shop."

Louise drifted through the Hallmark store, looking at all the bright displays competing for attention. The gift-wrap aisle had animated wrapping paper. Racecars silently roaring down ribbons of asphalt for boys. Galloping unicorns for girls.

Louise paused to finger the unicorns wistfully as they raced in elegant circles, manes and tails blowing on sparkling magical wind. The only thing that Louise held against Elle was that once a week she took horse-riding lessons at a farm in New Jersey. On Elle's profile on the school's secure social-network site were pictures of her doing English dressage on a beautiful gray mare with black mane and tail. The mare was prancing, ears forward, neck arched, right front leg and left back leg cocked high in mid-step. It was the most beautiful thing Louise had ever seen, and she *wanted* with all her being to know what it was like to commune with such an animal.

Jillian came around the corner and shoved a card into Louise's hands.

"Two cards?" Their mother followed on Jillian's heels.

"She invited both of us." Jillian snatched up the unicorn paper. "And we're only giving her one present. It's like one of us is going without a gift. If we go with only one card, then it's like one of us is twiddling our nose at her."

"The Pondwaters know that you two are at Perelman on a scholarship. They know we're not at their level..."

"Yes, Elle's parents know, but Elle is the one we have to live with, and she's nine." Jillian bumped against Louise to get her to back her up.

Louise raised an eyebrow at her twin. Normally Jillian would have been glad for a chance to twiddle her nose at Elle. Jillian was up to something. "It's just a little more for a second card."

"Do you want us to look like welfare kids?" Jillian added.

"It's the price of having us at a private school." Louise checked the back of the card and winced. Between the barcode and copyright information was the price. It was more than a few dollars. This required work. "You should see the website of the party planners for this. It's going to be a dress-up tea party like we're a bunch of first-graders. There's going to be roses on every table, real china and silver candelabras, and people dressed up like the characters from the movie."

"And silk ball gowns and crowns for us to wear," Jillian added.

"And a hair stylist and someone to do our nails," Louise finished.

Their mother visibly melted. "Oh! That's sounds so wonderful. You're going to be so cute!"

"Mom!" they both cried.

Their mother sighed, shaking her head. "I swear, you two were never little girls. It's like I gave birth to teenagers."

As they headed for the checkout counter, Louise looked at the card in her hand. She half-expected it to be some odd joke card. It was surprisingly elegant. It took her a second to register that it read "Happy Birthday to Our Sister."

"She turns eighteen on May first," Jillian whispered. "Shutdown is next week and then again on May eighteenth. So if we want to get it to her anywhere close to 'on time,' we have to mail it today. Postage to Elfhome is going to take all our savings, so Mom needs to buy the card."

Louise went breathless with the idea. They were actually sending their older sister a birthday card. She'd open up the envelope and be so surprised. There was no way she could know about them, since their parents had stolen their embryos. Would she be just as excited as they were? Would she want to see them? At eighteen, she would be free to travel back and forth between Elfhome and Earth.

It was thrilling to think they might actually get to see their sister someday, maybe even someday soon, because of the card. Still, Louise couldn't help feeling as if the birthday card was a terrible idea.

9: LEMON-LIME-FLAVORED FAME

Iggy was blown away by the video when they showed it to him. "This is awesome. I can't believe you did this. But that's Gage. And Mason." He named their classmates as they appeared. The Lost Boys reached the *Jolly Roger* and there was a pan-over to show the pirates.

"Hooo!" Iggy shouted and stabbed the pause icon, stopping the camera on their version of him as Captain Hook. They had taken his suggestion of Captain Jack Sparrow and gone in that direction with trinkets braided in among dreadlocks and a five-o'clock shadow shading into a goatee. Instead of the red of Hook's traditional costume—based on a reference in the book that he fancied himself an officer in the British Navy—they went with tattered black with just hints of gold. Iggy made a dark and exotic pirate captain. "Oh! That's awesome! That is so awesome! How did you do that? Are your parents like movie people? Did they help you?"

"Seriously?" Louise thought everyone their age could edit video. "Yes!"

She explained how they had used a rendering application to turn the photographs into skins for CGI models that could then be edited. "The stock running animation is fairly wooden if you spend a lot of frames showing it, so we move the camera angle a lot." She backed the video up to illustrate how they used just a few frames of the computer-generated movement intermixed with close-ups of the Lost Boys and shots of tropical rain forest that they had made to seem moonlit by manipulating the color spectrum and lighting. She let it play through to the sword fight.

"So cool. But how do you know how to do all this?" Iggy asked as the video ended.

"We make videos all the time." She pointed at their production company logo that she had put at the end out of habit.

"Lemon-Lime JEl-Lo?" Iggy cried.

"It's a production company name." Louise showed him how their names made up the word JEl-Lo. "Jillian Eloise and Louise. Lemon-Lime because there's two of us."

Iggy stood staring at her with his mouth open for a minute, and then he dissolved into laughter. "What I meant was, 'You're Lemon-Lime JEl-Lo?' My sister's got one of your posters above her bed. The 'Blast it all' one."

They had designed character sketches for their series. In their videos, Queen Soulful Ember had a quick temper that led to her blowing up everything that annoyed her. "Blast it all" was her catchphrase and often triggered extreme reactions from her bodyguards and servants as they tried—politely—to keep her from reducing everything to cinders. Queen Soulful Ember's character sketch for posters and whatnot showed her mostly buried under guards with only her madly twitching fingers visible and the words of her catchphrase flaming overhead.

The twins planned to use the artwork to make money off their videos. They'd tried to set up a store using an online retailer that would use their uploaded art to create customized items, everything from posters to coffee cups. For a small percentage of the profit, YourStore would handle everything from creating the goods to mailing them out to customers. The twins had gotten all the artwork in place and the prices set. The last step, however, required that they provide bank account information. Their parents wouldn't allow the use of their bank account, citing everything from possible identity theft to tax reporting. Their parents didn't want to be held liable for some financial mess that YourStore might suck them into.

Since the twins couldn't collect income, they'd assumed that the store never went live. Had the store been selling their stuff all this time?

"A Queen Soulful Ember poster?" Louise asked. "A Lemon-Lime JEl-Lo brand from YourStore?"

"Yes! You're famous!" Iggy laughed. "Don't tell me that you don't socialize online, either."

"We hang out at Sundance and Vimeo and Vicker."

He cocked one eyebrow in puzzlement. "What are those?"

"Filmmaker sites." They maintained gender- and age-neutral identities on the sites, posting so that no one would track the messages back to them. It was mostly because their parents were sure that they would be cyberstalked by dirty old men. Louise doubted that anyone would be interested in them, but the secrecy kept their parents from discovering their activities on questionable sites.

"So you're totally unaware that there are kids in this school that can quote all of *The Queen's Pantaloons*?"

"All of it?"

"They totally mess up the timing of the jokes, but yeah."

The news went through the fifth grade like a virus, visibly moving from kid to kid. The students that had been told they were Lemon-Lime JEl-Lo *stared* at the twins as if they had suddenly become conjoined. Which would have been totally annoying if it weren't for the state of their finances.

After the first bell, Louise had logged quickly into their store and checked their account balance.

"Oh my God," she whispered.

Jillian leaned over and frowned at the screen. "What is that?"

"That's what YourStore is waiting for us to claim. They've been selling our stuff. Lots of our stuff."

Jillian slapped a hand over her mouth to smother a squeal.

"We still have to figure some way to claim it," Louise said. "We need a bank account."

"We'll get Mom and Dad to set up an bank account for us. With that much money involved, they'd be crazy not to let us claim it!"

Louise squinted, trying to see the future events unfolding implied by the numbers on the screen. "I don't think they'll let us keep it."

"Why not?" Jillian cried. "It's ours! We earned it! It's not like we can give it back, either."

"I mean 'keep it' as 'spend it the way *we* want.' They'll want to put it all away for our college fund and things like that. Or at least, get us another playhouse. They're not going to let us buy an antique piece of computer equipment off some unknown vendor. Remember how they got with that special-effects software we wanted to order?"

Jillian huffed as she grudgingly acknowledged that their parents would take control of the money. "A new playhouse at least would be cool."

"We were saying we need a lot of money to save the babies."

"This is not a million dollars. It's not going to be a million dollars anytime soon. Besides, like Mom said, we can't just pay for the babies to be born. They need a mom and dad and a place to live."

Louise considered the possibility of using the money to talk their mom into having the babies. She was always snarling how she hated her boss. But she really did like her job, and knowing their mom, she'd feel as if she should quit working until the babies were in kindergarten. The money at YourStore seemed like a lot of money to them, but it didn't equal their mother's salary for four years.

"Think April would help us set up a bank account?" Jillian asked.

"No," Louise said. Their mother's work had made them aware of salaries and taxes. "If she did, this would look like taxable income for her. She would have to report it and pay taxes on it."

Jillian frowned at the numbers. "I wish Alexander could help us. It must be great to be all grown up and have all this stupid kid stuff over with. I would love for once to be able to stay up as late as we want, to eat pizza every night for a week, and not have to clean our room all the time."

Louise nodded. Claiming the money would be no problem for an adult.

"Oh! Oh!" Jillian cried and started to sort through data on her tablet. "We just need an adult's Social Security number. Someone that doesn't have to worry about added income. Esme is in another solar system. She doesn't have to worry about filing taxes. We can use her number as the adult on our account."

Louise ran the plan over in her mind, looking for dangers. They could set up a joint account, link YourStore to it, and then only use the money online. If they used it carefully, there would be little activity to draw notice to it. It seemed safe enough. "As long as we don't buy anything big and expensive."

"Like a pony?" Jillian said and did a little mime of trying to hide said animal. "What pony? Oh, that pony! It followed us home, can we keep it?"

Louise laughed out loud.

"Louise," Miss Hamilton said, "keep it down."

Louise smothered giggles.

"There," Jillian announced. "And done."

"Jilly!" Louise whispered fiercely. "You didn't!"

"I did," Jillian said without remorse. "And the flash-drive adapter ordered with express shipping, no signature required. It will be here tomorrow. We just have to beat Mom and Dad home."

Louise thought of Tesla sitting in their locker, waiting to escort them home. "And keep Tesla from ratting us out."

Louise won the flip of the coin. After they got off the train the next afternoon, she ran on ahead while Jillian followed slowly with Tesla. She had felt nearly sick with worry all day and hadn't slept well the night before. They had done things behind their parents' backs before but never to a point that involved thousands of dollars. Their baby brother and sisters, though, were completely helpless, and the deadline for their disposal was just months away. The task of saving them loomed huge and impossible. The money was their only advantage.

As horrible as hiding the YourStore sales from their parents was, they had to keep the new bank account secret. The delivery of the antique computer equipment to deal with Esme's weird mystery was putting everything at risk. If their parents opened the package and started to ask how they had afforded it, not even Jillian could spin a lie believable enough to save them.

Since Louise couldn't get to sleep, she had spent the late hours hiding under her blankets and downloading emulators and drivers. In theory, all she needed to do was plug in the flash drive and transfer whatever data it was holding. Once they had a copy of the data, they could hide all the evidence of their crimes.

Her heart fell when there wasn't any package on their doorstep. Had their mom come home early? Had someone stolen it? Or would it come tomorrow?

Louise fumbled through unlocking their front door and pushed it open. Lying in the hallway was a bulky envelope that the delivery person had pushed through the mail slot. Its address label read "J. E. Mayer."

Relief flooded through her. "Oh, thank God. This better be worth it."

Shaking, she ran upstairs. The faster they used the reader and got it hidden away, the less chance they'd get caught. She had it connected before Jillian came in the front door. She could hear her twin thumping around downstairs while she downloaded everything onto her tablet.

The television went on in the kitchen, blaring out the news, moments before Jillian charged upstairs. She must have parked Tesla somewhere downstairs, since she was alone.

"Well?"

"It came. It works. Here." She flicked files across their home system to Jillian's tablet. She tucked the flash drive back into the Chinese box. The last step was to hide the reader and the mailer away where their parents wouldn't find them. "There's just one large PDF file and lots of JPEGs. I think they're photographs."

"More pictures," Jillian complained as she scrolled down the list of files. "Etienne Dufae 1843. Roland Dufae 1880. Are those the dates the pictures were taken?" She tapped the thumbnail of the first picture and gasped. "Oh, wow!"

Louise glanced up from stuffing the reader into the back of the camera drawer. Jillian was gazing raptly at a boy who could be their older brother. The photo was in black and white, the clothes were ridiculously old-fashioned, but there was no mistaking the family resemblance. "Well, at least we know who he is."

"We do?"

"Doh, we're related to him." Louise considered the mailer. Their parents might see it if she just put it in their trashcan. She folded it neatly so that the mailing label was hidden and tucked it into the bottom of her backpack. Tomorrow she'd throw it out at the train station. "He's probably our grandfather or something."

"It says 1843. More like great-great-grandfather." Jillian tapped on the next thumbnail. "Etienne had his own store."

The boy stood under a storefront sign that read: E. DUFAE & CO., WATCHMAKERS AND JEWELERS.

"Where do you think that was taken?" Louise said.

"It's named 'Cambridge, MA 1843,' so I'm guessing in the Boston area."

Leonardo had gone to M.I.T in Cambridge. Orville had been born there, and his mother had been killed there. Louise felt like she suddenly had sunk roots deep into distant soil. It was an odd feeling, suddenly being anchored like that, making her aware how adrift they had been beforehand with no family history beyond where their parents had gone to college.

Jillian suddenly squealed loudly in pure excitement and leapt up to spring around the room, shouting and flailing her tablet.

"What? What?" Louise started to flick open photographs, trying to find the one that had gotten Jillian excited.

"We're elves!" Jillian shoved her tablet out to show Louise.

The female in the black and white photo could have been Jillian; she looked more her twin than Louise did. Only the female was an elf. With her dark long hair coiled like a crown on her head, there was no mistaking the point of her ears or the almond shape of her eyes. She sat in the high-back chair like a queen on a throne. From the Victrola beside her chair to the newspaper on her lap, everything said "Earth," while she remained wholly elf.

"That's—that's not possible," Louise stammered.

"She's an elf and she looks like me and she's a Dufae. Josephina Dufae."

Louise stared at the picture as her insides went all fluttery with excitement. This couldn't be real. It had to be like the Danish king comment on the back of Neil Shenske's photograph. She picked up her own tablet and started to open the other photographs for more proof. It was impossible to tell in the other pictures; the subjects all wore hats. Certainly, though, the earlier Dufaes had that elf look around the eyes.

One labeled simply "Dufae" proved to be a scanned copy of a handwritten document showing their family tree. The top branches were all in Elvish runes. The name that formed the trunk, merging all the Elvish bloodlines, was Guillaume Ruelle Dufae. Jillian was right in one regard; the Dufaes started out as elves. Somehow, though, they became Frenchmen. Guillaume had married a Bridget Dubois. There was no indication if she was human or elf; no information was given on her except the date of their marriage and her death. She apparently died giving birth to Etienne, because his birth date was the same day. For Guillaume's death, it was given as only September 1792.

Elves claimed to be immortal. Windwolf hadn't visibly aged during the last twenty-eight years. (At least once a year, a reporter would compare his appearance to a teenage pop idol. The twins parodied this by having Prince Yardstick enter *American Idol*.) According to anthropologists, elves were considered adult only after they were a hundred years old. Etienne was nearly sixty in his photograph, but he looked only seventeen. Was it proof he was full-blooded elf or did half-elves age equally slow? The Dufae family tree traced only the male bloodline. Wives were listed only by three dates: birth, marriage, and death. It gave no clue if the females were elves or not except by the fact that they seemed to live average human lifespans.

Etienne would father Roland and Josephina and die within ten years of when the picture was taken. Obviously he hadn't died of old age. Etienne's daughter never married and lived to be a hundred and fifty. The family tree stated that Roland died before he was fifty without explaining why. Was it because he inherited a human lifespan when his sister lucked into an elf's? Or had he been murdered like Leonardo and Ada? Roland left behind a young son, Adrien, who had been Leonardo's grandfather.

Which made the twins...what? Elves? Half-elf? Quarter? One-eighth? How infinitely small did the amount have to be before it didn't matter?

Jillian had found the family tree, too. "The note at the bottom says that Guillaume was beheaded during the French Revolution's September Massacres. We're French elves." Jillian obviously loved the idea. "French *noble* elves."

Louise refrained from pointing out that not everyone who was beheaded in the French Revolution was noble, at least not according to Charles Dickens, but he might not be an accurate reporter on the events. "We're New Yorkers."

Louise abandoned the photographs. They only raised more questions. She opened up the PDF file named Dufae Codex, hoping for answers. The scanned pages of the file were from a book, handwritten in Elvish. Page after page of runes. There wasn't a single French or English word in sight. The source material had to be a thick bound journal, as there were over a thousand pages. She checked random pages to verify that it was entirely in Elvish. After the first dozen pages, though, the text changed from handwritten notes to elaborate symbols and circles and glyphs. She recognized the format from the only scientific paper they'd ever found on spell-casting.

"This. This," she whispered, having to force the words out one at a time. "The Dufae Codex is a book of spells!"

Jillian squealed with excitement. "Oh! Oh! Lou!" Jillian went speechless as she scrolled through the book, and when she finally could talk again, she sounded like she could barely breathe. "This is so awesome! We can learn magic!"

"There's no magic on Earth," Louise pointed out despite the giddy feeling that was racing through her. An entire spell book of Elf magic. This was better than Christmas. It couldn't be real. She didn't want to get all excited only to be disappointed.

"Well, the elves were getting to Earth somehow if the Dufae were in...oh! Oh!"

"What?"

"Leonardo was an elf!"

"Barely. And?"

"No one knows how the gate works!" Jillian jumped up and started to pace, words tumbling out with her excitement. "That's the reason Pittsburgh goes back and forth between the two worlds. If someone could come up with another way of doing it, they'd do that instead. All the scientists on Earth have tried, but they can't figure out what Leonardo did. It's not based on any science that they understand. Because it's not science, it's magic!"

Louise nodded along with the deductions. It made sense, but she was missing why Jillian was so excited by this. "So?"

"We can't figure out how to save our little brother and baby sisters using science—so maybe we can use magic."

"Magic?"

"We know what science can do. There's no artificial womb yet. We're not going to be able to implant our brother and sisters into—say—a pig."

"Ewww! Why would you say that?"

"I'm just thinking outside the box."

"Too outside!"

"And we're not going to be able to talk a woman into doing it!" Jillian nearly shouted to override Louise. "Not without lots of money."

"There's the money from YourStore."

"Yeah, with that we could get the babies born, but then what? We need enough money to raise them. We can't make enough to do both—not legally—in a few months. And if we do it illegally, we could get taken away from Mom and Dad."

Louise wasn't completely sure about the last one. Their parents had explained—several times—in the past that parents who couldn't stop their kids from breaking the law lost custody of them. She had tried to research this claim, but most kids who made the news had done something really horrible—like torturing cats or killing another child. There wasn't any data on nine-year-old bank robbers. Louise wasn't sure if this was because other nine-year-olds hadn't attempted it, or had their identities protected because they were minors or simply too smart to get caught. Still, the risks were too high to explain her doubts. Jillian was always sure they could get away with everything but was sometimes painfully wrong.

"But if we focus all our time on learning magic and it turns out we're wrong..." Louise started to argue her sister's logic.

"If we don't figure it out, we'll track down Mrs. Shenske and tell her."

"What? No, no, that's bad, we talked about that. Esme's mother might have Mom and Dad arrested."

"We do it anonymously. First we fiddle with Dad's company's records. It'd be easy. We change the number of embryos so no one can tell any are missing, and we wipe out Dad accessing the racks on our conception date. Boom. Everything that ties us to Esme goes away—"

"We should do it anyhow—just in case," Louise said.

"Okay." Jillian sat down and picked up her tablet. "But we wipe out everything that links us to Esme and then send some secret message to her mother telling her about the embryos. Last-ditch plan."

"Do you think she'll actually do anything with the information?"

Jillian shrugged. "I don't know. She might not. That's why it's a last-ditch plan. A better plan is to see if the codex has a spell that will let us save our baby brother and sisters."

"We'll need magic for a spell to work." Louise picked up her tablet.

Jillian paused in the middle of hacking their dad's work account. "You have an idea?"

"If Dufae's hyperphase gate uses magic, then it's generating its own magical power source. I'm going to see if anyone else has realized that and found a way to re-create his method."

"We're elves. We're *elves*! We're elves and we have a spell book!" The words wanted to leap right out of Louise's mouth as they set the table for dinner. Jillian obviously wasn't having the same problem. Only the speed with which Jillian put out dishes and silverware betrayed that she was impatient to get back to their room and work at translating the spell book.

Their mother, however, had brought home Ethiopian takeout from Queen of Sheba. It was a sure sign that she was very upset about something. Another indication of their mother's mood was that she'd bought more than they could possibly eat. There was dabo bread with awaze dip, menchet abesh wot, gored gored, gomen besega, ater kik alecha, shiro, and cabbage wot. She cranked up Rob Zombie in a declaration that she was not to be talked to until she'd had time to calm down. She moved through the kitchen, stripping off the uncomfortable work shoes and jewelry, head bobbing in time with the music, eyes angry.

Certainly it was all the more reason for Louise not to blurt out their secret. She fought the urge, filling up glasses.

Their father came home, stood in the dim foyer a moment, eyes wide, listening to the loud heavy metal music. After a visible "did I do something wrong" mental check, he came cautiously into the kitchen. He opened his mouth several times, reconsidered what he was about to say, and closed it each time. He settled at the table and asked with a glance, *Do you know what's wrong?*

Jillian shook her head, looking innocent.

Louise bit down on *We're elves and we've got a spell book* and shook her head, too.

Following her own rule on quiet for meals together, their mother turned off the music and sat down for dinner in silence.

After several minutes of furious eating, she sat back and sighed. "Anna Desmarais is a raving loon."

Their father braved a comment. "I thought you were done with the Forest Forever event."

"She's also on the board of trustees for the Stars Align Gala in June. Part of being filthy rich and having a guilty conscience means she's connected to a dozen different charities."

"You've worked with some whack jobs before."

"She implied at the meeting today that I embezzled from Forest Forever."

"You're kidding!" their father cried as the twins gasped.

"She didn't call me a liar and thief, at least not in so many words." Their mother growled. "She danced all around actually accusing me, but she made it fairly clear what she thought. She wants all the books checked for Forest Forever before releasing the next round of funds for the Stars Align Gala."

"You're not going to lose your job, are you?" Jillian asked.

"Taliaferro and I butt heads, but he trusts me. He knows how careful I am with the expense accounts. You have to be to avoid this kind of finger-pointing with charity work. He thinks Desmarais might be a racist because she made it clear from the first time she laid eyes on me that she didn't like me."

"That totally sucks," Louise said.

Their dad reached out and took their mother's hand. "It's going to be okay."

"Of course it is," she snapped but squeezed his hand tightly. "We're being audited on Monday. Taliaferro wants me to come in Saturday and Sunday to get ready for it."

"So . . . we don't have to go to Elle's stupid birthday party?" Jillian smiled at the idea that they'd have all of Saturday to work undisturbed on the spell book.

Louise glared at her sister; this was not the time to push their mother.

"You're going if I have to FedEx you there. This is exactly what I was talking about. You have to learn how to deal with these rich bitches while it's just the school play up for grabs and not your job. You're going to this party, smile until it hurts, and make friends."

"Yes, Mommy," Louise said, and Jillian echoed her.

"How is Plan Invade-and-Conquer going at school?" their mother asked.

"Okay." Louise wasn't sure what was safe to talk about since everything was kind of tangled together with the secret of the bank account and flash drive and codex and them being elves.

Jillian tried to work her way around their mother's edict. "We've got all the boys on our side since we showed them our music video. If two girls back us, or come up with another play, we'll win. We vote on Monday."

"Good! Never let your guard down until the fight is over." Their mother tapped hard on the table to drive home her point. "You keep your guard up. You watch for an attack and you take every opening that you're given."

"Yes, Mommy," they said together.

10: THE QUEEN'S PANTALOONS

Elle had a kitten.

She also had a huge brownstone townhouse filled with gleaming hardwood floors and crystal chandeliers and oil paintings, but none of that mattered to Louise. A kitten beat everything Louise had, even being part elf and in possession of a spell book. Louise wasn't pretty like an elf. Without magic, there was no point to being able to cast spells.

The emotional minefield of keeping so many big secrets from their parents had put Louise off-balance the entire week. On top of it all, yesterday had been Shutdown and they'd failed to contact Alexander. Even on the Pittsburgh Internet, they hadn't been able to find a phone directory.

The last thing Louise wanted to do was engage in social warfare. Besides, with a real living pet, Elle had already won. While the rest of the party giggled and shrieked somewhere downstairs, Louise curled up on the second floor landing with the chocolate tortoiseshell kitten.

About an hour later, Zahara came creeping up the stairs. She was still in her silk tribal wrap dress with thick gold bracelets that gleamed rich against her dark skin. While nothing had been done to tame her curly hair, someone had carefully applied glitter to her face, rich blue makeup to her eyes, and lip gloss to her quiet smile.

"You're not going to be made up?" Zahara asked.

"I don't feel like I'm seeing myself when I put on makeup," Louise said. "I feel like I've put on a mask and am trying to fool people."

Zahara settled on the stair just below her. "It's not like a mask. It's like a bracelet." She slid off her thick gold band and twirled it so it caught the light. "This is beautiful as a piece of art. My arm is beautiful as part of my body." She held up her arm, slim and graceful, as dark chocolate as the tortoiseshell. "Gold does not make you beautiful. Your arm does not make gold beautiful." She slid on the bracelet and twisted her hand to show off the band in all its golden wonder against her warm darkness. "The two come together in a celebration of beauty. We exist. We are. One does not detract from the other. So you cannot claim that they add to each other."

"But they do add to each other. I don't think that would be nearly as pretty on Elle."

Zahara giggled, and her quiet smile broke into something younger and joyous. "Everyone has been talking about your videos all week, but I don't think anyone has been talking to you."

"No, they've been just staring." If the twins hadn't been so wrapped up with decoding the spell book and finding a method for generating magic, it would have been very upsetting. As it was, it was embarrassing and annoying.

"My mom is a model; she's really famous. She meets all these amazingly talented people, and they all act like it's a big deal to talk with her. But really, she's a normal mom that gets up in the morning hoping that there's enough milk for everyone's cereal and nobody overflows the toilet before she has to go to work."

It so wasn't where Louise thought the conversation was going that she laughed. "Your toilet overflows a lot?"

"Constantly. It's an old building, and my little brother is an idiot with toilet paper. When you meet enough 'famous' people, you start to realize that at the core, everyone is the same."

"So—you're not impressed with us being Lemon-Lime JEl-Lo?"

Zahara giggled. "I am impressed! I could fangirl all over you about how funny your videos are, how amazing the costumes are, how beautiful the sets are and everything. According to my mom, though, having someone suddenly gush all over you is a little creepy."

"Yeah, it is. A little."

"Is that why you've kept such a low profile? Every time you'd release a video, people would start trying to guess who you are."

Louise shook her head. "We just thought our lives wouldn't be interesting to anyone. We just go to school." And school was so boring that they made up games like pretending not to know French in order to make it bearable. After several attempts to write up biographies, including one that ironically claimed that they were elves living in secret in New York City, they'd decided to leave off all information about themselves.

"Most people think you must live in Pittsburgh because everything is so detailed and accurate. Also because you always post your new video during Shutdown."

It was a little bit creepy that people had figured out their posting schedule. Since the date floated, they didn't think anyone would make a connection. "We make a lot up."

"There's scientists saying that you're getting most of it right. How do you know everything that you don't make up?"

Real scientists had seen their videos? Did any of them recognize themselves? "Remember the paper we had to do in first grade about Elfhome? While we were doing research for it, we ran across this funny article."

Their classmates had been happy to regurgitate commonly known facts like how Elfhome was a mirror Earth in a parallel universe complete with identical continents. The twins, however, realized that there was too little known about the elves themselves. It was easier to find out information on ancient kings of Babylon on Earth than the current royal court on Elfhome. Even though there were big communities of scientists in Pittsburgh, there was nothing publicly available about their findings. Obviously the information was being hidden someplace. The twins rose to the challenge and started to hack university e-mails, looking for clues to what the scientists were doing with the data they were collecting.

What they found was ripe for parody.

Apparently elves knew that the humans would view them as lab rats. There was an entire section of the treaty forbidding the collection of genetic material from elves. It went so far as to specifying "stray DNA" of dandruff, fingernail cuttings, and stray hairs. Because the elves were immortal, most questions about ancient history were viewed as personal and rude. While the enclaves had public areas open to the humans, a bulk of the compounds were deemed private and off-limits to close study. The elves were also reluctant to talk about private issues to anyone outside of their household.

It forced researchers to become super-secret spy scientists that the twins parodied by making them ninjas in their videos. In every scene, they had one or more ninja anthropologists, sometimes well hidden, sometimes badly. It made every video an Easter egg hunt for scientists.

The true trigger for their videos was an "eyes only" paper on elf names and why they were taking English nicknames.

"When elves are born, they're taken to Summer Court and the royal fortune-tellers give them these amazing, lyrical names with great deep meaning. Their real names are really like 'Pavana Gali Vento Ceyandalo Nagi Taeli,' which kind of means 'bare branches swaying in night wind.' There are rich layers of meaning to the entire name, since most of the words don't really have matching English words. Like 'Ceyandalo' means the 'alive but not in foliage' kind of 'bare,' not the 'naked' kind of 'bare.' Then the word order is different, so the name really is 'moving back and forth to brush dark hair, branches that are bare from winter, in the night wind.' All the elves in Pittsburgh are Wind Clan, so their 'last name' is always some form of 'wind.' Humans, being humans, started to shorten the elves' names, chopping off the wind part and such like. Since most humans didn't understand the nuances of Elvish, they were really butchering names and pissing off the elves. Like they accidently called that elf 'Hairbrush.' The elves started taking English nicknames to stop that."

Zahara giggled just like they had when they'd first read the paper. But then she gasped as she followed back the implication. "Wait. You mean there's a real Hairbrush and Umbrella?"

"Kind of. Hairbrush actually uses the name 'Winter' and Umbrella is 'Sunny.'"

"Really?" She laughed. "What about 'Suppository'?"

"We made that one up."

"Prince Yardstick?"

"That's Viceroy Windwolf. His real name is Wolf Who Rules Wind. Ruler. One-third of a yardstick?"

Zahara giggled again. "That's so funny. My sister loves Prince Windwolf. She's got this poster of him on her wall. But she thinks Prince Yardstick is a stick-in-the-mud."

Technically Windwolf wasn't a prince even though he was a cousin to Queen Soulful Ember. All the reports on him stated that he was unflappable and resolute. The twins translated that into a character who was completely unfazed by the madness that they unleashed around him. Usually he didn't appear until the video hit maximum insanity, which he would then view with mild confusion but utter calmness. Often he also was the person that put the world back in order—usually with a massive show of magic. She found it odd that anyone would consider him as dull, fussy, or old-fashioned. Maybe Zahara's sister didn't know what "stick-in-the-mud" really meant.

Mrs. Pondwater came to the bottom of the stairs and looked up. "Zahara, it's your turn for photographs."

"Come on." Zahara hopped up. "You should try the makeup. It's fun. And your parents will love the photos."

Their mother would. Considering everything they'd been doing behind their parents' backs, it would probably be good to do something nice for them. Scooping up the kitten, Louise let Zahara lead her back downstairs.

The makeup artist blinked at her in surprise. "Didn't I...oh, wow, your sister didn't tell me she had a twin! She had me make her up as an elf princess."

"She did?" Louise thought they were going to keep that secret.

"I have a whole box of these cool ear prosthetics." The makeup artist held up ear tips. "Elfhome parties are very popular."

Louise's heart leapt in her chest and she blurted out, "Oh, yes, please," before she even thought it out.

"Your sister is so cute and funny." The artist tilted Louise's head and painted something cool onto her ear tips.

"Yes, she is." Louise felt the familiar uncomfortable twinge of envy. She couldn't understand how it was that most people couldn't tell them apart and yet it was always Jillian who was described as "cute." What was it that made Jillian prettier? They had nearly the same hair—well, before Louise's was burned off. Same shade of brown eyes. Same chin. "Can you make me just as cute?"

Thirty minutes later, Louise looked like an elf. The makeup girl somehow made her eyes appear very almond-shaped. The elf ears peeked out between hair extensions braided with ribbons and little silk flowers and pinned cleverly into Louise's blast-shortened hair. She was dressed in a lovely copper lamé ball gown and had her face and bare shoulders dusted with glitter.

If she ignored how short she was, she looked completely like an elf.

There was the small matter that everyone else was probably made up to be a princess or a mermaid. At least, Jillian was also an elf—wherever she was. Louise hadn't seen her twin since they'd arrived. Still carrying the purring kitten, Louise went in search of Jillian.

The rest of the party was down the hall, laughing and shrieking loudly. As Louise walked cautiously toward it, she realized she could hear Jillian's voice slightly above the rest, quoting from their video, *The Queen's Pantaloons*. Louise stopped at the doorway, surprised to find that Jillian was the center of attention. Obviously Jillian was using their fame to take over the party. Elle had a stone-hard smile locked into place even though her eyes stormed. All the other girls, though, were laughing as Jillian played the part of the clueless anthropologist, the extremely nearsighted Dr. Forthwright, the only non-ninja scientist from their videos.

"Such fancy needlework." Jillian held up a facial tissue that was standing in for a lacy pair of oddly shaped underwear. The scene was based on odd wording used in academic papers to describe the elves' method of dealing with no elastic or zippers to create clothing. "What do you suppose it is? A table doily? A handkerchief? It has such wonderful perfume."

"The—the—the queen's pantaloons!" Zahara was standing in as Hairbrush, who they often portrayed as a hapless victim of cultural misunderstandings. She always managed to say the worst possible thing and then react wildly to the resulting confusion.

"Pantaloons," Jillian muttered as she mimed typing the word into a translator. "Pantaloons. Pan-ta-loons. Pan. Ta. Loons." She paused, eyeing the tissue that was standing in for the lace panties. "Canadian water bird? No, I think not. Forgiveness. What are pantaloons?"

Zahara did a very good job of copying Hairbrush's wild takes—that was half the humor of the scene. "Knickers. Drawers. Bloomers. Tanga."

"Hmm, tanga." Jillian consulted the nonexistent translator again. "Currency of Tajikistan. Ah, I see: it's money. What's the exchange rate?"

"Once per day?" Zahara sputtered out after a full minute of surprised and confused looks.

Jillian tossed up the tissue and the room burst into squeals of excitement. One girl after another snatched the white tissue out of the air and quoted a ninja anthropologist line and then tossed it up again. Not all the quips were from *The Queen's Pantaloons*, displaying a slightly scary range of knowledge.

Elle's smile started to tremble, and the anger in her eyes turned to hurt. It was her birthday party and she was about to cry.

Louise darted forward, caught the tissue, and tossed it to Elle. "The queen! The queen!"

Elle's eyes went wide in surprise.

Jillian quirked a frown at Louise but sketched an elaborate bow. "Queen Soulful Ember."

Elle's eyes narrowed but she rose regal as a queen. "Hairbrush? Hairbrush? We have laws against mimes."

Zahara did a perfect triple take. "Mimes? We do?"

"Surely we do. Frightening things: mimes. What will humans think up next? If we allow mimes, Kabuki is sure to follow."

"Kabuki?"

Elle struck the first pose of the Noh play *Tamura* or *Dance of the Ghost*. Amazingly, she had the dance fairly well approximated. Anyone who hadn't spent hours researching and re-creating the dance with Barbie dolls and CGI animation wouldn't have been able to tell the difference. Why did Elle know the dance so well? Was she a closet fan or had she learned it merely because she knew all the other kids liked the video? The other girls supplied "music," acting out the parts of the ninja anthropologist/musicians, drumming on side tables and pretending to be playing flutes.

"Noh!" Zahara cried. "Your majesty, Noh!"

"Are you telling your queen no?"

"Of course not!"

"But you just did!"

"But...But...But..." Zahara did Hairbrush's whimper as she once again found herself in verbal quicksand. "That is not Kabuki, it's Noh."

A withering look from Elle, probably for Zahara's part of stealing the spotlight during Elle's party. "There is a strange female in the garden." Elle pointed with the same circling flourish as the video, a subtle clue that the queen was on the verge of leveling everything with fire strikes. "We think she might be a mime. She's moving her mouth but nothing is coming out. We can't allow mimes; next thing you know we'll be up to our armpits in all sorts of scary things. Clowns. Frenchmen."

"Oh! Oh! Her! No! I—I—I mean to say she isn't a mime, your majesty. She merely swallowed the gossamer call."

Elle did a perfect comedic pause, hands cocked like a gun-fighter's, fingers twitching, as the other girls screamed with laughter. She finally broke her silence only when the laugh died to excited giggles. "What?"

"The gossamer call. It generates a sound audible only to gos-samers...and mimes."

Elle let her hands flutter up, fingers twitching madly, and the girls all shrieked with laughter. "Blast it all!"

Mrs. Pondwater came in, clapping her hands for attention. "Jillian. Louise. You're the last girls for photographs. The pho-tographer is waiting for you."

They allowed themselves to be shooed to the formal living room, where a thronelike chair had been set before a smoky-gray backdrop. The photographer eyed them with surprise.

"Elves? Are you sure you two are at the right party?"

Jillian waved off the comment. "We're just killing time until the next Shutdown. Then we're heading to Elfhome."

Louise shivered as the words raised the hair on the back of her neck.

11: RECIPE FOR DISASTER

-◈-═◗◖═-◈-

Louise couldn't shake the feeling of impending disaster all the next day. While she crawled through the Internet, looking for some hint that someone had created a magic generator, Jillian worked on translating the Dufae Codex.

To their dismay, the first few pages of the codex were incomprehensible. The author seemed to be making shorthand notes with only the minimum explanations. It was only when she reached the sixth page that she found a solid piece of translatable text.

"Finally!" Jillian cried. "I should have just skipped ahead to this."

"Another dead end. Literally." Louise stared at the police report detailing the death of the scientist she'd been researching. Or at least, the police were assuming he'd been murdered, as they hadn't found enough of him to verify it.

"This is what page six says." Jillian scrolled back to read her translated text.

"My theories are correct and incorrect. Yes, because the landmasses are identical on both worlds, finding the mirror site of our most powerful *fiutana* was as simple as following a map. Yes, power does leak through fissures between worlds at sites of *fiutana*. It is impossible, however, to set up a reliable resonance to the Spell Stones, which leaves me woefully unprotected. Also the magic seems, for lack of a better word, dirty. Even fairly simple spells have unpredictable results. Three different sites have produced the same failures. If I'm to stay on Earth, I will have to find a way to purify the magic. If I fail, I will need to return home. I should plan carefully, though, before returning. Who can I trust with this? How do I protect those I love when I do not know who is friend and who is foe?"

It was a disquieting echo to Louise's findings. "So the first five pages are test results?"

Jillian scrolled back through the original text. "Yeah, I think you're right. He says here that 'three different sites have produced the same failures.' Each of these pages has mystery words that don't repeat, and three words that do. I'm betting the repeated words are the locations, and the nonrepeating are the spells he's measuring. The numbers under them indicate the variation in the results."

"So this codex is a record of his experiments in magic."

Jillian flicked the digital pages. "I wonder how many years he was here on Earth before he was killed. There are hundreds of pages here."

Louise considered her own research. "If we could find one of these fissures, then we wouldn't need a generator. The way he said 'three different sites' seems to indicate they're fairly common. I wonder if he included a map."

"I'll check." Jillian started to scan quickly through the pages.

Almost immediately, though, Louise realized the mistake in her logic. "Dufae was in France and he died in 1792. Windwolf didn't colonize Westernlands until 1930. That's the whole point of him being the viceroy; he was the only *domana* on the continent when Pittsburgh was first transported to Elfhome. Dufae's map would only show the *fiutana* in Easternlands."

"Yeah, but there could be fissures here in North America. If they were common in Europe, they're probably common all over the world. If we figure out the conditions that form the fissures by studying Dufae's European map, we might be able to predict where they would appear in the United States."

"Dufae said the magic is dirty."

"One." Jillian held up a finger. "There are a thousand more pages to his codex." She held up a second finger. "Two. He didn't go back to Elfhome."

"So he figured out how to clean the magic?"

"I'm figuring that's what this is all about." Jillian held up her tablet and showed off a sketch of some odd-looking device. "This is page twelve."

Louise continued to wade through a flood of information on Leonardo's hyperphase gate. Every time she thought she was getting close to an answer, the information trail would stop. The last one filled her with so much uneasiness that she got up to pace.

"What?" Jillian asked.

"I have a weird feeling," Louise said. "Like we're doing something bad."

Jillian snorted. "We're always doing something that other people think is bad. Everyone wants us to 'be good,' and what they really mean is 'make it easy for them' and has nothing to do with 'good' or 'bad.' Like talking in the library. If no one is trying to get work done, why is it still bad? Because Miss Jenkins believes in learned behavior instead of rational thought. What we should be taught is compassionate response."

Louise growled as Jillian veered totally off subject. "That's not the point. Besides I can't blame them. Learned behavior is a fairly simple punishment-and-reward system. I wouldn't even know how to start to teach compassionate response."

"We're not animals. They wonder what is wrong with our country, but isn't it fairly obvious that if children are being treated like animals instead of rational beings, as adults they'll respond like monkeys?"

"Shut up or I'm going to fling poo at you!"

Jillian frowned as she realized that Louise was angry. "What's wrong?"

"I—I don't know. It's just this weird feeling. Here, look. See this?" Louise pulled up the last data trail she'd followed. "It's a micro blog post from three years ago."

"The Dufae gate uses magic!!!" Jillian read. "You were right; someone figured it out."

Louise impatiently waved her to wait. "The guy that posted this was an M.I.T. student by the name of Michael Kensbock. This is his posting history. He put out something on average every ten minutes. Two months later, his stream stops. This is his last post."

The message said: "Eureka! I haz magic. Nobel iz mine! Party time!"

"He made one!" Jillian cried excitedly.

"Yes, right before he disappeared." Louise pulled up the page that his family had put together in an attempt to find him. "He was at a bar with friends and went to the bathroom and never came back. Here's the weird thing. Right after he disappeared, someone took down all his content. His vlogs, his e-mails— everything that could be erased—was. His micro blog posts are the only thing not erased, although I'm finding evidence that this service had undergone a massive virus attack at that time."

"Maybe his disappearance didn't have anything to do with the generator."

"And his entire web presence erased?"

Jillian sighed and changed the subject. "Did you find a copy of the magic-generator thing?"

"It took some digging." Louise pulled up the site. "I noticed that he liked to use a cartoon icon of himself. So I did a pattern-recognition search on the image and a few of the most basic spell symbols, assuming that he would need a spell to test the generator."

"So you could hit anything that a normal search would miss?"

Louise nodded. "He obviously was going to publish the page to announce his work, but he didn't want it found until he'd verified his findings, so he carefully didn't use any words that would point a search at his page."

The page had everything needed to create a generator with a high-end 3D printer. It looked simple: a molded plastic box with two power ports. One was a normal male 220 plug, which would indicate that the generator required power on the level of a clothes dryer. The second set of connectors was mere thin wires coated with plastic with flat tabs at the end. They didn't look like anything that Louise knew, and they were identified as "magic connectors," which normally would have made her giggle. There were complete schematics on building a matrix of parallel Casimir plates a few micrometers apart and detailed explanations of how the electricity was turned into magic. It was complicated, but Louise could understand it.

After building the generator and running careful studies on its output, he'd used it to cast a simple detection spell designed to map out ley lines.

"I'm worried," Louise said. "This was his super-secret personal site he had stashed in the cloud. He had three public sites, but they're all toast. Someone did a very good job of worming into even cache copies of his sites and making them unreadable."

"Who knows what else he might have been doing that pissed someone off?"

"The thing is, he's not the only one." Louise flicked open windows of earlier dead ends. "Torbjorn Pettersen was a Norwegian who disappeared two years ago after publishing an article in *Scientific American* on field manipulation using quantum particles in an attempt to explain how Leonardo's gate moved Pittsburgh to Elfhome. After him, there was a scientist named Lisa Sutterland who was doing similar work and was killed when someone tried to kidnap her six months later. Marcus Shipman published work on the gate, and he's also missing. And Harry Russell. He went missing while he was under house arrest. He had a GPS microchip implanted on him as part of his punishment. Police should have been able to find him using that, but they couldn't until two months ago. The chip turned up inside a fish in St. Louis."

"As in the fish ate part of him? Eeewww!"

"That's what they think. Everyone I've found that has come close to figuring out how Leonardo's gate works has either disappeared mysteriously or been killed."

"Well, we're not going to tell anyone what we figure out. You were careful and made sure you couldn't be traced?"

"Of course I was!" Louise said. "After the first two guys turned up missing, I went into silent-running mode."

"Good. Let's copy the source and then not hit this site again."

They copied everything. Once they were safely isolated from the original site, they studied the plans.

"We'll need a very high-end 3D printer," Louise pointed out. "Our printer can't build at the nanoscale level that this is going to need."

"We could buy one." Jillian pointed out that they now had money.

Louise snorted. "It would eat up a huge chunk of our funds, and how would we hide it? We couldn't even carry it out of the foyer."

Jillian sighed. "Yeah, you're right. Forget about it. There's one in the technology annex to the art rooms that the high school kids use for Mr. Kessler's robotics and computer-design classes." Mr. Kessler taught their computer literacy class.

"We need to be careful to cover our tracks," Louise stressed.

"We'll be like ninjas."

✧　　✧　　✧

Their plan started to go wrong two blocks from school. They had intended to arrive early and go straight to the art rooms. As they stepped off the subway train, however, they literally ran into Iggy.

"Hi!" He grinned brightly as he patted Tesla's head. "Today is the big day!"

They gazed at him, mystified for a full minute.

"The play meeting!" he cried. "Don't tell me you went to that girly party and Elle sucked your brains out or something."

They'd totally forgotten about the joint-class play meeting, even with Elle's party. They'd spent all of Sunday researching magic.

"We have other things going on," Jillian said.

"Finishing the newest video?" Iggy asked. "I saw the filler you put up on Friday."

Strange how it was easier to lie to strangers than to people who might remotely be their friend. Could Iggy be considered that? Having gone through the process so few times—say never—Louise wasn't totally sure of the steps. It seemed for something so important there should be some ritual—a declaration of intent or a solemn vow or at least a handshake. How could people keep track otherwise?

"Yes, another video," Jillian lied, but added truthfully, "The girls at the party kept asking what the next one was about."

"We—we had an accident in our studio," Louise countered to explain why they weren't going to be producing said video anytime soon.

Jillian made a face but after a moment of thought nodded. "We kind of burned it down."

"Kind of?"

"Well, we blew it up first, and then it burned down," Louise said.

Iggy giggled. "Blast it all?"

"Yeah, exactly!" Louise said. It felt good to admit that much of the truth. "So we're trying to figure out how to finish the project."

Louise started them toward the school. Jillian could keep Iggy distracted while she went to the art rooms alone. On Mondays, Mr. Kessler had hall duty on the first floor. Mr. Kessler unlocked the art rooms and left them open on the expectation that Miss Gray would arrive shortly. Since Miss Gray didn't have a class until second period, though, she tended to arrive at school at the last possible moment. It was a habit that the twins were counting heavily on.

They stopped at the corner to wait for a walk light. Iggy seemed focused on petting Tesla, so Louise pulled out her tablet and activated her tracking program for their art teacher. Miss Gray was still at her apartment, running about in frantic circles as if she kept forgetting things in her bedroom as she tried to get out the door on time.

"You know Tesla's not real." Jillian kept Iggy's attention as the walk light turned white and they started to cross.

"Doh!" Iggy laughed and then blushed and glanced around to see if any of the kids from their school were nearby before confessing, "I love stuffed animals."

"And?" Louise couldn't see how the two related.

"My parents don't think boys should play with stuffed animals. They're too girly because they're too cute! Boy toys have to be fierce and strong. My parents won't let me have any stuffed animals, but I can have robotic ones, because they're robots."

"That doesn't make any sense," Jillian said.

"Welcome to my life." Iggy patted Tesla's head. The robot completely ignored it. "My mom won't let me have any pets, either. She calls hamsters and guinea pigs 'livestock,' which is kind of funny because they got me this really cute ox."

"Ox?"

"I'm a metal ox." Iggy patted his chest. "I'm logical, positive, and filled with common sense, with all feet firmly planted on the ground."

Iggy was several months older than they were, since they were Tigers, which came after Ox. Louise had never considered the accuracy of the Chinese Zodiac before, but it seemed like a good description of Iggy.

Jillian laughed. "All four feet firmly planted?"

Iggy grinned at the jibe. "We consider it being pragmatic. Others see it as obstinate."

"So your robotic ox." Louise measured possible ranges of sizes with her outstretched hands. "How—how big is it?"

"Bonk is just a little thing." He demonstrated with his hands barely a foot apart. "He's so cute!"

"Bonk?" Jillian said as they hit the door. Louise prepared to slip away as her twin held Iggy's interest.

"He has depth-perception issues or something." Iggy illustrated by tapping his palm against his forehead. "He makes this noise when he runs into things head-first. When he does it he makes this sound kind of like 'baa' crossed with 'moo.' I think they may have given him some goat programming."

"Baaamoo?" Jillian attempted as Louise started her feint toward the girls' bathroom to explain why she was walking away unannounced.

"No, not like that." Iggy made a very cute "booonnnk" noise.

"Louise! Jillian!" Zahara came bursting through the door and spotted them in the hallway. "I'm so excited I could barely sleep. I didn't tell you, but I want to be a pirate!"

"Shiver me timbers!" Iggy cried. "Are ye three sheets to the wind?"

"Arrr, ye scurvy dog!" Zahara cried back. "Are ye blind in both eyes? I be a corsair out of Barbados and the greatest pirate queen that ever sailed the seven seas!"

Jillian's eyes widened and she glanced to Louise for help, completely destroying any chance that Louise could slip away. "There's—there's no pirate queen in *Peter Pan*."

Zahara laughed. "I know, but there should be. Maybe we can rewrite parts of it."

Jillian's eyes went a little wider. "They won't let us rewrite it. Not after what happened in second grade."

"No, not you two." Zahara grinned, her nose wrinkling with delight. "All of us."

The morning set the pattern for the day. As hard as Louise tried, she couldn't find a single chance to slip away unnoticed. At recess they played jump rope with Zahara. Even at lunch, where they normally sat alone, they ended up with Iggy, Zahara, and a handful of boys from Iggy's class, all talking in pirate. By then, it was obvious to Louise that they would have to wait until the play meeting was over and forgotten before staging the raid on the art-room printer.

Jillian was not taking the delay well. She was doing a good job covering it, but inwardly she was obviously seething. "Why can't they leave us alone?" she muttered darkly as they were herded from the lunchroom back to the fifth-grade floor.

"We'll just do it later. Tomorrow."

"Tomorrow is the one day Miss Gray comes in early."

"Then Wednesday. Or even next week. We need to find a spell that will help save the babies first."

Jillian glared at her as Louise coded open their joint locker.

"What?" Louise whispered as Elle stopped beside them to get things out of her locker.

"I want to learn everything, not just what we need for them." Jillian used vague terms so Elle wouldn't understand what they were talking about.

Elle snorted, guessing wrong that they were discussing their next class. "The way you butcher French, you'll be lucky to know enough to pass the tests."

She yanked out her tablet and flounced away.

Louise bumped Jillian, who was about to shout something after Elle. "We're about to yank the rug out from under her in public." Zahara wasn't the only girl speaking in pirate at lunch. If all the boys and at least two other girls besides the twins voted for *Peter Pan*, they were going to win. "Let her score points. Besides, we're the ones screwing around in class pretending not to understand. It's karma if people don't know how fluent we are."

Jillian muttered some very rude French that wasn't in any textbook.

"We're going to have to learn more Elvish." Louise tried distracting her. "Dufae uses a lot of words we don't know. We can use an online translator to get the basic gist, but we can't trust it to be accurate. Everything we've read said that magic is as exacting as chemistry. We need to be sure we're translating things right or it's going to end like the flour experiment did—and we're running out of places to safely blow up."

Jillian harrumphed at the knowledge that they weren't as fluent in Elvish as they were in French. "We planned that explosion."

Louise made sure no one was nearby before whispering, "We planned *an* explosion, but not that one. If we screw up a magic spell, God knows what might happen."

"There's a reason we're not more fluent," Jillian said vaguely as Giselle opened up her locker on the other side of theirs. "*Nicadae.*"

Someone in Pittsburgh had mistranslated the phrase to "hello" without realizing that the elves were actually saying "Nice day" in butchered English. All in all, the official dictionaries were a joke, consisting of only a few thousand words of Low Elvish and pidgin commonly used in day-to-day transactions in Pittsburgh. "Nicadae" and its like were viral; all the dictionaries had the same mistake. If there was a more accurate dictionary, it had been hidden by a scientist with mad ninja skills. "We've never tried the University of Pittsburgh."

"That's because it's only on Earth one day of the month, and that was Friday." Jillian slammed shut their locker, and the twins headed down the hallway since their French class was about to start.

Louise groaned as she realized Jillian was right. They'd spent all Friday searching Pittsburgh's limited Internet for a trace of Alexander and had gone to bed after midnight, frazzled and worried. They would have to wait until next Shutdown before they could hack the university's computers.

Jillian stopped as something occurred to her and her eyes went wide.

"What?" Louise asked.

"Do you think...?" Jillian threw up her hand and wriggled her fingers.

"Blast it all!" someone cried from down the hall.

Louise grabbed Jillian's wrist and pulled her hands down. "People watch us now!" she whispered fiercely.

Jillian rolled her eyes. "Forget about it! What about us? Do you think we can?"

Could they? Were they like the queen and able to wreak havoc with a wave of the hand? The idea was thrilling, but seeing the gleam in Jillian's eyes, Louise caught hold of her excitement and attempted to drown it under logic.

"The ninjas haven't figured out how they do that." Louise pointed out that the more humans understood how magic worked, the more they didn't understand how members of Elfhome royalty created wildly powerful effects. Earth scientists were still writing papers with conflicting theories even after twenty-eight years of covertly studying the elves. Their stumbling block was the amount of energy that a noble *domana*-caste elf could channel. Written spells obeyed Einstein's physics: energy output could be calculated in proportion to available magic. Of course there was the problem that the scientists hadn't come to agreement on the nature of magic. Unlike Earth, Elfhome had an ambient magical field. It seemed pervasive as magnetism or gravity, but it was fluid in that it flowed like water, creating streams of power called ley lines. A written spell was fueled by local magic and could deplete the area of power, just like fire would use up all available oxygen in a closed system.

While the scientists couldn't explain the source of magic, they could measure it. Windwolf had been recorded discharging energy on par with a nuclear reactor for over an hour. No human knew how he channeled so much power, and the elves refused to explain. Scientists could only secretly video the elves and attempt to figure it out.

"The ninjas are stupid." Jillian waved away her point, doing the flourish that Queen Soulful Ember made right before she started to throw fireballs. "Since all elves use written spells on a daily basis, the ninjas are still not sure if the gesture-based spells are limited to the *domana*-caste or not."

"Just because we haven't seen a dragon, doesn't mean dragons don't exist." Louise stated the logic of why the scientists were reluctant to commit to a theory.

"It's obvious that it's just the *domana*! Metal interferes with magic, so anyone who can cast spells with their hands couldn't wear rings or bracelets. There's not a single photo of Windwolf wearing jewelry, but all the other elves of Pittsburgh do."

"That's hardly empirical evidence." Louise stated as they walked into their classroom. Everyone was still standing around talking because their French teacher, Mr. Newton, hadn't arrived.

"I love it when Queen Soulful Ember loses it." Giselle butted in as if they weren't having a private conversation. Apparently she'd listened to them the whole way from their lockers. Giselle's comment made everyone turn and look at them. As Louise wished she could go invisible, the other students joined in.

"Blast it all!" Claudia cried, hands over her head, fingers wriggling. "And then boom! How does she do it?"

"Yes, how do they do it?" Elle obviously didn't think they knew. "Or did you just make all that up?"

"We didn't make it up," Jillian cried.

Louise didn't want to draw even more attention to them, but Jillian wouldn't back down now. "All we had to do was study videos of the elves casting spells frame by frame. They do a two-step command sequence. It's kind of like selecting a toolbar on a computer screen and then selecting an app to run."

Or at least, that's what they'd observed. They hadn't been able to find any scientific studies on the subject, even though it seemed obvious.

Jillian demonstrated the finger positions on the first command.

"It's the combination of both the position of the hand and a spoken word." She held her right hand within an inch of her mouth. The queen always used the same first command, but Windwolf varied between two, depending on which type of spell he was about to cast, Fire or Wind.

As Jillian spoke the Fire command, Louise explained the rest.

"After the queen activates 'the toolbar,' she changes her hand position and uses another command word to choose which spell she's actually going to cast from the toolbar. Each spell has a different hand position and word."

By measuring the effects, the twins had determined that the caster then used additional hand movements to enter the spell's area of effect in terms of direction and distance from the caster, and the amount of damage they wanted to inflict. Jillian demonstrated the queen casting a flame strike directly on top of Elle strong enough to probably reduce the entire school to ashes.

Louise turned her startled laugh into a cough. "We needed to analyze the spell-casting so we could draw it. We wanted to get it right."

Elle looked confused. "It would have been easier to just make it up. Nobody would know."

"We would know," Jillian said.

"Finding out how they do it is half the fun," Louise said.

"*Être assis.*" Their French teacher, Mr. Newton, commanded as he walked into the classroom. He waved at their chairs in case any of them still didn't understand the phrase. And thus started yet another period where Louise hadn't been able to slip away to the art room.

The play meeting was the last period of the day. They filed into the auditorium to find that the other fifth-grade class was already sitting in the front row.

With broad shoulders, square jaw, and a buzz cut, Mr. Howe looked exactly like what he was: a retired Marine master sergeant. He stood at parade rest, hands clasped behind his back, eyeing the twins' class as if they were unruly invaders. Miss Hamilton was laughing as usual as she gently but firmly herded them in.

She saluted Mr. Howe. "Class 501, reporting for duty, sir!"

Mr. Howe grinned and returned the salute. "Thank you, Miss

Hamilton. All right, listen up, today's mission is the joint fifth-grade class play. Today, we're going to vote on a play..."

Elle's hand shot up. "I think we should do *The Little Mermaid* this year. MTI has a junior version of the script for middle school students. The cast has been enlarged to ensure parts for an entire class, and all the music has been simplified so it's easier for kids to sing. Not that that would be a problem for me, since I take voice lessons. We can get a director's show kit from MTI that has budgets, press releases, sample programs, cue sheets, glossary, and audition sides."

"We would call that jumping the gun, Elle," Mr. Howe said coldly. "I haven't finished."

"I'm sorry, Mr. Howe. I just wanted to point out that we could get everything we needed already polished and tested."

Louise realized that everyone was looking at her and Jillian. They hadn't prepared a pitch for the teachers. Nor did she have any clue where to find press releases or sample programs. Every other year, teachers took care of getting what was needed after the class voted. Under the stare of their classmates, Louise put up her hand.

"Yes, Louise?" Miss Hamilton said.

"I have a play, too—when we get to nominating."

Miss Hamilton turned to Mr. Howe. "I think we should jump to nominating, since Elle has opened the floor. We can cover the changes to how we're doing the play this year after the vote."

Mr. Howe considered and linked his tablet to the theater's screen. "Okay, we have *The Little Mermaid* as play number one." He wrote the title in small letters on the far left. "Louise, what's your play?"

"*Peter Pan.*"

Mr. Howe grunted slightly as if surprised by the choice. He wrote it close beside *The Little Mermaid*. "And who else has an idea for a play?"

There was silence as everyone waited.

"Anyone?" Mr. Howe eyed his class as if disappointed that none of his students had a suggestion. "Iggy? I thought you had a play you wanted to do."

"I want to be Captain Hook!" Iggy stated firmly.

There was a sudden chorus of "Arrrrr" and "Aye, matey!" from Iggy's class.

"Lost Boys live forever!" one of the boys in the twins' class shouted.

Mr. Howe and Miss Hamilton exchanged looks.

"So some of you already discussed this?" Miss Hamilton said.

"We want to do *Peter Pan*," Zahara said.

"*The Little Mermaid*," Elle and Giselle cried.

"Let's vote. All for *The Little Mermaid*?"

All the other girls except Zahara and Nina from Mr. Howe's class put up their hands. It was a depressing show of hands. Mr. Howe and Miss Hamilton both counted, and once they were sure, Mr. Howe wrote the total on the board.

"Hands up: Who wants to do *Peter Pan*?"

They counted and then counted again.

"All right. It's *Peter Pan*."

A cheer went up, and Elle visibly struggled not to pout. Somehow, though, Louise felt like they hadn't won.

"Settle down. We have lots to go over yet. Louise, do you have a scene and cast list for the play?"

"I do." Jillian raised her hand but started to talk before either teacher called on her. "There are five acts, the first and last are both in the nursery, so we would need to build four sets. For the nursery, we only need three beds and a window. It can be very *Our Town*-like. The second set is the forest of Neverland, the third is the mermaid lagoon, and the fourth is Hook's pirate ship."

"I think it would be cool if we did a Kansas/Oz comparison between the real world and the fantasy world." Louise defaulted to set design. "Do the nursery in grays or neutrals. The original set design had details that stressed how poor the Darlings were and outside the window were treetops to give the impression of skyline seen from an attic room. We could modernize it by having a brick wall as backdrop with graffiti and maybe use a flickering light and sound to make it seem like trains are passing by."

"So the forest of Neverland would be colorful?" Jillian asked.

"Yeah, we could do flowering trees and different shades of green for foliage of trees."

"Sounds costly," Jillian complained.

"The biggest challenge would actually be scene changes. They need to be quick and easy while still giving visual depth to the stage. What we might be able to do is build out something that opens and shuts like umbrellas."

"We could get yards of fabric in different shades of green," Zahara said. "Everyone could cut a couple dozen leaves for homework, and then, on stagecraft days, we could staple them to the umbrella rigging."

"Girls!" Mr. Howe held up a hand for silence. "I'm glad you're jumping in with both feet, because this is exactly how this year's play is different from other years. The class play is a yearly exercise on working together as a team. Unlike earlier years, where your teachers would set work schedules, assign projects, and oversee the work, you will now be responsible for all of it."

"Mr. Howe and I will simply be advisors to help you find solutions when you can't find a way to deal with a problem by yourself," Miss Hamilton said.

"This year, you will pick out a director, a stage manager, a costume designer, a props director, as well as assign who will get what roles." Mr. Howe opened a new window on his tablet and wrote down "Peter Pan" and started a list of jobs.

Louise took a deep breath as their future was suddenly unveiled. As Lemon-Lime JEl-Lo, she and Jillian would be the best candidates for most of the responsibilities. The play took up nearly three months of daily work, both at school and at home. Jillian already had sold the idea of her starring as Peter, who appeared in every scene.

But their siblings were going to be disposed of in three months. They should be focusing all their time and energy on the babies. They had to make a magic generator, translate the Dufae Codex, and experiment with spells.

"I want to be Captain Hook!" Iggy put up his hand.

"Aye!" the pirates shouted.

"Captain Iggy Hook!" the Lost Boys cried.

They all cheered as Mr. Howe started the cast list with "Captain Hook: Iggy."

"If we're doing *Peter Pan*, I want to be Wendy!" Elle cried, and her friends clapped when Mr. Howe, hearing no objection, wrote it down.

"Jillian's going to be Peter!" Zahara said.

"And the director!" Iggy added. "Louise can be stage manager."

There was another cheer, and their names went up on the screen.

Louise sank into her chair, trying to keep dismay off her face. This was the worst thing that could happen.

12: DECODING THE CODEX

It proved impossible to sneak away to the art room to use the 3D printer. Everyone wanted their attention.

Except the Girl Scouts.

As Jillian had predicted, Mrs. Pondwater didn't take well to their *coup d'état* with the play. She ambushed them outside the troop meeting on Monday afternoon and politely informed them that if they wanted to stay in the Girl Scouts, they'd have to find another troop. With Nigel Reid's appearance on the *Today Show* less than two weeks away, there wasn't time to infiltrate another group and set up a field trip. They had no real guarantee that it was the real Nigel who had contacted them. If Nigel did mention them on the show, then there would be opportunities later to interact with him. Besides, it was a relief that they didn't have troop meetings to attend on top of everything else.

Jillian was swamped with rewriting the play to more modern English and planning on how they were going to do the complex sword fights and flying scenes. Louise needed to design the sets, create a work schedule for the stagecraft period, and create a blocking mock-up on the floor of both classrooms and the fifth-grade hallway so actors could learn how to move around sets that didn't exist yet. They also found themselves managing the other kids, who had never tackled such a large project before. They needed to help Zahara with the costumes, Reed with props, and Ava with the advertising.

With every minute of their time at school eaten up, they had no choice but to wait until stagecraft started. At that point, Louise could slip the magic generator into the work schedule. It required her to design decoy equipment into set designs.

Jillian hated the idea. She wanted to start trying out the multitude of spells in the codex. They hadn't found anything that resembled basic magic lessons, and Louise was afraid to experiment blindly. Louise pointed out that their goal was to save their siblings, not blow up the neighborhood. Reluctantly, Jillian agreed.

Since Louise's evenings were being taken up with finalizing the conception art for all the sets and costumes, Jillian handled the translation for the next few days.

Jillian plowed onward through text peppered heavily with completely unknown words. Dufae's story unfolded in awkward bits and often incomprehensible pieces, such as: "I miss the moon spinners and the dark-eyed widow." And: "I feel like a duck with a puddle. At least it keeps the house warm." And: "What is this obsession with stone people?" And: "He shapes stone with coarse hands, rough as rock, unyielding."

It was another day before they could translate another large section into something understandable and not a song. (At least, they thought the odd sections with what might be musical stanzas were songs and had nothing to do with magic. Maybe. Rough sketches of a kitten also started to appear in the margins, growing on each page to a slightly pudgy cat.)

I am so very lonely. Why do they put so much importance on the count of years? It disregards that some will never grow out of childish spite, and others, like myself, leap to wisdom at a very young age. If they had recognized me as an adult as I know myself to be, I would have been allowed to take as Beholden those whom I could trust completely. I would have had more options than to run and hide. The irony being that I have succeeded this much because I am still a child in their eyes. I was allowed freedom to do what no adult could—to move unwatched and unchecked through the very camp of the enemy. I worry now that my actions might have brought danger down on my parents. I can only hope that their true ignorance of my actions will guard them against attack. That I hope this in vain eats at me at night.

"I wonder how old he was." Jillian made notes on the page and indexed it. "Not how many years old, because elves take forever to grow up, but, you know, was he the equivalent to our age? Or was he older, like a teenager? He did get married and have a kid, but he could have been on Earth for years and years."

"I don't know, but whoever he was hiding from—they're probably still alive."

Jillian looked surprised, and then her eyes went wider as she realized the truth. "Elves live forever."

"What he was working on might still be dangerous," Louise said.

"Oh. Oh!" Jillian said. "His parents! They're probably wondering what happened to him."

It felt as if reality had shifted around them. Dufae was no longer an old person who had died hundreds of years ago, but a child who should still be alive, still young, still with his loving mother and father. On Elfhome there were people who knew his face and the sound of his voice, people who probably missed him horribly and were praying in vain that he come home safe. Or worse, what Dufae feared had happened, and the people he was hiding from had killed his parents.

"We need to be careful," Louise whispered. "This is dangerous."

"Oh! Oh!" Jillian leapt to her feet close to bedtime. "Listen to this!" She paused to find her place again in the translated codex and started to read. "*I still think that I might need to open one of the* nactka.'"

"What's a *nactka*?"

"I don't know. This is the first time he mentions it. But listen!" Jillian went back to reading.

"*It stands to reason that since I can't set up a resonance, opening one should be perfectly safe. If I'm cut off, the spell surely cannot trigger. Logic prevails that I should delay opening a* nactka *until I fully understand the nature of the spell, but I'm not sure I can grasp the spell without fully studying one.*"

"Open one? So they're like jars?"

"There's more!" Jillian went back to reading, holding up one finger to indicate that Louise should wait.

"I don't believe that there have been any changes made to the fundamental nature of the nactka *itself. The object inside is held as if time has been stopped until the* nactka *is open. A flower would remain as if newly picked. Ice will not melt even in the hottest of summer. A chicken egg will not hatch for a hundred years, and yet when taken out, the chick will emerge unharmed."*

Louise gasped and then caught hold of her excitement. "But we don't have one of these."

"But we know they exist! Magic can save our baby brother and sisters."

"We don't have one, and he might not describe how to make one."

"He had one here on Earth."

"Three hundred years ago in Paris."

"Grandpa Dufae has this codex and the old photographs. He might have it. I'm sure he would let us use it."

"And he might take us away from Mom and Dad!"

Jillian waved away the objection. "He already knew there were other embryos. If he wanted more kids, he would have arranged for them to be born."

"He didn't have the money to pay for surrogate mothers. Esme did."

"He gave Esme copies of all the Dufae family stuff. He must have thought she was arranging more kids to be born or something."

They both paused and frowned as the logic of their mother once again escaped them. Why had she left the puzzle box with April? Except for the odd mystery photographs, there had been nothing of her in the box.

"They would have never made her captain if they thought she was crazy," Jillian pointed out.

"There is that," Louise agreed. They had to be missing some vital information that made Esme's action logical, but so far Louise couldn't even guess what that might be. "We need more information."

Jillian growled in frustration and sat down at her desk and started to link her tablet to the house computer.

"What are you doing?"

"This is taking too much time. I'm speeding it up."

"How?"

"I'm going to machine translate the entire document so we can do text searches and see everything he says about the *nactka*."

Needless to say, the spells made the translation software have hissy fits.

The next entry of *nactka* came a hundred pages later and explained little.

> *It was pure childish curiosity that made me unlock the box, but I had recognized the dozen primed* nactka *the moment I saw them. I might be still a child, but I'd sat at my grandmother's knee and heard all the dark stories of our enslavement. I knew that I had to act. My first thought was to merely disarm the* nactka, *but I was afraid I might accidently trigger whatever spell they were meant to activate. Nor would simply destroying these twelve solve the true problem. He couldn't have made these; he lacks the intelligence and talent. Whoever created these might be able to make more. Might have already done so. These* nactka *pose no threat on Earth; they are inert. They remain dangerous, however, until I understand what the spell they're linked to does.*

"No, not another song!" Jillian cried as the next paragraph started out with "Knock knock, pick the lock, open the box..."

"Well, we know that the *nactka* are in a box." Louise started a separate search. "Let's see what he has to say about the box."

Luckily Dufae obsessed about the box. He drew pictures of it. He considered changing the keyword of the lock spell and made elaborate notes on how to make lock spells and then decided that the magic of Earth was too "dirty" to guarantee a success.

And then they made an amazing discovery. The last few pages weren't in Elvish but French. The hand that made the letters was more impatient, gone was the elegant perfection.

> *Today my wife has born me a son, and we named him Roland Dufae. His ears are as pointed as mine. I was born fifty-some years ago, but I still look like a youth. I realize that my father would have lived forever on his native world*

and could not imagine that his life would be cut so short in such a tragic way. I have no idea how long I will live, but I must be sure that my child knows of his heritage, for it is stamped upon his face and determines how fast or slow he may grow. I will teach him to read and speak my father's tongue. When he is old enough to understand, I will tell him of how my father traveled to Earth from the world of elves and why. When the crown of France fell, taking my father with it, I was still an infant. I was carried to safety in America. The codex and many of my father's things were brought with me, but the nactka *that were his whole reason for fleeing his homeworld were not among them. I do not know what happened to the box containing the* nactka. *For his soul, I pray that they were smashed by ignorant fools, but from what I know of the box's construction, this is unlikely. Protected as it was, it was virtually indestructible. It must exist somewhere in France along with all the crown jewels looted from the palaces. The fools will not be able to open the box, so it will continue to be, until I or one of my children search it out."*

On the next page was English done in careful precise lettering, nearly as if printed by a machine.

"My beloved grandchildren, Leo was killed by his efforts to build a gateway to Elfhome. Dufae's enemies have been on Earth all this time. It is possible that they already have the contents of Dufae's lost box. Stay hidden. Trust only each other and no one else. Keep yourself safe."

How do you find a box that was lost three hundred years ago on another continent? Once upon a time, it might have been impossible, but the data age had put cameras into the hands of billions of humans, all with the curiosity of monkeys and a weird drive to share what they knew. Louise created a rendering of the box based on Dufae's sketches and tied it to a spider to crawl through the web, comparing the image to the trillions of pictures stored on the Internet. Someone, somewhere, had to have seen the box.

13: THE QUEEN'S PARTING GIFT

-◆-➡◎⊂◆-

May first was Alexander's birthday. She turned eighteen, a full and legal adult. Louise and Jillian celebrated alongside her and yet a universe apart, with cupcakes they bought on the way home. They risked a birthday candle because their mother was working late, stuck at work because her company needed to counterbalance growing protests with more security measures at upcoming events. The lone candle, though, reminded Louise that their baby siblings might never see a single birthday, and it made her cry.

"Make a wish, then blow it out," Jillian choked out.

Louise wiped away tears, thinking how stupid "wishing" magic sounded. She didn't even know what it was she needed to wish. For more time? For everyone to forget that they were supposed to be doing a play at school or that Jillian and she were shouldering a monster-load of the work? That they could find a *nactka* that had been lost for hundreds of years tucked away in their parents' basement?

Somehow they needed to save their sisters and brother.

She blew out the candle, and they ate their cupcakes while searching the world for Dufae's lost box.

"Jillian! Louise!" Zahara had bounced up beside Louise at the twins' locker. Since Jillian had cut her hair Peter Pan-short, their classmates couldn't tell them apart from behind. Jillian had already

113

been sucked away to deal with some play-related emergency. It left Louise feeling horribly aware that she rarely dealt with the world without Jillian beside her. It nearly felt like she had lost her right hand. "Did you see the *Today Show* this morning?"

Louise gasped as she realized that it was the day that Nigel was going to be a guest. She'd forgotten in the search for the *nactka*. "No!"

"Nigel Reid did a shout-out to Lemon-Lime."

"He did?" Louise cried, at once crushed that she'd missed seeing him, and yet excited at the idea that the real Nigel Reid had mentioned her and Jillian.

"He said he was a big fan. And he had Wembley with him."

"What?" Wembley was one of their running jokes in *The Queen's Parting Gift*. The Court had told the humans that the queen was giving them a "wembley" as a gift and meant at first a beautiful songbird. After the bird dies, they come up with a series of increasingly uglier animals to offer up as a wembley, that all meet bizarre deaths, until they get to a woolly-mammothlike *kuesi*, which are so ugly that they've crossed the line to cute.

"Well, the two *kuesi* at the Bronx Zoo had a baby, and they've named it Wembley."

"They did?" It had been the gift of the two *kuesi* that the twins were making fun of. It nearly seemed like a joke that of all the possible animals that the elves could give the humans, they had chosen two *kuesi*. The reason, though, was because most Elfhome animals required magic to function normally. Apparently the *kuesi* had been bred to be indifferent to the levels of magic around it.

"He's so cute!" Zahara cried and pulled up a video clip on her tablet.

The video started with Nigel already onstage with Wembley. The baby *kuesi* looked vaguely like a very hairy elephant with nubs of tusks. Its trunk was in hyperactive overdrive and developed a fixation on exploring up and under the host's dress. The first time the woman squealed and jumped. She spent much of the video circling Nigel with the trunk in chase while the man explained about how the *kuesi* had been used to build the first railroad on Elfhome. Nigel seemed torn between amusement and confusion to what could possibly be attracting the animal so strongly.

"Do you have some peanuts hidden down there?" Nigel asked.

The host glared at him for a moment, which unfortunately

distracted her long enough for the trunk to find its target again. The video clip ended with the host squealing a second time.

"That's the shout-out?" Louise managed to say after she stopped laughing.

"No, wait, it comes before. Let me see if I can find it." Zahara went to a website that was labeled Lemon-Lime Love. "Ugh. No. No." She changed sites to one called Jello Shots.

Louise's stomach flipped weirdly at the site names. "Oh, tell me that those aren't what I think they are."

"Fan sites dedicated to your videos? Okay, I won't tell you then. Here."

The clip was labeled "Nigel Reid is a Jello Shot!"

The clips started with Nigel leading the baby *kuesi* out onto the stage. Despite being only a few months old, it was already as tall as the Scotsman. Its long hair was silky and unruly, making it look like a shambling mound of hair with a trunk.

"Thank you for having me. This little fellow is a six-month-old Elfhome *kuesi*..."

"*Kuesi*? I thought he was a wembley." The host double-checked her teleprompter. "I thought... it looks like a wembley."

Nigel laughed. "Yes, everyone thinks so because of the video *The Queen's Parting Gift*. The people at the zoo have gotten so tired of having people insist that the sign is wrong that they've named this little guy Wembley. But he really is a *kuesi*, which is a cousin to Earth's woolly mammoth."

"Oh, he's so cute," the host said and then went wide-eyed as the beast beelined over to her and loomed above her. "And big!"

"I asked the Bronx Zoo to borrow him because I hope to be working with Lemon-Lime JEl-Lo in the near future."

"Wow!" For a moment the host was more interested in the news than the animal standing beside her. "I love Lemon-Lime JEl-Lo."

"Yes, they're a wonderfully creative and knowledgeable production company." Nigel dodged around gender, age, and number of people involved, probably because he didn't know any of it.

"How in the world did you make contact with—" Whatever she was going to ask was cut short by the *kuesi* fondling her under her dress. She jumped, squeaking loudly, and the clip ended.

The comments under it exploded with speculations on what work he'd be doing with Lemon-Lime. The thread quickly grew ugly as the Jello Shot fans decided that Nigel was merely trying to capitalize on Lemon-Lime's fame and that he was lying about the entire thing.

"Holy shit," Louise whispered as she realized that despite being posted just an hour before, there were twenty pages of comments already.

"What are you doing with Nigel?" Zahara asked.

Louise stared at her, full of horror. It had never occurred to her that anyone who knew the truth about them would connect them up to Nigel. "You can't tell anyone about this! We'd get into so much trouble if our parents knew!"

"They don't know?"

"No! They think the Internet is full of pedophiles, and we're not allowed on any adult site until we're at least fourteen."

"Wow. That's like really fossil-age thinking."

"My mom knew *one* person that got into trouble like that, so she's super protective. If they found out that we've posted our videos online and are commenting on filmmaking sites and set up the YourStore—"

Louise stopped being able to talk, because she was completely breathless at the idea of how much trouble they'd be in. They'd be grounded for months without Internet, and they might never get their video equipment back.

"I won't tell," Zahara promised. "And I'll tell everyone else not to say anything. But this was on television. Does anyone else know that you're Lemon-Lime?"

Their Aunt Kitty had helped them pick the name, but she didn't know about their videos. Also she didn't watch morning shows. She wasn't a morning person. Any time they did see her in the mornings, it was usually because she'd been up all night and hadn't gone to bed yet. It was part of the reason she often babysat in emergencies.

"So what are you doing with Nigel Reid—that your parents know nothing about?"

It sounded horrible when Zahara said it that way.

"He wants to ask us questions about the gossamer call."

Zahara's eyes went wide. "But didn't you just make that up as a joke?"

"Yes. I mean, no. We know there is a whistle for the gossamers, but we haven't found any references to what it looks like or how it works." Louise pulled at her hair at the sudden realization that they didn't have anything concrete to tell Nigel. Her research had been detoured by everything else.

"So what are you going to do?"

Louise stared at Zahara as her mind raced. Was it possible that the codex had some information on it? Once they had a magic generator, they could experiment with any spells that the elves might have embedded into a whistle, but they didn't have any gossamers to test them on. They could build a virtual simulator of a gossamer if they could find anything about their physiology. So far they hadn't found any studies on the massive living airships. The fact that the creatures were translucent made all pictures of them blurry and difficult to figure out where the flying jellyfishlike animal ended and the sky began.

"Louise?"

"Um..."

"You should at least thank him for the shout-out," Zahara said.

"You think so?"

The bell rang for homeroom. There was a sudden and massive movement of bodies as everyone in the hall headed to their classroom.

"My mom always thanks anyone that says something nice about her to the media."

Louise nearly protested that they weren't on the same level as Zahara's fashion-model mother, but then remembered the *Today Show* host's reaction to the name Lemon-Lime. They might have been unaware of it, but apparently they were famous. "Okay, I'll thank him."

There were hundreds of messages under Nigel's original post. The first was "Seriously? Nigel Reid? THE Lemon-Lime? I don't know which one to disbelieve the most." The second stated, "Dude, Lemon-Lime talks to no one. They're like ghosts!" A random reply on the next page showed that the comments turned ugly as fans decided that the shout-out was just a way to steal Lemon-Lime's fame.

Louise winced. Poor Nigel. Zahara was right; for all the grief he was getting, he deserved a thank-you. She opened up a private message and gave it a subject line of "Thank you for the great shout-out." After that, she didn't know what to say.

Famous people are all just normal people at their core, Zahara had said. It was certainly true for her and Jillian. Well, they were normal if one ignored them being elves, conceived after their male genetic donor was dead, and smarter than just about everyone else....

She stared at the blank screen for a while as the cursor blinked. They had nothing to give Nigel right now. All they had was a handful of observations that anyone could make. They should be sure before they told him anything, and that would take time. Meanwhile the poor man was going to get dragged through dirt. In public.

If they released a Lemon-Lime video acknowledging Nigel, then they could clear his name. They had planned on doing filler anyhow.

"Oh, great idea!" Jillian reacted to the news with wide-eyed amazement. "A video reply will confirm we're really Lemon-Lime. We could crank a filler out in a few hours."

By the end of homeroom, they had a short storyboard laid out. Normally, they did stop-motion with Barbie dolls on green screen; it gave their work a distinctive style. Unfortunately, they'd blown up their entire cast. Louise always thought they should acknowledge the accident by having Queen Soulful Ember blast the royal court to cinders. The addition of Nigel to the mix gave them the idea of changing who got vaporized. In the new video, the queen lets loose a series of blasts, aiming at one precious treasure after another. Her court barely manages to deflect her spells' damage onto what seems to be unoccupied space. After the court leaves the area, however, ninja scientists rain out of their smoldering hiding spaces.

The second act was solely a shot of the Cathedral of Learning to symbolize the University of Pittsburgh. Jillian was writing the dialogue for the first section, but Louise had an inspiration for the middle section. She typed dialogue that would later need to be read in. The first male would say, "Good God, not again. And those were the last of the anthologists, archeologists, biologists, and botanists. What's next on the list? Ah, entomologist. Yes, we do need to learn more Elvish. This dictionary we have sucks."

"I do not think that word means what you think it means," some unseen male says with a slight Spanish accent.

"Get me entomologists!"

The third act was a shot of a crude box trap baited with ants. Nigel Reid and his cameraman stumble into the trap and ninjas hammer it shut and cover it with mailing stickers, addressing it to Elfhome. They could use sound bites from Nigel's documentary on fire ants—painfully short to stay within fair use limits—specifically the discussion on the queen, since applying the factoids to Soulful Ember would be funny. Once Nigel was trapped inside the box with the ants, she could use a slightly muffled version of the section where he was cheerfully describing the pain of being stung. Repeatedly.

Louise pulled old backgrounds from their home computer to build the needed sets. Giggling, Jillian told her between first and second period that the "precious treasures" would be various plot McGuffins from earlier videos. They could get around not showing the queen and her court and use only dialogue to progress the story. They spent the break between second and third period recording the lines in the girls' restroom.

After a great deal of consideration, Louise decided to insert one frame of the raw footage from their playhouse explosion as an Easter egg with each fire strike. The first would be subtitled, "We decided to experiment with special effects on the fire strike." The second would state, "We blew up our studio." The third would end with, "There will be a short hiatus in production until we manage to replace our equipment."

They had always operated on the assumption that they had at least one die-hard fan that liked finding the Easter eggs. They'd even given the fan a name: Harvey. It was weird to know that they had thousands of Harveys and one of them was sure to analyze the video frame by frame for Easter eggs. This hidden message would definitely be read. Maybe by hundreds of people.

Louise was just adding various Foley effects, like hammering nails, out of the copyright-free archive when Jillian suddenly kicked her. She looked up, aware for the first time that the room had gone completely silent.

"Louise!" Mr. Kessler, their computer literacy teacher, was bearing down on her.

She blinked up at him, surprised. She and Jillian sat in the back of all their classes and rarely drew the attention of any of their teachers. Up to this moment, she wasn't even sure that Mr. Kessler knew their names, since the few times he'd called on them, he addressed them as Twin One and Twin Two.

"What are you doing?" He came to loom over her. He held out his hand for her tablet.

As Louise hesitated, hands covering her screen, she saw Jillian quickly copy everything off her tablet. "I was just watching the new Lemon-Lime JEl-Lo video."

There was a murmur of excitement from the other kids in their class. She cringed slightly as she realized that Elle could and probably would fully explain how she had the new video. Then again, maybe Mr. Kessler was a fan.

"That stupid tripe?" Mr. Kessler snapped his fingers, demanding her tablet immediately. "Those videos are nothing but a glorification of the rich and selfish elf royalty."

"They are not!" both Louise and Jillian cried.

"It's believed that there are fewer than ten thousand elves on the whole North American continent, and yet the queen lays claim to all of it. Nine point five four million square miles for just ten thousand selfish bastards. That's over nine hundred square miles per elf. Alaska's population density is less than two square miles per human."

"Mr. Kessler." Elle waved her hand, making Louise shrink. When he didn't acknowledge her, Elle pressed on without lowering her hand. "Mr. Kessler, you shouldn't use the b-word in class. It's very rude. And what you're saying is very bigoted. Can we stay on topic?"

Mr. Kessler snorted and handed back Louise's tablet. He'd deleted all her work and purged her cache. She gasped at the hours of work she might have lost. "I want you to solve the problem on the board, Louise."

She took a deep breath against the anger boiling in her. He had no right to delete work off her tablet. Yell at her, yes, but not destroy her work, much of which she'd done before his class started. They were only five minutes into class, too; it wasn't like she'd spent a long time ignoring him.

"Sometime soon." He pointed at the board.

She glanced to the front of the room. The wall screen had a quadratic equation. She locked her jaw against the first two things that wanted to come out. "I don't understand."

"Oh, then you agree that this is a class and I am a teacher and if you were paying attention to me you would understand—"

"I don't understand why you're asking me to solve that equation. This isn't math class, and we're not up to quadratic formulas yet. We're still doing pre-algebra work."

"Yes, this is computer literacy class, and if you were listening, you would know—"

"That x is negative four and one?"

"Huh?" Obviously, he wasn't expecting her to be able to solve the problem since he didn't recognize the correct answer when she gave it.

"You're asking me to solve y equals x squared plus three x minus four. The solution is negative four and one."

He glanced at the board and then at her. "What?"

Did he even know how to solve the problem himself?

"Quadratic equations with two variables have countless solutions," Louise explained because she suspected he didn't know. "The answers create a continuous line in the shape of a parabola. The 'correct' answer to this equation is the two points where that parabola hits the x-axis: negative four and one. What I don't understand is why you're asking us to deal with an equation like this. Our class has just started to graph straight lines. How do you expect anyone to use a computer to calculate this if they don't know how to check the result? They could get a nonsense answer like 'forty-two' and think it's right."

He stared at her, slack-jawed, for a moment and then said angrily, "My point is that you should be paying attention to me."

"I will when you start teaching something I don't already know."

He scanned the room, taking in the hostile stares of the other kids. "Fine." He went back to his desk, deleted the equation from the wall display and typed in a simple addition function. "Reed, can you set up a four-column, four-row spreadsheet that uses this to produce totals in the fourth row?"

At lunch, the entire fifth grade gathered around their table, worried that Kessler had deleted all their work.

"We saved it." Jillian pulled it up on her tablet and played what they had finished.

"Wow!" Iggy said when it came to the end. "You did this all during class this morning?"

"It's only five minutes long, and we're using a lot of old stuff," Louise said. "Hopefully people won't think that someone forged this since it's all rehash."

"If we use the new song for *Black Willow Wicker*, the music would establish the video as one of ours."

Louise tugged at her hair as she considered the pros and cons. Their soundtracks were heavily influenced by the fusion music of garage bands in Pittsburgh. The groups combined guitar-heavy rock and roll with Elvish musicians playing traditional instruments. When the twins started writing their own songs three years ago, the fusion music was insanely hard to find. They had stumbled across a handful of tracks during a research raid on the Pittsburgh Internet during Shutdown. With their Aunt Kitty being a composer, they knew better than to use the songs without permission. To create their own version of it, though, they had to digitally recreate the off-world instruments. It had taken them months to dig up enough information and code it all in. Since then, fusion music had been discovered by the masses, unfortunately fueled by mass piracy and pale imitations. None of the groups based on Earth could match the twins' music, because no one else had the right instruments.

The new song for *Black Willow Wicker* had been written for the humorous battle between Queen Soulful Ember and an army of black willows protesting Hairbrush's attempts at magical topiary that created a roving flock of boxwood penguins. ("They had to be flightless birds. Flying topiary would have been simply ridiculous.") Louise used a series of bugle calls starting with reveille to mirror the trees' strategies. It was bit of geek humor they didn't expect Harvey to get.

It didn't quite match the feel of the filler video, but everything from the *zalituus* horn to the *olianuni* marked it as one of their pieces. To write and record something else would take days. Louise wanted to get their reply video posted as quickly as possible.

"Yes, let's use it." Louise ported in the song and started to fiddle with the video's story beats to match up with the music. Because the battlefield scene had been punctuated with explosions as the new storyboard, it actually wasn't as hard as she had thought to make the two mesh together.

"What do we call this one?" Jillian asked. "*Thank You for the Shout-Out?*"

There was a groaning outcry against the title from the kids around them.

"*It's a Trap!*" Ava suggested.

"*Where in the World is Nigel Reid?*" Iggy said.

"*Missing Treasures,*" Zahara shouted to be heard over the sudden loud flood of possible video titles.

"*Missing Treasures,*" Louise repeated. There was a nice double meaning that the queen was missing her original targets, the various treasures, but also that Nigel Reid was going to go missing. "I like that." Louise glanced to Jillian, who nodded. She quickly created a title screen. The only ending credits that they did were to claim copyright to everything in the video, from the art down to the music, and assigned them to Lemon-Lime JEl-Lo. "We're ready to load."

A cheer went up from the other kids. As the boring part of waiting for the video to upload wore on, the other kids scattered to get food and claim tables.

Since they needed to hide their data trail while loading, normally they only loaded their videos to one site, Filmcraft. They never were staff pick, had more than a hundred comments, and never reached the thousand mark of "likes." The low response was why they never thought they were widely popular. While Jillian uploaded the new video to Filmcraft, Louise did a search for *The Queen's Pantaloons.* Where were all these people seeing their videos if not on Filmcraft? The search term brought back over two million hits. Filmcraft wasn't even on the top page of results. The first hit was YouTube, a site that Jillian considered the ghetto of video sites and they never used and rarely visited. Unlike Filmcraft, YouTube listed the number of times the video was actually viewed. The number made her squeak.

"What?" Jillian asked.

"Five hundred million views!" Louise cried.

"For what?"

"*The Queen's Pantaloons!*" Someone using the screen name of JelloShot01 had copied their video from Filmcraft. He had all their other videos, too. In the "recommended videos" on the side was *Culotte de la Reine,* which was their title translated into French. When she clicked on it, their video started to play with French subtitles.

"You really didn't know how famous you were?" Iggy asked.

Dumbstruck, Louise shook her head. This explained all the money in the YourStore account. How much more could they make if they advertised? How did they go about advertising?

Zahara returned with three sandwiches and drinks. "Here. I figured you'd want to see it uploaded."

"Thanks!" Louise wasn't sure if she should offer money to

Zahara. If the food was a gift, it would be kind of insulting to offer it. They had, however, all that money from YourStore. They weren't the poorest kids in school anymore.

Once it was uploaded, they posted a link at the Pittsburgh Forum under the heading "For Nigel from Lemon-Lime JEl-Lo."

Louise had left her tablet on the JelloShot01 YouTube channel as they ate. Before lunch was over, *Missing Treasures* was added to his list and already had fifty thousand views. She stared at it in surprise and dismay. How had they missed that they were this famous?

Louise spent the rest of the day searching through the rough translation of the codex for some references to the gossamer call while watching the numbers soar on JelloShot01's channel. Debate broke out on the fan website as to whether this was a real video or a fake created by Nigel. The doubters pointed to the odd posting time, insisting that Lemon-Lime was based on Elfhome and wouldn't be able to upload during any period other than Shutdown. Others pointed out that if Nigel was working with Lemon-Lime, then he could have arranged for work visas for Pittsburghers. This triggered a spirited debate between people who thought the twins had to be elves and those who believed that they were Elfhome "natives"—Pittsburghers born after the first Startup.

Fifty-three minutes after JelloShot01 copied their video, the first report of the frame-by-frame analysis hit the boards. Louise imagined that she could hear the massive wails of dismay as they discovered the hidden messages. Another twenty-eight minutes and their fans had decided that Lemon-Lime had sought Nigel out in order to raise money to replace their equipment. This completely ignored the fact that Nigel had posted a very public message seeking Lemon-Lime. Another theory surfaced after someone decided to take the video's storyboard as gospel truth. Obviously, this new camp stated, Lemon-Lime was trying to warn Nigel that he was about to be tricked into a one-way trip to Elfhome. This was quickly refuted by fans that were also followers of Nigel's work. Apparently Nigel had been fairly public in his attempts to get to Elfhome; the production company that handled his nature documentaries had been denied travel visas by the EIA for several years. His fans also pointed out that Nigel was in New York for the *Today Show* as part of his pitch to NBC to do a series on Elfhome. Nigel had reached out to Lemon-Lime before the April Shutdown. Lemon-Lime, they theorized, could have left Pittsburgh last month and joined Nigel in New York.

This triggered a furious reexamination of Nigel's appearance on the NBC morning show and the phrase "hope to be working." Some stated that this and the video indicated that Lemon-Lime hadn't agreed to anything. Others claimed that the "hope" meant that Nigel hadn't locked in the NBC backing yet, and Lemon-Lime was only defending Nigel from the backlash of his shout-out. Yet another group suggested that NBC was waffling on their decision, and Lemon-Lime's video was an attempt to sway the network by adding their fanbase to Nigel's.

"Wow, they really overthink everything." Louise closed the window on the seemingly endless debate. "They're making it all more complicated than it really was."

"Maybe," Jillian said. "We had no idea if it was really Nigel Reid trying to make contact with us and we don't know why he's in New York and we didn't expect such a huge shout-out from him. Face it, we didn't even know we were famous, and from what I can tell, we're up there with blockbuster movie stars. Some of what the fans are saying might be right."

Louise didn't want to believe that Nigel had used them. He always seemed so genuinely nice on camera. She wanted it to honestly be what it be appeared to be—Nigel had only contacted them to learn something interesting to him. She had to admit that she could be wrong.

"Do you know what really sucks?" Jillian sighed. "If we could go public, then everything would work out. We could sign a movie deal with some big studio and use the money to save the babies."

Louise's stomach sunk at the idea of so many people focused on them. "No one is going to offer us a deal. Even if they did, as soon as the studios found out we're nine-year-olds, they'd back out."

"I don't know," Jillian said. "People in Hollywood make some pretty crazy decisions."

"We're still minors. We can't sign contracts on our own. Mom and Dad would have to agree to anything, and you know what they'll say."

"That we should have as normal a childhood as possible," Jillian growled with frustration. "Alexander was so lucky. Her grandfather didn't make her be normal."

"He must know what it was like, growing up and being like us. Mom and Dad are doing the best they can, but they can't know how boring it is to try to keep at everyone else's speed."

"This might be the perfect way to nail a Hollywood deal, and it's going to just slip away. Everyone loves us now, but how long is that going to last? A year? Two? It's not going to last until we're eighteen."

Louise liked doing the videos, but she wasn't sure she wanted to do them another eight years. Hollywood was Jillian's dream. If Louise had a dream that included Hollywood, it'd be doing nature documentaries like Nigel. "Well, maybe not *The Adventures of Queen Soulful Ember*, but that doesn't mean we can't come up with something just as cool."

Jillian harrumphed. Being a Hollywood director had been her dream for years. It had to be hard to see the possibility dangle within reach and yet know that she couldn't claim it. She probably didn't realize, though, that it made Louise feel so small and unsure beside her. Louise didn't know what she wanted to be when they got old enough to do anything and everything. She did know she didn't want to be in front of a camera, having everyone watch her, and she didn't want to be behind the camera, having to tell everyone what to do. And that knowledge made her feel even smaller.

Hating how she felt, she focused back on searching the codex for information on the gossamer call. There was nothing on gossamers. Not on how they were controlled. Not on how they were created. She flipped through the book, pausing here and there to study the spells traced on the pages. So much to learn, so little time.

They knew that the gossamers were called with whistles. The *domana* triggered their magic with different words. Every written spell had an activation phrase. Sound seemed to be a basic part of magic. Each *domana* spell required a different finger position. Using motions and words, the elves operated their bodies like a human did a computer, selecting a spell and running it. No, not like a computer, like an instrument. The finger positions were like the fingering of a flute or guitar. The *domana* were producing a unique chord with each new gesture and word. Given two hands, ten fingers, two joints on the thumb, three joints on the other fingers, there was a staggering number of possible finger positions.

The written spells in the codex required phrases to trigger them. The phrases worked much like spell locks in that the main function was to keep the spell from activating until the caster wished it to activate. That each spell required a different phrase, though, seemed to indicate that there was more to it than a simple key turning in a lock. Perhaps the sound set up important resonance within the spell components....

So much they didn't know. Louise sighed and focused on what she did know.

The elves didn't have slides or valves on their instruments. A whistle with multiple tones then would be fixed and played like a flute or boatswain's call. The samples of gossamer calls they could find had featured only four tones that they'd already mapped out sine waves for. One was in the high ultrasonic range, but the others stepped down the hertz range to something audible to humans. It seemed to indicate that the gossamer's hearing was similar to whales and open-water species of dolphins. The Earth sea mammals used low-pitched tones in the seventy-five hertz range to communicate because those sounds traveled farther. They used frequencies in the one hundred to hundred-fifty kilohertz range for echolocation. Humans could only hear up to twenty kilohertz, so it would explain why three of the tones were audible. The twins had noticed that "turn" commands used the ultrasonic tone while the other three sounds triggered "docking" and "wait" activities. Obviously the elves were using instinctual behavior for their commands.

The question remained whether the commands were actually spells printed on the whistle itself or were like the *domana*-caste, genetically keyed within the gossamer. Considering the limited tones of the whistle and the wide range of words used as commands for both written spells and *domana* spell-casting, it seemed likely that it was the latter. If that was the case, then the "magic" of the whistle was that it needed to cross great distances in order to trigger the gossamer's genetically coded spells. Dufae actually discussed in length how the magic "jumped" distances via resonance, which allowed the *domana*-caste to channel the massive amounts of power from a distant location to where they needed it. He also took great care in determining the exact distance between the mouth and the hands to trigger the *domana* spells.

Louise flipped back to that section of the codex. Since Dufae was cut off from the Spell Stones, he had developed a set of spells to help him carry out his experiments. The twins needed a whistle that could hit all four tones with a magical spell that could amplify the reach of the instrument.

An hour later, she thought she knew how to build a gossamer call. They wouldn't even need to use the school's printer. Of course, until they got a working generator, there'd be no way to test it.

14: STAGECRAFT

-◆-►══○══◄-◆-

The next day they started the set construction during the joint stagecraft class. Louise had designed the sets so they broke down into many intricate pieces when they were dissembled, requiring three-dimensional models for each part to be understandable. The Darling nursery in a ghetto of New York City. The Neverland forest with trees that umbrella-opened and the Lost Boys' houses tucked under the roots of the trees. The mermaids' lagoon where "the ocean" would shimmer blue via a series of holographic projectors. And then, as a grand piece of design, the massive *Jolly Roger* pirate ship with three masts and rigging, which, of course, had to stay hidden in the wings until the fourth act.

Mr. Howe and Miss Hamilton reviewed the designs as they gathered in the art room while Louise's heart hammered in her chest.

"This is ambitious," Miss Hamilton said.

"Are you sure we can get all this work done?" Mr. Howe asked. "We have less than eight weeks now before the show, and we won't have access to the stage until the end of this month."

"These are the time schedules I've got worked out for the construction." Louise pulled up the lists. This was the first year that they would use the large auditorium. Every class put on a play; the productions were set up so each class had private use of the stage for only a month. Since the sixth-graders were currently erecting their sets and doing dress rehearsals, their class wouldn't have access to the stage until that play was over. "As long as we get the materials on time and have access to the machines like the printer. The big one in the annex."

"What do you need that for?" Mr. Howe asked. "Do you even know how to program it? Normally only seniors work with that for the advanced robotics and science labs."

Louise pointed out the magic-generator doubles. "These projectors are usually very expensive because they're very versatile, but if we use the printer to create them with limited functions, we could do the same thing for just a few dollars."

"And yes, we know how to program them," Jillian said.

"Why do we even need these?" Miss Hamilton asked.

"The lagoon is supposed to be a bunch of rocks in the water. It's basically a protected swimming cove. The mermaids are supposed to be slipping in and out of the water. The script calls for Peter and Wendy to attempt to capture a mermaid. She slips from their grasp and swims away."

"There's no explanation on how this is supposed to be staged." Jillian took up the narrative. "We think Barrie meant for the mermaids to enter and exit via trapdoors, but those were banned in New York schools before we were born."

Mr. Howe frowned, looking off vaguely as if he was considering time. "It really wasn't that long ago—was it?"

"It was," Miss Hamilton murmured. "So you're going to get around needing to have the mermaid just 'disappear' by projecting her?"

"Her and three other mermaids in these alcoves." Louise pointed them out. "Instead of them being stuck in a fairly seated position, we can pre-record part of their performances and splice them in, kind of integrating film and live action."

"This is just a fifth-grade play," Miss Hamilton said.

"We're within budget and time." Jillian gave her a carefully innocent smile. "And this is the Perelman School for the Gifted in New York City, not a public school in Detroit. It will be a play that will make parents feel like the money they spend on their kids' education is justified."

Louise thought Jillian was laying it on too thick and bumped her slightly. Jillian continued to smile brightly at their teachers and bumped her back.

Louise tried to detour the conversation. "These projectors will allow us to basically hand-wave most of the set for the mermaids' lagoon. We can do a 'painted' backdrop of rocky cliffs, kind of what they did for the movie." She pulled up a print from the Disney cartoon and a photograph of a Hawaiian cliff for comparison. "See, the real cliff has a black rock and the blues of the water as its primary colors. Disney went with a more purple color scheme; I think to suggest a woman's boudoir. Don't think we should go that direction."

"No," Mr. Howe said.

"Definitely not," Miss Hamilton said.

Louise closed the Disney print and centered the photograph. "So what I was thinking is blowing up this photo and printing it out on a color printer on the largest sheets of paper our printers can handle. I think eleven by seventeen inches is the largest. This is the cost of the paper, ink, and adhesive."

"And mount them on...?"

"We do both the nursery and the lagoon as a series of panels that lock together to make a full-size wall. The nursery backdrop will be on one side and the lagoon cliff would be on the other. Panels can be flipped as they're raised and lowered. This is the break-out of their cost, and here's the model rendering showing them being raised and lowered."

"You've put a lot of thought into this," Mr. Howe said.

Louise nodded, heart still hammering. She knew that she needed to be completely thorough with all of the set design or the teachers would feel as if they would have to watch over every little detail.

The teachers conferred in murmurs and then nodded in agreement.

"Okay." Mr. Howe clapped his hands. "Let's get started then."

Louise gathered her courage by focusing on what she knew well. "I would have liked to work from the largest item down. First step would be creating the walls for the nursery and lagoon. Since we don't have the panels yet, we can set up work on Marooner's rock and the Darlings' beds and the projectors."

"The projectors are large?" Mr. Howe asked, putting a tremble of fear through Louise.

"No, it's just that each one will take hours for the printer to create. We start one running now, it should be done by first period tomorrow."

"I'll set up crews to handle the rock and the beds," Jillian said. "And Louise can do the programming of the printer. We need to discuss with Reed how to do the swords, since he's prop master. And there are a few questions we have on the costumes with Zahara before the sewing starts."

They'd hoped that everyone would work on the assumption that the twins were interchangeable. Either one of them could do the programming. Louise was better at not getting caught, which made Jillian better at talking her way out of things. Since they would be in adjoining rooms, they figured that it would be best for Louise to handle the printing. If she was caught, Jillian could jump in to talk them back out of trouble. That weekend, in preparation for this class, Jillian had trimmed her hair to match Louise, saying it was so she looked more like Peter Pan.

They gave identical inquiring looks to their teachers.

"She's Louise?" Mr. Howe asked pointing to the correct twin.

Miss Hamilton paused a moment before answering. "Yes, that's Louise."

He picked up two cards and wrote "Louise" and taped it to her. The other went on Jillian with her name printed out. "Okay, let's roll."

The biggest hurdle to making the magic generator was Mr. Kessler. For computer literacy classes he came to their classroom, but the technology room attached to the art room was his official domain. Louise was upset with herself that she'd insulted him the day before. She knew that they would need the printers; she shouldn't have lost her temper. Considering how he treated them before Louise snapped at him, he probably would have blocked any attempt to use the printer even without her standing up to him. Now it was almost guaranteed that he would try and deny them access to the technology annex.

The twins had debated how to get around Mr. Kessler. Stealth was no longer an option. In retrospect, even if they had started the printing anonymously, odds were he would have killed the print job long before it came to an end. Because of the long run time, they needed hours of uninterrupted access to the printer that only the play allowed them.

Since stealth wasn't an option, they would have to use what they had.

After the class was engaged in building the one massive Styrofoam Marooner's Rock and the three Darlings' beds, Jillian took Zahara and ambushed Miss Gray with innocently worded questions about the mermaid costumes in terms of strategically placed seashells. Within minutes, Miss Hamilton was dragged into the whispered discussion of possibly scandalous wardrobe versus theater traditions. With the other two teachers occupied, Louise was free to corner Mr. Howe and ask him for help with the printer in the annex.

"I don't know anything about that equipment. You should ask Mr. Kessler for help. He's in the room right now."

"He picks on us." Louise was glad she could be truthful about it. "I don't know why, but he doesn't like us. He teases us in front of the whole class."

Mr. Howe's eyes narrowed slightly. "Let's go see Mr. Kessler."

She couldn't read his tone. Aware that he towered above her, she led the way to the annex. Did Mr. Howe believe her? Did he think she was making it up? Was she going to be able to use Mr. Howe to counter Mr. Kessler or were the men going to join together to create an adult wall of stupidity?

Mr. Kessler sat at his desk. He looked up sharply as Louise entered. "This equipment is for big kids, shrimp. Shoo."

Louise took a deep breath and clung tight to her courage. "I need to use the 3D printer in here."

"There's one in the art room for you squirts." He focused on closing up the windows on his desktop.

"I need the advanced model for our joint-class play. The art room one only prints at a hundred-micron resolution."

"No." He glanced up and visibly flinched at Mr. Howe at her back. "Bill? Oh, I didn't see you. Look, my stuff is not toys. I won't let the ninth-grade kids touch my printer, because they don't have the programming skills yet."

"It's not your printer, Mr. Kessler. It's the school's printer."

"I know how to program it." Louise held her tablet tight to her chest, afraid he'd try to take it and erase her work. "I made sure to run my job on a simulator to double-check my work."

Mr. Kessler stood up and paced a moment behind his desk. "Okay. Fine." He stormed to the 3D printer. "It's mine in that I have to deal with all the hassles of getting it replaced if it's broken."

"It's a printer for a high school. If it's that delicate, it shouldn't be here," Mr. Howe said. "And if it's here, my kids have a right to it."

Louise linked her tablet to the printer. She had really hoped that she could print the magic generator, but not with both men focused so intently on her. She carefully loaded the program to print the holographic projectors. After double-checking she had everything set up, she started the machine. The printer hummed, and the scent of chemicals tainted the air. Otherwise, it barely seemed like the machine was working.

As she fled the room, she heard Mr. Howe growl softly. "You seem to have lost sight that these are little kids, Kevin. You are here to teach, not to casually insult them, and you don't make them a target by singling them out. If I hear about you picking on any of the kids in my grade, or the school for that matter, I will do my best to see to it you no longer work here. I may even feel it necessary to give you a more personal understanding of the effects of being bullied. Hands-on, so to speak. I trust my position in this matter is clear."

Louise was not sure if Mr. Howe had been serious, but Mr. Kessler seemed to think he was. He avoided her and Mr. Howe for the next few days. She wasn't sure if that meant he'd peacefully allow them access to the printers. Half-expecting him to sabotage the print runs, she did the two hologram projectors first. Only when they finished successfully did she feel confident in attempting to print the magic generator.

While everyone was working attaching the leaves to the first umbrella trees, she slipped away to the technical annex and programmed in the last job.

"This is the last one?" Iggy made her jump by suddenly showing up beside her.

She nodded, not trusting her voice to answer. She focused on making sure everything was set correctly before pressing the start button.

Iggy perched on the edge of the nearest art table. "You don't like people paying attention to you, do you?"

"No." She glanced toward the art room and discovered that all the teachers were focused on the rest of the class dueling with the newly made swords. It was the first time she'd ever been alone with a boy and it made her vaguely uncomfortable even though Iggy had been acting like they were friends.

"Most people actually don't like being in the spotlight." Iggy swung his legs back and forth, probably unaware that it made him look very much a little boy. He was, though, the oldest kid in both fifth-grade classes. "Sometimes they find ways to keep people from noticing them. Little things. Like not smiling so much, not looking people in the eye. It's so little that they don't always realize they're doing it."

Was he implying that she wasn't meeting people's gaze? Certainly, considering everything she'd been doing lately, she had been trying not to draw attention to herself. Had he just caught her at stealing printer time? He probably didn't understand the programming, as it was years above what they were doing in class. She closed the window just in case.

"The problem is that those little things work too well," Iggy said. "People start to ignore you. But because you're not totally aware of what you're doing, you start imagining that there's a good reason that they don't look at you. You think you're ugly and awkward and all the horrible reasons why people wouldn't want to look at you."

"I don't..." And then she paused, as her breath caught in her chest with the realization that she did. Embarrassment burned up her face. He knew how she felt, like he'd found it written someplace and read all her secrets. "I don't think I'm ugly."

"Just not as cute as your sister?"

She ducked her head so he couldn't see her blinking. Crying in school; only kindergarteners did that.

"Your sister is shy, too."

"Jillian?" Louise snorted with disbelief. Jillian loved people watching her.

"She doesn't like people looking at her, but if she can become someone else, have a part she can act, then she doesn't mind them watching, because they're not really looking at her."

"That's silly."

"You don't like acting because you don't like becoming someone you're not. That's why you're fine with being the stage manager."

"How do you know? You barely know us. I bet, from behind, you couldn't even tell us apart."

"I think I could. Not a week ago, no, but now, yeah. Up to a week ago, you two were like some masked wrestling tag team. The villain type that always cheat by being in the ring at the same time."

"You watch pro wrestling? You know that's fake?"

"It's theater. And yes, I watch it with my dad. I think he's worried about me growing up with so many sisters, like I might be permanently warped by Barbie dolls and Disney princesses."

"He's afraid you might be gay."

"I'm not! But, yes, in a nutshell, he's worried I'll get to like pink too much or something under the pressure..." He trailed off, blushing red. "My oldest sister. When she's home and she's alone, she's really beautiful. But as soon as she knows someone is watching, she does all she can to make herself invisible. I didn't notice, not for a long time. I don't know when it went from being shy to something else. I saw the cuts sometimes on her arms, but I didn't understand what they meant."

Something quietly awful had happened to Iggy's oldest sister. The details were carefully hidden away, but it involved an ambulance outside the school late in the afternoon and her entire class going through counseling the following weeks.

"I'm not like that."

"I know you're not." He kicked at the table leg. "You're smart enough to figure it out. If you make yourself invisible, then people can't see how beautiful you are."

"You—you think I'm beautiful?"

His eyes went wide, and he blushed red. He hadn't meant it. He slid down off the table, suddenly focusing hard on his shoes. She looked away, her throat suddenly seeming small and raw.

He started to flee, but he paused by the door. "I—I think you're like my sister," he stammered without turning around to look at her. "All alone, you're beautiful. And I wish someone had been able to convince my sister of that when she was younger. It's okay to be shy, but by trying to hide, you might start to hurt yourself without even realizing it."

15: CROWD SOURCING

Jillian was being Peter Pan when the bell rang, announcing the end of last period. She was standing on one of the art room tables, practicing lines of the first scene with Elle as Wendy. Louise paused at the doorway, wondering if Iggy was right, that Jillian could only stand on the table, bigger than life, because at that moment, she was Peter and not Jillian.

Zahara shook her head at the lines. "I'm just saying, if he showed up in some girl's bedroom in Queens, she's not going to be all 'Boy, why are you crying.' She'd be either hitting him with pepper spray or calling 911."

"It's a fantasy!" Elle cried. "What part of fairies and pixie dust are you missing? It's not operating in our reality."

"Obviously, the Darlings just moved from some little town in England to New York City." Giselle held up one sheets of the backdrop graffiti that would be seen through the nursery window. "One of their parents has been assigned a menial government job at the British Embassy. Probably their father. He's the government type. Their mother is either a daycare aide or works at a Build-A-Bear or something like that."

"We've already changed the play to the point of breaking!" Elle waved her copy of the script. "It's a classic. It's like rewriting Shakespeare."

"People are rewriting Shakespeare all the time," Zahara said. "And making them newly arrived from some farm town kills the whole 'not in Kansas' angle we're going for with the sets! Our audience will relate more to Wendy if she's just a little freaked out about having some mental case show up in her bedroom."

"Maybe Wendy is a mental case, too." Mason was looking pointedly at Elle. "Or maybe she's retarded."

"Mason!" Miss Hamilton pointed at him and gave him "the look" that she used to control anyone that strayed over the line. As he ducked his head meekly, Miss Hamilton waved Jillian down off the table. "School is over. It's time for all of us to go home. We will discuss making changes to the script tomorrow."

"Next week we will also be working on choreographing the fight scenes." Mr. Howe got a cheer. He cut it short by whistling sharply. "Only people who e-mail back signed permission slips this week will be allowed to participate. If your parents don't reply to the e-mail, you will be given a non-fighting role. And we will be checking against signatures on file, since the chances that one of your parents will sue the hell out of us is too high."

Jillian had hopped down off the table and hurried over to Louise. Her eyes were full of questions that she couldn't ask in front of everyone. Louise nodded to the most obvious one; the print job was started. They wouldn't find out until tomorrow night if the generator worked, and only if they managed to get it home unseen. Jillian grinned brightly and bounced in place.

Iggy fell into step with them going down the stairs to their lockers. He was still blushing and avoided Louise's glance by focusing on Jillian. Strangely, Jillian shied slightly away from him, looking away.

"You are going to be able to get permission from your parents, right?" Iggy asked.

Jillian shook herself a little, as if putting back on a mask. She looked up, full of confidence. "Of course I will. Our mom wants us to participate in class projects."

"Are you?" Louise asked Iggy. She had gotten the impression that his parents were very protective of him. Certainly it explained why he'd be worried that someone else's parents would refuse.

"I'm fairly sure my dad will sign it. Hook is da man!" Iggy waved his left hand with his fingers still in braces.

"How much longer before your fingers heal?"

Iggy eyed his left hand. "We see my doctor next Saturday. The doctor said four weeks, maybe five, so I might get it off

Saturday." He seemed doubtful. "Knowing my mom, though, even if the doctor says they're healed, she'll want me to wear it another week or two, just to be sure."

Which meant it had been more than four weeks since they'd found out about their siblings. It didn't seem possible that much time had already gone by. They had less than two months now to find the mythical box with mysterious *nactka*.

They got their jackets. Iggy's locker was four down from theirs. As Louise activated Tesla, Iggy drifted back to pet the toy's head.

"Good boy, Tesla, keep them safe." Iggy waved his broken hand and headed back toward the stairs. "See you next week."

"'Bye!" Jillian called brightly. Louise forced herself to wave; that's what friends did, wasn't it?

Apparently the Chen family was still being paranoid after Iggy's brush with violence; his sisters were waiting for him at the staircase so the family could go home together. His oldest sister was hunched as if carrying a great weight, head bowed, long bangs covering her face. As Iggy joined them, she looked up, and for one brief moment, she was as beautiful as Iggy claimed. Then she ducked her head as if withdrawing into a shell, vanishing from sight.

"Who were you just now?" Louise asked Jillian.

"What?"

"When you said good-bye, who were you? Peter Pan?"

"Oh, no, not Peter. He wouldn't think to say good-bye. He isn't much on hello, either. I kind of like that about him."

Tesla tilted his head and said, "Squirrel," in his little-boy Welsh voice. Both of them jumped with surprise.

"What the hell?" Jillian laughed. "I forgot he could talk! Why did he say that?"

Louise squeaked with surprise. "Oh, I completely forgot!"

"Squirrel," Tesla said again.

"Alarm off!" Louise pulled out her tablet. "I linked him to the box search so he could wake us up if the result came in during the night." A squeal of excitement leaked out as a flashing icon on her screen confirmed a positive hit. "We found it! Dufae's box! We found it!"

They rode home, heads together over her tablet as Tesla stood guard. Luckily their subway car was blissfully empty. Louise's spider had found a dozen photographs taken of Dufae's chest. It matched her CGI sketch perfectly. The pictures were dated from last year. The text explained that the chest had been discovered in the basement of the Louvre. It was labeled "unidentified block of unknown wood with possible Elvish runes," with a side note that said it had been donated to the museum in 1897.

On that site there was nothing else about the chest, but there were hundreds of other photographs of objects found around the world at various museum and private collections. The common denominator was that they were all suspected of being from Elfhome prior to the first Startup.

"We were right that it must have been common for the elves to travel to Earth," Louise said.

"But it doesn't explain why they stopped," Jillian said impatiently. She pulled out her tablet and started to follow trails of data. "Okay, where is the box now?"

"All these objects are part of a crowd-sourcing project. Oh! The irony!"

"What?"

"All these objects are linked to Dr. Forthwright," Louise said.

"*Forthwright?* Our character?"

"No, the woman we based him on." They'd changed the woman's name to hide the fact that they'd raided her personal computer three years ago. Because they often played Forthwright opposite to Prince Yardstick and Director Maynard of the EIA, it felt weirdly sexist to keep the one non-ninja scientist female since they had made the character both extremely nearsighted and often clueless. It was like they were saying somehow that women shouldn't be intelligent. They'd changed the sex as well as the name of the anthropologist. "Dr. Cassie Banks."

"Okay, that's a weird coincidence."

"Dr. Banks has a sister that works at the Smithsonian. While doing inventory on objects in storage, her sister found a vase labeled 'Jefferson's Chinese Vase' with what appeared to be Elvish runes. She sent photos of the vase to Dr. Banks, who recognized the mark. It's a stamp that elves use to identify the clan and household who made the item."

"Jefferson's Chinese Vase?" Jillian said.

"Maybe they thought the Elvish Runes looked like Chinese characters."

"They don't look anything like Chinese!"

"The vase was last cataloged in 1912. They didn't have the Internet and translation software."

"It's the Smithsonian!"

Louise chased data to answer the question instead of theorizing. "They've since verified that it did belong to Thomas Jefferson. It was anonymously donated to the Smithsonian in 1898 by someone claiming that his grandfather had stolen it during the Civil War when the Confederates seized Monticello. At the time, they had no way to establish authenticity, so they left it in storage."

Jillian growled and focused back on her tablet. "But what about the box?"

"All the photos are part of a crowd-sourcing project Dr. Banks started with curators from around the world. They searched their museum storage facilities for buried Elfhome artifacts. Oh! The porcelain vase was thought to be Chinese because of its age. The method of creating porcelain wasn't introduced to Europe until 1712—"

"What about the box?" Jillian cried. "I don't care about the freaking vase!"

"I'm looking!" Louise scanned ahead faster. "All the pieces were gathered into one exhibit, and it's touring! Currently it's in, oh God, Australia!"

"You've got to be kidding! Paris is at least just on the other side of the Atlantic."

Louise found the exhibition site and then a list of dates and cities that it expected to hit. "It's coming to New York!"

"Oh, boy, is it ever." Jillian tilted her tablet so show an article titled *Secret Treasures Opening at American Museum of Natural History on June Fourteenth! Sign Petition Now!* "This site is run by Earth for Humans, the same group that's holding the protests against the expansion of the quarantine zone around Pittsburgh. The exhibit has their panties in a knot."

"June fourteenth! That barely gives us any time. We need to save the babies before the end of June."

The box had been given the name *"Louvre morceau de bois"* and careful noninvasive investigations had concluded that the box was solid Elfhome ironwood. The runes were being considered magical in nature, but so far the type of spell hadn't been determined.

Jillian started to bounce in her seat. "Oh, Lou, this is so cool! They have no idea what it is! They don't know it opens! The *nactka* are still inside."

Louise shook her head, fighting the excitement. "We don't know that."

"Even if they identified the runes as a spell lock, the only way to open it is with the keywords. We have the password but they don't, so they're not going to get it open."

"They could cut it open."

"They think it's a block of wood! Besides, they're museum people. They preserve stuff, not smash it open to see what's inside. What's even better: they don't know what's in the box. We open it up, take everything out, and seal it again and they'll never know we took anything."

"Are you serious? Steal from a museum?"

"It belongs to us! The French might be all 'finders, keepers,' but they murdered Dufae. He wasn't a French noble. He wasn't even human! They killed him just the same. They have no right to this box."

It all seemed morally clear until she imagined sneaking into the museum like a cat burglar, dressed all in black, to weave through laser-guided security systems and knock out guards. It got all weirdly murky ethicswise, but the idea was scary exciting. How would they knock out guards? Some kind of gas? Where would they get something like that? At their father's clinic?

Louise found herself laughing with the giddy joy flooding her. They were going to be able to save their siblings! She struggled to contain her giggles; they had so much to do in so little time! "We need to find out everything we can on the American Museum of Natural History."

16: SHATTERED

When had she become shy?

The next morning, Louise followed Jillian through Lexington Avenue Station trying to pinpoint some unnoticed moment in her life. With all the excitement over finding the chest, she hadn't thought about her conversation with Iggy until they were weaving their way through the rush-hour commuters. It started as a hyperawareness of all the people around them and the knowledge that in a few short weeks they were going to be robbing one of the world's largest museums. If people knew what they were planning, they would be staring in disbelief and dismay.

Luckily no one could probably guess, not even given all the time in the world and several broad hints.

So why did Louise feel like cringing every time someone noticed them? They had no hope but to stand out. Jillian had decreed they would wear matching outfits to help pull off switching the real magic generator with a fake they'd printed at home. Jillian had chosen their cutest dresses that made grown woman start talking in abnormally high voices. ("Oh, just look at you! Aren't you just so cute!" This wouldn't be so worrisome if it wasn't the same voice that women used with puppies.) Then there was Tesla, who really was quite massive beside them and at first glance looked real. He wore a big bow about his neck that matched their outfits. (Their excuse if people wondered why they hadn't left him at their locker was that they wanted to show off the bow.) Jillian sported a huge grin and was skipping with excitement.

Really, the only reason they were being ignored at all was because it was New York City at rush hour.

Once upon a time, the attention didn't bother Louise. Or to be more specific, it never even occurred to her to notice that she was drawing attention. Looking at her was something people did to see what was in front of them; it was how they kept from stepping on her. She hadn't been afraid that people would judge her on what they saw.

Was it simply that she had been too young to realize people formed opinions of others? Did the strangers only become frightening when she realized that they might be thinking negative thoughts? And was Iggy right, that the only reason strangers thought Jillian was the pretty one was because Jillian purposely did the "cute act" even as she was doing now? Everyone who noticed the two little identical girls with the big robotic dog would gaze longest at Jillian. She was the one smiling and skipping, whereas Louise probably looked vaguely uncomfortable. Jillian rewarded the strangers with an even bigger grin. Most would end up smiling back, charmed as usual.

Of course in the past, Louise would think the person saw her as less cute, less charming, and she would probably end up looking even more uncomfortable. It was an endless loop. But really, the people smiling at Jillian were probably only thinking about catching their connecting train, getting to work, and whatever difficulties lay ahead of them. Louise had been imagining monsters that didn't exist.

What started the loop? She had been running the cycle since before they started first grade. Their class photos from that year show Jillian smiling and Louise looking like she wished to be anywhere except in front of the camera. All their early photos, though, she had smiled happily. Kindergarten, then?

It had been an unsettling year. Since they hadn't attended preschool, the limit of their exposure to other kids had been chance meetings at public parks. Up to kindergarten, other children seemed like very clever puppies. They were something fun to play with but prone to peeing unexpectedly and occasionally biting. If those toddlers could actually talk, the discussions had only been about ownership of supposedly communal property. They barked words like "mine" and "gimme." Louise could remember vividly that she had been told that she was a girl and that the children they saw most often at the park were boys, and she had come to the conclusion that they were totally separate species, on par with monkeys and people. It was the only way to account for the difference in communication and cooperative play.

When they were four, they started kindergarten. The other children were a lot more verbal, but what they said was rarely nice. There was one girl whose favorite retort was "You're a ugly face."

Was that it? Did somehow that nasty little catchphrase dig in and bury itself deep in Louise's psyche? Or had it been just part of an onslaught that they suffered for being different? They were the only twins. They were the youngest and smallest. And most importantly, they already knew everything. Their mother had spent the first three years of their life attending an online university while being a stay-home mom. It had given the twins access (accidental at first) to classes from basic math to advanced physics. What they hadn't known was that no one liked a know-it-all. Not even teachers.

Group dynamics had led to a full-out quiet war against them, where the weapons were pointed looks and harsh words. Since no one could call them stupid, everything else was fair game. A new school had promised a restart with a clean slate, but by then the twins were battered and scarred. No one, not even Elle, had been outwardly mean, but that hadn't stopped the twins from expecting a new attack.

Louise needed to find a way to fight this mental monster that had been lurking inside of her, poisoning her.

She reached out and caught Jillian's hand for courage. Jillian squeezed her hand hard. She hated the idea that Jillian may have been hurt just as badly by that year but she had never noticed. At least her twin had found a better way of dealing with it.

Louise forced herself to smile. It felt so faked; she was sure she must have been grinning like an evil mad scientist out to take over the world. Skipping did help a little to let her feel strong and brave.

Miss Gray used the voice. She looked up when they walked into the art room and her voice came out all squeaky with that "oh, little puppy, you're so cute" tone. "Jillian! Louise! Those dresses are darling."

And then awareness of who exactly they were caught up with the cuteness, and her look changed to slight alarm. "Jillian. Louise. What are you two doing here so early? And why do you have your dog with you?"

"He matches us!" Jillian said as if it explained everything. She managed to seem unfazed that Miss Gray was in the classroom far earlier than they had expected. Louise's heart was jumping in her chest out of nervousness.

"Yes, I see, but why are you here so early?" Miss Gray had apparently decided to tackle one issue at a time.

"Our class had a job printing on last night." Louise pointed toward the Annex. "We wanted to see if it completed correctly and move the item to our class locker before the seniors come in."

"And the dog?" Miss Gray asked.

"His name is Tesla!" Jillian purposely misunderstood the question. "Miss Gray, we remembered that we forgot about Hook's hand."

This was the complete truth. Louise had only thought of it the night before as they got their parents to sign Jillian's permission slip for the stage-fencing lessons. Part of the fight involved Peter chastising Captain Hook for unfairly using his hook.

Jillian pulled out her tablet and moved to corner Miss Gray. "His left hand needs to be large enough to be easily seen as a hook by the audience. It needs to give the impression of a weapon, so it needs some point to it without it being dangerous to Iggy or anyone he might swing at. It also needs to be lightweight since he needs to carry it the entire play. We're not sure, though, how to make it without making Iggy's arm seem super long."

As Jillian pinned Miss Gray down by sketching out the all-important hook, Louise took Tesla into the next room. Thankfully Mr. Kessler hadn't arrived yet, so the Annex's lights were still off. Weak morning sunlight filtered in through the wall of windows. On the top floor of the school, the art rooms looked out over the distant Hudson River. Louise left the overhead lights off and hurried to the 3D printer. The screen was reporting the job completed.

Her hands shook as she opened up Tesla's onboard storage compartment and took out the fake generator. She set it down on the nearest table. As she took her hands away, she was filled with the certainty that she had put it in the wrong place. She snatched it up and then started to put it down, farther from the table's edge so it couldn't fall. It felt even more dangerous, but now that she was paying attention, there hadn't been any chance it could have fallen from the first place she put it. She slid it forward. When the fake generator teetered on the very edge, the uneasiness disappeared.

She frowned at the precariously balanced fake. That didn't make sense.

The hallway door was flung open and Mr. Kessler stormed in, flipping on lights. "Stupid freaking steps." He was panting as if he had just run up all twelve flights. "If I wanted a Stairmaster workout, I'd get a gym membership."

He hurried to his desk, logged onto his desktop, and quickly pulled up several windows, muttering, "Come on, come on."

What should she do? It was obvious he didn't realize she was in the room. She hadn't gotten the real magic generator out of the printer. The fake was sitting out in plain sight. She was going to get caught! Should she try and hide the fake, or hope that Mr. Kessler didn't notice that there was something still in the printer?

In the art room, Jillian did something that made Miss Gray raise her voice.

Kessler looked up, saw the open door, and hissed in surprise and anger. He jerked around to stare at her, the hiss becoming an explosive "Shit! What are you doing in here?"

"Me?" she squeaked as she slid sideways, blocking the view of the printer since she couldn't shove the fake back into Tesla without being caught. "I was just getting our job out of the printer."

"You're not supposed to be here alone. You shouldn't even be here with that big ape of a teacher. And what the hell is that thing you have in there?"

"You took it out?" Even as she said it, Louise remembered that the status light was still on, which it wouldn't be if he'd taken the generator out of the printer.

"I checked your code with the teacher-access option." He kept coming like a freight train without brakes. "The school board has made it clear that it will be my head on the chopping block if a kid used the printer to make bombs, drugs, or porn. Drugs or porn? What a complete joke."

Louise backed up until she was pressed against the printer, stunned and dismayed. What could she say? The magic generator was just the tip of the iceberg. Alone, it would probably seem harmless. The danger to their plans was anyone digging deeper into their activities. The scope of their plans would probably stay unfathomable even with the generator's discovery, but it would mean that they were watched closer and every action questioned.

"I took it out already." She pointed a trembling finger at the fake.

"I don't know what the hell you were trying to make, but this isn't a holographic projector like—" He started to reach for decoy generator.

There was a sudden loud roar, and the world shuddered. The fake toppled from the table. Louise squeaked in surprise, reaching out to catch it and then jerking her hands back as she realized that she wanted it to fall, wanted it to break. Her heart leapt and jerked as Mr. Kessler nearly caught it. It tumbled in his fingertips and crashed to the floor, smashing into dozens of pieces.

"Oh no!" Louise cried as she was filled with the sense that something horrible had just happened. "What was that?"

All the lights flickered and then went out, leaving them in the dim morning light. Outside, a dozen car alarms wailed and smoke billowed up from somewhere below. Mr. Kessler froze in place, staring at all the broken plastic littering the floor.

She hurried to the window and looked out.

Twelve stories down, people were littered on the ground like a collection of dolls ravaged by the neighbor's dog. The twisted wreckage of a large box truck sat burning. An explosion had gutted the building across the street, revealing an interior twisted beyond recognition as the façade tore away. Paper drifted like autumn leaves in the black oily smoke.

Mr. Kessler joined her at the window, mouth working but nothing coming out. Finally he managed to force out. "No. No. This is wrong. What could have happened?"

"Warning," Tesla said in his little Welsh schoolboy voice. "A bomb has been detonated within the city block where I'm currently located. Warning: a ten-alarm fire has been reported within the city block where I'm currently located. Warning: a 911 call reporting multiple injuries has been made from the building where I'm currently located. Initiating emergency response."

Louise had no clue to what "emergency response" might be,

but it didn't sound good. Tesla probably could drag her out of the building and back home. Most likely, though, it would be safer to stay in the Annex.... She squeaked as she remembered what she'd been in the middle of. *Oh no, the magic generator was still in the 3D printer!*

Tesla padded out from behind the art table and scanned the room until he spotted her. "Primary target found."

She pointed at him and in her most level tone commanded. "Cancel emergency response."

Tesla tilted his head. "Primary target appears unharmed. Cancelling emergency response."

Louise glanced at Mr. Kessler. The man was rubbing his face as he gazed down in horror at the street below. He was safely beyond sane action.

She hurried to the printer and fumbled with the locks. She glanced toward Mr. Kessler to make sure he was still at the window; his hands had crept up to grip his hair. She jerked open the printer.

She had expected the magic generator and the fake one to look like a diamond and a cut-glass gem, with only an expert able to tell the difference at a glance. The fake had been the same size, shape, and general color, but now, having seen the real one, she knew that the fake wouldn't have been mistaken for the real one. It was more like sterling silverware and plastic. The fake had looked like five dollars of melted plastic. The magic generator gleamed with perfection.

Gritting her teeth, Louise eased the generator out and gingerly placed it in Tesla's storage. She shut the lid and redid the locks hidden by his fur.

Downstairs there was an odd sound, growing louder. As she listened, she realized it was children shouting and screaming.

The PA clicked on and Principal Wiley said, "All students are to report to their homeroom immediately. Teachers are to take attendance and report all absences. No one is to leave the building. I repeat. No one is to leave the building. All students are to report to their homeroom so attendance can be taken."

He said nothing about injuries. Who had called 911? Who had been hurt? It was still another ten minutes until the homeroom bell. Anyone could have been out on the street when the blast went off.

Jillian ran into the room. "Lou! Lou!"

Louise reached out and gripped her twin's hand tightly. "I'm okay."

Miss Gray came into the room. "Louise. Jillian. You need to report to your homeroom." Her voice quavered; a frightening thing to hear in an adult. Then again, Miss Gray hadn't been "an adult" for very long. At the moment, she looked no older than some of the senior students. "Mr. Kessler? Kevin?"

Mr. Kessler turned from the window, his mouth still open in soundless protest to what he was seeing.

"The windows blew out on the first floor," Miss Gray said. "A lot of the children were hit with flying glass."

Mr. Kessler blinked at them. "What?"

"Go to the first floor!" Miss Gray cried and caught Louise's shoulder. "Come on. We need to go now."

"Miss Gray, we know first aid. Our father is a medical technician."

"You need to go to your homeroom." Miss Gray steered them toward the stairways. "First things first. Miss Hamilton has to know that you're here and safe before you can do anything."

They went down the stairs without talking, seven flights, the crying on each level growing louder. Each floor was a lower grade. Younger students. Closer to the destruction on the street. With each step down, Louise wondered, "Who would do this?" The gutted building had been nondescript, with offices on the upper floors and a failed art gallery on the first floor. Nothing that seemed to warrant a bomb of that level. What was the real target of the bombers?

When they reached their floor, Mr. Howe and Miss Hamilton were in the hallway.

Mr. Howe was shaking his head but then pointed toward them. "There they are."

"Oh, thank God, they weren't out on the street!" Miss Hamilton pointed across the hall to Mr. Howe's room. "We've moved rooms." Mr. Howe's windows looked over the auditorium's roof toward the school's loading docks and the back alley. The teachers didn't want them seeing what was on the street, barely fifty feet away.

Miss Hamilton reported, "Room 501, all students accounted for," via her headset as she herded them into the room. Mr. Howe, however, headed downstairs to help with the younger children hurt by the blast.

"We can help," Louise said. "We know first aid. Our father is a medical technician."

"No, that's very good of you, but no. This is our responsibility."

"We took the first-responders test."

"And probably aced it; yes. I know. You two are very, very smart, but you're still children. I know this might be hard for you to understand, but it is the right of every child to grow up innocent. And it's the duty of adults to protect that innocence."

Louise eyed her with confusion. "Is this a sex talk?"

"No, it's not about sex. This is about growing up enough that you can make wise and intelligent decisions for yourself instead of having decisions forced on you. It's something that being smart doesn't help you with without time to know yourself and the world around you."

"But we can help."

"You can't be a child if you're being an adult for another child," Miss Hamilton said. "You can't be a child and make life and death decisions for another child. And for me to allow you to be put in a situation where you have to act as an adult, I'd be denying your right to your full childhood."

"We know what to do—"

"Yes, I know. And the fact that you don't understand what I'm trying to explain just makes it all the more important that I do my duty and protect you. Now, go sit down."

Zahara was waving at them. Her little brother from kindergarten was clinging to her. Her eyes were bloodshot with tears. She hugged them tight, her whole body shaking. She didn't seem anything like the girl they knew, usually so calm and sure. It was like her little brother had sucked away all that was Zahara and left something fearful in her place. Was this why Miss Hamilton wouldn't let them go downstairs?

"We were late," Zahara cried. "We had just started up the stairwell to the first floor when it blew up!"

"It's okay," Louise said. "You're not hurt."

The frightening thing was how easily she could have been killed.

17: SMOKE AND MIRRORS

As if the blast had blown away all thoughts, they didn't remember the magic generator until late that night. By unspoken agreement, they were both in Louise's bed, after a long, hot bath to scrub away the lingering smell of smoke.

Jillian suddenly sat up with a gasp. "Did you get it?"

"Huh?" Louise had been already dreaming. She was babysitting several dozen of their baby siblings who all looked like Jillian miniatures. The babies were taking turns using the gossamer call and they had a host of monsters trying to break into the house. Louise was chasing the babies through the house, trying to get the whistle off them while arguing with a 911 operator who wouldn't believe that they had a black willow in the backyard. She wasn't sure if Jillian meant the whistle or the operator's cooperation, or film for Nigel Reid as evidence that the monster call actually worked. "Get what?"

"It!" Jillian cried and pointed at Tesla parked stoically in the corner of their bedroom. In a sign of how rattled the bombing had made their parents, they had hinted that the twins could sleep with them, something that the twins hadn't done since they were five. Secretly, Louise wanted to but she knew that their mother needed to get up early. She suggested a compromise of leaving Tesla on guard instead of setting him to privacy mode that shut off all his spy hardware.

Louise blinked sleepily at the robotic dog for a minute before understanding sunk in. "Oh! Oh, that! Yes, I got it."

Jillian threw off the blankets and scrambled out of bed.

"He's still broadcasting!" Louise whispered.

"I know." Jillian got her tablet and hacked into Tesla's systems. "There, he's looping the feed from two minutes ago."

"What about the time stamp?"

"I fixed that. Don't worry." Jillian tossed her tablet onto her bed and went to open Tesla's hidden storage compartment.

"We'll have all tomorrow to play with that." School officials had decided to suspend classes since the city had closed the street down.

"I want to see if it works. Besides, Aunt Kitty will be here babysitting us, and she's not going to let us 'play quietly in our room.' She'll want to do fun things."

Louise had to admit that was true.

Their grandmother had been a firm believer that love made a family, not blood. She'd taken in her daughter's best friend, Kitrine Green, when the teenager's mother chose her drug-dealer boyfriend over her child. Despite being poor, their grandmother had supplied Kitrine with an electronic keyboard and encouragement to follow her dreams. Now a successful composer and songwriter, Aunt Kitty had an extremely flexible work schedule and often acted as their emergency backup parent. Her babysitting, though, came at the price of entertaining her.

When they were little, she told them that she was their fairy godmother, appearing as if by magic with plastic glass slippers and costume-ball gowns. Their first introduction to creating videos came on Aunt Kitty's visits as they acted out fairy tales complete with original scores. Lately they had found themselves at fascinating places like behind the scenes of a Broadway musical production, or at a recording studio, or at the NBC television studios. Aunt Kitty would think that the twins were truly upset by the bombing if they resisted any adventure that she could cook up.

And if their parents thought they were emotionally troubled, there be no privacy for them until they'd "dealt with the trauma."

"What should we use to test it?" Louise slipped out of her bed.

"The ley line mapping spell." Jillian pulled out the package of transferable circuit paper they'd ordered online. The printer that could use the paper to print out digital circuits was hidden in the back of their closet. They were quickly running out of hiding spaces.

"It's not going to find any ley lines."

"Probably not, but we could be sitting on top of one of those fissures that Dufae talked about and never know it."

"In Pittsburgh, weird things happen around ley lines, especially with machines. Metal conducts magic, and it does nasty things to active spells."

"It's the one spell we know works with the generator. Kensbock used it to test his prototype."

Which would be more comforting if he hadn't vanished into thin air shortly afterwards. It had been his invention that caused his disappearance, not the spell he used.

Jillian continued on, getting the printer out of the closet. "We should make sure that our work environment is magic-free prior to any large-scale experimentation."

Jillian had a point and of all the spells they could cast, the mapping spell was probably the safest. Louise abandoned her reluctance with a sense of relief and growing excitement. They were going to cast their first spell!

Louise quickly copied the spell for printing while Jillian loaded the paper into the printer.

"Okay, hit it!" Jillian whispered with excitement.

Louise hit "print" and—the longest thirty seconds that Louise had ever experienced later—the printed spell came out. "Okay, now we need to get the pastry board."

Dufae had spent a page talking about building his spell-casting room. He needed a stone surface to act as insulator. Dufae had bought several four-foot by twelve-foot slabs and laid them as a floor, complaining about the seams he needed to bridge on the larger spells. The twins had ordered a twenty-four by eighteen inch white marble pastry board that weighed a whopping thirty-six pounds. It had taken both of them to carry it upstairs and hide it between Jillian's mattress and box spring.

Getting it back out was harder than Louise expected. Things at rest stayed at rest, especially with a twin-size mattress on top of it.

"If we just had a pulley and a rope..." Jillian whispered.

"...Mom would bitch at us for putting a hole in the ceiling!" Louise finished. "Wheel your chair over, we'll use that."

"We can just put it on the floor."

"We need to plug the generator in."

Jillian swore softly. "How long is the plug?"

Kensbock designed the generator with a stupidly short 220 plug. The only 220 outlet in the house was in the basement for the dryer. They had bought a step-up-and-down voltage converter transformer. Unfortunately, it too had a short plug.

"We need to make this a battery-powered unit," Louise whispered.

"Yes!" Jillian cried in agreement.

"Shhh!" If they got caught with evidence scattered all across their bedroom, they'd be so grounded.

Jillian slapped hands over her mouth.

They froze in place. Jillian's eyes flicked right to left a million miles per second as she thought up lies to cover what they were doing, just in case. After two minutes, it was obvious that they hadn't been heard.

All told, it took them half an hour to get the pastry board within range of the plug, the protective sheet peeled off the printed circuit, the spell carefully positioned on the marble, and the transformer plugged in. After a great deal of consideration, because the magic generator didn't have an on/off switch, they decided to connect the leads to the spell prior to plugging it in. Since Louise had more experience with the soldering iron from set making (still something their parents didn't know), she connected the leads to the spell. She had noticed that some of Dufae's spells were used for healing—how would they connect the leads to that spell without burning the patient? Obviously they would have to use something like clay or paste.

Finally it was time. They plugged in the generator. Louise noticed nothing different, but Jillian gave a slight "Oh" of surprise.

"Is it working?" Louise asked.

"Doh. Yes."

Louise frowned at the generator, wondering how Jillian could be so sure.

According to the codex, each spell needed a certain frequency of magic to operate. Apparently, naturally occurring magic was like light in that it contained a wide spectrum. Written spells used a narrow frequency to both limit and channel power. Dufae's description of "dirty magic" probably was because the magic that leaked across consisted of constantly shifting frequencies. It would be like trying to use a flashlight as someone kept switching the type of batteries. Dufae complained about the fact that his "magic cleaning system" gave him one steady source of magic at the cost of being limited to one frequency. Luckily for the twins, the next section of the codex was devoted to taking that one frequency and stepping it up or down via translation spells that Dufae created through trial and error. Because of it, every spell in the book was available to them.

Louise wondered how Kensbock ended up matching his generator to the one spell in his possession. Had he set the generator to the spell? Or had he rejected several spells before finding one that matched his output? The more she thought about it, the more she felt sure that his kidnapper had selected the spell and given it to him on a silver platter. Someone had been tracking his progress and acted quickly after he reached a successful conclusion. Kensbock had made extensive notes on everything, except where he had found the spell. Dufae had noted that the spell was one of the first ones taught children; he'd dissected and reconfigured it in trying to deal with his situation on Earth with the dirty magic. Had Kensbock been given it because it was so simple—or because it matched the frequency of another spell? If Louise had been the one manipulating the man, it would be the latter. But what spell would it be?

"Lou?" Jillian whispered.

"Huh?"

"Are you okay? You look like someone hit you with a cattle prod."

"Huh?"

"Lights are on, but no one's home," Jillian whispered.

Louise shook herself. "I'm fine."

Jillian watched her closely for another minute before leaning down to inspect the spell. Dufae stressed that the lines of the spell had to be solidly drawn without blemishes and that all conductive material, even fine dust, must be kept clear of the tracings. Jillian gave two thumbs up to indicate that they were ready to activate the spell. She turned her right hand sideways and tucked in her thumb to make a fist.

Jillian wanted to play "rock paper stone" to see who activated the spell.

Louise clenched her jaw in frustration. Part of her felt like she should let Jillian do it since obviously her twin *wanted* to—but she *wanted* to too. Jillian gave her a look that was a clear mix of impatience and confusion. Louise jerked up her fist.

Five games later—because Jillian was a sore loser—Louise took a deep breath and spoke the activate phrase as loudly as she dared.

The black lines of the spell suddenly gleamed like gold light. Jillian gasped. A glowing sphere rose over the spell and a confusion of landmasses and rivers and buildings took form in ghostly holographic perfection.

This of course called for a Dance of Joy, which consisted of leaping from bed to bed, with silent screams of delight.

Several minutes later, they were able to examine the spell in relative calm.

Louise was used to seeing the map of New York City as a clean, orderly collection of lines and labels with Manhattan at the center. This was a tiny exact miniature with their house in Astoria smack in the middle. The northern edge was the Bronx, and the western edge was a thin slice of the New Jersey shore of the Hudson River. The southern tip was just beyond East River Park.

"What's that?" Jillian pointed at an area of featureless terrain. "Some kind of park in . . . Flushing?"

Jillian scooted away from the spell and got her tablet to compare it to a map of the city. "It's Corona Park."

"Dufae said that ley lines were denoted by blue lines, the width and brightness indicating—oh no!" Louise jerked the plug of the transformer out of the wall outlet and the gleaming spell collapsed.

"What?"

"Mom and Dad!" Louise slid the marble slab across the floor and under her bed, vaguely aware that she ripped the leads free.

Jillian quickly set the transformer and generator into the shadows under her desk and scrambled into bed with her. They lay side by side under the covers, trying not to pant, feigning sleep.

"Are you sure?" Jillian whispered after a minute of silence.

"Shhh," Louise breathed, eyes closed tight.

A moment later, the door latch clicked open. A slant of light spilled into the room from the hall as their parents silently looked in on them.

Jillian faked a restless turn, threw her arm over Louise's shoulders and pressed her forehead to Louise's. They probably looked like sleeping angels. If Louise weren't so scared, she would have started to giggle.

"Oh, they're so cute," their father murmured.

Normally their mother would snort at his naïveté. This time she said, "Yes, they are," in a voice that was close to tears.

The door closed as quietly as it had opened. Louise felt at once relieved and horrible that they'd fooled their parents. Jillian started to shake with silent laughter. She rolled onto her back, hands against her mouth to keep the giggles in.

Louise smacked her.

Jillian leaned close and whispered into her ear. "We're elves! We did magic!"

Despite everything, the words shimmered through her, bright and joyous. *They were elves. They did magic.* Surely anything was possible, even saving their baby brother and sisters.

18: LEARNING THE LAYOUT

Aunt Kitty was in the kitchen the next morning, making French toast, her one and only dish. She was wearing three-inch heels, tight black leather pants, and a bright yellow blouse that accented her dark ebony skin. "You have to not let her get to you." Aunt Kitty waved a spatula, making all her many gold bracelets chime like a tambourine. "You control how you feel, not her. She can try and make you feel things, but if you don't let her, then she's not going to succeed."

Louise paused on the stair's landing, aware that she was interrupting a private conversation. She sat down on the top step, leaning forward so she could see her mother standing in the corner, glaring into her coffee.

"Do not quote my mother to me." Her mother was dressed for work in a quiet business suit and low heels. She was still half a foot taller than her "adopted" sister.

"Why not? She was the smartest woman I ever met." Aunt Kitty lifted a corner of the toast and checked to see how done it was. "Anna Desmarais is simply a paranoid racist. You control you, and you're not going to allow yourself to sink to her level."

"And I'm not supposed to be angry that she's involved my kids?"

"Oh, come on, you're saying that your girls wouldn't jump at a chance to go to this? You know how much Jillian likes everything connected to movies. And they wanted to go to the *Today Show* to see Nigel Reid and you wouldn't let them. You know how much Louise would have loved to meet him. You're going to tell her that you've got tickets to this and you're not taking her?"

Louise yelped with excitement and charged down to the kitchen. "What tickets? To some kind of event? Will Nigel Reid be there?"

Her mother sighed loudly, shaking her head. "Oh, now you've done it."

Aunt Kitty laughed and flipped the French toast.

"Mom!" Louise cried.

"Anna Desmarais has given me four tickets to NBC's charity gala in June. They're going to have a lot of their network stars there and a handful of 'special appearances' like Nigel Reid."

"Really?" Louise squealed. It was hard to rein in her excitement, but obviously her mother didn't think it was wonderful news. "What's wrong with the tickets? Are they fake?"

"They're real tickets." Their mother sighed into her coffee. "Honey, sometimes when people suddenly start acting all nice to your face, you have to start looking for knives behind their backs. After all this..." She caught herself about to swear and covered by sipping her coffee. "After calling me a thief, and dragging us through two audits in an attempt to find proof, Desmarais gave me nearly a thousand dollars' worth of tickets."

"The woman is married to a billionaire," Aunt Kitty pointed out with her spatula. "Everywhere she goes, she rides in that big limo with two drivers when the car can bloody drive itself. A thousand dollars is nothing to her. It's probably what she pays to keep her hair that blond and beautiful at her age."

"She says she doesn't dye her hair."

Aunt Kitty snorted. "You know what your mother would say to that? 'Maybe she was born with it, maybe it's Maybelline.' Seventy and still blond? No, she dyes."

Her mother pointed at Louise. "Don't you ever repeat that."

"Yes, Mommy."

Aunt Kitty served out the toast to Louise and her mother and started a second batch.

Louise wanted to beg and plead to go to the event. It would be the perfect opportunity to give Nigel the gossamer call without the risk of meeting him privately someplace. (Not that she was scared he would do anything, but their mother would simply kill them if she found out.) "Maybe Mrs. Desmarais is sorry about how she treated you, and that's why she gave you the tickets."

Her mother sighed, drank the rest of her coffee, and rolled up her French toast so she could carry it. "I need to go. We'll talk about this later." She kissed Louise on the forehead and waved the toast at Aunt Kitty. "Thank you. You're a lifesaver." In the foyer, she paused to shout upstairs. "George, you're going to be late. Jillian, come down for breakfast!"

Normally she would have left without waiting for Jillian to answer, but instead she stood at the bottom of the steps until Jillian came trotting down with Tesla on her heels. She kissed Jillian good-bye and gave her a hug.

Jillian came into the kitchen, so bright-eyed that she positively radiated "I've got a plan." She came to lean against the back of Louise's chair, presenting a united front. "Aunt Kitty, can we go to the Museum of Natural History today?"

"The museum? Really? I thought you would want to relax at home or go to the movies."

"Nothing good is playing," Jillian complained truthfully. "And the museum has this exhibit on the Alpha Centauri colony that we just found out about." Again, truthfully as they had started to research the AMNH just two days ago. "It's only there for a few more weeks. We really want to see it!"

Aunt Kitty looked to Louise to see if it was truly a joint decision.

Louise nodded slowly. They had planned to go alone to the museum to examine camera placements and security measures—things not easily found on the Internet. The bombing changed everything. The image of people scattered on the ground like broken dolls flashed through her mind and she shuddered.

"Are you okay, Lou?" Aunt Kitty gathered Louise into a hug.

"I'm fine." Louise had to be okay or everyone would start watching them closely. Normally the television would have been on, playing their parents' newsfeed. Obviously it was off because all the news was focused on the bombing and their parents didn't want them upset by it. "I just want something to think about that doesn't have anything to do with—with that."

Aunt Kitty hugged her tighter. "It's okay to be upset. Most people would be."

"We're fine," Jillian said in Peter Pan's carefree voice. "None of our friends were hurt. It was a bad thing, but it's over."

Their father careened into the kitchen, hair sticking out in every direction, looking like a startled scarecrow. "Louise. Jillian. Are you two okay? Is everything all right?"

"We're fine, Daddy," they said.

He combed both hands through his straw hair, making it stick out even more. "I should stay home."

"I got this covered," Aunt Kitty said. "Go on. The last thing this family needs is one of you losing your job."

He gazed at the twins as if they'd been horribly wounded by the bomb.

"Daddy, go!" Louise pulled out of Aunt Kitty's hug to give him a push. "We're not even going to stay home. We're going to the museum."

"Aunt Kitty is going to get us each something from the gift shop!" Jillian stated as fact.

Aunt Kitty laughed. "Oh, am I?"

"And we'll have pizza for lunch!" Jillian continued with the list of treats for the day. "And we'll bring home Thai takeout."

Louise looked at her twin with surprise. What was this greediness?

"Guess I can't compete with that." Their father nevertheless looked more relaxed at the idea of leaving. Jillian must have guessed that the adults would believe they weren't too upset if they were trying to milk the day for all it was worth. He took out his phone. "Here, let me give you some money to cover—"

Aunt Kitty waved off the offer. "No, this my treat to them. I missed their birthday because I was buried in work. Let me play best aunt ever."

"Thank you. Call if there's any problems." He gathered them both into one big hug, kissed them each on the temple, and went without breakfast or coffee.

It was impossible to avoid news on the bombing. Everyplace they went had newsfeeds spilling out updates. Everyone they brushed up against was talking about it. By the time they reached the 59th Street–Columbus Circle Station, they had learned that authorities had determined that the bomb had been in a truck rented by Vance Roycroft, who had ties to the radical group Earth for Humans. His target apparently had been an art gallery about to open in the building across from their school. Because of the riots, the owners had been careful not to draw attention to the fact they would be selling only artwork from Elfhome. There had been crate upon crate of elf-made pottery, woodcarvings, and clothing. The newsfeeds carried photographs of the artwork. As with most things Elvish, the pieces were exquisite and one-of-a-kind, handcrafted by people that had forever to master their art and the time to create stunning individual pieces.

Roycroft had attempted to pull into the alley behind the art gallery. Finding it blocked by a broken-down garbage truck, he'd double-parked in front of the building and walked away. Judging by the remains of the truck, police were able to determine that the bomb had been in a shipping crate identical to the ones that gallery used, complete with EIA paperwork from the Pittsburgh border. They theorized that Roycroft initially meant to deliver the bomb as a package delayed by customs. They also believed that detonation was controlled remotely by someone other than Roycroft who didn't realize that the delivery had gone astray. While the blast had been designed to do structural damage, it didn't contain shrapnel to cause harm to humans. If the bomb had detonated inside the gallery, police speculated, there would have been no loss of life.

Citing this "limited scope of intended damage" and the fact that authorities had already traced Roycroft's movements to Adirondack Park in upstate New York, the authorities had decided not to shut down the city.

Ironically, none of the targeted artwork had been damaged. The shipping crates and a state-of-the-art fire-suppression system had protected all the pieces. There was an odd undercurrent to the words used to describe the art gallery. The newsfeed repeatedly mentioned that the gallery was empty—except for the art—and heavily insured because of the riots.

"They're not saying it in so many words, but it's like they think the original plan would have been acceptable," Louise grumbled as they waited for the C train. Vance Roycroft's face remained on the wall while the feed continued with updates on the manhunt for him, along with factoids on the massive state park.

"Why blow up an art gallery in the first place?" Jillian complained. "It's stupid."

Aunt Kitty agreed. "Um-hmm. If they were smart, they would have figured out a better way to make their point than with a bomb. The Waldorf Astoria and the UN building are both well protected. They must have decided that the art gallery was a safe Elfhome substitute."

"Safe for them," Jillian muttered darkly and then leaned close to Louise for comfort. It made Louise angry that this stranger had blindly lashed out in such a stupid, selfish way.

"The elves won't ever know about this bomb!" Louise cried. "Humans bought the artwork on Elfhome and brought it to New York City. The elves were already paid; they're out of the equation. The only people who are going to be impacted are humans. And besides, the elves have nothing to do with how big the quarantine zone is—the UN negotiated the space between the United States and the rest of Earth's countries."

"Exactly," Aunt Kitty said. "The terrorists are protesting the expansion of the zone, and that's controlled by a vote of the United Nations ambassadors, who are all right here in New York City."

"They're trying to control the vote? By blowing up children? If I was an ambassador, I'd be pissed off that someone nearly hurt my kid."

The C train rumbled into the station, blocking the annoying newsfeed. For a few minutes they focused on getting on. Interestingly, the change in security level made Tesla much more aggressive in keeping between them and other people.

Once they got settled, Aunt Kitty asked, "Are there children of ambassadors in your school?"

"Yes. Several," Louise answered. "We're one of the top private schools in the city. I certainly wouldn't vote in favor of anything if my kid were one of the kindergarteners hit by flying glass. Certainly everyone knows that if their kid was running late for school, they could have been killed in the street. When I was asked to vote, I'd say 'screw those idiots' and expand the quarantine zone. It wasn't the elves that put Pittsburgh on Elfhome. It wasn't elves that were logging the quarantine zone. It wasn't elves that brought that artwork to New York. This is all a mess that humans made."

Aunt Kitty nodded and gathered Louise close. "I know, honey bear. People don't always think that clearly when it comes to hate. These terrorists hate elves, so their first target will always be something related to them."

✧   ✧   ✧

At some point along the way, unnoticed by Aunt Kitty or Louise, Jillian had gained a big bandage just above her left eye. To strangers, Jillian probably looked like a poor little war orphan. To Louise, the bandage gave Jillian pirate flair.

As the museum security stopped them at the entrance because of Tesla, Jillian explained with a convincing waver in her voice, "After what happened at our school yesterday, we feel safer with him. Can't we please keep him with us?"

Aunt Kitty eyed the bandage with hidden dismay, but played along. "They go to Perelman. The bomb was right across the street. They had a rough day yesterday and wanted to do something to take their minds off the explosion."

The girls had to produce their Perelman School for the Gifted student ID badges to verify this claim. After a quick conference with the powers that be and a search of Tesla's storage chamber, they were allowed to take their "beloved" nanny-bot into the museum.

"Girl, you are going to be dangerous when you're eighteen." Aunt Kitty seemed torn between dismay and amusement. "Turn the world upside down and inside out."

"I'm really hoping that I don't have to wait that long," Jillian said.

Aunt Kitty laughed then.

Louise cringed inside. She hated that they had to lie to their aunt. In many ways, she was a cohort in crime, but only to a point. Much as she loved to kidnap them away for adventures, she always kept in mind that they weren't her kids. She carefully never crossed any line that their mother set. Thus she never gave them Coke to drink, never let them stay up past their bedtimes, and never, *never* would let them rob a museum.

They'd programmed Tesla to search out security cameras and map out their field of vision. With what he was recording, they hoped to be able to find all the blind spots in the museum. His optic system abided by the museum rules on cameras since he wasn't using a flash. If the security people had known how his guidance system could be exploited, they probably wouldn't have allowed him to enter the building.

The twins picked up maps handed out at the ticket booth and glided upstairs on the escalators. Everywhere Louise looked, there was a security guard. The colony exhibit was in the Special Exhibition Gallery 3, which would also be the site of the Elfhome's

Lost Treasures. Judging by the maps they'd studied a few nights ago, the museum chose it because it was the largest space for traveling exhibits.

"You really wanted to see this?" Aunt Kitty asked as they pondered the first display.

"Yes." Jillian hesitated and then said in what sounded like the truth but wasn't, "We really thought it would be more interesting than this. And it closes at the end of the month, so this was almost the last chance to see it—just in case it was more interesting."

The first display was a very detailed model of the Chinese hyperphase gate in orbit. It looked very much like a bicycle wheel with a large inner ring that was the gate part of the station. Dozens of thin spokes connected the inner ring to an outer one where the crew lived. The long, slender needle of a colony ship was poised to thread through the eye of the gate and jump to the Alpha Centauri star system. A sign identified the ship as the *Minghe Hao*, which had left Earth three years ago.

While the ship and gate were in scale to each other, the Earth below was not. The two threw a massive shadow down onto the planet, blotting out everything from Malaysia to the Philippines. Because of the scale problem, the International Shipyard loomed beside the gate, closer than it really was. The next colony ship, the *Shenzhou Hao*, was being pieced together from segments shipped up in large prefabricated pieces from China. Obviously the scene was totally a figment of the model maker's imagination, as the *Shenzhou Hao* hadn't been started when the *Minghe Hao* slipped through the gate with little fanfare. The *Shenzhou Hao* wasn't finished; even through its original departure date had been years ago.

Louise wasn't sure why the display seemed so uninteresting. She studied it for a moment, noticing that they hadn't added weather patterns to Earth, nor sunlight to indicate the Earth's revolution. Maybe they thought people would be confused by what geostationary orbit meant if the entire display spun. There was no movement at all, not even lights blinking in the Shipyard to indicate construction of the various sections of the spaceship.

She had a sudden and awful feeling that she was looking at a frozen moment in time. A doomed ship, forever stuck on the event horizon of disaster. Had the *Minghe Hao* actually arrived safely? Or had it crashed?

"*Wǒ kàn bù dào!*" a child's voice complained loudly in what sounded like Mandarin.

Louise glanced across the room as she struggled to translate the complaint. *I can't see!*

A flock of children crowded around the last display: a life-size statue of Jin Wong, captain of the first colony ship. Faces reverent, the children lightly touched fingertips to the glass. There were too many of them to be one family, but their ages were too scattered to be kids on a school field trip. A kindergartener with long black pigtails stood on tiptoe, trying to see past the older children, who looked like they could be in middle school.

"*Wǒ kàn bù dào!*" the little girl cried again in Mandarin. This time Louise was certain that she was complaining that she couldn't see the statue.

A tall boy ghosted out of the shadows, gently shushing her. His quiet command was easy to translate. "Not so loud, Lai Yee Zhao."

The little girl eyed the boy with almost the same awe as being leveled at Jin Wong. "*Yamabushi zhànshì, wǒ xiǎng kàn tā!*"

Louise parsed through the sentence several times, trying to translate it and failing. She wasn't sure what *yamabushi* meant, although *zhànshì* seemed to indicate it was a type of warrior. The last part seemed to be a complaint again that she couldn't see the statue.

The boy scooped Lai Yee up so she could sit on his shoulder. She gazed in wide-eyed wonder and then pointed at the statue of Jin Wong.

"Is he dead?" the little girl asked, her voice still loud.

The *yamabushi* shushed her again. "We don't know. He went away."

"Why did he leave?" Lai Yee whispered loudly.

The other children half-turned to hear the answer.

The tall boy gazed at the starship captain for a moment before answering sadly, "To find another world for us to live on."

"Elfhome?" the little girl asked.

And all the children shushed her.

Lai Yee was right: the first set of colonists had opened the door to another world. Ironically, Elfhome wasn't light-years distant, but just an odd sidestep into another universe from any point on Earth. The distance to Alpha Centauri made all information on the colony four years out of date. Was that the reason the boy claimed that they didn't know if Jin Wong was alive or dead? He'd been middle-aged when he left Earth; surely life as a colonist could not be easy for a man nearly seventy.

And what of Esme? How had she fared in the eighteen years? The bios all indicated that she was still alive, but they could be wrong. Something could have happened to the colony, and Earth wouldn't know for years.

Jillian and Aunt Kitty were moving on to the next display, forcing Louise to guide Tesla into his next mapping position. Once Tesla was lined up, Louise pretended to study the model of the Alpha Centauri star system. As if to make up for the lack of movement in the first display, this one had the two stars whizzing through their complex dance with their various planets orbiting them. A red digital clock counted backwards, marking the time before the first reports about the *Minghe Hao*'s safe arrival would reach the Earth. Alpha Centauri was 4.37 light-years away; there remained four hundred and six days and a handful of hours before the fate of the ship could be known.

But there had been radio messages from the earlier ships. At least, Louise thought there had been. Why would the boy say that they didn't know if Jin Wong was alive or not?

"Those poor people." Aunt Kitty nodded at the crew photo of the *Minghe Hao*. "No one noticed when they left. No one will notice if and when they arrive. I don't know why they keep sending out those ships. Even the first one—there was a ton of fanfare—and then Pittsburgh vanished—and everyone just forgot about the Chinese. It wasn't until the Chinese started to flip the power on and off like a toddler with a light switch that anyone realized that the gate had anything to do with Pittsburgh blinking in and out of existence."

And Elfhome had continued to steal the limelight since then. Despite their wealth of information on Earth's mirror planet, the twins had known virtually nothing about the space mission that triggered its discovery until they learned of their own odd connection to it.

"The crews wanted to go." Jillian led the way past the group photo of the second ship, the *Zhenghe Hao,* to stare at the crew of the *Dahe Hao.* Esme Shenske stood front and center as the captain. She looked so determined and fierce, like she was going to war. "They walked away from family and friends and ever coming back. I don't think they cared a rat's ass if anyone noticed or not."

The tall boy glanced over as if he fully understood Jillian's comment.

Louise looked down out of habit and nudged Jillian before she realized that she didn't really know if he understood or what he thought. The twins were at the museum to plan a robbery to save their baby siblings. Until a month ago, they didn't even know the names of the spaceships or any of their crew. Surely there was little common ground between her and this boy that worshiped Jin Wong, even if her genetic donor was a spaceship captain in her own right.

Louise looked back up at Esme. *Don't care a rat's ass if anyone noticed or not.* That's how she had to be. Fierce and determined. They were going to war. Everyone better stay out of their way.

Only pretending to look at the rest of the Alpha Centauri exhibit, Louise focused just on the building. The hallway was one long, wide, vaguely boot-shaped corridor. There were only two openings, the toe into the reptile exhibit and the cuff into stair tower that faced West 77th Street.

According to e-mails between curators, it would take a week for the colony exhibit to be packed up and shipped to the Field Museum of Natural History in Chicago. The space would be cleaned as the Elfhome exhibit arrived from the Australian Museum in Sydney. The AMNH had scheduled a week to unpack and arrange the incoming display cases. During that time, Dufae's chest would arrive from Paris, escorted by an assistant registrar. On June fourteenth, the exhibit would open to the public.

At the end of June, the frozen embryos would be thrown away.

It gave them less than a month between the time that Dufae's box arrived in the United States and the last possible day to save their siblings. That narrow window opened in approximately twenty days. They had to be ready to slip into that opening and take what they needed.

At the end of the gallery, they continued through to the primates and then circled around through the North American birds, the New York State mammals and city birds and finally down through the African mammals to end up where they'd started. In the loop, the twins documented the two flights of stairs, the three elevators, the up and down escalators and the only restrooms on the floor. Since the access routes were grouped together into two tight knots, they only represented two main ways up to the level. A close examination of the map, however, showed that only one went all the way down to the lower level and access to the subway.

So while Jillian kept Aunt Kitty busy in the gift shop, Louise quickly mapped the second and first floors with Tesla. She noticed how many guards were walking around and the care that the staff was taking checking bags coming in and out of the museum. Even in the middle of the week, with the recent bombing canceling all school trips and most people's travel plans, there were hundreds of visitors scattered among the floors. The twins couldn't hope to set up the generator, open Dufae's box, take out what they needed and get it locked again without a visitor seeing them. Obviously they were going to have to stage the robbery after hours.

The idea of sneaking around like cat burglars was at once thrilling and nerve-wracking. How in the world were they going to steal the *nactka* out of the Dufae box?

Louise returned to the gift shop to find that Jillian had picked out a souvenir slickie on the Alpha Centauri exhibit. Louise never saw the point of slickies. They weren't connected to the Internet, so there was no way to share the data. They were barely indexed, so finding anything was a pain. And they often cut costs by making photos two-dimensional instead of three-dimensional with panning and rotation. She supposed that it allowed you to give something tangible as a gift instead of giving the "ethereal" download of a real book.

"You want that?" They'd planned on getting something in a box that was approximately the same size as a *nactka*, just in case they needed to get one through security the day of the robbery. Of course, they had to guess at the size.

"Yes." Jillian gave her a look that said Louise was to play along even if she didn't understand. Jillian held out the slickie flat on her left palm and flipped the digital pages with her right index finger. There might have been hundreds of colonists that went to Alpha Centauri, but judging by the quick flow of images, the only one that mattered was Captain Jin Wong. "It's all videos they took of building the gate and the ships and training of the crews." Jillian paused on the picture of Esme. Whereas the photo upstairs had shown her to be blond, this picture had her hair dyed a rich purple, the kind that only came with an expensive professional job. She hovered in midair, the Earth a blaze of brilliant blue behind her. She glared at the camera like she was going to plow it over. There was a bandage on her right temple, unexplained by the caption that read simply: *Esme Shenske, Captain of the* Dahe Hao, *during final days of her training.* "Isn't it cool?"

Judging by the fact that all the Chinese children held one or two in their hands as they lined up at the check-out counter, maybe it was.

"Are you sure?" Louise had hoped that finding the right-sized object didn't fall to her.

"Yes. And I saw some snow globes you might like."

Louise followed Jillian, cringing inside. People were going to start thinking she loved snow globes if she picked out a second one for her birthday. The Pittsburgh on Earth/Elfhome one had a coolness factor that she doubted could be topped. A snow globe, though, would require a box.

She bit down on a sigh when she saw the selection. There was a small but adorable red panda globe that Aunt Kitty pointed to. There were also a handful with various dinosaurs encased in indestructible plastic. Snow flurried around the poor creatures as if their doom were quickly approaching.

With face carefully set to "excitement," Jillian pointed to the largest, a replica of the *Tianlong Hao* suspended over Earth. Instead of snow, stardust littered the face of the planet, waiting for movement to send it whirling on a solar wind. In a band around the bottom were the words: *Spread your wings, fly free.* There was Chinese lettering, apparently repeating the sentiment, just showing on the curve of the band.

Two of the Chinese girls were intently inspecting it with surprisingly blue eyes. There was only one globe left, so if Louise wanted it, she was going to have to buy it out from under their noses, which were unfortunately large for their faces.

The *yamabushi* appeared between Louise and the girls. The tall boy was like a ninja or something; Louise hadn't noticed him until he was right in front of her. "No, Arisu," he told the Chinese girls clearly in English and then dropped to Mandarin. "It's too big. No."

"Mail?" Arisu apparently was the younger girl. She fumbled with the Mandarin word and then dropped to English. "Couldn't we have it mailed...?"

The *yamabushi* sighed and shook his head. He spoke slowly and clearly in Mandarin. "No. I'm sorry. We can't mail anything to Pittsburgh." The boy tapped his wrist, indicating a watch that wasn't present. "We need to go. Hurry."

Shutdown was on Saturday night at midnight, giving them less than three full days to get to the border.

The three Chinese children turned with easy grace considering the close confines of the gift shop and circled around, gathering up the rest of the flock. With speed unheard of in a group of American kids, the Chinese were gone without a trace.

It left Louise no reason not to buy the snow globe. Jillian sharpened her look. At least it wasn't expensive.

"Oh, it's wonderful. I just love snow globes, and this one is so cool." She did love that it took them one step closer to stealing the *nactka*.

They had Tesla's recording of the museum's security camera placements, the number of security guards and their positions, floor plans, verification that the floor where Dufae's box was going to be displayed was marble, train schedules from their house and school to the museum, and the gift-shop box (and the decoy snow globe). Louise wanted to get started on figuring out how to put them together into a logical plan.

Impatient as she was to get started on a plan, the twins had to entertain Aunt Kitty for the rest of the day. After the museum, they walked to Celeste on Amsterdam Avenue between 84th and 85th streets. The tiny Italian restaurant was packed with lunch rush. Louise would have been happier going home and ordering something delivered, or even a frozen pizza. Eating at the restaurant, though, maintained the image that the twins were perfectly fine.

The twins knew that they wanted margherita pizza, so they ignored the menu. They ordered Sprite. Aunt Kitty considered a glass of wine before telling the waiter that she'd have a San Pellegrino. She added in an order of the carciofi fritti.

While they waited for their drinks and food, Aunt Kitty checked her phone and answered a text. Whatever she read on the screen made her wince and sigh.

"What's wrong?" Louise asked.

Aunt Kitty sighed again. It was probably more bad news; she'd already warned them that if their performance of *Peter Pan* was changed because of the bombing, she wouldn't be in town for it. She had set up several business meetings the week after the original date. "Do you remember a little while ago—well, you probably think it was a long time ago, it was like the beginning of last year, I think—we talked about production companies?"

It had actually been three years ago, shortly before they posted their first video.

"Maybe," Louise said cautiously. Perhaps Aunt Kitty had talked to Jillian about it last year.

Jillian caught Louise's glance and gave Louise a surprised look to say she had no idea what Aunt Kitty was talking about. "No."

"I'd told you that when people did videos, they had a production company and a logo? Like Spike Lee's production company is 40 Acres and a Mule Filmworks, and the logo is the number forty over the letter A?"

That was the conversation from three years ago. Adults had a weird, loose concept of time. It was a full third of the twins' life and they still remembered it completely.

"We remember that," the twins said. Jillian added an impatient, "And?"

"Well, you picked out the name Lemon-Lime Jello."

Louise's stomach turned to stone and dropped to the floor. "And?"

"You can't use it," Aunt Kitty stated.

"What?" both girls cried.

"I just found out that someone else is using it," Aunt Kitty said.

"They are?" They glanced at each other. Was a musical group taking advantage of their popularity?

"I was approached to do a TV show soundtrack with an elf fusion music element to it. The network people brought with them a sample of what they're looking for, and it was from a company called Lemon-Lime Jello. I'm not sure if they're spelling it the same way you two were, but it's close enough that you'll probably have to find another production company name."

"We had it first," Jillian pointed out.

"Oh, Jilly, I know you thought of it first, but they got to market first. Apparently they've gotten quite famous even though they're based on Elfhome."

"Wait!" Louise realized that it wasn't another company; it was her and Jillian. "This was an elf fusion soundtrack from a film production company called Lemon-Lime Jello?"

"Yes, the network copied the music from one of their videos and played it for me."

"Did you see the video?" they both demanded to know.

"No." Aunt Kitty waved them down, mistaking their alarm for being upset with the supposedly stolen name. "It was a short meeting. They're after a very specific sound, something very authentic. People are starting to be elf fusion snobs and they want the sound of traditional Elfhome instruments."

Jillian started to sulk. Obviously she was thinking of all the money they could be making if the networks hired them. Louise had to agree that it sucked that so much of their problems could be fixed if their parents wouldn't be so focused on "letting them be children." What was so wonderful about being a kid? They had to lie to go anyplace that they wanted to go to, and they wasted hours sitting in a classroom, supposedly learning how to fit in with the rest of humanity when quite frankly it seemed fairly pointless to try. They weren't really humans; they were elves.

"So what are you going to do?" Louise asked as casually as she could.

Aunt Kitty looked at her in confusion.

"About the soundtrack?" Jillian clarified.

"I had to turn the gig down. They specifically wanted instruments that I don't have."

"Oh." The twins shared a guilty look. They could have given her their software, but that would mean explaining about the videos. They couldn't tell her the truth; everything would start to unravel. Lemon-Lime led to YourStore that led to a joint bank account under Esme's name that led to what they really were doing at the museum.

"I know you really like the name," Aunt Kitty continued. "But you need something new. I'm sorry to have to tell you, especially after such a bad day yesterday. If you promise me not to tell a soul, I'll tell you a secret that might make you feel better."

"Okay." At least they were good at keeping secrets.

"NBC is going to green-light a series on Elfhome by Nigel Reid."

"Really?" they both cried with amazement. Last they'd heard, Nigel had been blocked at every attempt to get to Elfhome.

"They do focus groups and such like that. And this Lemon-Lime Jello production group apparently used Nigel in one of their videos and suddenly he's the hottest thing on the face of the planet. So the network is going to do a pilot and see what the focus group thinks."

"Nigel got a visa for Elfhome?" Louise cried.

"No," Aunt Kitty said. "Apparently EIA is being a pain. They want NBC to commit to a full season before giving Nigel and his cameraman visas, and that's all they're willing to cover. Nigel will have to pull a full working crew from the affiliate in Pittsburgh."

Jillian tilted her head in confusion. "What are they doing for a pilot show if EIA won't let Nigel on Elfhome?"

"They're going to film using animals and plants here on Earth," Aunt Kitty said. "The *kuesi* at the Bronx Zoo. Some of the songbirds at the aviary at the Queens Zoo. And there's a herd of Elfhome red elk at the Philadelphia Zoo."

"Oh, that's going to be so lame!" the twins cried. Louise added, "The cool part of Elfhome is the forest and the elves and the weird monsters that need magic to survive."

Aunt Kitty nodded agreement. "Since they're calling the series *Chased by Monsters*, I think that's the general idea that they're going for."

Louise squealed. "Oh, that sounds so cool! Nigel is perfect for it." Although it did sound slightly dangerous, considering what had happened with the simple fire ants. "I hope he doesn't get hurt doing it."

"So this Lemon-Lime video made Nigel more popular?" Jillian asked.

"Yes," Aunt Kitty said. "So some good came from these people stealing your name."

The twins were saved from having to come up with an answer by the waiter showing up with their drinks.

19: THE PLAN

That night, they built a full-scale model of American Museum of Natural History in virtual space. They deleted out the Alpha Centauri exhibit. They used the museum's database and photos of the traveling exhibit at other museums around the world to create mock-ups of the display cases. The e-mails between employees showed where they planned to position the cases. Once they had the AMNH in June set up, the twins donned gaming goggles and considered the problem before them.

The museum database listed Dufae's box at two feet wide by two feet high by three feet long and weighing eighty-six pounds. Last week, the twins had used cardboard to create a mock-up and filled it with cans of foods. They only had twenty-seven cans, totaling thirty pounds. They could lift a smaller box filled with the cans, but the mock-up was too large and awkward. Their arms were too short to get leverage on its smooth surface. If they could barely shift the cardboard fake, they wouldn't be able to budge the real box that was nearly three times heavier.

Their only option was to set up a magic generator next to the box, open its spell lock with the keyword, and take out one or two of the *nactka*.

"Third floor sucks." Louise frowned at the ceiling of the gallery. "No skylights."

"Even if we came in through the roof, we'd have to get past two cameras."

176

They used color to represent the field of vision for the cameras, leaving the safe areas in stark black and white. In a glance, they could tell where they could walk without being picked up on monitors. Huge sections of the massive building were monochrome. Elephants could wonder through unnoticed as long as they kept to certain areas. Whoever had set up the museum's security system, however, had done an excellent job covering access points like doorways, staircases, and elevators.

They could hack into the monitoring system, but they couldn't actually loop the video like they could on Tesla. Short of teleporting, there was no way to reach the gallery without being seen.

Once they were actually in the hall, however, they could avoid the cameras. By the very nature of the area hosting traveling exhibits, the security hadn't been tailor-designed for the display cases. The squat box was screened by taller items on all four sides; as long as they stayed under four feet and three inches, they'd be hidden. Since they were only four feet tall, they wouldn't even have to duck. The Dance of Joy, however, was strictly out.

"It's going to be a popular exhibit." Louise blew a raspberry as she realized that their Lemon-Lime videos had probably helped to create a massive desire to see real Elvish goods. "We won't be able to open the box and ransack it with dozens of people milling around."

"We're not going to be able to get up to the gallery unseen after hours."

"There's the bathroom around the corner." Louise pointed toward the restroom in the tower stairwell. "There were no cameras in them."

Jillian shifted the virtual world and grumbled at what she saw. "A mouse couldn't sneak through here unseen."

Louise sighed. "Let's start over. We need to be able to get inside, to the gallery unseen, and then open the box without any other visitors seeing us. Get the *nactka*. Lock the box again. Then get out, without being searched."

"That's it in a nutshell."

"What we need is a cloak of invisibility and a time-stop device."

"We do have a book of magical spells." Jillian held up her tablet.

There was no time-stop spell, although the *nactka* suggested that the elves had one. What they did find, however, was a "light-bending" spell that was for all practical purposes the same thing as invisibility.

And entirely too cool not to experiment with.

20: COMPLICATIONS

Louise thought she'd walked into the wrong room on Monday. She jerked to a halt, momentarily disoriented. She didn't recognize the room, but they had just been at their locker, so they had to be on the fifth-grade floor. She yawned deeply, sure that it was the lack of sleep that was making it hard to think. They'd stayed up every night since last Tuesday, playing with the magic generator and planning the two robberies.

Jillian thumped into her back. "Ow! Lou! Why'd you stop?"

Louise rocked back so she could check the number over the doorway. Yes, it was their classroom. All the art hung on the walls had been taken down, the desks had been rearranged, and there was something odd about the windows that she couldn't put a finger on. What's more, no one was in the room, despite the fact that the hall was crowded.

Jillian didn't notice the changes; she was focused on her tablet. She stepped around Louise and continued walking to where their seats used to be. "We should get something like a floor safe that's fireproof . . . and . . . and put it in a cardboard box labeled 'time capsule, do not open until 2050' and put it into our closet. We could even draw a safe on the outside of the box. Or we can get something like this."

Jillian held up her tablet to show a bullet-shaped container made by the Smithsonian that had the words "Time Capsule" printed in large blue letters on it. There was a plaque to mark where the tube was buried.

"What if Mom and Dad make us bury it?"

Jillian made a face as she thought about it a moment. "That might work."

"How would you feel if your parents told you that they'd buried you in the backyard for twenty years? It would be worse than that cabbage-patch story Grandma Mayer used to tell us."

"Better than Nana." She fell into their grandmother's thick Jamaican accent. "We got you at Macy's. It was a half-off sale; that's why we got two."

"Forget about it. No burying the babies," Louise stated firmly. "It's just creepy."

Jillian blew a raspberry, reached where her desk should be, and stopped in surprise. "Where's my desk?"

"Over here." Louise pointed to the desk beside her. The powers that be had decided that fifth-graders were all now big kids and had put desks for high school students in the room at the beginning of the year. After five minutes with their feet dangling, the twins had demanded that they be given desks for little kids. "Or over there."

"No. No. We sit together." Jillian picked up the other small desk and moved it beside Louise. "Where is everyone?"

It was weird that they were the only ones in the room. Now that she thought about it, all the hallways had been crowded as they climbed the stairs. "I think they're too scared to come into the rooms."

"Really?"

The twins had rushed to the classroom to get away from the noisy crowd. It seemed very wrong, though, that they were more scared of the other kids than a bomb. Maybe because they realized the odds for an ugly encounter with peers was a million times more likely than a second bomb.

Claudia peered timidly into the room, saw that they rearranging the desk and hurried in. Normally she sat at the head of the first row but she claimed the desk beside Louise. "Did you hear? There's elves at the Waldorf Astoria!"

"Really?" the twins both shouted. "Which ones?"

Claudia winced. "I can't say the name. They only gave the Elvish name, and it was really long. It's the female with really white hair and the blue triangle thing on her forehead."

"Saetato-fohaili-ba-taeli?" the twins cried.

"Um, maybe," Claudia said.

It was an elf, only not one of the twins' favorites. The female's English name was Sparrow, the correct translation being Lifted Sparrow by Wind. The twins had called the character based on her "Jerked" but never had a reason to mention that in any of their videos, so she remained nameless to their fans. Sparrow was the viceroy's *husepavua*, which literally meant "loaned voice," so the twins had her carry around a megaphone, through which she shouted any order that Windwolf gave her. The few times the twins had raided EIA records, Sparrow seemed to act as an ambassador, meeting with Director Maynard and Pittsburgh city officials in Windwolf's place. Normally if there was video of some Elfhome diplomatic event, the cameras would stay focused on Windwolf. Which wasn't all that surprising—he was the viceroy, looked like a teen idol and had a rabid fan following of girls from ages nine through ninety.

If only it had been Windwolf instead of Sparrow. However, with madmen blowing up buildings, Louise was glad the viceroy was still safe on Elfhome.

Louise squeaked in realization that it was the worst possible time for the elves to venture to New York City. "Why on Earth is she here? Now?"

Claudia blinked in surprise. "You haven't heard? There's this really awesome exhibit of Elvish artifacts found all over the world. It's coming to New York in a few days. The UN decided that since humans have broken part of the treaty by logging the quarantine zone, the elves could reclaim any part of the exhibit that is culturally important to them."

"What?" Louise and Jillian both cried. They hadn't planned for elves seeing the exhibit. Sparrow would know Dufae's box was a chest and that it could be opened. At least the female elf couldn't open it, not on Earth without magic, and not on Elfhome without the key phrase to the spell lock.

"The elves will probably lie and claim everything in the exhibit." Elle hovered at the door for a minute, trying not to look scared and failing. Then with a deep breath, she marched across the room to the twins. She gave Jillian an odd measuring look, like she wanted something from Jillian but knew she couldn't get it from her, and then hugged Louise tightly.

Louise squeaked in surprise and then realized that Elle was trembling. The girl was really, really scared. Taking pity on Elle,

Louise hugged her back. "There, there." She repeated the non-sense her father always said at times like this. She understood now why; what the hell was she supposed to say? It was the first time Louise had ever hugged anyone outside her family. Elle seemed to be all fragile bones under her porcelain white skin. She smelled totally different than Jillian; if pink had a scent, Elle was delicately sprinkled with it.

Jillian gave Louise a confused look for hugging Elle. "No, they're elves. They won't lie; it's shameful to them to be deceitful. It goes against their sense of honor. They wouldn't say something was culturally important if it wasn't."

Which was the twins' only comfort in the face of the news.

"Bad form?" Elle quoted Peter Pan's criticism of Hook when he cheated. "There will always be villains that break the rules. Only children are naïve enough to believe that."

"Honor isn't about other people, it's about what you want to be," Louise said. "A hero does the good and noble thing. The villain allows fear or envy or selfishness to let him ignore what is right. If you can recognize the difference, then you're choosing to be one or the other. Which do you want to be? The villain or the hero?"

"Oh!" Claudia cried as she remembered something else. "And Sae-Saetoto..."

"Sparrow." Jillian saved Claudia from butchering the rest of the female's name. Really, how much harder was Saetato than Claudia?

"Sparrow brought *sekasha* with her. Five of them!"

The twins squealed in excitement. "Which ones? Which ones?"

"Wraith Arrow." Claudia ticked names off on her fingers. "Skybolt. Zephyr Blade. The blue-haired one."

"Stormsong?" The twins squealed for one of their favorites. Apparently at some point, Stormsong had had a stalker with an artist's eye. The twins had found hauntingly beautiful pictures of Stormsong doing unlikely things like skateboarding. The photographs had been on an abandoned website; it wasn't clear if the stalker had died of old age or come to a violent end for pissing off the female warrior elf.

"I think Killing Frost," Claudia continued. "Or it could have been Tempest Knife. You know a lot of them look like twins."

"They're not twins," Louise said. The ninjas had attempted to build family trees for the elves in Pittsburgh and were dismayed to discover that while the elves were all part of the Wind Clan, not one was actually related to another. None of Windwolf's bodyguards were even cousins to one another. But Louise had to admit that they did look like brothers. The Wind Clan *sekasha* were tall, strongly built without being muscle-bound, black-haired, blue-eyed, and model handsome. They were also all the same exact height except for the blue-haired Stormsong and the youngest of the *sekasha*, Louise's personal favorite, Pony.

Jillian was already checking her tablet for news stories. "Of course they don't name the bodyguards. Come on. Pictures. Pictures. Yes!"

Louise took out her tablet as Jillian linked the story. The elves had been photographed at the train station, unloading. There was something surreal about seeing them up against the familiar landscape of New York City. "That's Bladebite, not Skybolt, and Tempest Knife."

"How can you tell?" Claudia asked.

Louise frowned at the male, trying to pinpoint the differences. "Bladebite is wider across the shoulders. His features are squarer. He keeps his hair shorter, so the beads the *sekasha* braid into their hair are more noticeable."

"What are the beads for?" Elle sounded honestly curious, not like before, when she didn't expect them to know and thought she was setting up a trap.

The twins glanced at each other. They'd never been able to find the answer until they got hold of the codex. How safe was it to explain to their classmate information that they shouldn't have?

"They're like batteries," Jillian decided to tell them. "The beads store magic so that the *sekasha* can trigger the protective spells tattooed on their arms in areas where there is little or no magic. It only buys them a minute or two of time on Earth, but presumably they'd kill their attacker in that time."

"Oh, so cool!" Claudia bounced. "We should go see them!"

"What?" the twins both cried.

"Wouldn't it be awesome to meet a *sekasha*? I think they're totally the coolest elves. Sword Strike is my favorite; he's so dreamy!" Claudia cried and dropped her voice to say the catchphrase of the captain of the queen's guards. "*Sonai Domi.*" She sighed deeply. "It's so cool when he says that. You can tell that he loves her so much."

"What does *'sonai domi'* mean?" Elle asked. "And are they really lovers? Or did you make that all up?"

Okay, Elle was totally freaking Louise out. Elle sounded like she really wanted the answer to be "Yes, they're in love." Elle had to be a fan of the videos.

"We think they are." Louise linked to their home computer and found the clip she wanted. "Normally we grab everything we can of a person talking and then build a phonetics library using their voice. After we write the script, we record Jillian reading it to get the timing and inflection that we want. We merge that with the right voice for the character to get natural sounding dialogue."

"But the real *sekasha* almost never talk," Jillian grumbled.

They had run hundreds of hours of video through an application that watched for lip movement, and only uncovered a handful of spoken words, most of them on the order of "yes" and "no." The bodyguards stood in the background, faces set, silently vigilant.

The *sekasha* were, however, so omnipresent that the twins felt that they had to have at least one active character who was part of the holy warrior caste. Finally they found a voice sample. In a Pittsburgh television station's news archive, they unearthed a video taken during the signing of the peace treaty between the humans and the elves. In a total of twenty-seven frames, Sword Strike's expression changed to utter tenderness as he gazed down at his queen and murmured the two words in a deep, rich rumble. It felt extraordinary to witness the sudden transformation, as if they had accidently seen into the male's soul.

Louise played the clip, first at normal speed, and then in slow motion.

"Wow," Elle whispered. "They're into each other."

Louise broke the phrase down. "The ninjas have translated *sonai* to 'kind' and *domi* as 'the female I'm beholden to.' Literally it would mean 'my kind lady,' but we ran across some other places where elves used *sonai* and a more correct translation seems to be 'have mercy.' We're fairly sure at this moment Sword Strike isn't saying 'my kind lady' but 'please don't kick their butt.' See, she starts off looking annoyed, and then blushes, and then looks a little embarrassed. It's what started the whole 'blast them all' running joke."

Claudia and Elle both giggled, which was good.

Jillian wasn't completely happy that Louise was admitting that they weren't perfect. She gave Louise a dark look, but explained the rest of their reasoning. "We wanted to use him as a character after that but no one ever caught him talking on video again, so we couldn't get a full phonetic sampling. We couldn't find any human voice that we liked in the free archives, so we decided we'd use the undoctored sound bite as his automatic response to anything going on."

"It works well," Elle said.

Claudia bounced again. "So, we can go see the elves. Right?"

Louise was glad that Elle seemed slightly horrified by the question as well.

"Going to see them would be bad." Giselle came into the room and joined the conversation without so much as saying good morning. "The Jello Shots are going nuts. Some of them are pissed that Queen Soulful Ember and Sword Strike didn't come to Earth, and the others are mad that Wraith Arrow isn't here with Prince Yardstick because they ship the two together."

"What?" Louise didn't understand what "ship" meant. It sounded like they were two dolls in one package, but that didn't make sense.

Giselle misunderstood the question. "Yeah, I know. Anyhow, all of the Jello Shots are talking about coming to see the elves. Not just the Jello Shots in New York City. California. Japan. England. China."

They had fans in China?

"And Earth for Humans is all worked up, too," Elle added. "It's the only reason my mom sent me to school. She said that with elves in New York City, no one is going to even think about the undamaged art at the gallery."

Louise had never considered the fact that the terrorists' original goal had gone undamaged and thus remained a target. She glanced toward the window. Roycroft had been killed in a shoot-out in upstate New York, but the police were saying that what they recovered indicated that he was working in a terrorist cell with at least two other people. Earth for Humans claimed that Roycroft had gone rogue and that they had no knowledge of who he was working with, or of the bomb. No wonder Elle was scared. But when Louise weighed all the factors, what scared Louise more was that the elves might take Dufae's box back to Elfhome before the twins could get their hands on a *nactka*.

The rest of the day was devoted to getting caught up on the four days of school they'd missed. While the other kids were scrambling to learn material that would be on the upcoming state achievement tests, the twins multitasked between working on the class play and tracking the museum's suddenly frantic level of e-mails. Dufae's box was in France, and France was balking at sending its three treasures. Like Elle, they were worried that the elves would simply claim all the items on exhibit to be culturally important and ask for everything to be returned to them.

France obviously didn't care about the box, because it rarely made an appearance in their side of the conversation. Their focus was on a crown worth a king's ransom. Because it bore a resemblance to the Grand Duchess Vladimir tiara, the crown was believed to be the inspiration of the Russian court jeweler Bolin. A stunning piece of fifteen intertwined diamond-encrusted circles with fifteen flame sapphires, which could have only come from Elfhome. In addition, there was Elvish inscribed on the inside (although the twins couldn't find a translation of the Elvish online). The history of the piece vanished during the Russian Revolution, along with the tiara. Somehow it was found by the Nazis and recovered after the Second World War by the French. France's claim on the crown was nebulous since it had originally belonged to Imperial Russia, and the equally fabulous copy was part of the British Crown Jewels by some odd chain of bloodlines and events. The French clearly wanted to state "finder's keepers" without being completely politically rude. They pointed out that unless Queen Soulful Ember or her father, King Ashfall, had lost it while sightseeing on Earth, the only way it could be in France was that the elves had sold it at some point to humans.

Of course, this circled back to the point of the exhibit, which was that the elves used to be frequent visitors to Earth, all the while keeping humans ignorant of Elfhome's existence.

Because the elves were on Earth and the exhibit opened in two weeks, the curators of AMNH were in a frenzy to get the dispute settled as quickly as possible. In so many words, they pointed out that crowds came to see sparkly things like gold and gems, and that children would not be impressed by the carved wood and rich fabrics that made up much of the exhibit. France wanted a promise that the United States wouldn't give the crown to the elves, but since the United Nations were debating the issue, the AMNH would have to obey the world's decision.

"I could just scream," Louise whispered to Jillian. "None of it is really theirs in the first place. Just being little pigs about the matter."

Jillian nodded glumly. "Here comes Mr. Kessler. You should probably at least pretend to pay attention to class."

Louise groaned quietly and closed up the web browser. Mr. Kessler paused at the doorway, obviously disoriented by the changes to their classroom. He eyed the new windows, the bare walls, and the desks rearranged by Miss Hamilton in an attempt to distract her students from the ruin of the building across the street. He spotted Louise and headed toward her.

What did he want? Louise sunk lower in her chair, wishing she could hide under her desk.

"Twin—Louise. Here." He set a magic generator down on her desk.

Louise blinked at it, confused by its presence. "Where—where did you get that?"

Mr. Kessler opened his mouth, caught himself before saying something cutting, and forced out a level, "I made it. Since I dropped your original—by accident—I ran your program a second time. And I tried it out. I have no idea what you think this does, but at least it doesn't burst into flames when you plug it into a 220 outlet."

Louise gathered it up, wanting to hide it so no one else would have the chance to examine it closely. "Thank you. Can I put it in my locker to keep it safe?"

Mr. Kessler flicked his hand toward the door and started for the teacher's desk.

Louise hurried to their locker and stuffed it into Tesla's storage compartment. What could they tell Mr. Kessler? Did they have to tell him anything? He seemed not to really care what the generator did, which was weird. Why would he even give it to her until he knew what it did? She was glad he had, but it seemed stupid of him.

"Seamus!" Mr. Howe barked in his classroom across the hall. "Sit!"

Oh. Yes. Mr. Howe had told Mr. Kessler not to bully the twins. Apparently Mr. Kessler was worried that breaking the fake generator would be considered being intentionally mean to Louise. He was making sure that everything was good before the joint stagecraft class, where Louise would have to give Mr. Howe a report of her progress or lack thereof. Eek! They hadn't made a second fake generator! They'd just assumed that Mr. Kessler would report the first one smashed and that would be the end of it. Oh, how could they be so stupid? Of course, one way or another, they'd have to produce an unsmashed fake generator because they'd said it was necessary to put on the play! If she took the magic generator upstairs during stagecraft, Mr. Howe would insist it be stored with the rest of the play equipment— which was the whole point of having the fake in the first place. She needed a fake, and she needed it to be able to do something demonstrable.

What could it do?

She leaned against the cool metal of her locker, thinking. Something to do with the play that she had overlooked but would seem vital. The holographic projectors were to deal with the mermaids. What else was Peter Pan canon? Pixie dust? No, they were going to go with just glitter, and that was the most intelligent method. Wait—Tinker Bell! Traditionally the fairy was represented just by a pin spotlight and a shimmer of bells as the character spoke. The twins were planning to do a traditional Tinker Bell, but they could do it bigger.

She hurried back to her desk. Mr. Kessler glanced at her as she came in but didn't stop his lecture on spreadsheets. She quickly checked his class schedule for the next few periods. As she'd hoped, he was floating from class to class today, spending the next four periods on the lower floors. It'd be unlikely he'd climb the eight flights up to the art rooms.

She then quickly checked a run time on a hybrid projector. Only three hours. Good. It gave her forty minutes to spare. If there was a teacher mode on the printer, then she should actually be able to load the program remotely. (Since the school was filled with gifted students, it really should have had a beefier security system. She and Jillian had hacked in as first-graders and set up a back door that no one had seemed to notice in the last five years.)

She winced at the printer's log that showed who accessed the printer and copies of the programs they ran. Judging from the few times that the printer had been used, Mr. Kessler really did see the printer as "his." In the last month, she and Mr. Kessler were the only ones using it. It felt wrong to leave any evidence of the magic generator anywhere in the school system, so she changed the log, swapping out the magic-generator program with the hybrid projector.

Twenty-three minutes later, she started the print job. Once the printer was finished, she would delete out all evidence that she—or rather Mr. Kessler—printed anything new. The only hard thing left was getting the hybrid projector off the 3D printer and into storage with the other play items. Since the entire class saw Mr. Kessler hand her the magic generator, she had fourteen witnesses that she *had* to go to the art room.

The end-of-period bell rang, and she followed Mr. Kessler out the door and watched him head to the stairs. His next class was with the second-graders, two flights down, but he did have time to run upstairs and back.

"Go down. Go down," she whispered.

He paused at the stairs, checked his watch, and trotted downwards.

"Oh, thank God." She collapsed against the wall with relief.

Jillian was grinning hugely.

"What?" Louise asked.

"We've got a second generator!" Jillian whispered. "It means we both can go to the museum."

Louise gasped. She hadn't even considered that side of things. "But it's all useless if France doesn't send the box."

"They'll send it." Jillian's grin didn't waver. "Even if we have to get tricky about it."

A full agonizing ten days later, the EIA talked France into sending just the box. Suddenly they had seventy-two hours to be ready to rob a world-famous museum.

21: KNOCK, KNOCK, OPEN THE BOX

Louise felt like she was going to be sick. She was so nervous her stomach was a queasy roil. At the same time, she couldn't stop grinning widely. They were going to do it, actually rob a museum like two cat burglars.

Part of her really wished they were going to do a traditional middle-of-the-night entrance through a skylight, but it was far easier and simpler to slip into the museum in broad daylight while it was still open. With the museum closing at 5:45, they could even be home before their parents could deeply question their "working late on the play" alibi.

The American Museum of Natural History had its own entrance from the 81st Street Subway Station. There were beautiful tile mosaics of a coral reef with sharks and fish. The twins stood, pretending to study the art while everyone who arrived with them swept out of the station.

They backtracked to a blind corner and quickly assembled their gear. The spell needed to be printed onto a three-dimensional surface that stayed rigid while the magic was active. After a lot of experimenting, they'd found that wardrobe moving boxes worked best. The forty-eight-inch-tall cardboard boxes covered them head to toe and were sturdy enough for the spell to work while they moved around.

Louise was all fumble-fingered as she carefully taped up her box. It had to be fitted together completely square. Then, seeming impossibly slow, she peeled the protective sheet off the circuit tracings and stuck them to the box. Everything had to match perfectly or the spell wouldn't work.

When she was done, she glanced to see if Jillian had finished her box.

Jillian was gone.

"Where are you?" Louise called.

Jillian's muffled voice came from near the tile mosaic. "Over here."

"I can't see you," Louise said without thinking.

"Doh!" Jillian's voice grew nearer. "Hurry up. We only have a few minutes before they shut the doors!"

"Okay, I'm almost ready." She lifted up the box and let it slide down over her. In the darkness, she activated the magic generator. She gave it a minute and then spoke the words that triggered the spell. "Did it work?"

Jillian huffed nearby. "Wait a minute, I'll check." There was a muffled scuffling noise. "Well, I can't see you, so I guess it worked. Let's go."

The drawback to the spell was that they couldn't cut eyeholes in the boxes. Nor could they mount cameras to the top of the boxes. They were basically running blind. Keeping the subway wall to their right, they started forward. Or at least Louise assumed they were both walking forward. She couldn't hear anything but her banging heart, nervous breathing and the soft scuff of her shoes. The scent of cardboard seemed nearly suffocating; why hadn't she noticed it before?

She went as carefully as possible down the subway hallway, toward the museum. They'd marked the edge of the museum's surveillance with a piece of tape. Once she crossed it, she turned on her phone and used the back door they'd created in the museum's surveillance system to watch the flow of people coming and going. They'd discovered if they moved sideways quickly, there was a slight blur in the video. It let them track their own movements with a small risk of discovery counterbalanced by the ability to dodge other people. She wove around a woman with a stroller and a group of Japanese tourists.

Her heart jumped as they passed the threshold into the museum proper. They were almost safe. There were people coming and going from the bathrooms on the right, so she kept to the left. At the end of the hallway, she turned left and went back toward the lunchrooms for school groups on field trips. The doors were shut and locked, but it gave a safe spot to crouch, out of the way, until the museum actually closed. There was a time stamp in the corner of the surveillance video. 5:32:03. They had cut it close.

At 5:35, the second closing announcement was broadcast, echoing through the nearly empty museum. After the English request for visitors to leave the museum, it repeated in Spanish and then Japanese.

Guards went into the bathrooms around the corner, their voices echoing on the tile. "We're closing. Anyone in here?" They heard the thud of bathroom stall doors being swung open to make sure no one was standing on the toilets.

At 5:45, the recording of "The American Museum of Natural History is now closed" played in three languages as the big metal shutter rattled shut, closing off the subway station.

They'd done it. They were inside the museum after closing! They were now officially cat burglars.

"Meow," Louise whispered.

The hardest part was going to be waiting another ten minutes before moving to be sure they avoided any last-minute sweeps of guards. There were still cleaning crews and guards and employees working late to dodge, but they should be few and far between.

Louise opened another window and checked on Tesla via a traffic camera. They had bought him the climbing feet attachments and had him scale the forty-foot granite pedestal to hide at the feet of the Chinese astronaut Jin Wong. The bronze statue of the man had odd wing-things spread wide behind him. Even after close study, and an extensive Internet search, Louise and Jillian weren't sure what they represented. Its location across the street from the museum, its height, and the wings made it a perfect place to hide Tesla. Even on the high traffic camera, the robot dog was invisible.

Reassured that Tesla was still safe, Louise closed the window and waited.

At 5:54:30 something collided with her. She yipped in surprise.

Jillian whispered a curse word. "It's just me."

Louise checked her phone. The screen showed the hallway clear. It should be safe to talk, and they needed to keep from running into each other. "You take right. I'll keep left."

Jillian's feet appeared on the screen as her twin lifted up the box to hear better. "What?"

"Stay on the right side of the hallway." Louise repeated and moved to the left side of the wide hallway. "I'll go left."

"Okay." Jillian's feet vanished as she dropped down the box.

They needed to get to the third floor from the basement without colliding with anyone. The fastest way would be the elevators, but guards would see and hear the cars moving. They were hoping that the escalators wouldn't be turned off immediately. They'd found going up stairs in the boxes cumbersome.

The good news was that if they moved slowly, there wasn't even a blur of motion on the monitors.

The bad news was that if they moved slowly, it was easy to lose track of where they were and run into walls. The hallway did a weird dogleg and they found themselves in a dead end, bouncing off each other.

Jillian was stuttering in frustration. "Ompfh! No! Ah! Don't."

"Shh!" Louise hissed.

"Stand still!" Jillian whispered.

So Louise stood still as Jillian moved forward quickly to establish her location on the screen and bounced off another wall with another muffled swear word. Louise used her twin's voice and the blur on her phone to orient herself. She was facing the exact opposite direction they needed to go. Jillian turned and headed the right way in a quick shuffle. Louise turned around and cautiously followed.

Luckily the escalators were still on. It felt odd riding up inside the box, not able to see where they were going, knowing that they couldn't be seen.

At the top, she bumped into Jillian again.

"Go right!" Louise whispered.

"Are you sure?"

Louise flipped to the online map. They should be right off the Theodore Roosevelt Memorial Hall on the first floor. They needed to walk around to the next set of up escalators. "Yes."

Second floor. Akeley Hall of African Mammals. Theodore Roosevelt Rotunda.

Third floor. Reptiles and Amphibians.

Her phone's screen showed the exhibit area empty of people, but the lights were still on. The glass display cases were full of taxidermied reptiles. A Komodo dragon gleamed in the perpetual dimness. She had been worried that the museum staff would start turning off lights, but now she was starting to wonder why they hadn't. It was now after 6:00.

The Lost Treasures of Elfhome exhibit was in the hall beyond the reptiles. When the twins had checked earlier, there had been a barrier up, directing the visitors back through the upper level of the African Mammal hall. While they'd been on the train, the barrier had been taken down.

Dufae's box sat against the west wall, screened on all sides by the taller displays. According to e-mails, the case would receive a glass lid after the elves visited the exhibit. The lighting had been aimed so it gleamed off the gold inlay of the spell-lock glyphs.

Louise had won the flip of the coin earlier. She shimmied the box up and off. She checked her phone's screen. It was still showing the empty exhibit hall. Wetting her mouth, she spoke the keyword to unlock the spell.

The band of glyphs gleamed and a seam appeared in the wood with a quiet *thunk*. The lid slid up and off easier than she'd imagined for not having been opened for hundreds of years.

Inside were a dozen spheres nestled in velvet-lined holes. They were much bigger than chicken eggs, but had the same oval shape. A spell had been etched into the surface of the *nactka*. When she picked one up, it seemed oddly warm and heavier than she expected. It wasn't made of gold as she had first thought; the material felt more like ivory under her fingers, feeding her impression that it had once been the bone of some magical creature, cut into an egg shape and hollowed out. She shivered and carefully placed it into the snow globe box from the gift shop.

Jillian's voice came out of nothing on the other side of Dufae's chest. "Incoming!"

Louise quickly put the lid back on the chest and spoke the locking word. The glyphs gleamed and with another quiet *thunk* the seam vanished. Back toward the reptiles, the elevator dinged quietly.

"Go," Louise whispered as certainty filled her. "If we're both here running blind, we'll get caught. Take the backup route. Go! I'll catch up."

Jillian gave a muffled curse, but she went because she always got caught when she didn't listen to Louise.

Louise tucked the boxed *nactka* into her backpack, felt around to find her invisibility box, and lifted it up and shimmied it down over her. There were footsteps coming quickly in her direction.

She was almost to the door out of the exhibition area, into the primates, when the elevator in front of her also dinged and its doors opened. She bit down on a squeak and skittered sideways until she hit a wall and backed into a blind corner.

On her screen, Louise saw that three people had gotten out of the elevator. The first was a man with a museum badge pinned to his shirt pocket. She nearly squeaked in surprise to see that the two people following him were elves. It was the queen's delegation to inspect the exhibit for culturally important pieces! What were they doing here now? They were supposed to come tomorrow during a big black-tie event.

Despite the grainy texture of the surveillance camera, Louise instantly recognized Sparrow Lifted by Wind. The female elf wore a fairy silk gown, and her gleaming hair spilled down to the floor all braided with beads and jewels and ribbons and flowers. In the center of her forehead was the blue bindi triangle that she alone wore. Most importantly, the female elf was trailed only by Bladebite. Where were the other four *sekasha*?

"Look out!" Louise frantically texted to Jillian, who was moving somewhere through the museum below. "Elves!"

Bladebite was stating something forcefully as he gestured about them. He was using High Elvish, which Louise couldn't follow at all.

"It is a treasure house," Sparrow answered in Low Elvish. She flicked her hand, dismissing him. "The doors are locked. There are dozens of guards. It is safe. Go. Look."

Bladebite continued to protest even as Sparrow moved away from the elevator.

"Go. Look." Sparrow walked past Louise without pausing to see if the *sekasha* followed.

Nor did he. Far below in the stairwell there was a slight noise, like a muffled sneeze, that Louise knew in her heart of hearts *had* to be Jillian.

The warrior glanced toward Sparrow and then, shaking his head, started down the stairs.

Oh, for once, Jillian, please don't get caught, Louise thought as hard as she could. Blindly charging after Bladebite, though, seemed like the wrong thing to do. If for no other reason than the fact that the museum staff member was walking in circles, trying to keep both elves in view. Louise was afraid that she'd collide with him.

The man wasn't sure which person to follow. "Um, I thought we were going to, um, wait, I'm not sure if you can...Right." He turned and spotted someone across the room. "Yves? What are you doing here?"

"The EIA asked us to facilitate this since we're trustees for most of the museums that donated to this exhibit. I brought Ambassador Feng with me. He's the United Nations' representative for these negotiations. His translator has taken ill. *Parlez-vous Français?*"

Ambassador Feng could have been mistaken as an elf even though he wore a dark business suit. He was tall and elegant and handsome, with long black hair and almond-shaped dark eyes. Only his round ears marked him as human. He stirred uncomfortably, looking annoyed at the museum staff person.

The staff person blinked in surprise. "Um. That's French. No. I took Mandarin in high school. *Nǐ hǎo.*"

Yves waved the implied offer away. "I doubt very much that the *husepavua* knows Mandarin, and mine is quite rusty." He turned in question to Sparrow.

"*Oui, je parle Français.*" Sparrow answered that she spoke French and proved it by continuing the conversation in that language. "What is this stupidity? I have guard dogs with me."

"They are distracted." Yves waved his hand in a circle to take in the museum. His back was to the camera so that Louise couldn't see his face. "This is the most inconspicuous place we could meet. If I need, I can have your holy dogs killed off."

"We should not be meeting at all," Sparrow stated. "And please don't kill my dogs. Yes, I loathe them with all my heart, but it would make my position tedious."

"There has been a change in plans," Yves said. "You must return to Elfhome as soon as possible. Go back to the border and wait."

Sparrow hissed out what might have been a curse and flicked a glance toward the museum staff member. "We need more privacy than this."

Yves turned and addressed the staff member in English. "Do you have the insurance paperwork?"

"No. I thought—do we really need them?"

"Yes. Please, go get them."

No, no, don't go! Louise didn't want to be alone with these people. She felt like she was in shark-infested waters; if they found her, they'd kill her instantly.

"Oh! Okay. I'll be right back." The man hurried away.

Louise shrank back, putting her hand over her mouth.

Sparrow waited until the elevator dinged closed before growling out, "You demanded I come, and I set all my plans in motion and came, and now you're telling me I must go back? I will not be able to stop what I have started!"

"Shut up and listen," Ambassador Feng snapped. "We do not have time for this. Your dogs might return at any moment, and I do not want them sniffing at me."

"They will not recognize you, especially in those ridiculous clothes."

"At least I'm not in the same rags I was in four hundred years ago."

Sparrow glared angrily at the male who seemed more and more an elf.

Yves moved between them. "Dufae has an heir!" His voice was full of annoyance at their petty fighting. "A child by the name of Alexander Graham Bell. We need him."

It was good that Louise had her hand already over her mouth. She muffled the whimper of fear. *Alexander!*

Sparrow huffed slightly in exasperation. "What does this have to do with me?"

"He is in Pittsburgh."

"He is human." She flipped her hand toward the Chinese ambassador. "He's the one with the spies within the EIA. I can do nothing with humans without attracting attention."

"Dufae's child tested fluent in Elvish, both in oral and written sections of the application, and claimed our gods as his religion. Obviously he's been raised by an elf. His guardian might turn to the Wind Clan when we take him. We cannot afford to get the *sekasha* or anyone else involved. You need to be there."

"Are you sure that he will be useful? Neither Dufae's sister nor his nephew matched his genius. This child could be an idiot."

Yves still hadn't turned to face the camera. It almost seemed as if he knew exactly where it was located and how to avoid it. "Someone in the NSA had the brilliant idea of screening college applicants for prodigies. They came up with test questions on building a gate that weren't meant to be answerable. For almost three decades, no one has been able to. During the last Shutdown, Dufae's child applied to Carnegie Mellon University and answered all the questions."

Yves paced in the camera's blind spot. "The humans have noticed our activities and have decided to put Bell into protective custody. The NSA has borrowed some operatives from another American agency to go to Pittsburgh and fetch Bell. They'll be heavily armed and difficult to eliminate. It is possible that the Americans can make Bell disappear so not even we can find him. You two need to reach him first."

Sparrow huffed again. "This would not be an issue if that idiot cat didn't keep killing everyone who could build us a gate."

Ambassador Feng reacted as if struck. "The scientists are not cooperating once they understand the situation. They're smart enough to know that opening a gate between the worlds will result in full-out war."

Yves waved aside the male's comment. "She is right. We cannot afford another dismembered genius. Tell that cat of yours that if he harms Dufae's child, we'll have him skinned. Alive. Slowly. I'll make him into a coat for my little sister."

Ambassador Feng gave a slight bow. "I'll have it explained so even he understands."

What did they mean? Surely they didn't mean an actual cat with fur? And yet that was what the words seemed to suggest. Was she mistranslating the French? And why were they even speaking French? Why weren't they speaking Elvish?

"Can this not be delayed?" Sparrow seemed determined to not be involved in the plan. "Was that not the point of infiltrating the EIA? So that we controlled what humans came and went from Pittsburgh?"

"We cannot delay the visas for the two agents," Yves stated. "The United States is expediting the papers using the fact that Dufae's child claimed joint United States and Elfhome citizenship. The EIA has to give full cooperation to allow the USA the ability to protect its citizens; it's part of the United Nations agreement. You must return to Pittsburgh immediately."

"I can't be there when Wolf Who Rules is killed." Sparrow took a step backwards. "Your summons was the perfect excuse to be absent when he was attacked. Everything is set. He's in Pittsburgh. I've brought one of his Hands with me to weaken him. A trap has been set that Yutakajodo says will succeed. I cannot compromise my position by returning until the deed is done."

"My father commands it," Yves stated coldly. "You must obey.

Finish up here and return immediately to Monroeville and wait for Shutdown. Do what you must to make sure that you arrive in Pittsburgh first."

"But—But—" Sparrow struggled to refuse.

Yves cut off her protest. "By the time you cross the border, the viceroy will be dead. No one will lay the blame on you."

Louise realized she was crying. Alexander was an idea of a perfect older sister and a handful of photographs. Windwolf was much more a real person to her. Louise had watched hours of video of the viceroy and pored over all the known facts of his life. She knew him better than most of her teachers. How could they talk so casually about killing him?

Yves turned to Ambassador Feng. "We will need Shoji on this. He is the only one we have clever enough to verify that the work we get out of Dufae is correct. You have him on leash now?"

"Firmly. We've got the child caged in an obscuring spell at a secret compound. Shoji will not be able to find him."

"Be sure to keep him well hidden and unharmed. We've missed our chance at taking the other children of the Chosen bloodline. Without the others, we'll lose our hold on the tengu if the child we have is killed or freed."

"We have Shoji."

Yves snorted with contempt. "The male would kill himself before being used that way. It's the dragon influence on the bloodline. If it comes to that, you'll have to cage him."

There was the scrape of boots and they all went silent, turning, clearly frightened.

Stormsong stood in the doorway of the Lost Treasures exhibit. She frowned at the three assembled in the hallway. She asked something in High Elvish.

"Good God, tell me that she doesn't speak French," the ambassador murmured, although neither his tone nor his face betrayed the fear of his words.

Louise muffled a whimper, remembering how Yves had so casually mentioned killing off the holy warriors if they learned too much.

Sparrow snorted. "Not a word." She switched to English to address the warrior. "Not all humans speak English. We are speaking French."

Stormsong studied Ambassador Feng for a minute and then

asked in fluent Mandarin, "Why aren't you using the Chinese official language? Would not that be more polite?"

Ambassador Feng went white and took a step back. He caught himself and bowed, stuttering out, "I'm—I'm amazed. I did not know that you spoke my language."

"We're not speaking Mandarin because I don't know it." Yves returned the conversation to English. His tone was bold and fearless. "This is a common problem with humans. Earth has nearly seven thousand distinct languages. We have a legend that at one time we tried to reach the heavens and one of our gods cursed us so we would fail. He made it so not one man spoke the same language as his neighbor. And in a babbling of voices, the people abandoned their great work and fled in confusion."

"The tower of Babel. I know the story. I've read your Bible."

"Singing Storm of Wind has helped the viceroy study human culture since they were doubles. Wolf Who Rules hired tutors to teach them several of Earth's languages. Together they have read most of the classic works of human literature."

"But you didn't teach them French?" Ambassador Feng asked in French but proved that he had been following the English conversation.

Sparrow locked down on a flash of anger, trying to pass it off as thinking carefully before answering the question in French. "I'd been banished to the farthest corner of hell by his father. I did not join Wolf's household until after the first Startup."

The elevator dinged and the staff person tumbled out, shuffling through papers. "Yes. Sorry. I should have had these ready."

They all turned to face him. Yves, however, was the one who addressed him.

"Yes, we're going to have to prepare claims on three items. You can ship them tomorrow."

"Tomorrow? We were hoping that the elves would allow us to keep the exhibit together until the end of this show."

"Tomorrow," Yves said firmly. "Let me point them out."

Ambassador Feng frowned as Yves swept the staff person back into the exhibit room. "I know your people still see him as our emperor," he murmured quietly to Sparrow alone. "But much has changed since the pathways between the worlds were closed. Our goals are no longer strictly the same."

Sparrow sniffed with disdain. "It seems to me that your people are the ones who lost sight of the truth. Playing with your ugly little monsters. We are meant to be gods with angels serving our every whim."

"We needed an army to take back our world. Monsters were the only way to build one quickly. Once we have what is ours, we'll go back to making angels." The ambassador glanced toward Stormsong. "More obedient ones this time."

Sparrow and Ambassador Feng followed Yves as Zephyr Blade came trotting upstairs. Stormsong nodded to the male warrior in greeting.

"This is the strangest place I have ever seen." Zephyr Blade eyed the primates in the glass display cases down the hall. "Those are not real humans mounted downstairs?"

"I doubt it," Stormsong growled. "I believe they're cleverly made dolls. Like that mechanical dog at the hotel. Humans are very good at deception."

Louise huddled inside her invisible box. What should she do? Should she reveal herself and explain what she'd overheard? Would they believe her? Would she even have a chance to explain if she suddenly popped up out of nowhere? The warriors sounded somewhat freaked by the museum.

"Is something wrong?" Zephyr Blade asked Stormsong.

"I'm not used to being surprised." The female started to pace in a wide circle, nearly brushing up against Louise's box. "I feel half blind and half dead."

"It's because this world has no magic. It's blinding your ability. All of us are feeling it. It's like we've been coated with lead. How long are we staying?"

"Sparrow will not say. I'm not sure that she knows. It will depend on how cooperative the humans are. It could be months. I'm not sure why she felt the need for us to come; almost everything on Earth, we sold to the humans outright."

"She is right that something important might have been lost when the war broke out and we pulled down the pathways."

Assuming that Louise didn't trigger some automatic "hack first, ask questions later" response, what would she actually say? That Sparrow had laid a trap for Windwolf? Louise didn't know where or when or how. Nothing but honor would stop Sparrow from denying it, and everything Louise had witnessed indicated that Sparrow would do anything and say anything to keep her secret. Obviously she had lied about why she wanted to be on Earth. According to Stormsong, humans like Louise were "good at deception," and Sparrow was her trusted leader.

And even if the warriors believed Louise over another elf, could they save Windwolf?

By the time you cross the border, he will be dead.

Obviously the assassination attempt was scheduled to happen before Shutdown. No one could communicate with Elfhome until Pittsburgh returned to Earth on Tuesday.

No matter what Louise did, she couldn't save Windwolf. Yves said that if the *sekasha* proved troublesome, he'd have them all killed. By warning the warriors, Louise would merely make them targets when they were most vulnerable. The three people plotting at the museum represented an unknown number of powerful, hidden people. Their organization had obviously infiltrated both the EIA and the Chinese government. Hundreds, maybe thousands, against five warriors stranded on Earth.

How would the warriors even stop the three here? Kill them? Louise shuddered at the sudden image of blood splattering across glass display cases. What else could the elves do? If they tried to follow human laws, the assassins would be free to contact others to carry out their plans. Their massive organization would kill the five *sekasha* before they could carry the news back to Elfhome.

And every action had a reaction. If Louise acted against Yves, he could act against her. Even if she slipped away without giving her name and address, the security cameras would record her face. A quick check of elementary schools in the area would find her and Jillian. These people that so casually kidnapped and dismembered scientists, murdered elf nobles, and caged children to be used against their family would know where the twins lived.

No, she couldn't warn the *sekasha*. She could do nothing to save Windwolf.

Louise could barely breathe as grief and fear formed a huge burning knot in her chest. She felt like she was teetering on a crumbling edge and any moment she was going to go crashing down.

"Why," Stormsong whispered in Elvish, "do I feel so alive?"

Louise blinked back tears and realized that the female had stopped pacing right in front of her.

Suddenly her box slid upward, exposing Louise.

Stormsong held the box over her head, gazing down at Louise with confusion.

Louise gazed up at her in utter terror.

For an eternity they looked into each other eyes. Louise knew not what the warrior saw within her, but Louise saw grim determination settle on the face of the female.

"Go," Stormsong whispered in English. "Quietly. Now."

And she settled the box back over Louise.

Louise gasped, startled back into breathing.

"Now," the warrior growled lowly and gave the box a slight nudge.

Louise bolted, running blindly to the stairs and then down, and around, and down, and around, flight after flight until she was in the Grand Gallery of the first floor. They'd assumed that they wouldn't be able to get out the way they'd come in. The backup route took her through the Northwest Coast Indians and the Imax Corridor and then to the glass-walled Weston Pavilion. It wasn't until she was at the Columbus Avenue Entrance that she realized she had done the entire run completely blind.

Was she really in the museum's proverbial back door?

She flipped her phone to the GPS screen and checked.

She was.

How had she managed that?

And where was Jillian?

She checked her twin's coordinates. According to Jillian's phone, she was just a few feet away.

"Are you okay?" Jillian texted.

Louise had to try three times to type a simple "yes" and then twice to send "here."

"Me or you?" Jillian texted. They both had an exit kit just in case they were separated and needed to escape quickly.

"You," Louise tapped in. She was so rattled that she screwed the spelling up, but autocorrect fixed it.

"Okay. Keep watch."

As far as they could determine, the museum had a maze of office areas and work spaces tucked between the windowless visitor areas and the building's façade that showed four stories of windows. They had picked their exit point because it was one of the few places where they were sure that the interior wall actually gave direct access to the outdoors and not into "staff only" areas. The sleek modern pavilion was one giant cube of glass.

With muffled thumps and quiet mutters, Jillian got the Hoberman megasphere out of her backpack, shoved it under the bottom of her box, and flicked it to expand the tight bundle of plastic into a bright-colored, four-and-a-half-foot-wide, loosely woven ball. Louise winced slightly as the sphere seemed to appear out of nowhere on the museum security monitors. They had practiced this, but they weren't totally sure it would work. They hadn't used it to get in, since they hadn't figured out a way to keep the sphere invisible while using it to breach a wall.

Jillian reached out from under her box to adjust the megasphere. Her disembodied hand turned the ball so that the loop threaded with wire was lined up with the window. With the soft murmur of Elvish, Jillian activated the spell. Another slight push, and the loop slid into the glass and the glass temporarily vanished. Then came the scary part, actually stepping through the loop, box and all. The spell affected only what it was touching at the moment of activation, but Louise couldn't help but imagine that they would end up in the quantum space where the glass molecules were suspended.

"I'm through," Jillian called from outside.

Louise carefully lined her box up with the loop and stepped through. "Okay, I'm out."

Jillian's hand appeared and jerked the loop out of the glass and canceled the spell. "It's out. Let's go!"

Louise checked the security camera feed. It showed the glass back in place and the multicolor ball bouncing away as it trailed behind Jillian, still connected by the wire. With a quiet thud and a muted "oomph" Jillian hit a tree and bounced off it.

Wincing, Louise checked the other security cameras. There were no guards heading toward the Columbus Street exit, so no one must have noticed the ball for the minute it was inside the museum. Breathing out with relief, Louise followed after Jillian into the wooded safety of Theodore Roosevelt Park.

22: SURROGATE MOM

April Geiselman jerked open the door. She was in a bathrobe, and her makeup was weirdly smeared. She glared down at them. "What are you doing here? It's after dark. Do your parents know where you are?"

"We need help." Jillian slipped past her into the apartment. Tesla followed Jillian in, unstoppable as a tank. They'd safely retrieved him from Jin Wong's statue. The mini-Tesla was still in school, broadcasting from their locker.

"Alexander is in big trouble. We need to warn her!" Louise ducked around April the other way.

"Some people want to kidnap her!" Jillian cried as Louise dumped the flattened wardrobe boxes on the floor.

"Hey! Wait!" April cried. "You can't come in; I have—what?"

"We were at the museum . . . and we heard these people talking about Alexander." Louise realized that they probably shouldn't dwell too much on where they heard all this and certainly never mention when. "They said they're going to kidnap her! We need to warn her, but we don't know how!"

"Okay, okay, calm down." April made calming motions with her hands. "Who are 'they' and where is she? I thought she was still on Elfhome."

"We don't know who 'they' are!" the twins cried, and Louise added, "At least not all of them."

A tall figure in the hallway brought the conversation to a halt.

The shirtless man had lipstick smeared across part of his face and his hair sticking out every which way. "April? What's going on? Whose kids are these?"

They all gaped at him for a moment.

April finally broke the silence by pointing at him. "Stephen! They're—they're . . . It's complicated. Look, I'm really sorry, but this is going to be a while. Can—can we do this another time?"

April herded the man into her bedroom, where the muted conversation continued in awkward and embarrassed starts and stops. Mostly it was April apologizing and Stephen saying that he understood. Since they'd missed dinner, the twins raided April's fridge for Diet Coke, still-warm Chinese takeout, and three different types of pickles.

April had changed into a tank top and yoga pants when the two adults emerged from the bedroom. There was an awkward good-bye at the door, where both adults seemed hyperaware that the twins were watching closely.

"I feel like I'm in high school again," Stephen whispered.

"I'm sorry," April said for tenth time since the twins appeared on her doorstep. "It's a family emergency."

"So they're family?" Stephen asked.

April shot the twins a cryptic look. "Yes, it's complicated, but they're family."

"With family, is it ever anything but complicated?" Stephen hesitated and then kissed April good-bye before allowing her to shove him out the door.

"Call me," April cried and then slammed shut the door and chained it. She leaned her head against the door for a minute. "I just knew the negative karma was going to bite me in the butt one day. Walk away from one kid and two will come breaking down your door."

"Sorry," Louise called.

April pounded her forehead against the door a few times before joining them in the kitchen. "Okay, let's start at the top. You found out that someone is going to kidnap Alexander. Who?"

Since Louise was the only one who had actually seen and heard the elves, she told the story without explaining where they were when they overheard the conversation. April got out a cold Diet Coke, poured it into a glass, and added rum to it.

"They were just standing out in public, planning this out loud?"

Put that way it did seem unlikely. Sparrow's movements, though, were highly publicized, as hordes of fans and protesters followed her. If someone came to the Waldorf Astoria, the *sekasha* would have paid more attention to the individuals. The Lost Treasures gave an excuse for the group to gather in relative innocence.

"They were talking in French," Louise said.

"So how did you understand them?" April asked.

Jillian slurped down the chow mien noodle she'd been fighting with and explained. "We're fluent in French."

"And Spanish—but in New York, how could we not be?" Louise felt that confessing to trivial things made up for leaving out the whole museum robbery thing.

"And Low Elvish." Jillian apparently felt the same way.

"And Hindi and Mandarin." Louise started to tick off on her fingers the languages they knew.

Jillian waved her chopsticks to negate that claim. "That's more 'limited working proficiency' than fluent."

"Hindi and Mandarin?" April added more rum to her drink.

"We learned Hindi by watching Bollywood musicals," Louise said.

"And Mandarin from Chinese historical dramas," Jillian said. "And a smattering of Korean, for the same reason."

"But that doesn't matter," Louise said. "I was hiding, so they thought they were alone while they planned to kidnap Alexander and kill Windwolf."

"Whoa! Wait! Kill Windwolf? Holy shit! You said this was Sparrow and Windwolf's bodyguards!"

"Well, that's why Sparrow was talking in French. None of the *sekasha* understand it, so even if they overheard her—and they did—they didn't know what she was planning."

"Who cares what language they were speaking in?" Jillian cried. "We have to warn Alexander!"

"We can't." April took a big swallow of her drink. "At least, not until Shutdown. Are you sure about this?"

"Yes!" both girls cried.

"We can't call her because we don't have a phone number for her," Jillian said. "And we haven't been able to find a Pittsburgh directory."

"Oh, I have one," April said.

"You do?" the twins cried.

April went to her bookcase and pulled out a paper book. "Pittsburgh is completely last century. They do old-fashioned paper directories."

The twins leapt at her with a cry and snatched the book from her hands. "Bell, Bell, Bell." They chanted, flipping pages. "Bartley. Bowles. Bruton. Burger. There's no Bell!"

"Their number might be unlisted." April got out another Diet Coke.

"Why would anyone do that?" the twins cried. "What's the point of having a directory if everyone isn't in it?"

April shrugged and added rum to the new soda. "I don't know. My folks are in it. They mailed me that copy as a hint to call more often. Maybe the reason Tim Bell's phone stopped working was because they moved to Earth."

"No, on the application to CMU, Alexander said she lived on Elfhome." Louise flipped to the *W* section. "Maybe Orville is listed."

"Well?" April asked as the twin frowned at the only Wright listed.

"There's an Oilcan Wright. Who names their kid Oilcan?" Louise stared at the simple listing of name, street address, and phone number. "How are you supposed to cross-reference this?"

Jillian gave a small scream of frustration. "We can't call him and say 'If you have a cousin named Alexander, Sparrow is going to try to kidnap her and kill the viceroy.' What if it isn't him and we just told a stranger this secret that could get him killed?"

April motioned for her to stay calm. "Are you really, really sure that you understood what they were saying—in French?"

"Qu'est-ce que vous ne comprenez pas dans je parle Français couramment?" Jillian shouted.

"I'll take that as a yes," April said. "Look, there's nothing we can do today. It's probably too late for me to get train tickets to Elfhome; normally the seats are booked months in advance. I can try, but we shouldn't count on it. Usually if I want to go home for Christmas, I have to get the tickets before March. I'll probably have to drive down a few days before Shutdown and hope I can get through."

"Couldn't you fly in?" Louise knew that the airport still operated, but she'd never heard of flights into Pittsburgh. Airports equaled planes, though, didn't they?

"No. Passenger flights aren't allowed in the airspace during Shutdown. Everything in and out is either cargo or military planes, and that's only after dawn. There's always some residual magic in the zone, and it wreaks havoc on mechanical systems. The risk is too high for passenger flights."

"They have to let you through, don't they?" Jillian asked. "You're a native Pittsburgher!"

April added more rum to her drink. "Yes, but this isn't driving across the river to New Jersey. This is going to another planet. Elfhome. The world of elves. Different stars. Different moon—well—looks the same, but it's not the same moon. Totally different sun. Not our world."

"Yes, but you can drive to it," Jillian pressed.

"It's like going to another country." April took a drink and shuddered slightly. "Canada or Mexico—if they dropped off the face of the planet for thirty days at a time. There's only four highways still connected to Pittsburgh. A concrete trench and three fences topped with barbwire surround the rest of the area. Even returning residents need a passport, and all vehicles are searched for stowaways. Trucks start to line up two days before Shutdown in special parking lots, and they have first priority for getting in and out. New EIA employees are second-level clearance, and scientists are third. I'll be last in line."

"So you might not get in?" Jillian started to cry. Louise struggled not to start, too.

"Oh, oh, don't do that. Here, have ice cream." April pulled out several pints of Häagen Dazs, three bowls, and a half dozen spoons.

Louise couldn't see how ice cream could help, but April did have exotic flavors like Bananas Foster, Caramel Cone, and Midnight Cookies and Cream. The last proved to be fudge and chocolate wafer cookies in chocolate ice cream. The twins were distracted by sampling each of the flavors.

"I have one edge: I'm a native Pittsburgher." April hunted through the freezer and added Dulce de Leche and Rum Raisin to the selection. "Normally the last hour or so, the only vehicles they let through are the returning residents."

Louise gasped as she realized that if April went to warn Alexander, she probably would have to stay until the next Shutdown to come back. "What about your work?"

"I might lose my job over this." April took a big swallow of her Coke and rum and winced. "Oh, that's strong."

"I'm sorry," Louise said.

"It's okay. It's a crappy job. I've been meaning to look for another."

"We could call...someone," Jillian said. "There's Esme's sister, Lain. She's in Pittsburgh. She could warn Alexander."

"I don't know if Lain knows about Alexander." April waved her spoon loaded with Bananas Foster. "Esme didn't want me to tell her family. And phones are very unreliable during Shutdown. All of Pittsburgh tries to call out to do business that one day a month. You basically start dialing at midnight and listen to 'all connections are busy, please try again later' for a couple of hours. No, no, don't cry! I'm going to drive to Pittsburgh!"

"You said you might not get through!" Jillian wailed.

"I can call people while I'm waiting at the border. I won't have anything better to do. My whole family still lives in Pittsburgh. My mom and dad, my uncle and three cousins—I'll call them all. They still live just across the river from Old Man Bell. I'll have one of them go over and warn Alexander and see about maybe getting her to Earth. She can stay with me."

"Really?"

"It probably would have ruined both our lives if I had tried to keep her when she was a baby. I was stupid young and had a lot of growing up to do. I couldn't even keep a plant alive. Old Man Bell, he has a world of patience and was ready to make Alexander his entire world. But I always regretted having to let her go."

If or rather when they found surrogate mothers for the babies, would they be able to let them go? April had done the hard thing because it was better for Alexander. Whatever they chose for the babies, they had to remember to do what was best for them.

"We should go home," Jillian announced, pushing away her empty bowl.

April snagged her purse from off the floor by the couch. "Okay, I'll take you home."

"We can take the train." Louise wasn't sure how sober April was.

"What kind of mother would I be if I let you go home on a train alone at this time of night?"

"You're not our mother," Jillian pointed out.

"I could have been." April was completely right there. A fraction of an inch in the right direction and they would have been born eighteen years ago. "Come on." April paused at the door, wavering. "Remind me to let the car drive itself."

23: SHUTDOWN

The alarm woke Louise. She lay in the darkness for a minute, confused. Then she remembered that it was Shutdown and Pittsburgh was back on Earth. They had gone to bed early so they could spend all night trying to reach Orville, assuming that he was the Wright listed in the phone book. Her eyes adjusted to the dimness and she made out Jillian sitting on her bed, sheets piled around her, face illuminated by the screen of her phone. A quiet voice said, "All circuits are busy, please try again later." Jillian grunted as if hit, and her fingers moved on her phone's keyboard.

"Go back to sleep," Jillian said after her third attempt got the same error message. "I'll wake you up if I get through."

"I want to stay awake."

"If I don't get through before three, you're going to have to take over trying to get through. We have to keep trying until midnight tomorrow."

April had said that it was unlikely they would get through during the first few hours, but it was upsetting to think that three hours might go by without success.

It was still dark when Jillian woke Louise. "I didn't get through. I never even got a connection."

"April got to the border Saturday; she'll get in," Louise said with more confidence than she felt. She glanced at the clock.

It was three-thirty. Jillian had let her sleep an extra half hour. They needed to be awake for school at five-thirty. Louise reset the alarm.

By failure number seven, Jillian was breathing deeply.

The world was strangely quiet as Louise sat dialing her phone. It seemed as if the whole world were holding its breath, just as afraid for her sister as she was.

At four twenty-three, the phone clicked instead of immediately giving Louise a recording. Her heart leaped up and then sunk down to her toes as it gave a standard busy signal. She hung up and redialed. It clicked, and after a moment of silence, gave a busy signal again. Her heart had done the same dizzying loop of up and down and back to rest.

"Oh, you do have a phone!" Iggy said when they met him at the subway platform shortly after eight. It had become a ritual at some point that Iggy walked with them to school from the subway station.

"Doh!" Jillian hit dial to try yet again. "Everyone has phones, even the Amish."

"Isn't that against their religion?" Iggy asked.

"I report it, not explain it," Jillian stated.

Jillian's phone suddenly connected, and a man spoke over her phone. "Hey, this is Oilcan. My life imploded, and I'm not going to be home until *probably* Wednesday. I ran over my headset. It's in a zillion pieces that not even Tinker could fix. If you really, really need to talk to me, call Tinker. Be warned that she's in full Godzilla mode. If you don't have Tinker's number, call Roach."

They stared at Jillian's phone for several heartbeats.

"Normally you leave a message after something like that." Iggy pointed to the still connected phone.

"That's not the right number." Jillian disconnected the call.

"Ah, okay, I was wondering. Those sound like gang names. And headsets? Only bikers use those."

Jillian glanced to Louise as she put her phone away. "I'll have to look up the right number later."

"So." Iggy bounced in place. "Are you psyched?"

"Huh?" Louise said.

"Tomorrow you start flying!" Iggy meant for the play.

Jillian swore slightly as the twins traded glances. They had totally forgotten about the play again in the flood of other concerns. Because of the bombing, all the school activities had been pushed back a week, including the sixth-grade class play. They'd made up for lost time on stagecraft with after-school sessions. They hadn't had access to the stage, however, until last week. It meant they spent the first few days moving pieces of the sets into place, assembling them, and testing their blocking.

Jillian and Iggy started to practice lines, which left Louise to consider Oilcan's answering machine message. They still didn't know if this man was their cousin, Orville. They'd scripted out a series of questions that they could have asked to establish his identity. If he wasn't going to be home during the Shutdown window, then they could only leave a message. Should they without knowing if this was really Orville or not?

It was painful to feel exactly nine years old.

"We could just say 'Alexander is in danger' and not give any other information on her, not even her gender, and if it isn't Orville, he'll have no idea who we're talking about."

They'd hidden themselves in the girls' restroom to discuss the problem before the homeroom bell rang.

"I don't know. Two kids call and leave a message about elves kidnapping your cousin—who's going to believe that? It's going to sound like a joke."

"We can have Tesla leave it." Jillian dropped her pitch to the gravelly tone of Tesla's original deep voice, before they changed it to sound like Christopher Robin. *"Ohayougozaimasu, Orville-san."*

"That could work, but do we say who is going to kidnap Alexander? Sparrow is a double agent working inside the Wind Clan. We don't know whom she's working for or why. It isn't Windwolf; he's a target, too. And Sparrow probably isn't going to carry out the kidnapping herself."

"I know! I know!" Jillian cried. "Okay. We'll call Lain."

"What? Lain?"

"She's Alexander's aunt."

"But she might not know that. Esme didn't want April to tell her about Alexander."

"While Esme was still on Earth." Jillian wrapped her arms around Louise. "If I were leaving Earth like that, I would know that I was never coming back. And that I would never see you again. I would want the last time we're together to be all good memories—and that certainly wouldn't work if I dropped a shitload of crazy on you."

Louise shuddered at the idea of losing Jillian. "So, you think that Esme would have left a note or something that Lain could read after they'd said good-bye?"

Jillian nodded. "I would. A big long sappy note of everything that hurt too much to say."

"Like what?"

"You know. Like how I was going to miss waking up in the middle of the night from a nightmare and knowing that I wasn't alone. And how scary everything was going to be without you with me. You're the brave one. I couldn't do half the things we do without you leading the way."

"Me? Brave?"

"Yeah!" Jillian squeezed her hard and then let her go, embarrassed. "Anyhow, I'm betting Esme did tell Lain before she jumped."

The homeroom bell rang, ending their moment of privacy.

"Okay," Louise said. "We'll call Lain."

Mr. Howe was standing in the hallway with Miss Hamilton. They had Elle with them plus the two boys, Darius and Carlos, who were playing Wendy's younger brothers. Darius had been picked for John because he was the best of all the fifth-grade boys at remembering lines after Iggy. Carlos was the smallest of the boys and thus had been picked to play Michael, the baby of the Darling family.

"Girls, there's been a change in plan. The flying instructor is here. They've installed the wires for the play, and you're going to be spending today learning how to use it."

Jillian breathed out a curse that only Louise could hear.

"Today?" Louise asked fearfully.

A weird side effect of playing with the spells was that the residual magic seemed to be giving Louise horrible nightmares. One of the recurring ones was Jillian falling, and it had them both a little edgy about the flying.

"Yes, we were originally scheduled for last Wednesday but..." She paused as the sentence led her to the bombing. The teachers seemed reluctant to discuss it, as if they had been repeatedly told not to bring it up.

"But I thought it was moved to tomorrow," Louise said.

"There was a conflict in schedules, and we got bumped to today. Go down to the theater with Mr. Howe."

He held up his hand to check them and stepped into 502. "Behave!" Mr. Howe growled at his class. "I'll get a full report, so don't think I won't know."

With that warning, he led them downstairs. The twins followed, exchanging glances that spoke volumes. The flying instruction was a full-day affair. Jillian was better at lying, but she was going to be strapped into a harness and suspended from the ceiling all day. Louise would have to be the one to call Lain.

The flying instructor was a giant. He towered over the twins and was nearly a foot taller than even Mr. Howe.

"I'm Rob Noble. I'm with Flights of New York. In the next two days I'll teach you how to operate the equipment and help you choreograph the entire play. I've done hundreds of productions of *Peter Pan*, so I know the characters and I know the scenes. I can give you complete blocking instructions or I can just make suggestions. This is your production, not mine. Today we'll get you comfortable at flying and then choreograph everything but the fight on the *Jolly Roger*."

He held a harness that was a belt with wide suspenders and straps that looped through the legs. The reinforced back had one large ring. "We'll be using these flying harnesses, and only them. Safety is very important, so never try to hook the wire to something like a belt or a piece of clothing and expect it to hold. The harness goes under a costume. It can't be dyed or painted, because that might weaken the material. You'll want a T-shirt on under it; you don't want it up against your skin. Stage manager?"

Louise put up her hand when she realized he was asking who was acting in that position.

"Okay. Before any practice or performance, it's your responsibility to check the harness for wear. If it looks like it's fraying or breaking in any way, you have to tell your teachers that it can't be used. I'm leaving lots of spare harnesses with your teachers, so don't try to jury-rig something. Do you understand?"

Louise nodded.

"I will be double-checking the equipment, too," Mr. Howe said.

"The more eyes on it, the better." Mr. Noble pointed to a

dangling rope. "Yesterday we installed the equipment and tested it. This here is called a flying wire." He took out a flashlight and pointed it up to the ceiling to show where it connected and then followed its path down to a complex set of pulleys and cams. "It's controlled by what we call a lift line. It used to be that for every flyer, you would need one or two humans on this line. We now have these robots that we will be programming in the choreography. It will be a little tedious, so you have to be patient, but once we have the movement entered, it's actually easier and safer for the flyers."

He tucked away the flashlight. "Who is Peter?"

"I am." Jillian moved up to lean against Louise.

The instructor did a double take. "Oh! Twins! I think you're going to be the smallest Peter I've worked with."

Jillian put her hands on her hips, jerking Peter's boldness up like a shield. "Size has nothing to do with talent!"

He grinned. "Of course not. Have you ever taken dance classes?"

"Yes." The twins had taken a variety of dance classes at the YMCA.

"I take classes at the Dance Conservatory." Elle stepped forward with ballet flourish. "I'm playing Wendy."

"Good, good, that will help. Let's get you into your harness."

Louise took her place at the lighting board. She needed a stool to reach the array of monitors and switches. Mr. Noble had linked the lift operator robots to the stage's computer. By design, the board was out of sight from anyone in the audience. Half-blinded by the lights on the stage, the teachers wouldn't be able to see her if they stayed with the actors. Louise took out her phone and dialed Lain's number. The call went through, but the line was busy. She hissed out a swear word. She wouldn't be able to use an auto-dialer since she had to stay focused on the flyers while they were in the air. She couldn't drop everything if the auto-dialer connected unexpectedly. She tucked her phone among the various buttons, switches, and slide controls. She hit disconnect and then redial.

She found a rhythm to her work. The action suggested a melody to her, so she would write a section of song, dial Lain's number, program in the newest flight movements, check her phone's screen, tweak the lighting, and disconnect from the busy signal.

Carlos and Darius as Michael and John Darling were going to stay comic relief as they struggled with the flying. Jillian and Elle astounded Mr. Noble with the speed at which they learned the basics. He shifted them from the simple single harness that they started with into a three-point harness that would allow more complicated movements.

"Who designed your sets?" Mr. Noble asked as they started to program in the choreography of Peter's secretive arrival at the Darling nursery.

"Louise did." Mr. Howe's focus was wholly on Jillian as she cartwheeled through the air, fifteen feet up. "In fifth grade, we turn everything over to the kids. Louise designed them and the class built them."

"Really? Wow." Mr. Noble gave a tip of a hat to Louise while keeping his eye on Jillian. "Your set is amazing for flying. Most productions forget about the three-dimensional aspects of the play and just do one level. And I really like the New York skyline twist. Never saw that before."

Louise blushed. She'd considered possible flight movements when she designed the set, but it had been only a few minutes of thought, now lost in a flood of all the other considerations such as visual impact, ease of construction, cost, movability, and convertibility. The little loft area of Wendy's bed was actually the flipside of the *Jolly Roger*'s poop deck, the ship's railing hidden behind the princess bed. The two sets of steps joined together to make the *Jolly Roger*'s grand staircase. The long elevated landing between the steps turned to become the gun ports. She'd actually been feeling guilty that she'd designed something fairly plain considering some of the work she'd done on sets for their videos. Then again, those sets had been virtual and didn't need to be moved down twelve stories when done.

Because the four actors were taking turns getting individual instructions, they didn't take a break until the third-period bell.

"It's been three hours!" Jillian cried after Louise updated her on the series of failures to connect with Lain. "Who the hell is she talking to?"

"Earth."

"All of Earth?" Jillian flailed slightly on the stage floor, too tired to do more of a display of frustration.

"Everyone she knows only has one day a month to call her."

"We're running out of time. We only have until midnight and it's almost eleven already. Half the day is gone."

"We'll just keep calling until we get through," Louise said.

"Peter!" Mr. Noble called.

"Coming!" Jillian leapt up and bounded lightly onto stage as if she weren't tired and struck a pose. "What need do you have of the great Peter Pan?"

Louise was still wondering why Jillian thought she was the brave one. She didn't feel brave. Her heart jumped in her chest every time she hit redial. The only thing she'd done all morning was listen to busy signals. Jillian seemed fearless, leaping into the air, doing flips and cartwheels, sparring verbally with Mr. Noble while trading lines with Elle.

Did Jillian really think she was the one that led the way? Louise always thought of Jillian as the one who led. It was because Jillian wanted to be a movie director that they did the videos.

Distracted, she wasn't prepared for the phone to actually ring and then be answered before it rang a second time.

"Dr. Shenske's residence; can I help you?" a man's voice snapped over the speaker. "Hello? Anyone there? Oh, freaking hell, stupid phones!"

"Hello? I'm here!" Louise cried before he could hang up. She dropped her voice to a lower, more adult pitch. She should have brought Tesla to act as a filter. "I—I need to talk to Lain Shenske."

"Dr. Shenske is busy at the moment. She's supervising loading the van with botanical specimens. There was a big twenty-car pileup on I-279, so the van is way behind schedule. It will be at least two hours until she can come to the phone. I'm fielding all calls from Earth."

"Who are you?"

"I'm Richard Hill. I'm a post-doc from Cornell; I'm doing research for Dr. Karen Purcell. I'm helping out now, but I'm going have to fly shortly if I want to go back to Earth today. Startup waits for no man."

"I really need to talk to her. This is an emergency. Life and death."

"Oh, geez, you interns are all the same. You're the third to call this morning. Suck it up and learn how to deal with standard procedures. There's no cutting corners in field research paperwork." And he hung up on her.

Louise stared at the phone, dismayed. Should she call back? Try to explain before he hung up on her again? No, the man would hang up as soon as he recognized her voice. She should hook Tesla into the loop and use his filters to disguise her voice. Actually, she could get Tesla to do the calling and have him loop her into the conversation only if he actually got through to a human.

So the day went. The telephone number was busy every time Louise tried, except for one time when the connection went through and she heard someone shouting in the distance. "Watch! Watch! Don't yank out the leads or the spell will collapse!" a woman cried and then they were disconnected.

Louise eyed the phone. If Pittsburgh was on Earth, how were they casting spells? Did Lain have a magic generator, too? Did this mean Lain knew Kensbock? Did Lain know where the M.I.T. student was?

"We have time for one more run. Can we give it a go?" Mr. Noble called.

Louise had been working on lighting and music to go with the action as she endlessly failed to talk to Lain. She waited until everyone was in their places and then dimmed all the lights except the nursery's nightlights. She was aware that Mr. Noble and Mr. Howe had come to bracket her as she stood on a stool and worked the control boards. There were half a dozen monitors on the system. There were cameras that showed the audience and what was onstage. There was the screen that showed the programming for the lift-line robotic operators. The controls for the Tinker Bell projector. The sound mixing display. And her phone, cycling through dial, busy signal, disconnection.

This would be the worst possible moment for the phone call to actually go through.

Trying to ignore her phone, she cued in the gleaming figure inside a ball of light that represented Tinker Bell. She zoomed the gleaming circle about the nursery, leaving a contrail of glittering motes.

"Oh wow," Mr. Noble breathed. "That is cool. I've never seen that before. What are you using?"

"A holographic pinpoint projector." Louise moved the light about as "Tinker Bell" searched for Peter Pan's lost shadow.

"Where'd you get it?" Mr. Noble whispered.

"I made it," she admitted since Mr. Howe was standing right

there. "I recorded a silhouette of my Barbie doll using stop-action for the wings' flapping and then looped it."

"Oh! Really?" It was impossible to judge if his whispered question was just surprise or disbelief.

"This is a school for the gifted, Mr. Noble," Mr. Howe said.

Onstage, the window opened and Jillian peered in, impossibly high and half upside-down. Then she flew in and landed in a crouch. She was just in T-shirt and jeans, but she'd mussed her hair so she looked half feral.

"Tinker Bell," Jillian gave a stage whisper as she slinked across the nursery like something wild. "Tink, are you there?"

"You two are scary good," Mr. Noble whispered.

Louise caught the flash of light on the auditorium camera as someone opened the door and stepped into the darkened room. She didn't catch who it was, but she had the sudden sense of impending doom. She glanced at her phone. It was dialing again. She made a big sweeping gesture with her right to cue up Tinker Bell's gentle tinkle of bells that was J.M. Barrie's "fairy language" and with her left quietly cancelled the phone call.

After Jillian did Peter's joyous flight at finding his shadow, she shortcut through the scene to get to the flying. "I'll teach you how to jump on the wind's back and then away we go."

Carlos and Darius were still awkward, despite the day's work, but luckily in a silly, laughable way. Elle was graceful and refined. Jillian managed to impart boyish swagger as she zoomed about the stage as if she had been born with wings.

As Jillian landed, crying "Now come!" and pointing out the open nursery window, Louise's phone rang. Mr. Howe looked down at her phone as "Mom" displayed on the screen.

"Louise," he chided.

"I was expecting my mom to call, so I had it out," Louise lied. "Can I answer?"

The lone person in the audience clapped, distracting him.

He huffed. "Yes. Since it's your mother." And he stalked out to see who was on in the auditorium, applauding.

"Hello?" Louise tentatively answered her phone.

"Louise, I forgot all about the fact that you two need gowns for the gala." Her mother sounded like she was juggling a hundred things at once. Death would fall on anyone that made her drop what she had in midair.

"Gowns?" Louise cautiously tried to weasel out of whatever her mother had planned.

"Gowns, like dresses, only fancier."

Louise gasped as she realized who had to be in the dark auditorium. "You want Aunt Kitty to take us shopping?"

"I called the school and let them know that she was picking you up. I didn't want you to miss her."

Louise brought up the auditorium lights and verified her guess. "She's here now."

"Be good for your aunt. Love you." And she hung up with no idea that she'd just thrown all their plans into ruin.

There was a conspiracy to put little girls in pink and yards of tulle. It was tempting to agree to the first dozen they saw, but since they'd failed to reach Lain for almost fifteen hours, they held their ground. On the fourth store, they found a black satin full-length dress that the twins loved at first sight. It had a ruched sleeveless bodice and empire waistline wrapped with a matching black pleated sash.

"Are you sure?" Aunt Kitty asked a dozen times. "It's awfully grown-up."

"It's perfect." Jillian turned in a circle to show it off to full effect.

Aunt Kitty took a video and sent it to their mother. "We'll see what she thinks."

A minute later a firm "No black, it's not a funeral" text came back.

Two stores later, just shy of closing hours, they found two matching tea-length dresses of soft shimmering yellow with wide black belts. The dresses had poof skirts thanks to layers of crinoline but were fully lined, so the itchy material didn't touch bare skin. With their mother's texted approval, the dresses were bought and they headed home, exhausted.

They spent the last hour getting ready for bed with phones in hand, dialing, disconnecting at the first tone of the busy signal, redialing. The minutes ticked down and then Shutdown was over.

They stared numbly at the clock as it turned to midnight.

"What do we do?" Jillian asked.

Louise called April, who answered on the first ring.

"Hello?"

"Ugh!" Louise flopped back in bed. If April answered, she wasn't on Elfhome.

"Hello?" April said again.

"It's us," Louise said.

"Oh." It wasn't a good sounding "oh" but a "but I've got bad news" kind of "oh."

"What happened? Is it Alexander? Did something happen to her?"

"No, no, it's that I didn't get across the border." April sounded tired, but not stressed, yet somehow Louise was sure that she had horrible news. "I'd gone to Cranberry to try and get across. Normally it's the best bet. There was a shoot-out on Veterans Bridge, though, and things got all screwed up."

"A shoot-out?" The post-doc had mentioned a twenty-car accident but nothing about a shoot-out.

"I'm not sure what happened—the details are really sketchy—but apparently there was a big pileup on Veterans Bridge. There was a heavily armed group of smugglers in one of the cars, and they tried to kill the cops that showed up to direct traffic. They shot at least one person, and they rigged a bomb to take out the bridge. The EIA bomb squad managed to defuse it. Then the rescue teams used Earth-based life-flight helicopters to fly out the wounded."

All of which would have stopped traffic incoming from Cranberry completely.

"I did get through to my parents and cousins," April continued. "At first they didn't know whom I was talking about. I think my mom is going senile early; Old Man Bell saved my life, and she didn't remember him at all. She was no help. I had more luck with my cousin, Ellen. It took ten minutes of describing the hotel on Neville Island, Old Man Bell, and his two grandchildren who build go-carts, for her to figure out who I meant. Apparently Alexander doesn't use her real name."

"What name does she use?" Dufae would be just as dangerous.

"Tinker."

"Tinker?" Louise echoed, mystified.

"As in Tinker Bell?" Jillian cried. "Eewww."

"She doesn't seem to use a last name. I think she just goes by Tinker. And Orville is Oilcan. My cousin saw the two of them last week. They're racing hoverbikes professionally."

"Hoverbikes?"

"Alex invented them!" April sounded surprised and proud. "They use magic to hover, but they also have a gasoline engine. I'm not sure I understood that part completely. Racing them is a big sport event that everyone follows. Ellen says that she only knows it's the same two kids because my folks lived down the street from them for years. She thinks that Sparrow's people are going to have a hard time finding her if all they know is her real name."

"How much did you tell your cousin?" Louise cried.

"Not everything." April sighed. "Nothing about you two. But it was getting obvious that I wasn't going to get through, and I didn't want Ellen drawing attention to herself or Alexander by talking to the wrong person. I warned her that it's not safe to talk to the EIA or the police or anyone else outside the family. I told her that this is a widespread conspiracy, and it being elves, their moles could have been put into place shortly after the first Startup. The first time I talked to her, she thought I was an utter loon."

"And the second time?" Because it sounded like there was a second phone call that had gone totally differently than the first.

"She heard on the news that one of the *sekasha* had been killed, and Windwolf was missing."

"Oh no! Which one?" Oh, please God, not Pony!

"I don't know. It might make the Earth news tomorrow. I wasn't thinking about the elves. I was worried about Alexander."

Louise tried to take comfort knowing that at least Alexander was well hidden. But what if Sparrow's trap succeeded? What if both Windwolf and Pony were dead? Tears started to burn in her eyes.

"Ellen promised me that she'll find where Alexander lives and go see her and tell her about Sparrow. And she'll tell her that I'm willing to have her come live with me in New York. I'm not sure if Alex will take me up on the offer. I would have at eighteen, but I always thought of Earth as my home, not Elfhome."

Louise would jump at a chance to visit Elfhome, but to stay? To leave behind everyone she knew? No. If Alexander were anything like her and Jillian, she would never leave her grandfather and Orville.

"Ellen will warn her," April repeated firmly. "You can stop worrying."

They said good-bye and hung up, feeling raw and drained. April was right in that there was nothing they could do now until next Shutdown. In the meantime, they still had the babies to save.

24: JOY

The news was full of the attack on Windwolf and his disappearance. Lacking concrete details, the media filled in with speculation. What was known as fact was that the viceroy and his bodyguards had been traveling in two separate Rolls-Royces from the south edge of the Rim. At some point the two vehicles had been separated. Near dawn, Windwolf's car was found in an area called Fairywood, along with the body of his driver. To Louise's guilty relief, the *sekasha* that had been killed was Hawk Scream; the warrior's neck had been broken by a large animal. Since the police were involved in the shoot-out on Veterans Bridge, the search for Windwolf had been left to the EIA.

Knowing that the very people that attacked Windwolf also controlled the EIA, Louise was afraid that he might be dead. The only thing that gave her hope was an odd dream she had about him surviving the night without magic to protect him.

Certainly the media had decided that the viceroy was dead; they debated who would replace Windwolf and what his death would mean to Pittsburgh. Would the elves declare war on the humans? Should the UN pull in extra troops just in case to protect the human population? Or would the elves consider that a sign of aggression? Analysts pointed out that this wasn't the first time that a *sekasha* had been killed by an animal while guarding Windwolf. Five years earlier, humans had a caged saurus on display at the fairgrounds. When the massive lizard broke free, it had wounded the viceroy and mauled one of his bodyguards before Windwolf killed it with a flame strike. The elves hadn't threatened war at the time; they had simply deported the humans responsible.

Other sources, though, pointed out that Windwolf had been the one who meted out the punishment on the criminally negligent. Sparrow's sense of justice was unknown. Analysts were optimistic. Louise was not.

It was surreal to stand on the train platform, hear the endless speculation, and *know* what the rest of the world didn't. Surely this is what a sighted person would feel like in a country of blind people.

Sparrow would take command of the Westernlands until Queen Soulful Ember could choose a new viceroy. Between the moles in the EIA and her leadership of the Elves, Pittsburgh had fallen into the hands of the very people who had attacked Windwolf. There had been a reason that Sparrow wanted Windwolf dead. It may have been solely for the ability to start a war. By secretly controlling both sides, Sparrow could easily manipulate conflicts until humans and elves were at each other's throats.

Zahara ambushed them at the top of the stairs to the fifth-grade floor. "Did you see the news?"

"About Windwolf?" Louise felt guilty. Guilty that she hadn't been able to warn anyone on Elfhome. Guilty that she hadn't told any of her friends. Guilty that they needed to go on acting like they knew nothing about forces of evil trying to destroy the peace that existed between humans and elves.

"No. Not that. That sucks. I mean about Nigel Reid."

"What happened to Nigel?" Louise cried. The last twenty-four hours had been nothing but bad news.

"He's going to Elfhome!" Zahara obviously thought this was good news. "NBC announced it this morning! He's going to be doing a show called *Chased by Monsters*, and they're going to start filming next Shutdown."

"Last I heard, he was filming the pilot here on Earth." The twins had verified Aunt Kitty's news while arranging to give Nigel the gossamer call at the gala.

"What? No. The network pulled serious strings yesterday and pushed the visas through."

"Why?" Louise cried. "This is the worse time possible for him to go!"

"Taggart," Jillian muttered darkly.

"Huh?" Zahara was lost in the conversation.

"Taggart is a famous war correspondent," Jillian explained. "He left CNN to team up with Nigel to do nature documentaries. NBC must be counting on war breaking out and want someone there that can cover it for them."

"Why would a war break out?" Zahara asked.

The bell for homeroom saved Louise from having to answer.

With the addition of Iggy and three of his biggest pirate class-mates, they were trooped downstairs to the auditorium for an entire day of flying. They were going to choreograph the fight scene on the *Jolly Roger*. The main focus of the battle was Hook and Peter's duel, but the three Darling children would flit about on the edges, having their own moments as they took on and conquered a pirate. Louise had written big sweeping fight music for the battle, but it needed logical pauses in the score for Jillian and the others to deliver their lines.

Louise took her place at the control board and opened up a browser to the Internet. As Zahara claimed, NBC stated that Nigel would be sent to Elfhome next Shutdown to film *Chased by Monsters*. Horrible, horrible title for such a noble, gentle, and intelligent man. What was he thinking? She checked Nigel's website. He had the same information that he'd featured a week ago. It was possible that the sudden change had flooded him with things that needed to be done since he had only twenty-some days to prepare for filming on another planet and get to the Pittsburgh border. The NBC press release said nothing about Windwolf or Taggart or EIA or visa problems. Zahara's state-ment about the network pulling strings sounded right, but where would she get that idea, since she clearly wasn't thinking about political ramifications?

Louise checked Jello Shots. The website was in furious debate. The source of Zahara's comment was obvious as the fans weighed in on how NBC had rammed Nigel through the EIA's visa bottleneck. What would their beloved Lemon-Lime do about Windwolf's death? Would Lemon-Lime ignore it and continue on with Prince Yard-stick or herald in Sparrow as the new viceroy of the Westernlands?

The question made Louise want to rage. She would never acknowledge Sparrow's character, Jerked, as viceroy, even if the real person claimed the title. Prince Yardstick would survive the attack in their videos.

A new thread popped up: Did Lemon-Lime put Nigel in the last video knowing that Taggart would be needed on Elfhome?

Louise stared at the heading in dismay and anger. They had made the video before they had overheard Sparrow plotting. And certainly, they had never expected to be able to influence anyone to the point of getting Nigel a visa to Elfhome. If they'd known all that was coming and the extent of their fame...

They did know what was going on. They knew Sparrow and others were kidnapping scientists to build a secret gate between worlds. They knew that the scientists were balking when they discovered that their work would plunge Elfhome into war. They knew that Sparrow and Ambassador Feng had been behind the plot to kill Windwolf. They knew that there were moles in the EIA, using that agency to keep out anyone who might investigate their activities.

They knew. And as Lemon-Lime, they could do something about it.

Louise took a deep, cleansing breath. Right. Lemon-Lime was going on the warpath. It was a good thing that she needed to write fight music already.

"You did what?" Jillian cried as they detoured to the grocery store after school. It was odd walking through the store knowing that they could afford to buy anything they wanted.

"I had a dream last night that Windwolf survived the attack. Peter Pan and Tinker Bell—the fairy, not our sister—saved him while riding hoverbikes, so I turned it into a video. I called it *The Queen's Salvage.*"

"What—what—what?"

"I think Orville was supposed to be Peter Pan in my dream because Tinker Bell looked like Alexander." She picked up a bag of cheddar-flavored goldfish crackers. Their mother usually insisted on healthy snacks like carrots and grapes.

"This is all kinds of wrong. First off, we don't know if Windwolf survived."

"No one will know until next Shutdown, but everyone is acting like he was killed. If we don't remind people that he might be alive, the UN is going to steamroll through several votes, including the quarantine zone expansion, which they were putting on hold. Oh! Chocolate-covered strawberries."

"*Okay.*" Jillian looked at her as if she'd grown a second head.

Louise shook the strawberries at Jillian. "The person most vocal about pushing through the votes? Ambassador Feng. They're using this attack to leverage what they want. And we've got to stop them."

"Us?"

"We're the only ones that seem to know the truth." Louise added the strawberries to her basket.

"What if they get mad and start to look for us?"

"Jello Shots have been trying to figure out who we are for the last two years. We apparently are like world-class ninjas because a hundred thousand geeks haven't been able to find a clue."

"I don't know if that's scary or sad."

"I think it's both." Louise picked up premium beef jerky that their mother would never, never buy because of how horribly expensive it was.

"Yeah, both." Jillian eyed the basket. "Why are you buying so much junk? You know we'll have to hide it all."

"Because we can," Louise said. "Besides, I want something in case we get hungry. We've got lots of work to do. Thank God we're nearly done with saving the babies."

"So this video is of Peter Pan and Tinker Bell saving Windwolf?"

Louise laughed. "No, I just riffed on my dream. Two Pittsburghers save him. I don't even name them. The guy is dressed up as an African explorer. The girl looks like Tinker Bell with the blond hair and the breasts, but she has a flamethrower. They kill this saurus chasing Windwolf and take him to the Neighborhood of Make-Believe."

"That is so weird. Why?"

"I had a dream about Nigel in Pittsburgh. I just smashed the two dreams together to protect Alexander."

"Okay, that works." They stopped in the kitchen equipment aisle and considered the tools. They needed heavy gloves, tongs, and something to stand in for the rack holding the vials of frozen embryos so they could practice stealing them out of the liquid nitrogen vaults. "Did you check on the snake?"

"Yes, we can pick it up tomorrow afternoon. All we need to do is make sure ice doesn't melt in the *nactka* and we're ready to roll."

They'd been so upset the night of the robbery that they'd just brought the *nactka* home inside the gift-shop box and hidden it away in the back of their closet. There it had stayed, untouched.

They set up for the experiment on their desk, arranging the magic generator, oven mitts, scissors, a thermometer, and a glass of normal ice. They'd toyed with stealing a cup of liquid nitrogen out of the chemistry lab at school, but the long commute on the crowded train made it unsafe and impractical.

Her first impression of the *nactka*, as Louise lifted it out of its box, remained of a delicately etched monster-size egg. According to the codex, much like Dufae's box, it required magic to open and close, but once sealed, it would hold whatever was inside in stasis without magic. Louise suspected—if she had translated the Elvish and understood quantum physics as well as she thought—that the device acted like a miniature gate, teleporting whatever was inside from the moment the *nactka* was sealed to the moment that it was unsealed.

They set the *nactka* carefully on the magic generator. While Jillian filmed the experiments, Louise took an outside reading of it with the thermometer and made note that it was the same temperature as the room.

"We need to test the ice before it melts." Jillian pointed her new camera at the glass filled with ice.

"I'm hurrying." Louise spoke the keyword to unseal the *nactka*.

The dome of the device cracked at the lines and unfolded like a flower, as if the cream-colored shell was on hinges. They both yelped in surprise as a creature popped up out of the trap and hissed angrily. Before Louise could get a clear look at it, the creature sprang to the edge of the desk, then to her footboard, and then bounced off the glass of the window.

"What is it?" Jillian backed way, trying to film the animal as it bounced around the room like a rubber ball.

"Umm." Louise got the impression of a small snaky body and a mouth full of teeth. No snake she'd ever seen moved with leaps and bounds. It landed back on the desk beside the *nactka* and shoved it aside to stand on the magic generator. "I don't know."

Louise tore open the bag of goldfish crackers and put one of the bright orange fish on the edge of the desk. She softly snapped her fingers; might as well start training it now. "Cracker?"

She sat on her bed, giving the creature an opportunity to investigate the food.

"I don't think snakes eat crackers." Jillian worked the zoom controls on her camera.

The creature sniffed loudly and then darted forward to snatch up the goldfish. It opened wide and shoved the cracker into its surprisingly large mouth.

"I don't think it's a snake." Louise slid another goldfish onto the edge of the desk after the creature retreated back to the generator. She snapped her fingers together softly. "Cracker? Snakes don't have legs."

"Gecko?" Jillian guessed.

The goldfish was snatched up, crammed into the mouth full of teeth, and chomped loudly. Crumbs rained down on the desktop to be picked up with delicate claw-tipped fingers.

"I-I don't think geckos have hands."

Jillian attempted to keep filming and turn on her tablet. "Logically, it's most likely an Elfhome species of lizard, meaning that it's dependent on magic to exist, which is why it's staying near the generator."

"I think it looks—" Louise squeaked as the thing suddenly leapt onto her shoulder.

They eyed each other nearly nose to nose. It was only about six inches long, covered in scales of a delicate rose color. It clung to her with tiny little pinpricks as claws poked through her shirt. There were five claws on each foot. It had a mane of long slender filaments that seemed too thick to be hair.

It snapped its tiny fingers, opened its wide mouth full of teeth, and said in a tiny, childlike voice, "Cracker!"

Louise blinked in surprise and then fumbled out a small handful of goldfish and held them up to the creature, forgetting to give the training prompt.

It used both front paws to grab up the crackers and shove them all into its mouth, one by one, at express speed. When Louise's palm was empty, the creature snapped its fingers again and commanded, "Cracker!"

"It can talk!" Jillian whispered.

"She has thumbs." Louise fed it another cracker while carefully shifting closer to the generator.

"She?"

"She feels like a girl to me." Louise wondered if the crackers were actually good for the little thing.

The creature snapped her fingers and commanded, "Cracker!"

"Where are the strawberries?" Louise asked.

"Here!" Jillian found the clear plastic container with the chocolate-dipped strawberries.

Chocolate could be fatal to dogs, so Louise picked it off.

"Cracker!" There was impatient snapping of tiny fingers. "Cracker!"

Louise offered the bare strawberry. A giant of its type, the fruit dwarfed the head of the little creature that eyed it dubiously. It looked from Louise to the massive strawberry to Louise and then back to the fruit.

"Strawberry." Louise took a bite to show that it was edible. "Strawberry?"

The creature plucked the fruit out of her hand, turned it around and around in puzzled study, and then sniffed it. It took one cautious nibble and then, eyes going wide, crammed the entire fruit into its mouth.

"Oh, she's so cute." Jillian zoomed in with her camera. "Nom, nom, nom, nom. But what is she?"

"You know, she looks like one of those dragons on Chinese menus."

The dragon looked up. "Nom, nom, nom, nom." It snapped its fingers. "Strawberry!"

They took turns feeding her the strawberries and looking up information on Elfhome dragons.

"There's almost nothing here," Jillian complained.

"While apparently dragons vary in size, they are reported to be very large, fire-breathing, and dangerous," Louise read what she found aloud. "Approach with caution. Maybe she's a baby dragon."

"Do you think she can breathe fire?" Jillian asked.

They stared at the baby dragon who was munching on the last strawberry.

"Nom, nom, nom." She licked her fingers and then snapped them. "Cracker!"

"She eats a lot," Jillian said.

Louise broke open the bag of beef jerky. The baby dragon had learned that new containers equaled new food. The little creature grasped the bag of beef jerky in one hand and with the other was stuffing pieces of the dried meat into its mouth as fast as it could chew. "Nom, nom, nom!"

"Good thing you got so many snacks," Jillian said.

"We should give her a name."

"We're keeping her? What do we tell Mom and Dad?"

"We don't have to tell them. We'll keep her in our room. We could get a little aquarium for her when we're at school."

Jillian shook her head. "That's not going to work. Sooner or later, they're going to find out."

"We just need to buy some time until we can figure out what to tell them. We can come up with some story about finding her in the subway or something." It couldn't be "buying," because they'd try to make them take the dragon back to the mythical store. There was also the uneasy question of where they'd gotten the money to buy an exotic pet. "Think of it as a challenge."

Jillian flopped onto her bed. "I never thought I'd get tired of lying."

"We need to name her."

"Let's call her Greedy Gut." Jillian patted the bed beside her. "Greedy Gut! Greedy Gut!"

The baby dragon stuck out its tongue and blew a raspberry.

"I don't think she likes that name."

So while the baby dragon polished off the beef jerky, they tried out names. They had named lots of characters in the past, but nothing alive with a personality that they couldn't change at whim.

Louise felt like a name was floating on the edge of her awareness, but she couldn't quite grasp it. "It should be something bright, and happy, and female."

"Bossy." Jillian got another raspberry for the suggestion. "She reminds me of some senile old grandmother."

The name finally came within reach. "Joy. I think her name is Joy." No raspberry. "See, she likes it."

Jillian came to eye the baby dragon. "No, she's just falling asleep now that all the food is gone. I think her name is Bottomless Pit."

"Her name is Joy," Louise repeated more firmly. "And you can't blame her for being hungry; she hasn't had anything to eat for hundreds of years."

Jillian gasped. "Oh my God! Lou! What's in the other eleven *nactka* still in the box?"

"Oh no!" Louise leapt to the codex and quickly looked up the longest passage regarding the device. "Twelve loaded *nactka*! They all have something in them!"

"Eleven more like her?" Jillian eyed the baby dragon. "What would we do with twelve of them?"

Louise was amazed that Jillian even asked the question. "She's obviously very intelligent. She might even be smarter than a human. It's been—what—five minutes and she already knows three words of English."

"'Nom, nom, nom' is not a word," Jillian said.

"We need to get them out of the box!"

"What if the elves took the box? They were going to take three items."

They hacked into the museum and checked the security monitors, but the box had always been screened from the cameras. There was no way of telling if the box was still there.

"They would have to tell France that the elves took the box." Louise dove into the e-mail system to sift through the curator's mailbox. Dated late Friday night was an e-mail to the curator at the Louvre explaining that the elves had asked for the return of the box. Not surprisingly, there was no answer until early Monday morning Eastern Standard Time—or normal business hours for Greenwich time—objecting and asking the AMNH not to allow the elves to take the box. The answer was short and simple: the elves had already returned to Elfhome with it.

The Louvre sent back a caustic answer that ended with, "Thankfully the EIA spared us the loss of the tiara."

Jillian swore softly. "That's right. The EIA told the French just to send the box."

Louise checked on the other two items. They were both small pieces of jewelry, obviously worth a good deal in terms of gold and gems but otherwise insignificant. "These are decoys. If they just took the box, everyone would talk only about it, but with the obviously worthwhile items, the box isn't interesting."

"If they wanted it, does that mean they know what's in it?"

"Dufae said he stole the box on Elfhome. Maybe he stole it from Sparrow."

Joy had crawled into Louise's lap and fallen asleep. She looked so cute asleep. She was sprawled on her back, front paws on her full tummy and one back leg twitching in time with her soft little snores. Louise stroked one finger over Joy's buttery-soft hide. The baby dragon nuzzled into her palm with a small purr and then lapsed back into snores.

What was Sparrow going to do with the other eleven?

25: GOING TO SEE A MAN ABOUT A DOG

"Hello," the receptionist said as the twins walked through the door to their father's clinic. According to the human resources records, her name was Laura Runkle. She'd only recently graduated from business school and started working at the clinic a month ago. She was young, pretty, and very uncertain about her power. Her face and tone said, "Are you lost?"

Louise had Tesla take up an "off-duty" position beside one of the waiting room chairs, and then made a visible production of settling into said chair. She put on her reading glasses, flipped through the projected pages of her holographic book, and squirmed into the chair to read.

Jillian aimed the receptionist's attention on Louise by staring at her intently and then sighing loudly. "Bookworm." And then, having established that Louise was the quiet one of the twins, Jillian turned brightly to the receptionist. "Hi, I'm Jillian Mayer. I'm here to see my dad. He works here."

The receptionist started to smile, and then she came to a full, horrified stop. "Oh! You're George's twins."

Unsaid was "You're the two that blew themselves up." Really, do it once and people don't let you live it down.

"Yup!" Jillian juggled the big box she was carrying, nearly spilling it, to point in the direction of their father's office. "Our dad is this way—right? I got something to show him." She started to march down the hall, all but commanding that she be followed.

235

"Wait. I don't know if he's back there!" The receptionist glanced at Louise, who seemed nose deep in a book. Swallowing the bait, she headed after Jillian. "Which one were you again?"

Louise counted to five, and the shrieks started. According to Laura's social network page, she was terrified of snakes. While Louise loved the ball python they'd found at a small and possibly illegal pet store, Jillian could better act out "accidentally" dropping the box and setting the snake free.

"Follow," Louise told Tesla and hurried down the hallway toward the cryo-room. They had practiced the extraction at home, using all stand-in material. It should take her only three minutes, but that was assuming that nothing went wrong. Louise swiped the copy of their father's keycard through the lock. Jillian could keep the office distracted for several minutes but probably not more than five.

There were skintight gloves, big blue protective gloves, a heavy lined apron, and a full-face plastic facemask. She pulled them on quickly as she scanned the blue-capped cryogenic tanks. In an odd design flaw of the security system, there was no camera in the room. They hadn't been able to determine how the tanks were labeled. There were two tall square units and two tall cylinder tanks and then a host of short tanks tucked under a work counter. The taller units were simply labeled "1" or "2," while the short ones counted up to "6." She knew that the babies were stored as H-2-3-2-753694. The initial seemed to indicate a size, but which of the three units labeled "2" was "H"?

"Hello?" Joy suddenly appeared on one of the small tanks under the counter. "Who's there?" She patted the side of the tank, claws clicking. "Hello?" Without an aquarium for her, they'd been forced to keep her locked in Tesla's storage compartment. Luckily, like any baby animal, Joy mostly ate and slept.

"Shhh!" Louise cried. Why did the baby dragon have to wake up now? Louise picked up Joy and put her on her shoulder. The tank was a "2." Was it the right one?

The small tank was on wheels. She rolled it out from under the counter. Louise swiped her father's keycard through the reader on the cap and typed in 753694. If the vial was inside, the lock would acknowledge the code...and unfortunately make a record that it had been accessed.

The reader blinked from red to green. It was the right tank.

Louise flipped up the lid and took out the polyurethane cap under the lid. Instantly the air hitting the opened pit turned to misty clouds. There were six wire handles of the racks suspended within the liquid nitrogen. Each was etched with a number. She wanted the second box off the third rack. She unhooked the handle labeled "3" and carefully raised up the rack, wisps of freezing air flowing off it. On the rack were five little boxes inside wire frames, pegged into place by a restraining bar. She removed the bar and wriggled free the second box. She slid off the lid to the box, revealing four frozen vials standing inside slots. She took the first one out and peered closely at the label.

"Hello?" Joy pointed at the one on the far end. "Who's there?"

Louise put the first vial back into the stand and checked the end vial. 753694. "Score!"

She opened up Tesla's storage compartment and used the keyword to open the *nactka*. Once the vial was safe inside, she activated it. The babies safe, she replaced the lid on the vial box, put it back into the rack, put the retaining bar back on, and carefully lowered the rack back into the liquid nitrogen. She was pushing the tank back under the counter when she realized she'd forgotten to put the polyurethane cap back into place.

Swearing, she pulled the tank back, flipped up the lid and put the cap in place.

She started to shake once she and Tesla were back in the hallway, Joy tucked into the wide front pocket of Louise's hoodie with a bag of Cheerios to keep her quiet. The shrieks were still at full volume, and dozens of loud adult voices were coming from the direction of their father's office.

Jillian was still in full distraction mode. Time for damage control.

Laura Runkle was the one shrieking. She was standing on a desk, prancing, as if she were trying to run up invisible stairs to get even higher. Several other people were sitting on their desks, trying to look nonchalant but asking loudly, "But is it poisonous?" as if such a thing was in the range of possibilities.

Their dad was at least standing on the floor, his back to the wall, looking terrified while trying to seem in control.

Louise felt guilty. It had never occurred to them that their father might be scared of snakes, too.

Her entrance line was "What happened?"

Jillian glanced up and managed not to grin ear to ear with triumph. "I dropped the box." She did a little voice waver of distress. "Wiggly got loose."

"Oh no!" It was Louise's last scripted line. At this point she was supposed to bravely pick the snake up and put it back in the box. She scanned the room, but the python was nowhere to be seen.

They'd rehearsed "the distraction" in their bedroom with a rolled-up towel cord standing in as "Wiggly." They'd discovered they couldn't contain Joy anywhere. Somehow she escaped from everything they put her into except Tesla's storage compartment with a lot of snacks. With her loose, they couldn't practice letting the real snake loose and catching it again. Somehow they'd overlooked the fact that the python might actively attempt to escape. The videos they'd watched on handling big constrictors all featured very slow-moving snakes.

She glanced questioning to Jillian, who shrugged and spread her hands.

"Louise." Their father's voice cracked. "Get the snake and put it in the box. Please! Now!"

"Okay," she said to at least seem like she was obeying him. She dropped down to hands and knees to peer under desks and behind filing cabinets. So many places it could hide.

"Is it poisonous?" one of the men sitting on a desk asked.

"No, it's a constrictor." Jillian joined Louise on the floor. "They kill their prey by coiling around it and choking it to death."

The man had been extending his foot down, and he paused, freezing in place. "Kill its prey?"

Where was the python hiding? There were many nooks and crannies, but most of them Jillian would have seen the snake moving across the floor to reach. The box canted sideways marked where Jillian dropped it. The desk that Laura Runkle was standing on, still screaming, was next to it. Just beyond the desk was a door marked "Masturbatory Chamber." She had a weirdly strong feeling that the snake must have slipped unnoticed into the room beyond.

Her father let out a yelp as she opened the door and stepped into the room.

The snake was on the floor, as she expected, coiled in a pair of men's pinstripe trousers. There was a businessman perched on a table, clutching a magazine to his front.

"No! No! Don't come in!" the businessman cried.

And her father snatched Louise up and carried her out of the room.

"I need to get the snake." She squirmed in his hold.

"I will get it," he said firmly.

"But—but—" She didn't want to say he was scared of it, but obviously he was.

"I will deal with it." He caught Jillian by the shoulder as he walked past her and pulled her in his wake. He carried Louise all the way to the back of the warren of cubicles and sat her down in a chair. "Stay here."

A minute later he returned, looking ashen but holding the box.

"I'm sorry, Daddy," Louise said. "I didn't know you—you didn't like snakes."

"I grew up in rattlesnake country. I know that they're not the same, but fear is not always rational. I'm sorry. I know you want a pet, but Daddy just can't deal with the idea of a snake in the house."

Tesla kept faltering as they backtracked to the pet store, returned the snake, and made their way to the subway. She had forgotten to turn off the magic generator. She was afraid he was breaking down, but she didn't want to call attention to it. If their father decided he could troubleshoot Tesla, he might find all her changes to Tesla's programming and the *nactka* in his storage bin.

Luckily, just as they reached the stairs down to the subway, their father's work called and he wasn't able to push off their demands.

"Let me put my kids on the express and then I'll be back."

He kissed them both on top of their heads. "Go home. Straight home. I'll be tracking Tesla and will be worried until I see he's home."

Jillian barely waited for their father to be out of earshot. "You got it?"

Louise nodded, watching Tesla's head twist and turn. The subway train came rumbling in and the robotic dog shuddered and pressed up against her.

"Come on, boy." She patted the wide shoulder. "Keep it together until we get home."

If Tesla broke down before then, they were going to have a

complete mess on their hands. There was no way they could abandon such an expensive machine on the subway system, but if they had to call their parents, they could discover everything.

She pulled Tesla toward the subway train and, as the door opened, dragged him on board. "Just a little longer, Tesla. Please. We need to get home."

By the time they hit their stop, Tesla was walking in a wavering line, drifting this way and that on the sidewalk. As they neared the house, Louise stopped being worried about getting home and started to feel bad for the robotic dog. What if they'd totally broken him so he couldn't be fixed? She'd thought she would be happy to be free from an ever-present spy, but the idea of him going away completely was making her eyes burn.

At the corner of their street, he came to a complete halt.

"Tesla!" she cried.

"Stupid dog." Jillian caught him by the collar and tried to pull him toward their house.

The dog flinched. "But it's so big!" he said in his Christopher Robin voice. "It just keeps going and going. And where is this home we're going to? How far away is it?"

"Tesla?" Louise said.

He cocked his head. "What? We think it's a reasonable question. We want to stop and see something. Everything is so interesting, but we keep on moving! Why can't we stop here and look, just for a minute?"

"Oh. My. God," Jillian whispered as Louise stared open-mouthed at the dog.

There was movement in Louise's pocket. Joy poked her head out. "Strawberry."

Tesla cocked his head at the baby dragon. "Hello."

"Hello!" Joy patted Tesla's black nose inches from her. "Who's there?"

Louise took a deep breath as she remembered that Joy had said the same phrase in the storage room as she pointed at the vial holding the babies. "Oh."

"We think our name is Nikola Tesla." He tilted his head the other direction. "Or that might be just my name and . . . and the others have their own names. We're not in agreement about that."

26: A DATE WHICH WILL
LIVE IN INFAMY

Nikola Tesla explored their room, clumsily handling everything with his awkward dog paws. They rescued their tablets, the lamp on the nightstand between their beds, their alarm clock, and their matching china piggy banks. Nikola Tesla paused to examine his front feet. "Why do our hands look like this?"

"Because you're a dog," Jillian said.

"We are?"

"Well, at the moment, you are," Louise said. "It's complicated."

Which seemed to be the theme for their life lately.

Nikola tried to pick up their new camera and nearly dropped it. Louise yelped and snatched it out of his paws. He gazed up at her with puppy-dog eyes. "We want to look at it."

Louise was sure April Geiselman would label this as karma. They wanted their baby brother and sisters so bad, and now they had them, with all the chaos that implied. How, though, mystified Louise. Somehow magic had weirdly combined the frozen embryos and the robotic brain of Tesla. It seemed impossible, but there was no denying that Nikola was a whole different creature than their nanny-bot.

Louise held the camera down to Nikola's eye level and wondered how differently he might be seeing the object. "It might break if you drop it. Let me hold it while you look at it."

"So, you're a boy?" Jillian moved around the room, putting treasures away while Louise kept the dog—puppy—boy—babies—distracted.

Tesla peered closely at the camera, tilting his massive head back and forth. "What's a boy?"

Jillian gave Louise a pleading look for her to answer the question. Louise shrugged; she had no idea how to explain when the person in question lacked any reasonable body parts.

Jillian tugged at her hair in frustration. "A boy is—someone who is not a girl."

"What is a girl?"

"We're girls." Louise tried to head off that route of questioning.

"Well, then, we must be a boy, because we're not you."

"That works," Jillian and Louise agreed.

Nikola was distracted from the camera by the snow globe of the hyperphase gate in orbit over Earth. (The Elfhome one was the first thing Jillian had put up out of reach.) He gave a little "oh" of amazement when the glitter swirled. Louise struggled not to snatch the globe out of his paws. She really didn't like it that much; it still felt vaguely dangerous to her for some reason. She supposed it could be worse; there could be four babies fumbling through the twins' belongings, in mass confusion.

"What are we going to do?" Louise whispered to Jillian. "Mom and Dad are going to freak if they find out. And they will, if he keeps talking."

"We'll tell them we figured out how to upload a personality, and we chose Christopher Robin. Nikola, can you say, 'Silly old bear'?"

He tilted his head with confusion. "Silly old bear?" He had a perfect Christopher Robin lilt, but the intonation was wrong.

"No, no. Silly old bear." Jillian gave the correct tone of an older person addressing a child.

"What's a bear and why is it silly?"

"We are so screwed," Louise whispered.

"We can work with this," Jillian said.

"But what about tonight? We can't leave him alone!" She was imagining all sorts of awful things like him getting out of the house and getting stolen.

"We can't take him to the gala."

"What's a gala?" Nikola asked.

They stared at him with slight horror.

"It's a party to raise money for some charity." Louise attempted to define it in words that he might understand. "People get dressed up fancy, and there's music, and pretty decorations, and..." Actually, she wasn't completely clear what the gala was going to be like, so she fell back on the parties of Jane Austen. "People dance and say snarky things to each other, and there's food and—"

"Food?" Joy woke up and joined the building disaster.

"Oh, now you've done it." Jillian sighed.

"I'm hungry!" Joy cried.

"You're always hungry, you bottomless pit." Jillian opened the lowest drawer, where they'd hidden all of Joy's food. "Oooh, you've eaten everything!"

"So hungry!" Joy clambered into Louise's arms and gazed up at her pleadingly. "Open can!" She made the sound of the can opener. "Yummy, yummy, stinky food in can!"

Louise wished she knew how much Joy was supposed to eat. Was she actually starving like she seemed or was she just pigging out? She didn't seem to be getting any fatter. After she'd eaten her fill, she would sleep for hours. "We should feed her before Mom and Dad get home."

They moved to the kitchen since Joy was a messy eater. Jillian spread out paper towels for Joy to stand on as Louise used the can opener to open up the organic cat food that they had bought for the baby dragon and hidden under the sink. Joy sat on her haunches and clapped her hands together. Nikola watched with interest.

"Gimme!" Joy cried the moment that the can was open, releasing its pungent smell. She grabbed fistfuls of dark moist meat and shoved it into her mouth as quickly as she could shovel it in.

"Do you think we should move her to baby food?" Jillian asked.

Louise shrugged. They'd started with little three-ounce cans with pull-top lids that Joy mastered after they opened the first can in front of her. During the night she raided the kitchen and left the empty cans all over the floor. Luckily, Louise woke up and found the mess first. They'd moved to the twelve-ounce cans, which meant the little dragon was eating nearly a quarter of her weight in one sitting. "She likes these."

"Nom, nom, nom," Joy mumbled around the mouthful.

"Why is she putting it in her mouth?" Nikola asked.

How did he know it was her mouth and not know about food? It made Louise's head hurt.

"It's yummy." Joy held out a handful to him. "But stinky."

"No!" The twins both cried and leapt to intercept Nikola's attempt to eat the food.

"That's dragon food," Louise said.

Nikola eyed the half-empty can. "It says 'cat food,' not dragon."

He can read the word food *but not understand it?* Louise glanced at the clock. They had exactly one hour before this became a complete disaster.

"Nikola, do you understand danger?"

He tilted his head to the right and then to the left. "Danger is when the primary target is in an area that might harm the primary target."

That sounded like robotic logic. Louise supposed that if Nikola could move the dog's body and talk over its speakers, then the full robotic brain could also be accessed.

"Until we tell you otherwise, only talk to Jillian and me."

"Joy!" the baby dragon cried, waving her hand to be included. The hand held food that dribbled through her clawed fingers.

"And Joy." Louise supposed Nikola might be able to teach Joy more English. So far she seemed only interested in learning words that got her more food. "If you really need to say something to us, and there's someone else there, you need to say 'Tut, tut, it looks like rain.'"

"Tut, tut, it looks like rain," Nikola quoted solemnly.

"Yes."

"But there's only a thirty percent chance of rain," Nikola complained.

"We're so grounded." Jillian sighed.

They washed out the empty cat-food can so it wouldn't smell, buried it deep within the trash, ran the range exhaust fan, and sprayed the kitchen with air freshener. Joy needed to be washed carefully, and she squirmed like an earthworm as they tried soaping her up and spraying her down in the kitchen sink.

"Just hold still!" Jillian cried.

Joy stuck out her tongue at Jillian.

After they were all dried off, they went back upstairs to get dressed for the gala and plan for their parents' arrival. Nikola followed them up, murmuring Christopher Robin lines that they'd taught him and complaining.

"Tut, tut, it looks like rain. It still doesn't make sense. Silly old bear. But what bear? You are braver than you believe, stronger than you seem, and smarter than you think. That one at least makes sense."

Louise stared at the mirror, trying to gain the confidence to actually leave the house. She felt like everyone was going to be looking at them, knowing the impossible and illegal things that the girls had been doing the last few days. Stealing magical artifacts from a museum. Baby dragons. Robotic dogs possessed by unborn siblings. She wanted the comfort of knowing that she and Jillian were drawing attention because they were cute and not because people *knew*. Jillian looked cute, and they were twins. It stood to reason that Louise must be just as cute. All she needed to do was believe.

"We should just leave him here," Jillian said as Louise tied a big yellow bow onto Nikola.

"No! We have to take him." Louise's whole insides went queasy at the idea of leaving their little brother behind. "It's part of having a baby; you can't leave them alone just because it's inconvenient. Something might happen to him."

"We were going to put him in the time capsule in the back of the closet."

In truth, they had only given a little thought about where they were going to store the *nactka* once it was loaded. It seemed unlikely that Nikola would be safe in the back of the closet for years and years. The plan had seemed so solid until it hit that "and then what" gray zone. Tesla wasn't really a good compromise. They needed to do more, but until then, they needed to take care of Nikola like he was a real baby.

And real babies had to have someone with them all the time.

Tesla would just have to be added to the list of things they had already planned to take. Speaking of which, she needed to pack them. They needed to take their tablets and the gossamer calls they made. The magical whistles were hidden with all the other things related to the codex. She shoved the calls into their purses, and then in a near panic, added the flash drive and photographs.

"If we take Nikola, we'll end up having to take Joy, too." They weren't sure what taking the magic generator out of Nikola would do. Until they could carefully test it, they'd have to keep one running inside the nanny-bot while the other recharged. So far, they hadn't been able to separate Joy from the generator, which made them suspect that she needed magic to thrive.

"Gala food!" Joy cried.

Leaving Joy at home seemed even worse than taking her.

"No. We all go. We're a family."

The trick, however, was to get Nikola to the gala at the Waldorf Astoria without their parents noticing. By secreting him in the car before their parents got home and careful redirection from the parking garage to the gala, they were able to keep him quietly following behind, unnoticed. He was being good, although part of it seemed to be that he was overwhelmed by everything. He kept twisting his head, trying to see everything.

When they checked in, however, one of the women manning the ticket window glanced beyond their parents and said, "Oh, that's not really real, is it?"

As their parents turned, Jillian threw both arms around Nikola and grinned brightly. "No, he's not real. He's our nanny-bot."

"What is he doing here?" their mother cried while their father looked too surprised to speak.

"He's going to record us all together!" Jillian cried. "We both want to be in the picture—you can't tell we're twins if we're not in the shot together. And we never have any video with Daddy in it when we're together."

Which was something their mother complained about constantly.

"We can't bring him in with us." Their mother started to scan the lobby.

Nikola cringed away from their mother.

Louise petted his head, trying to comfort him. "Why not? He wouldn't bite or bark or pee."

"He's just one big self-moving camera." Jillian pointed to a couple with their phones out, taking video. "They're filming."

"We'll have to check him in the coat room," their mother growled.

"Someone might take him!" Louise cried.

"You should have thought about that before bringing him." Their mother turned back to the woman at the ticket window. "Where's the coat-check room?"

"It's the middle of June." The woman looked surprised at the question. "We didn't set up a coat check."

Their mother stopped scanning to glare down at them. The hand went out. The finger pointed. "You. Two. Are. In. Trouble."

Louise swallowed hard and gripped Jillian's hand tightly.

"How much trouble depends on the rest of the night," their mother continued. "You two be good and charming to Anna Desmarais and much will be forgiven."

"Do we really have to be nice to her?" Jillian had the courage or stupidity to ask. Louise squeezed her twin's hand hard in warning.

"Don't push me now," their mother growled quietly so no one around them could hear her. "You will be nice if you ever want a life again."

"She's been awful to you!" Jillian cried. "Why do you have to be the one that's nice?"

"Because I am better than her!" their mother snapped. "I do not let other people define me. I am who I am, and that is an intelligent and gracious human being. And as such, I do not drop to the level of bullies and trade insult for insult."

"But isn't that just letting them win?" Jillian ignored another squeeze.

"No, it's called standing your ground without sinking to their level." Their mother held out her hand to Jillian. "Come on. Let's get this over with."

With Jillian linking Louise to their mother, they went in search of Anna Desmarais. A cold dread flowered in Louise's stomach and grew. This was going to be the worst night ever.

They went into a big ballroom full of richly dressed people. At Louise's eye level, it was a confusing wall of silk dresses and black tuxedoes. They wove right and left, avoiding groups of people standing and talking and laughing. The wall of black parted, and a woman stood alone in the crowd, quietly distanced from everyone.

She noticed them coming. For a moment, she watched their mother approach without a change in expression, like an ivory statue. Then she noticed Jillian, and a slight frown crossed her face.

Louise's feet stopped moving out of sudden fear. Nikola bumped up against her. For a moment, Jillian was pulled between their mother and Louise. Her twin looked back, impatient, and jerked Louise forward to follow.

"Don't piss her off," Jillian whispered. "She's killing my hand!"

The exchange had drawn the woman's attention to Louise, and her eyes widened in surprise. Louise felt something leap the space between them, a spark of knowing, powerful and dangerous.

In that moment, she knew that this was Anna Desmarais, her mother's nemesis. That the woman felt she was smarter than those around her. That she felt she was able to do anything she wanted, take anything she needed, and go through anyone that stood in her way. Louise knew because there was an answering echo inside her, a resonance of being. She recoiled as if suddenly seeing a mirror and it showed how selfish and wrong everything she'd done in the last few weeks had been. What she could become.

Did Anna see that Louise was just like her? Could she guess what Louise had done in the last few weeks?

"Mrs. Desmarais." Their mother pulled them into a line before Anna. Their father was trying hard to look at ease and failing. "This is my family. My husband, George. Jillian and Louise."

"What beautiful girls," the woman murmured without taking her eyes from Louise. "Yours?" The tone was polite, but it put shivers down Louise's spine.

"Yes, mine," their mother said coldly. "I have the stretch marks to prove it."

"Ah, I didn't realize you had children. Twins, no less? Are they clever, just like their mother?"

Her mother lifted her chin as if sensing a hidden insult in the question. "Yes, they are. They go to Perelman School for the Gifted."

"Perelman?" Anna cried. "Wasn't that the school that had so many children hurt by the bomb?"

"Yes, but they were nowhere near the flying glass. They're putting on *Peter Pan* for the school play. They were in the art rooms on the top floor checking on props when the bomb went off."

"I'm Peter Pan." Jillian beamed full-on cute at Anna. "We're fraternal twins, not identical. I want to be a movie director when I grow up. Louise wants to be a naturalist. We're both huge fans of Nigel Reid. We're really excited about meeting him tonight. Thank you so much for the tickets!"

Louise nodded, glad that Jillian was handling it. Which one of them was the brave one? She added a quiet "Thank you" and forced herself to smile.

Anna smiled at the thank-you, but her eyes remained troubled.

"I've heard that the art gallery might still be a target for the terrorists since the queen's delegation returned to Elfhome."

"Vance Roycroft is no longer a threat." Their father avoided saying the man had actually been killed in a shoot-out.

Jillian continued with megawatt-level cute. "Our friend Zahara was late that day. She and her little brother were at the front door—the good side of the front door—when it went off. Boom!"

Louise nudged Jillian to get her to stop talking about the bomb. It felt wrong to be talking about it so casually. Zahara and her brother had nearly been killed.

"Zahara is Mbeya's daughter." Their mother stooped to name-dropping.

"They haven't caught all the members of that terrorist group." Anna looked honestly worried. "Are you sure it's safe for them to go to Perelman with all that's going on in the city? Maybe they would be safer at a boarding school."

"That is what the terrorists want," their mother said. "Us so frightened that we run and hide."

"You're making a statement with your daughters' lives," Anna said.

Their mother straightened to full warrior-queen height. "I feel safer with them home with us, where I can check on them anytime."

"Do you have children?" Their father tried to run interference on a brewing fight.

Both women gave him a hard look.

Anna relented first. "Yes, I do. They're all older than even you, and unlikely to give me any grandchildren. My sons have a genetic disorder, and my two girls are both grown women who chose lives that didn't include husband and children."

"Oh, I'm—I'm sorry." Their father gave their mother a slightly panicked look.

"You should rethink your decision on Perelman," Anna said. "Children are your greatest treasure. When you lose your children, it tears a hole in your heart. Without my children to fill it up, my house is too big and empty. I would just rattle around it at night if I stayed home, so I go to events like this to fill my time."

She laughed as if this was a joke, and their parents were forced to join in. This night, Louise realized, wasn't the end of the war, but the start of a new battle. She could take no more;

she attempted a rescue. "Can we go find Nigel Reid and get his autograph?"

"We have Tesla with us!" Jillian reminded their parents. "So you could keep on talking."

Louise wanted to kick Jillian; couldn't she see that their parents needed to be saved?

Jillian caught her glare and patted her purse, reminding Louise that they wanted to hand over the gossamer call in person. They wouldn't be able to do that with their parents in tow. They'd assumed that at some point one of them would slip free, but it would be more fun if both of them got to talk to him.

"Adult conversation is so boring to them at that age," Anna said. "Let them go. We have things to discuss."

"We do?" Their mother nearly growled the question.

"I have a Christmas event in mind at the Natural History Museum that I think your company would be perfect for."

Their mother took a deep breath and flicked her hand, dismissing them. "Yes, go on."

Jillian caught Louise's hand and dragged her way. Louise wished she didn't feel like she was abandoning her parents to evil.

There was face-painting, balloon animals, clowns and jugglers, and herds of squealing kids. Since they still had time before the meeting, they got their faces painted on the theory it was like a mask. The artist did them both as Bengal Tiger cubs that complimented their yellow dresses and black belts. As an additional precaution, they went past the buffet table and loaded a plate full of cookies for Joy, just in case the baby dragon woke up.

They had picked out one of the smaller meeting rooms that they knew would be empty and hacked into Waldorf Astoria's event scheduling system to make sure it would be unlocked for the night. Louise led, still uneasy from her encounter with Anna Desmarais, the uncomfortable feeling of looking in a mirror and seeing something ugly reflected. All they had done to set up their meeting was have the room unlocked. They couldn't expect a private conversation with Nigel any other way; the stars were all being mobbed by crowds of excited fans who were being lined up and timed for their few moments of interaction. They only planned to do good things, so a certain level of ruthlessness could be forgiven—right?

Distracted by her thoughts, she was off-balance when they walked into the room and found Nigel waiting. He'd taken advantage of the table and had a slickie, a tablet, and a phone laid out. His blond hair was better contained than when he was on camera, and he wore a tuxedo instead of his normal bush khakis and white linen shirt. There was no mistaking, though, his merry blue eyes and gentle smile.

He looked up, surprised. "Ach, what bonnie wee lasses!"

They circled the table like tigers, checking the room for spy equipment. Louise doubted that there would be any, but Jillian had wanted to be sure.

"I'm sorry, but this is going to be a private meeting." His Scottish burr faded as he gained control of his surprise. "Go on back to the party. I'll be out in a short while."

"You're meeting with us," Louise said.

"I am now?" He smiled despite the fact he didn't seem to believe them.

"Yes, we need to talk." Jillian positioned Nikola by the door. "Watch the door."

"Watch it do what?" Nikola whispered, apparently unsure if he was supposed to talk in front of Nigel or not.

Jillian covered her face with her hand just as their mother would. "Just warn us if someone is coming in."

Nigel stood up. "Lassies—"

"We're Lemon-Lime JEl-Lo," Louise stated before he could order them out again. "We're the ones you're meeting with."

"You're..." he started but trailed off, looking puzzled.

"Lemon-Lime JEl-Lo!" Jillian snapped.

"He was probably expecting someone older," Louise pointed out.

"Well, yes, and taller." He came to crouch down in front of them so they were eye to eye. "You're truly Lemon-Lime?"

He seemed so disappointed.

"We have the gossamer call like we promised you," Louise cried.

"I'm sure you do." His voice was heavy with sadness. "It's just that when I saw your last video, I thought that you must know more than the news we got from Elfhome prior to Startup. I thought you knew that the viceroy survived the attack on him."

"You can't tell anyone that we don't know!" the twins cried.

"We do know who attacked him," Louise said.

"At least some of the people involved," Jillian said.

"They're doing a lot of horrible things like kidnapping children and killing scientists," Louise continued. "And they want the quarantine zone expanded. They attacked Windwolf, and now they're using his disappearance to push through the vote."

Nigel made a surprised, pained sound like someone had punched him in the stomach. "So humans murdered the viceroy?"

"He's not dead!" Louise felt sure of it, although she knew that she couldn't prove it. "Everyone has to stop acting like he is."

"And we're not sure what they are," Jillian added. "They might look human, but we don't think they really are."

"They might be elves," Louise said.

"Evil anti-elves," Jillian cried.

Louise winced. The extremely short version sounded stupid. She wasn't sure, however, how to condense three years of secretive information gathering. "The Museum of Natural History has an exhibit of things created by elves found on Earth over the last two thousand years. The elves were getting here via natural 'hyperphase gates' found in cave systems; basically magic-created fissures between the two universes. These pathways were their equivalent to the Silk Road. Elves used to come to Earth to sell these items. Around two hundred and forty years ago, they had a war with someone. Someone so powerful that they destroyed all the pathways between the worlds to end the war."

Nigel tilted his head in confusion. "I visited the exhibit yesterday. I noticed that they didn't explain how the items ended up on Earth. How do you know all this?"

"Some of it is deductive reasoning," Louise admitted. "Windwolf already knew English when Director Maynard met him during the first Startup. He had copies of maps that King Charles the Second issued to the Hudson Bay Company when he founded their first expedition in 1668. His copy also showed an English trading post where Pittsburgh stands. It dates the map between 1740, when William Trent established that outpost, and 1758, when Fort Duquesne was built by the French."

"I never heard that about the map before," Nigel said.

Jillian waved it off as unimportant. "One of the EIA archive videos from Maynard's first contact with Windwolf has a close-up of the map. The EIA has restricted access to their videos, so no one has actually studied them at length."

"I see." Nigel clearly was afraid to ask how they'd gotten hold of it.

It seemed safe to lump the codex in with data they'd seen but didn't own. "We've also found the journal of an elf who was in France during the 1700s. We're not sure when he arrived, but he was there for several years prior to being killed in the French Revolution in the 1790s. When he attempted to travel back to Elfhome, the way was unexpectedly blocked. He traveled to several points and was dismayed to find all the pathways closed off."

"Where did you find that?" Nigel asked.

"We can't say," Louise said. "There are a lot of things we've done that weren't technically legal."

"So let's just not go there—okay?" Jillian gave Louise an annoyed look for bringing up the codex in the first place. "The thing is, there's no way to know how many elves were trapped on Earth or what side of the war that they were on. But the ones we saw didn't look like elves. We're only guessing that they were because they talked about being alive for hundreds of years."

"The important thing is that they have moles in the EIA and the United Nations and possibly among the police force in Pittsburgh."

"You have proof of this?" Nigel asked.

"Nothing we can show you," Louise said. "But this isn't a guess. We know this for sure."

Jillian nodded. "It's why you haven't been able to go to Elfhome. They're using the EIA to block visas of anyone that they don't want in Pittsburgh. But NBC bypassed their normal channels and pushed your paperwork through."

"We don't know why they've been trying to keep you out, but they don't want you there. They might try and kill you."

"But you need to go," Jillian said. "The people in Pittsburgh have no idea that they're about to be in the middle of war."

"A war between...?"

"The elves and the anti-elves. The anti-elves have been building up an army—someplace—and they've been kidnapping scientists to make a gate like the one in orbit, only on land." Jillian took his tablet and linked it with theirs. "Here's a list of scientists they've kidnapped. We know that everyone on this list is dead, except for Kensbock. We're not sure they're the ones that took him; he wasn't doing the same type of work. We also know that the NSA is looking into the kidnappings, but we don't think they've realized who is behind them."

"And this is really important." Louise sent him all the pictures of the Dufae box copied from the AMNH's server. "This was part of the exhibit. Sparrow took it back to Elfhome. It might look like a block of wood, but it's a box. And it has eleven of these inside." They had carefully taken pictures of the *nactka* inside a light box and erased all GPS tags on it. No one would be able to trace the picture back to their bedroom. "It's really important that you find the box and get it back to Earth. If you can't get it back to Earth, get it to the *sekasha* and have them open them."

"What are these?"

Jillian opened her mouth, and Louise was suddenly overwhelmed with the sense that she was going to say the worst possible thing.

"We're not sure!" Louise cried before her twin could reply. "The elf that died in the French Revolution believed that they were linked to a powerful spell. He brought them to Earth where he thought they could be safely studied. We're not sure yet what the spell does, but it would be very bad if they're used."

"Sparrow took this box?" Nigel asked.

Jillian gave Louise another dark look for telling the truth about the *nactka*. "She's one of the anti-elves. She's the one that set the trap for Windwolf."

"Sparrow? The viceroy's secretary is the one that tried to kill him?"

"*Husepavua*," Louise corrected him. "We don't have any proof. It would be our word against hers. She's an elf—or pretending to be an elf—or something—and other elves are going to believe her first."

"You can't tell anyone!" Jillian said. "We wouldn't be telling you except we don't know anyone already on Elfhome, and someone should be looking for the box and we can't go ourselves."

Nigel's eyes widened with alarm. "Ach, no, ye cannae do that! Ye are just wee lasses."

Apparently Nigel's Scottish burr went into overdrive when he was extremely rattled. Louise felt guilty for alarming him. The truth was that if they went to Elfhome, they would be focused on finding Alexander. They couldn't trust Nigel, though, with all of their secrets. They couldn't tell him anything about her.

"Here." Jillian opened up her purse and handed him the whistle. They'd brought two just in case only one of them managed to make the meeting. "This is the gossamer call we promised you."

"You'll need it on Elfhome." Louise showed him how the tones could be changed by pressing his fingertips against the holes.

Jillian pointed out the spell etchings on the call. "We've found a spell that works as an amplifier for the ultrasonic frequencies. It needs magic to work, but it will make the call's range to be... well, we're not sure of the range. We haven't been able to test it, but we think it's close to a thousand miles, or one *mei*."

"You'll have to be careful on Elfhome not to blow it with anything metal in your hands—that could twist the magic, and the results could be bad," Louise warned. "Here is a list of gossamer commands we've pieced together from analyzing video. It's kind of like Morse code. We're guessing on these, so don't take them as God's word."

"Thank you so very much. I never expected Lemon-Lime to be two little girls. You didn't come here all by yourself, did you? You have someone...?"

"Our parents," Louise said.

"They're here?" Nigel glanced toward the door.

Louise jumped a little. "Someplace."

"But they don't know about our videos!" Jillian said.

"They don't?" Nigel looked concerned.

"They're super-protective, and they were afraid that if we posted our videos, we'd pick up creepy stalkers. They're not very computer smart, so they didn't believe we could stay anonymous. We knew that if we were careful, no one could trace our posts back to us, so we—kind of—went around them."

Like Anna Desmarais probably would. Louise cringed inwardly.

"So they don't know how popular you are?" Nigel asked.

"No!" the twins cried.

"We didn't even know," Jillian grumbled. "We apparently use the Internet in a much different way than the average person. We know about all the social media, but we don't hit those sites." Until recently, they didn't have anyone to be social with. "We do research." Hack into secure sites. "And post our videos."

Embarrassed, Louise turned the conversation back to the whistle. "The elves seemed to be exploiting instinctual behavior with the gossamer call. Elves have stated that the wargs are bioengineered for war. If the elves found a way to make sound trigger certain responses in all animals, then this whistle might effect anything they've created."

"So it works on wargs?" Nigel tried the various finger positions.

"We think it will, but the commands and reactions aren't going to be the same as for the gossamer. You would have to use trial and error, and that could be dangerous."

Nigel suddenly lifted the call and blew on it.

"No!" both the girls cried.

Joy appeared perched on Nigel's shoulder. She was smeared in frosting. "Who's there?" She leaned in close to peer nose to nose at the man who had gone still with surprise. "Cake?" She held out a fistful of white cake.

"Oh, you bottomless pit!" Louise cried and reached up to pry her carefully from Nigel's shoulder. "What have you done?"

"So hungry!" Joy crammed the cake into her mouth. "Nom, nom, nom."

"We fed you before we came." Jillian tried to wipe the frosting off Nigel's shoulder but only smeared it more.

"Cake yummy!" Joy licked her hands.

Nikola, who had been watching the door intently, suddenly announced, "Tut, tut, it looks like rain."

"Nikola!" the twins cried.

"But-but-but mother is coming!" Nikola cried and then grumbled, "Silly old bear."

Both girls yipped in fear. They hurriedly opened up Tesla's storage and shoved Joy into it.

Jillian pointed fiercely at Nigel. "You saw nothing!"

Nigel blinked for a moment and then said, "Yes, nothing, nothing at all."

"She's using her phone to track me," Nikola whispered.

"Oh God, did she hear anything we said?" Jillian cried.

"No, I don't think so." Nikola was torn between looking at the door and at Nigel, who was watching with eyebrows raised. "She keeps pushing buttons on her phone and swearing. I don't think she knows she's already connected to my command system."

Jillian caught Nikola by the leash. "Come on, let's head her off. We can't let her catch us alone in a room with a stranger."

Louise let Jillian go on ahead. She wanted to say good-bye properly instead of tearing off like a pair of headless chickens. "It was nice to actually meet you. Be careful on Elfhome." She didn't know what else to say; she had never had to say good-bye like this before. "Maybe we can get together when you get back."

"Yes, I would like that." Nigel calmly pocketed the whistle. "I'm sorry, but I have to ask: what exactly did I just not see?"

He meant Joy.

Louise blushed hotly. "We're not sure. We—we found her in the box before Sparrow took it to Elfhome. We think there are eleven more like her still inside it. You have to save them."

Nigel took a deep breath as he realized that saving the baby dragons meant facing down Sparrow with a small army at her bidding. "I will do my best." He reached out and took both her hands in his. "You should tell your parents."

"Tell them what?"

"Tell them everything. You two are very intelligent. Your videos—now that I know how young you really are—they're just breathtakingly clever, but you're just wee things, and I'm afraid you're getting in over your heads. These are dangerous people you've stumbled into. You two shouldn't be doing this all by yourself."

27: ENDING THE NIGHT WITH A BANG BANG BANG

Louise huddled in the back of the car, hugging Nikola tightly. She really wanted the whole night of bad to be over. The only good thing was meeting Nigel Reid, and Joy had totally screwed that up. It was one thing to hand over the whistle and tell him about Dufae's box. It was another to show him Joy and forbid him from studying her closely. Now they had to worry that Nigel wouldn't keep his word and pretend that he hadn't seen the little dragon. That he wouldn't follow his natural curiosity and try to find out their names and who they were and where they lived . . .

At least there was some comfort that he would be on Elfhome in less than thirty days and a universe removed from them for months after that. She wanted to believe that they'd done the right thing in trusting him so much.

Certainly if she didn't trust someone, it was Anna Desmarais. The gala was supposed to signal the end of the war between her and their mother, but Louise got the distinct impression that it had been a false peace treaty. A new battle was about to break out, and it was going to be worse. Much worse. There was no word or look or action, however, that explained why Louise felt this so strongly. Anna had been polite, smiling, listening carefully to their mother's conversation and nodding in response.

Ironically their mother had judged their interaction with Anna successful enough to warrant forgiveness for sneaking Nikola into the gala. "I'm still mad that she cornered me for hours, but at least I knew you were safe with Tesla. Were you able to see Nigel Reid?"

"Yes, we saw him," they said.

"He was awesome," Jillian added without explaining that the man had dropped everything to spend time in private with them.

Tell them everything. Louise felt as if disaster was about to crash down upon them. Nothing felt safe to say. She curled tighter into a ball and let Jillian answer questions about the face-painting and other things they'd supposedly done before their mother rejoined them. Before she knew it, they'd turned on to their street and were driving up to their house. They were one of the few houses with a basement garage instead of apartment. The big door sensed them approach and slid upward just as the car turned into the driveway. A light flashed on the dashboard.

"Huh," their father said as the car slotted itself perfectly into the garage. "Security system just crashed. I hope it doesn't call the police."

The mother swore softly at her phone. "I can't get it to respond."

"I'll reset it from the keypad in the kitchen." Their father hopped out of the door and trotted up the steps.

"No!" The word slipped out of Louise. It tore something loose, and she was flooded with sudden certainty that if she didn't stop him, she'd never see him again. She lunged between the front seats and slammed down on the horn. In the enclosed garage, the sound seemed like a sudden loud cry of pain. She beat on the horn, blaring it again and again.

"Lou?" Jillian cried while Nikola yelped in surprise.

"Louise!" their mother cried. "Louise! Stop that."

Louise leaned against the horn, pressing hard. It screamed warning even as shots rang out upstairs.

"Warning!" Tesla barked in his deep Japanese man voice. "Intruders! Home security has been breached. Response code five! Secondary target requires assistance."

The car doors all opened, and Tesla sprang out. Louise followed.

"Louise! Jillian! No!" their mother shouted.

Sounding like a grizzly-sized dog, Tesla went snarling up the steps.

There was an odd roar in the kitchen and a scream of human pain and another gunshot, this one sounding farther away.

"Louise, get back in the car! George!"

A moment later her father had swept her up and was carrying her back down the steps.

"Nikola!" Louise shouted, and then she realized that it was the robotic dog responding, not her baby brother. "Tesla, cancel response code five! Nikola! Nikola come back!"

Seconds later, she and her father and Nikola were all trying to fit into the front seat of the car. One of them leaned against the horn and it blared and everyone shouted in fear. And then the car was traveling backward out of the garage, horn still blaring, Louise, her father, and Nikola all flailing in the bucket seat.

"Get in the backseat!" their mother shouted.

Nikola tumbled into the backseat and Louise followed and the car swung around, its headlight picking out a man rolling on the sidewalk, his black shirt on fire. There were two more men getting into a black SUV parked two doors down.

Then they swept past the SUV, and the gunmen were left behind them.

The house looked like a tornado had hit it. All the drawers and bookcases had their contents scattered on the floor. The little television screen in the kitchen and the big screen in the living room were both shattered. Random holes had been punched into the walls and furniture overturned, its lining cut.

They had driven straight to the police station and then, with a squad-car escort, cautiously returned to the now-empty house.

"It was dark, and it happened so fast." Their father was recounting what had happened while they huddled together on the front porch. "One of the girls started to beep the horn, and then something small—like a rat—jumped onto my shoulder—and then there were these flashes at the end of the hall, like bottle rockets going off—and some people ran out the front door. When we pulled out, it looked like one of the men was on fire."

Their dad's shoulders were covered with cake frosting. The rat obviously had been Joy. They'd been calling her a baby dragon—did that mean she'd actually breathed fire on one of the gunmen? Where was she now? Had she been hit by a bullet? She wasn't inside Tesla.

The two police officers had checked the house to make sure it was clear and were now collecting evidence.

"Casings," one cop said from near the door. "Nine millimeter. One, two, three, four—looks like a full clip. One lucky"—he glanced toward Louise and Jillian and changed what he was going to say—"dog."

The other stooped and picked up something on the kitchen floor. "This is a slug. Here's another. Looks like it hit something and deformed." They looked around the kitchen, apparently searching for evidence of ricochets.

Louise wanted to search for Joy. "Can we pick stuff up or is this still a crime scene?"

"You can clean things up, sweetheart," the police officer said.

"Aren't you going to dust for fingerprints and . . . and . . . such?" their father asked.

"They only do that on television. For a robbery where no one is actually hurt, we just file a report."

In unspoken agreement, the twins started to pick up in the kitchen. This was Joy; unless she was seriously hurt, she'd be near food. Their parents went upstairs with the policeman to assess the damage up there. She wasn't in the pantry as Louise expected. Nor was she under the sink where they had hidden her cat food.

"Where is she?" Jillian's voice quavered.

"Who?" Nikola had been pressed against Louise's side since they arrived at the police station. "Joy?"

"Yes, Joy."

"She's in the refrigerator."

"How did she get in there?" Louise opened the door. The inside was almost as bad as the rest of the house. All the little Tupperware containers of leftovers had been torn open and licked clean. The fruit bin had little greasy handprints across the inside of the glass front, and only a few apple cores and some orange rinds remained. The baby dragon was asleep among the well-gnawed bones of the roast chicken. "Oh! Oh no! What a mess!"

"I'll clean the fridge. You get her." Jillian swung the trashcan around to beside the open refrigerator.

Louise scooped Joy up. Over the layer of frosting, she now had butter and various types of grease. She smelled of rosemary and garlic and chicken fat, with hints of oranges. The baby dragon yawned but otherwise slept through the quick warm bath in the sink with a large dose of dish soap to strip off the grease.

"What are we going to tell Mom and Dad?" Louise cried as she quickly dried Joy with a clean tea towel.

"That those men also took all the food in the fridge." Jillian dumped the chicken bones into the trashcan and covered them up with the torn foam from the living room couch.

"Why would anyone break into a house and steal leftovers? Mom and Dad are never going to believe—"

"Why would anyone steal our toothbrushes?" their father said as he came down the steps with the police officer. "That doesn't make any sense."

"Was it an expensive electric toothbrush?" The cop made notes on his tablet.

"No, they were just normal toothbrushes like you get at the supermarket. They're—what, ten dollars? I don't know. Who takes *used* toothbrushes?"

"You got me," the cop said. "First time I've seen it. So, what was in the safe in the bedroom?"

"Just paperwork. It was basically a fireproof filing box. It had our passports and marriage license and birth certificates and things like that. God, what a nightmare."

"You're alive and your family is fine," the cop said. "Count your blessings."

28: FLYING MONKEY FIVE

Riding to school with Nikola Tesla Dufae was totally different than being with Tesla the nanny-bot. They'd learned that he was enraptured by any shiny new situation and would fall silent, satisfied to just look and listen. Once things became familiar, however, he started to ask questions. Sunday had been a hell of an effort to get him to stay quiet as their parents cataloged all that had been taken from the house. Halfway to the city, on the crowded train, the questions started.

"Where are we going?"

"We told you that you shouldn't talk unless we're alone," Louise whispered as the high school student standing beside them glanced down at Nikola. She tightened her hold on his leash.

He gave a little whimper. "It just that Joy is dreaming of cake and she's wiggling her fingers and it tickles."

At times he said things that hurt Louise's brain. How did he know that Joy was dreaming of cake? Was he somehow aware of her thoughts? How was he aware at all? He was a couple of frozen cells inside a magical egg-shaped thing riding on top of a magical generator within a robotic body.

And how exactly was he feeling Joy wiggling her fingers? The storage bin didn't have sensors.

She petted his head to give them both something else to think about. He laid his head on her lap and thumped his tail.

Jillian hadn't noticed the exchange. She bent over her tablet, memorizing lines to the play. Between stealing the *nactka* and the embryos, they'd ignored the play but it was nine days away. It would have been less if the bombing hadn't pushed it back.

"We're going to school," Louise whispered. "And I know you're going to have a lot of questions, but you need to not ask us any of them until we're alone."

He whimpered again and sighed deeply.

Louise felt bad for him. It would kill her not to ask questions all day. Maybe there were other ways of getting around him not talking. "Can you text?"

"Yes! We can!" He'd gained more control over Tesla's body over the weekend. His pointed ears dipped in worry. "Can we?"

"Yes, you can text me." She hugged him. "But you'll have to be patient for me to answer. I might not be able to text you back immediately."

Jillian surprised Louise by introducing Iggy to Nikola Tesla. He'd been waiting at the top of the station's staircase. As usual, he went to pet Tesla even as he called hello to them.

"Iggy, this is Nikola Tesla." Over the weekend, it had become apparent that Nikola was their little brother, while Tesla was his robotic body. They'd debated on his last name. Should they use "Mayer" or "Bell" or "Dufae?" In the end they'd decided to use their biological father's name, even though it was too dangerous to actually say aloud. "Nikola, this is Iggy."

Iggy paused with hand outstretched, a smile tugging at his mouth, as if he wasn't sure if what she'd said was a joke or not.

"We downloaded a personality and gave him a real name," Jillian lied. "Say 'hello,' Nikola."

Nikola tilted his head in confusion and then leaned close to Louise to whisper. "We're so confused. When can we talk?"

Louise glared at Jillian for making things harder. Jillian rolled her eyes, indicating that she had a plan but couldn't discuss it right now. Louise sighed and patted Nikola, "When we introduce you to someone, you can say 'hello' and 'nice to meet you' and such."

Nikola stared at her for a minute and then turned to Iggy. "Hello. Nice to meet you." He looked back at Louise. "Silly old bear."

How did she get to be the bad guy in this?

"Do you have your lines memorized?" Jillian changed the subject.

"Yes. I think." Iggy held up his left hand like it was a hook and waved it. "Spirit that haunts this dark lagoon tonight, dost hear me?"

"Are you talking to us?" Nikola asked.

Louise groaned and pulled him on ahead via the leash. "Why don't you two practice in private?"

"He wasn't talking to us?" Nikola whispered.

"No!" Louise whispered.

Flying Monkey Five was in their classroom.

Louise had paused in the doorway at the sight of a weirdly familiar strange boy standing in profile in front of Miss Hamilton's desk. His focus was on Miss Hamilton, letting Louise stare unnoticed as she tried to figure out where she knew him from. He was as tall as Iggy and slender without seeming weedy. Handsome and obviously rich, he would have been a perfect prince for Elle's Little Mermaid princess.

Prince Charming made her think of Crown Prince Kiss Butt, and, with a gasp, she realized who the strange boy was. She jerked backwards into Jillian, who'd been trying to convince Nikola to stay in their locker instead of exploring the new landscape.

"What's—" Jillian started to ask what was wrong and then yelped slightly in surprise as Louise caught her wrist and dragged her down the hall at a half run. "What's going on? Where are we going?"

Louise banged open the girls' restroom door and pulled Jillian and Nikola in with her. Most boys would rather die than go into a girls' restroom; she was praying that Flying Monkey Five was the same. But he was one of them: kidnappers and killers. "Oh my God! Oh my God!"

"What's wrong?"

Louise opened her mouth to answer and then thought to check the stalls for anyone who might overhear them. She went down the row, swinging open the doors one after another. The metal doors clanged loudly in the tiled room.

"Lou!" Jillian complained. "You're scaring me."

"One of them is here. Flying Monkey Five. He's in *our* classroom."

Jillian gasped and skittered sideways from the doorway, looking scared. Louise really wanted her to be the brave one, because if she wasn't, it meant Louise would have to be the brave one, and she didn't feel ready to be it.

"What—what is he doing here?" Jillian whispered.

"I don't know. I don't know." Louise paced in front of the sinks. The mirror reflected back her twin's fear twice fold. "Esme warned us about the Empire of Evil, and he's one of them. She said that they're dangerous. He's probably here to do evil things—like kidnap us or steal Joy or something." She didn't want to scare Nikola by adding him to the list of possible targets. It was suspicious, though, that right after they'd saved the last of Esme's babies, the Flying Monkey had showed up.

Jillian went into one of the stalls and shut the door and locked it. She stood in the stall for a minute before asking fearfully, "Do you really think so?"

Louise forced herself to ignore the fear that was jittering through her. "Why else would he suddenly show up at our school?"

Jillian unzipped her pants, pushed them down and sat on the toilet. She was stalling though—she wasn't actually going pee. "How would anyone know about Joy? And even if they figured out how to open Dufae's box—which I'm betting it would take them more than a few days to do—how would they know that Dufae or someone else didn't take the *nactka* with Joy in it? It has been sitting around locked for nearly three hundred years."

"I feel weird," Nikola whimpered. "What is this I feel?"

Louise suspected he was afraid for the first time in his life. She hugged him tightly. "It's okay. We won't let anyone take Joy."

Jillian growled softly in the stall. "We've missed something if he's here. We've never been fingerprinted, so they couldn't have found us that way. We never showed up on the museum security system while the chest was at the museum. We erased everything at Dad's work, so no one should even be able to link us to Esme or Dufae. Even if they did, they couldn't know that we know anything about unlocking magical boxes."

"April knows," Louise said.

"She knows that Esme left us something, but we haven't told her about being elves, or Dufae, or any of that, so she couldn't have known we were going to take anything from the museum. And why would anyone suspect two nine-year-old girls of robbing a museum with magic?"

"But the Flying Monkey is here," Louise pointed out since it was undeniable.

"The only reason he'd be here is..." Jillian trailed off.

"Why?" Louise asked.

"I don't know!" Jillian stood and zipped up her pants. "I was hoping you'd answer the question."

Jillian came out of the stall and washed her hands.

Nikola glanced back and forth between them. "We're confused. Who is the Flying Monkey? Is he one of the men with the guns?"

They hadn't stopped to consider that Ming the Merciless might have robbed their house. It was a frightening thought. "Maybe."

Because of the robbery, they had decided to bring everything irreplaceable with them to school, and that included the photographs. Louise dug them out of her backpack and flipped through six pictures. The third photo made her stop with a gasp.

"What is it?" Jillian asked.

Louise held out the photograph of the blindfolded woman. "Is this who I think it is?"

Jillian frowned in concentration. "It might be her. I'm not sure." She swore. "Our stupid genetic donor! Why give us a photo of a woman and then draw a blindfold on the picture so we can't recognize her?"

"Who?" Nikola moved so he could see the photo. "Oh, Anna Desmarais."

"How do you know?" Jillian growled.

"Facial recognition is at ninety-six point three percent. The blindfold doesn't cover all of the bone structure of the eyes, so the match is positive. We could be a hundred percent sure if we could see the eye fold and retina."

Jillian snatched the photograph out of Louise's hand and read the words off the back. "Why did Esme write 'Queen Gertrude of Denmark' on this? Why not Anna Desmarais? And why did she use so many literary references? What does *Hamlet* have to do with *Flash Gordon* and the *Wizard of Oz*?"

"Maybe Anna isn't her real name," Louise guessed. "Maybe Esme didn't know anyone's real names, only that they were using fake names, and guessed that they would change their names again before we would ever meet them."

"But why then call her father the king of Denmark? Is Edmond Desmarais Neil's brother? Why would either one of them be king? Wouldn't this be like Prince Albert and Prince Philip? If you married the queen, you don't become the king! You stay a prince; your son is the one that becomes the next king."

Louise had no idea how to answer any of those questions.

The bell rang, and they were now officially late.

"What are we going to do?" Jillian cried.

Louise fanned the photographs so she could see all of them at once. Other than the old vintage photographs and Esme's cryptic labels, they had no idea who the people were or why Esme considered them dangerous. "We need to find out who they really are. Either we go back home or we go to class."

"He's in class," Jillian pointed out. "If we cut class, the school will call Mom and Dad."

Louise shook her head against that possibility. They needed to keep their parents safe.

"We could do it," Nikola said.

"Do what?" Jillian said.

"I don't know..." Louise didn't want Nikola to use his taser. She'd actually considered it for one second when Jillian asked what they were going to do. That would end badly. They were in deep enough trouble without adding assault and battery.

"We can search databases for pattern matches," Nikola said. "It's part of Tesla's programming."

"These are old photos. You might have to search back in some old archives to find matches."

Nikola nodded. "We will. It's a little distracting. We'll have to focus on it."

"It will be better if you stay in our locker. You'll have Joy with you. The two of you together should be safe." *Or cause enough chaos to bring down the building.* Louise really wished she felt better about leaving the two alone, but taking them into the classroom with the Flying Monkey seemed like a worse plan.

Once they had Nikola hidden, they walked slowly to the classroom, hand in hand.

Louise listed out the reasons they had nothing to fear but fear itself. "They can't know about the babies. They can't know about the codex. They can't know about Joy. So they can't suspect us of being anything but normal fifth-graders."

"What about Lemon-Lime JEl-Lo?" Jillian whispered. "Nigel could have ratted us out."

Louise shook her head. "No, the photographs are eighteen years old or more. Flying Monkey is here because of something that happened before we were even born. Maybe why we were born—or at least why Alexander was born. The way our life has been going lately, I don't think we can even guess what the hell is going to happen next."

Jillian hugged her tightly. "We're innocent, normal fifth-graders."

It was an act that they weren't scared, so Jillian walked in first, giving the performance of her life. Louise followed, hoping that she wasn't blowing it for both of them.

Flying Monkey Five was still at Miss Hamilton's desk. He glanced toward the door as they came in, and his gaze sharpened in interest. It took all of Louise's control to keep fear off her face. She should look curious. An innocent, normal fifth-grader would be interested in a new kid. Oh, God, she hoped she looked curious.

He did look like Crown Prince Kiss Butt. He had the same strong but nearly too sharp lines of his face. His hair was pale blond. His eyes were blazing green; it looked like he had to be wearing contacts to make them that vivid. He locked gazes with her, and the corners of his mouth turned up slightly.

Something about it made her angry. She didn't know who or what he was, but she had spent a lifetime getting around people smarter than him. She gave him her best "I have no idea what you're talking about" smile. As his smile faded, she felt stronger, like she'd already defeated him.

She settled in her seat beside Jillian and ran her hands over the desk. The school had tried to keep them apart in first grade. It was a simple matter to lay siege to the adults' patience and slowly but surely push for what they wanted: seats together. It had taken a month to wear down two sets of teachers, the principal and vice principal and both of their parents, but in the end they had won.

Game of wits, she could win.

"Class, this is Tristan LaClaire. He's going to have a very hard time as there's only a few days of school left, so please be nice to him."

There was already a desk for him as if produced by magic. Thankfully it was across the room, but still he had direct sight of them without needing to turn around.

Elle put her hand up as Tristan settled into his seat. "What will he be doing during the play? All the parts have been taken?"

Miss Hamilton considered. She probably thought about the fact that they were short on pirates but also knew that the pirates were losing popularity in her class as the rehearsals continued. A new student didn't need an immediate strike against him. "He can be one of the Lost Boys."

"But we already have all the Lost Boys."

"We can have an unnamed one. It won't be a problem."

Unnamed Lost Boy. Louise shivered slightly at how fitting that felt for the boy seated to her far right. Tristan LaClaire? She felt sure that wasn't his name any more than Flying Monkey Five.

He was here, reason unknown. The key to what he wanted might be connected to who he really was.

It was nerve-wracking to have Tristan, or whatever his real name was, in class. He was there, in the corner of her eye, no matter how hard she tried to ignore him. Every time she glanced his direction, he would meet her gaze and smirk.

It was the smirk that annoyed her the most. He knew that she had no idea why he was there and was feeling superior about it. Worse, she couldn't even guess. If her life didn't include baby dragons and robots possessed by unborn brothers and books of magic, she could easily come up with a dozen reasons why Tristan was in their classroom. With all normal logic removed, though, it was dangerous to try and guess.

In art class, they were doing team projects. Tristan was assigned to Elle's team since they were short one person. Louise worked to ignore him, making it a point to sit with her back to them. Unlike class, though, they were allowed to talk in the art room.

"I don't think they like me much." Tristan's tone was more smugly amused than hurt.

"They're just really shy." Elle surprised Louise by coming to their defense. "Until recently they didn't talk to anyone. Which is kind of sad. They're actually very nice once they get over being too shy to talk."

"Oh." He sounded almost concerned. Was he simply changing his tone because he thought that Elle was a friend of theirs? "What brought them out of their shell?"

Louise nearly forgot how to breathe as she realized that Elle could spill everything. Their contact with Nigel made it clear that they'd put too much into the videos; anyone who watched them would assume that Lemon-Lime knew everything about Elfhome.

"They joined the Girl Scouts." Elle misled him brilliantly.

By lunchtime Louise was jumpy and short-tempered. She just wanted to lock herself in the girls' restroom and scream. Jillian seemed fine, at least on the surface, but she'd retreated behind Peter Pan's fearless personality.

Still, Jillian flinched just as much as Louise when Tristan sat down at their lunch table.

Zahara eyed him warily and asked the question that everyone had avoided all morning. "Why did you come to school so late in the year? We're almost done."

"I'm on a fact-finding mission," Tristan said.

"Facts on what?" Louise forced herself to ask.

"This and that." He poked at his lunch. "How good the food is, for one. It made more sense for me to come now and see if I like this school enough to go in the fall than to wait until September and find out I hate it."

"You hate it, then?" Jillian dared to ask.

"I'd have to be fairly shallow to make up my mind I hated something in less than four hours," Tristan said.

Louise was tempted to say it had only taken her four minutes to hate him, but she clenched her teeth against the impulse.

"Why did you change schools so close to the end of the year?" Zahara asked. "Did your family move?"

Something like pain flashed through his eyes, and he focused on his plate. "Yes. My father's work keeps me moving around. I was in Pasadena, California. Bird-watching."

After all of Nikola's "we" comments, Louise noticed that Tristan said "I" when he talked about moving and work. It seemed that, if he was telling the truth, he'd been in California alone. Who would send a nine-year-old alone to the other side of the country?

Ming the Merciless, obviously.

Did that mean that Ming was the Flying Monkeys' father? There had been a family resemblance between all the males.

"Do you surf?" Iggy asked.

Tristan shook his head. "Apparently Scandinavians are great boaters and ice skaters but as swimmers, we suck. I stuck to skateboarding."

It was agreed that skateboarding was cool, too, most likely because almost everyone had some experience with it. Even Jillian and Louise had done their share of collecting bruises.

"You don't look French," Jillian said in a very Peter tone.

"Ah, yes, the eyes." Tristan vaguely motioned to his eyes, which had an epicanthic fold. "My family were originally Sami, it's a small tribe of indigenous people of Scandinavia. We were in France only long enough to pick up a French name. My father moved to New York before I was born."

Only the very last part sounded like the truth.

"So where do you live?" Iggy asked.

"I've got a condo in Queens."

He had used "I" again. Did that mean he lived there alone? Surely someone who was nine years old didn't live alone. Or did it mean he wasn't actually nine?

Nikola blinked at them when they opened their locker. "We found them."

"Shh." Louise petted him. She felt guilty. She hadn't checked her texts, since Tristan seemed to be watching them like a hawk. "Don't talk until we say it's safe."

He nodded.

With heart hammering in her chest, she and Jillian walked out with Nikola tucked between them.

Tristan was doing a bad job of pretending that he wasn't waiting for them at the front door. "A nanny-bot?"

"Yes," Louise growled.

"I guess no one is picking you up, either." Tristan waved to the line of luxury cars that were picking up the other students.

"We have Tesla." Louise gripped the leash tightly.

Tristan pressed a hand to his chest. "I feel safer already."

They attempted to hurry down the street toward the subway station, but he fell into step with them.

"What are you doing?" Louise snapped.

"I'm going home," Tristan said. "I was afraid I was going to have to go all alone, so I'm glad that I can go with you."

Louise stopped and faced him. "What?"

"We all live in Astoria." He smirked. "So I can go home with you. It's much safer that way."

They walked to the subway station in tense silence. The twins had the excuse that they were shy, but that would only work for so long. They should find something safe to talk about. Something like school. Or him.

"What do your parents do?" Louise tentatively went down the safest route once they boarded the train and found seats.

"Oh. My mother is a fortune-teller. My father is a king in exile."

"What?" the twins both asked.

Tristan laughed. "Well, that's the cool way to put what they do. My mother is a hedge-fund manager. It means she guesses the future and invests in it. She's very good at it."

"And your father? The king?" Somehow that rang very true.

"He's very, very rich, so he really doesn't do anything at all, except collect people that make him richer and more powerful. People like my mother."

"What country was your father king of?" Jillian asked.

"Nailau Peshyosa. It's changed its name since he was forced out. And he wasn't the king per se. He was Aumvoutui. King is a whole lot cooler sounding."

Louise leaned down to mess with her shoelaces to hide her face. She recognized the name Nailau Peshyosa. It was ancient Elvish for the Inner Sea or the Mediterranean Sea. Ashfall had been Queen Soulful's father and the first king of the elves. When he was crowned, the name was changed—over two thousand years ago.

She swallowed hard as she suddenly realized that Tristan looked the same in his photograph that Esme had left for them eighteen years earlier. He'd looked nine years old in the picture and he still looked nine now.

He wasn't human.

She took a deep breath, fighting to stay calm. He could be lying about his father being a deposed elvish king. But why would he pick such a set of lies? Or had they been able to convince him that they were nothing but normal fifth-graders? Was this some kind of elaborate final test? To see if they reacted to the obscure names that only elves would know?

No matter what he thought they were, the fact remained that he wasn't human.

Was he an elf?

Elves might be immortal, but they were born infants and needed to grow up first, just a lot slower than humans did. It took elves a hundred years before they could reach the physical maturity of a human eighteen-year-old. It meant at thirty-something they would be like an eight-year-old and at fifty they would be like a nine-year-old. There wasn't a big difference between eight and nine.

So he was a young elf born approximately fifty years ago. The photograph would have been taken when he was in his thirties. If his father was an exiled "king," then maybe it was why Esme had used the name Ming the Merciless. Ming was an emperor, which was kind of like a king.

It seemed as if Louise's life was going to stay strange and impossible to guess.

Louise straightened up to study Tristan. Sunlight and shadows passed over his face as the train carried them toward home. Except for the slight almond shape to his eyes, and the fact that he should be really old, there were no real indications that he was an elf. His ears looked as round as hers.

"What?" He actually seemed leery of her.

"What year were you born in?"

"Same as you."

Louise shook her head. "It depends if your birthday is in the spring or in the fall."

He had to do the math. He did it fast, but he had to think. "Twenty-twenty-two."

Most kids said it two-two or twenty-two.

"Ah, spring birthday." Because fall birthdays would make him a fourth-grader now. "Are you Water Tiger or Earth Monkey?"

"What?"

"Chinese New Year starts in February. You're either a Tiger or Monkey." She lied, since Ox fell before Tiger.

"I—I never paid attention to that," he stated. "What are you?"

"We are Tigers. We're lucky and brave, but we can't pass up a challenge, especially when honor is at stake or when we're protecting the people we love."

"Ah, I must be a Monkey then. I was born in January."

She hadn't told him on what side of the divide she and Jillian fell. He knew their birthday. She tried not to feel like this was the most frightening thing she had ever stumbled across. Wait—he'd known that they lived in Astoria, too. She wanted to run screaming, but they still had a long way to go. They were only now pulling into Queensboro Plaza.

Luckily some boys got on, loud and smelling of alcohol, and he focused fiercely on them.

The twins collapsed in the front hall in a quivering heap when they got home.

"I can't believe this!" Jillian cried. "This is horrible!"

"Why can't we talk to people?" Nikola whimpered. "Or at least, why can we talk to some people and not others? What's the point of being able to talk if not to do it?"

Joy somehow escaped Tesla's storage compartment to bounce on Louise's stomach. "No! No! Food first! Joy was good. Feed Joy!"

"Okay!" Louise cried. "Okay! Food and talk!"

Since Jillian seemed even more stressed by the events, Louise took charge of Joy's feeding. They had moved the growing supply of cat food to the back of the drawer of baking supplies since their mother rarely had time to actually bake. Joy bounced impatiently in place, clapping her hands as Louise opened the can.

Nikola stood and watched the process, his size putting him nearly level with the counter. "We don't understand why Tristan said he was born in 2022. He wasn't. Why he would say that? He didn't even like saying it; he found it very stressful."

"How can you tell?" Jillian asked.

"His breathing changed and his heartbeat went up."

"Nom, nom, nom." Joy shoveled in the cat food, dribbling it everywhere. They'd forgotten the paper towels, so Louise scooped up baby dragon and can and carried them both to the sink.

"Louise!" Jillian cried. "It's all over the floor now. Nikola, don't walk in it!"

Nikola looked at his paw and then shook it through the microtremor clean cycle.

Louise sighed as Jillian shrieked. How were they going to keep Nikola and Joy hidden from everyone? It was all becoming overwhelming. It was one thing when it was just their parents and the punishment for being discovered the loss of Internet and other privileges. It seemed like a logic puzzle without a solution. They couldn't go to school without Tesla standing guard. The *nactka* didn't need magic to keep the embryos frozen; they had made several test runs with ice prior to robbing the clinic. What the lack of magic would do to Nikola mentally, they were loath to find out. They had discovered by accident that moving the *nactka* and generator out of the Tesla body, however, made Nikola blind, mute, deaf and paralyzed. Needless to say, none of them wanted to deprive him of his "body."

They had the second generator but its battery pack needed to be charged during the day while they were at school. They could make another battery pack—actually they should, just so they had a spare—but they couldn't finish it and have it fully charged by tomorrow morning. The twins weren't sure what would happen if they separated Joy from the generator for any length of time. The baby dragon refused to cooperate in any experiments. It was possible that the lack of magic would kill her, so they didn't force her. Also a plan of leaving Joy home alone had "bad idea" written all over it.

So they were stuck with the foursome: Nikola and Tesla, Joy and the generator.

With Flying Monkey Five in their classroom, taking all four to school seemed like a recipe for disaster.

"Please listen to us." Nikola pressed up against Louise. "We've waited all day to speak with you. Please let us talk!"

"Okay, we're listening."

Nikola opened his mouth and then stood there a moment. Finally he admitted in a quiet little voice, "We don't know where to start."

"What is Tristan's real name? It's not Flying Monkey Five. No one names their kid that."

"We're not sure. When he was born, he was given the name of Tristan Jacques Desmarais, but if we understand names correctly, that's his real name. Maybe. His father's name is listed as Edmond Desmarais and that's not his father's real name, so Desmarais can't be his real-real name. Right?"

"Wait. Desmarais? He's *Anna* Desmarais' son?"

He nodded. "Here. We'll show you." He looked toward the new kitchen television, and it clicked on. A sepia photograph of Ming the Merciless scowled down at them. "This is the earliest photo I could find of Ming. At that time he was known as Pruet Lalumiere. It is dated April 16, 1853."

"Ming is an elf?" Jillian cried in surprise as Nikola flashed more photos of Ming on the screen. "Whoa, slower, we can't see that fast!"

"Sorry." Nikola slowed down to a few seconds per photo. Nearly too fast to follow except that they were all of Ming, unsmiling, in old-fashioned clothes. After the first one or two photos, which seemed to be portraits, the following pictures were candid shots where Ming barely seemed to realize he was being photographed. Horses were replaced by Model T Fords and then color slowly leached in. The time between the photos grew longer, as if he became more and more cautious of having his picture taken. As an elf stuck on Earth, he most likely didn't want proof that he was immortal just lying around.

"I think Ming is an elf king exiled from Elfhome," Louise said. "I think that Tristan was telling the truth about his father. He just didn't expect us to take him seriously."

"Weird. Why would he do that?"

"Tristan is an elf." Louise pointed out what she'd realized on the train to support that. "And elves don't lie."

"It's socially frowned upon," Jillian grumbled. "It doesn't mean they can't. It's just extremely dishonorable to lie."

"If we were normal kids, we wouldn't have believed what he said, so it's fairly safe to tell us the truth."

"But if he thinks we're normal kids, why is he at our school?"

"I don't know." The obvious answer was that Anna Desmarais had sent him there. But why?

"I could only find four photographs of Crown Prince Kiss Butt. His name is listed as Yves Desmarais." Nikola flashed through the pictures on fast-forward.

Yves? As in the man who'd ordered Alexander kidnapped and Windwolf killed? If Ming was the exiled ruler of the elves, then that would make sense. The crown prince had met with his father's still-loyal subjects to pass on orders. As viceroy, Windwolf represented Queen Soulful Ember's presence in Pittsburgh. Not only would Windwolf report any troop movements, he had the power to reduce them to slag. If the twins' research was correct, then there weren't any other *domana*-caste elves in Pittsburgh.

"Wait!" Jillian cried. "Back up to the second photo!" The picture showed a collection of people, all unaware of the camera as they stared at something horrific. Only Yves seemed unaffected by whatever they were looking at. Jillian pointed at a woman with both hands covering her mouth. "That's Esme!"

Nikola tilted his head as he chased info down on the Internet. "Yes, that's Esme Shenske. Anna Desmarais is her mother."

"What?" Jillian and Louise both shouted.

Nikola cringed away. "Anna Desmarais is Esme Shenske's mother."

"Oh my God, she's our grandmother?" Jillian and Louise both cried.

Nikola gave a complete report. "Anna Cohan married Neil Shenske and had two daughters, Lain and Esme. Eight months after Neil was killed, she married Edmond Desmarais and had two sons, Lucien and Tristan."

"Flying Monkeys Four and Five." Louise ticked them off on her fingers. "Crown Prince Kiss Butt—Yves—was child one. Lain and Esme are two and three. Their little half brothers were four and five."

"Oh geez, we've been going nuts trying to figure this out, and it's been her family all along." Jillian gave a scream and waved her hands over her head. "What the hell? Why didn't she just put their names on the photos?"

"Because Edmond Desmarais isn't Ming's real name any more than Ming is." Louise paced as her stomach churned. "We know Tristan is the baby of the family, and Esme left eighteen years ago. She might have assumed he would grow up. If we hadn't recognized him from his photo, we certainly wouldn't be able to identify him by the name he gave us. The obviously fake name of Flying Monkey Five forced us to do an extensive search."

Jillian growled. "I still say it was a stupid way of warning us! Her way didn't do any good at all. He's in our class! He followed us home! He knows where we live now."

"He knew before he got on the train," Louise said. "Remember? He knew we were going to Astoria. And he knows what our birthday is."

Jillian eyes went wide. "Really?"

Louise bit her bottom lip while trying to remember everything their mother ever told them about Anna Desmarais. In the light of this new information, things looked strangely different. "Oh. Oh. Oh shit."

"What?"

"Anna kept going on and on about Mom stealing something from her. She tore Mom's offices apart trying to find what Mom took from her. What Mom stole was us! Anna knows, and she wants us back."

"How could she know?" Jillian cried. "We erased all the records."

Louise squinted as she watched Joy stuff handfuls of smelly

cat food into her mouth. It was like a jigsaw puzzle. They'd been missing pieces and hadn't been able to put anything together. Now they had lots of pieces, but it didn't make sense. Were they still missing too much? They had erased all the information connecting Esme to all her children: Alexander, themselves, and Nikola. They hadn't been able to remove Esme's billing records without raising certain data flags in the system. So anyone checking could see that Esme had been a customer, and that she'd been paying for storage for eighteen years, but there wouldn't be information on any of the genetic material she'd deposited. Their parents were never billed, not for the twins' embryos or Nikola's, so there wouldn't be any records of what was taken. The company could have done a manual inventory, but their father would have mentioned that. What had the twins missed? And how did this fit with Yves wanting Alexander, Dufae's box, and Joy?

Joy finished eating by sticking her whole head into the can and licking it clean. They'd learned that they couldn't stop this ritual. Joy added a new twist by flinging the empty can over her shoulder. It bounced off the upper cabinet and, either by luck or design, landed in the trashcan.

"Joy! You broke the cabinet!" Jillian pointed to a section of bare wood in the frame.

"No, that's a bullet hole from the robbers that—" Louise gasped as she realized what they'd missed. "We didn't erase all the records! Mom and Dad would have copied everything they could get their hands on about our donors. Family history of illnesses. Genetic disorders. They would have records here at the house."

"And the robbers took everything." Jillian swore. "That bitch! Anna Desmarais wasn't burying the hatchet by giving Mom those gala tickets, she was making sure we were all out of the house so she could have our home robbed!"

Louise nodded slowly as she double-checked her twin's logic. "If she hadn't insisted that Mom and Dad bring us along, they might have hired a babysitter to come to the house. Any random day, someone could be home sick or waiting for a delivery or have a doctor's appointment. The only way she could be sure no one was home was to make a big stink about how she was being noble by giving Mom enough tickets for the whole family. Once she knew we were at the gala, she kept Mom busy so we couldn't leave."

Jillian growled more curses while making sure that the cat food can was buried deep within the trash. Louise turned on the sink's faucet and washed Joy with hand soap. By now the baby dragon loved the combination of warm water and attention. She purred like a kitty, rubbing against Louise's hands.

Jillian made a small sound of discovery and pulled their old toothbrushes out of the trash. Their mother hadn't wanted the twins using them just in case the robbers had touched them. "DNA! That's why the thieves took the toothbrushes: they have Mom and Dad's DNA on them. With these, Desmarais could prove that we're her—wait—no—the robbers didn't take ours. So why did they just take Mom and Dad's?"

Louise considered as she wrapped Joy in a clean dishtowel. "It could be that they wanted DNA to confirm Mom and Dad's identities, in case they were using fake ID."

Jillian snorted at the irony. "Pot calling kettle black." She frowned at the toothbrushes, obviously debating if she should actually put them back in the trash where a dumpster diver could retrieve them. "Maybe that's why the Flying Monkey is at school then. They didn't get DNA samples from us. Maybe he's trying to steal our DNA."

"That doesn't make sense." Louise started to pace. She thought better in motion. "Why send in an undercover kid when you could do something like put someone in as the substitute school nurse and have her check the fifth grade for lice? They could have had someone follow us on to the train and pull a hair or two out without us noticing. Hell, they could have paid a janitor to clean the floor of our locker; there's probably lots of our hair with tags intact."

"Because they're not smart enough to think of it?" Jillian shoved the toothbrushes back into the trash.

"If I could think of three things in one minute, they should have been able to think of *something* in a shorter period of time than it takes to enroll a kid in a private school like Perelman."

"He's definitely at school because of us! There's no way it could be anything else; he stuck to us all day. I think he would have followed us into the bathroom if it wouldn't get him into trouble."

"Maybe he's supposed to kidnap us."

"Him?"

"He's half-elf; he's probably a lot stronger than he looks. And he might know jujitsu or judo or something. He's fifty years old;

he's had time to get a black belt in every martial art there is. He could be super ninja."

"There's two of us!" Jillian said.

"Three." Joy proved that she could count.

"Eight." Nikola shrank back from the collective stare. "Maybe? Not all of us think we should count Tesla, but if we did, we would be eight."

Smart as Louise was, trying to understand how Nikola existed made her brain hurt. "I don't think he's going to try to kidnap us. If he was, he could have done it today easily."

"Kill us?" Jillian guessed and then shook her head along with Louise. "No, all the same things apply. It doesn't make sense to send in your kid to do your dirty work. You use someone that can't be connected back to you."

Nikola stared at Jillian. "It bothers us that you know that."

"Muhahaha!" Jillian gave an evil laugh and Nikola ducked behind Louise.

"Jillian!" Louise wasn't sure if it was a good thing or bad that she sounded like their mother.

Jillian snickered. "It's been a standard thriller trope since Hitchcock did *Strangers on a Train*. Most people are killed by someone that they know, so cops always consider family and friends as their first suspects. Anyone with half a brain knows that. So it stands to reason that the Desmaraises wouldn't use their kid to do their dirty work."

"But if the cops believed he was a really a nine-year-old stranger, would they even think to question him?"

Jillian's eyes went wide with fear.

Nikola tilted his head as if listening to something and then announced, "Mom just got off the train. She'll be here shortly."

The twins yelped in unison.

"We should tell Mom!" Louise cried as she ran upstairs with Joy. Nikola started to chase after her but then stopped on the stairway landing when he realized that Jillian was staying in the kitchen.

"Everything? Are you insane?" Jillian shouted as she hurriedly wiped clean the floor and sink. "They won't believe us. At least for most of it. And the rest? They're going to kill us for!"

"What?" Nikola cried.

"Jilly!" Louise ran back down the steps to where Nikola crouched on the landing in fear. "They're not going to kill us." A shiver of fear went through her as she realized that their parents would never believe that Nikola was alive and real. They might not "kill" the twins, but they might do something awful to the frozen embryos stored within Tesla. "Come on. It's going to be all right. We won't let anything happen to you. Okay?"

They ignored two calls from their mother to come help with dinner while they argued in heated whispers. When they heard their father arrive fifteen minutes later, they had reached a tentative agreement as to what to say and who should say it. They crept downstairs only to find their parents in the middle of their own whispered discussion.

Their mother hissed a curse word and growled softly, "You've got to be kidding me."

"No, due diligence starts next week."

"This is beyond insane."

"It's a holding company that they own. It could be just coincidence."

"Yeah, right." Their mother slammed shut the refrigerator door and yelled, "Girls!"

"We're here," Jillian answered for them as they'd agreed.

Their mother's visible anger vanished when she saw their faces. "What did you do?" she asked warily.

"We know who robbed us and why," Jillian said.

"What?"

"After we blew up our playhouse and found out where we came from, we got curious and went through your computer and found the names of our genetic donors."

"Their names? On our computers?"

Jillian nodded and lied. "It was on some documents listing out their racial and religious and medicals records. White. Jewish. Which of their parents were still alive. Hereditary diseases. That kind of information."

"I—I—I didn't think we ever got their names."

"It was there," Jillian insisted. "And we copied their names and started to look up information on them. We just wanted to know if we had any older brothers or sisters."

Their mother covered her face with her hands, which meant she didn't want them to know what she was feeling.

Louise ignored the plan and jumped to the point. "Our eggs

were from a woman named Esme Shenske. She's Anna Desmarais' daughter."

Jillian frowned at Louise going off-script. It forced her to jump ahead without all their quickly plotted arguments as to why they were right without incriminating themselves more. "That's why we were robbed. Anna Desmarais is trying to find proof that we're her granddaughters."

Louise braced herself for her parents' outburst. They stood silent for a moment and then looked at each other.

"Just coincidence?" Their mother finally broke the silence.

Their father spread his hands helplessly. "It is damning."

"What is just coincidence?" Louise asked.

Their parents exchanged a look.

"I don't think—We don't know—It's just going to scare them," their father stuttered.

Their mother shook her head. "It's better that they hear it from us first."

Their father sighed and nodded. "Desmarais is buying my company."

Louise swallowed down on the fear that jumped up inside her. They'd erased all the information tracing back to them. More importantly, everything that connected Nikola to Esme. At least, everything that was online and easily searched. If the company used offline backup storage of data, then the twins hadn't gotten everything. Normally no one would have realized that there was a difference between online and offline databases, so the data would be safe. But if Desmarais was buying the company, they could do a more detailed search than anyone normally could.

"Now it could be just coincidence that they're buying my company," their father continued. "They own lots of companies. It's mind-boggling how many they own. Edmond Desmarais is a very, very rich man."

"They've given over three hundred million dollars to charities in New York City over the years," their mother said.

How much of that was to the Museum of Natural History? If they'd given millions of dollars to the museum, it would explain why Yves Desmarais was walking around it as if he owned the place.

Their father nodded as if this proved something. "And it doesn't mean that they had anything to do with the robbery. We have no proof, so we can't go around saying that they did."

The Flying Monkey at their school was proof that the Desmaraises were closing in on the twins, but Louise and Jillian had agreed not to mention him. Anything related to elves and baby dragons and magic was too dangerous to Nikola to bring to their parents' attention.

"They took your toothbrushes because they wanted samples of your DNA!" Louise clung to the only proof they had to offer.

"Honey, you don't know that." Their father patted Louise on the head like she was still three.

Louise breathed out instead of screaming. "Why else would anyone steal toothbrushes?"

"That is damning, but it's still not proof." Their mother took four plates out of the dish cabinet and handed them to Louise. "Dinner is ready. We're eating."

Dinner was frozen lasagna, green beans, and a tossed salad. Simple. Inexpensive. Louise wondered what the Flying Monkey was having for dinner. Lobster? Steak? Were the Desmaraises making small talk of murder and kidnapping as they ate on fine china with real silverware instead of stainless steel? What were they planning? Why was Tristan at their school?

That night, Louise dreamed of the babies. They were playing in mud with nothing much more on than underwear. Brown hair and walnut skin and eyes full of mischief. They looked like peas in a pod, but she *knew* only one was a boy and three were girls. They had a string that they were making into one giant cat's cradle. With their tiny little hands, they plucked at the strands, deftly changing the pattern.

"What are you doing?" Louise knelt beside the little boy that had to be Nikola, wondering what were the names of the three little girls.

"We were bored." Nikola snuggled into her arms, puppy warm and soft, smelling of baby powder. "So we're looking to see what we can find."

The string shimmered between his fingers, and she realized it was fiber optics that they were weaving.

"Oh, you have to be careful. People can notice what you're doing."

"We're being careful," one of the little girls said. It was the same tone and cadence Jillian would have used a few years ago.

Full of confidence, not always correct in her assessment of her abilities. "See." The little girl held up a gleaming web run through her fingers. "This is Flying Monkey Five."

When Louise peered at it, it was as if she were watching footage from a web camera. Tristan sat on a big leather couch that made him look all of six years old. He apparently was multitasking, with a tablet balanced on his bare knees and a headset linking him to a bigger screen that held the camera. The soft flickering glow of the television showed he was in a small ultramodern apartment furnished in stark, lean lines. A Power Rangers water bottle and a box of Chinese takeout sat on the coffee table in front of him. He blew a raspberry while considering the information displayed on the big screen. Then, shaking his head, he started to type, muttering, "If it was going to be easy, someone else could do it."

"There he goes again," another girl cried. "Dig. Dig. Dig. What is he looking for?"

"You're spying on him?" Louise cried. "No, no, he's dangerous!"

"We know!" they said in unison, although some said it with exasperation and others with fear.

"We want to help," Nikola added. "We can do this."

"We'll be careful," the girls promised in unison.

The babies started to sing then. "Half a pound of tuppenny rice, half a pound of treacle. That's the way the money goes, Pop! goes the weasel. Every night I get home, the monkey's on the table, take a stick and knock it off, Pop! goes the weasel."

"No, no, don't knock him off the table. That will make him mad."

Louise woke up. By the clock on the nightstand between her bed and Jillian's, it was 4:26 a.m. She peered at it sleepily while she marveled at how vivid the dream had been. The alarm was set for 5:00 so they could feed Joy before her parents woke up. Should she even try to get to sleep again? The play was on next Wednesday and she hadn't worked on it much, what with Joy, Nikola, and everything taking up her attention. She could spend the half hour making sure she was ready.

She sat up, stretching.

Nikola padded out of the darkness to snuggle into her arms. Unlike her dream, he felt of unyielding metal bones and hydraulic muscles, but at least his fur was the same warm softness. "Don't worry, it's just a song. We don't really knock him off the table."

She gasped. "You know what I dreamed?"

"Yes." Nikola seemed to think it was perfectly natural for joint dreams. He pressed closer. "It was nice that you could come and visit us."

"Do the others have names?"

"We're discussing possibilities. We think Nikola Tesla Dufae is awesome. We all want great names, but we're in disagreement as to what is cool."

Nikola's use of pronouns was now frighteningly clear. Louise had slipped into the idea that he was only one person, but in truth there were four little people trapped inside one very limited shell. Four lives that were dependent on her and Jillian. And even if they found someone who was willing to act as surrogate mother, there was a chance that only one or two of them would be born.

She hugged Nikola tightly. She had thought that if they got the embryos stored someplace safe, she and Jillian would have years to plan. Now she wanted to find a way to make them real as quickly as possible.

Nikola tilted his head as if listening to something distant. "Oh, my, that can't be good."

"What?"

"The monkey just looked up 'how to build a bomb.'"

29: FLYING MONKEY DOES WHAT FLYING MONKEY DOES

Tristan waited for them at the train station. Except for one yawn, there was no evidence he'd been up late, endlessly digging through the Internet. The twins tried to act surprised and not annoyed at all by his presence; they'd suspected he might be waiting for them. Their plan was to tag-team him so they could take turns reading over his search history.

"So, does your family have plans for next Friday?" Jillian started her distraction run. Louise slid on her gaming goggles so Tristan couldn't see what she was accessing. He'd started the night by hacking into the school's computers and pulling up student records. No surprise there. But he'd also tapped the records of all the employees too. Odder yet, he'd done detailed background checks on a weird selection of them. Mr. Howe. Miss Hamilton. Those made sense. Miss Gray. Less sense. Teachers whose names she didn't recognize. No sense at all.

"Next Friday?" Tristan seemed completely confused.

So was Louise. She went back and checked which student records he'd pulled. He had only looked at seniors and juniors. He'd ignored the fifth-graders completely.

"Next Friday is the Fourth of July!" Jillian said. "It's why we're having the play on Wednesday instead of Friday. Everyone who goes on vacation leaves early Thursday so the school made the last day on the second."

Actually they were supposed to get out of school the second

week of June. By law, the school had to hold classes for a hundred and eighty days. A broken water pipe in the fall, a blizzard in February, and then the bombing had pushed the last day into July.

The babies said Tristan had been researching bomb-making.

Earth for Humans said that the bomber Vance Roycroft had gone rogue from their organization and claimed that he'd built a terrorist network totally separate from them. Police had confirmed that they found evidence that he hadn't worked alone but so far hadn't released any information on the other bombers.

To find a bomber, someone would need to know the basics of bomb-making. Tristan obviously thought that Roycroft's accomplice was a teacher or one of the older students. But why did Tristan think someone at Perelman was a terrorist? Pure location? Or did he know something more? And why had Ming sent Tristan alone to Perelman to find the bomber?

"The Fourth! Oh, yeah, I forgot. Jet lag and everything." Tristan yawned again, this time wider. "It's still the middle of the night for me."

"The fireworks are a big deal around here," Jillian babbled, hopefully intending to work around to something more interesting. "We go to our Aunt Kitty's place in Hoboken; she has a balcony overlooking the Hudson River. We have chicken and corn on the cob and apple pie."

"How cliché," Tristan said.

"Not cliché, traditional." Jillian kicked the platform, obviously wanting to kick him. "The chicken is Jamaican jerk, not southern fried, and we have black beans, rice and peas, and ginger beer."

"You don't look Jamaican," he teased, because he knew exactly what they were, at least as far as their mother's side. Did Anna know who their father had been?

"Our grandmother was," Jillian stated. "And she was a very wise woman. She always said that family meant what you made it to mean."

The train squealed into the station. Louise pushed up her goggles and focused on following Jillian on to the train. All the cars were crowded, and they had to huddle together around Tesla.

Louise's phone vibrated. She checked it, careful to keep the screen angled away from Tristan.

"We want to see the fireworks!" the text read. "Take us with you!"

She glanced down and Nikola gazed up her, face surprisingly hopeful for it being robotic. His tail thumped against her leg.

She typed "Ok" and put away her phone. She had no idea what to tell their parents, but there was no way she was going to leave Nikola alone. She patted Nikola on the head, and he leaned against her, tail thumping with happiness.

"He's looking for the bombers." Louise explained her theory while they camped out in the girls' restroom before homeroom.

"Here?" Jillian cried and dropped her voice back to a whisper. "At the Perelman School for the Gifted? Are they nuts as well as morally retarded?"

"The target was right across the street." Louise pointed toward the art gallery, which was still full of artwork from Elfhome. None of the teachers had left mysteriously, so if Tristan was right, the person was still here and possibly waiting for another chance.

"There's like a million people within range of the remote control." Nikola had been prancing around them singing "Fireworks! Boom, boom, fireworks bloom." He paused and said, "Actually it's estimated at three million during the daytime."

Jillian pointed to Nikola as if that totally proved her point.

"What do Sparrow, Yves, and Ambassador Feng want?" Louise said.

"What do those three have to do with the bomber?" Jillian cried.

"They want the zone expanded," Louise said. "How could they make sure that happens? By convincing a bunch of racist idiots that setting off a bomb in Manhattan would be a good idea."

"Wouldn't that mean they know who the bombers are? Tristan wouldn't have to be digging for a name."

"Spy cells work by no one knowing all the other people in the network. There's one point of contact and that's it. Yves' contact could have been Roycroft, who is dead now, and all he knows is that the trigger man was at Perelman."

"What does he want with the bomber?" Nikola asked. "Is he going to arrest him?"

Louise glanced to Jillian. Her twin shrugged.

"I don't think so," Louise said.

Jillian ticked off possibilities on her fingers. "Either they're afraid that the bomber can identify them and they're going to kill him or her. Or they want to supply them with another bomb."

Louise hadn't thought it was possible that Tristan's presence could get more frightening, but it just had. Fear was skittering around in her, urging her to run someplace to hide. They couldn't go back home, not without having to confess more to their parents and putting Nikola at risk. "I think if he was here to supply a bomb to a mad man, Tristan wouldn't be following us around. Anyone could do the research and deal with the bomber. Tristan is here because he can be with us all the time. Even Miss Hamilton isn't constantly watching us. I think he may be protecting us."

"Protecting us?" Jillian sneered at the idea.

"Anna wanted Mom to pull us out of school. Since Mom wouldn't do that, Anna sent Tristan here to protect us." That didn't feel right. "Or Ming did, to stop Anna from worrying about us." That felt more possible.

Jillian took it to its logical end. "So Tristan is looking for the bomber to kill him or her."

The homeroom bell rang, ending their war session. Reluctantly they left the safety of the restroom. Louise wished she could find comfort in the fact that Tristan probably didn't mean them harm, but it meant that one of the teachers or other students had already killed several innocent bystanders and might do it again.

Nikola gave the locker a dejected look and then gazed pleadingly at them. "You'll answer our texts?"

"Yes." Louise patted him on the head and then nudged him toward the tight dark hole. "I'm sorry," she whispered. "But you'll be safer this way."

With a whimper, Nikola backed into the space and let them close the door on him. Louise felt horrible doing it. People went to jail for doing this to children. If the twins weren't fifth-graders, they wouldn't have to be doing this to Nikola. If they were adults like other parents—because they were Nikola's parents—they could be working at home or work different shifts or arrange for a nanny. With time they might be able to think of better options, but there hadn't been time.

It had been over a month since the bombing. The FBI tip line gave the official profile of the suspected terrorists.

The most vocal members of Earth for Humans were the people living in the affected zone who stood to lose their homes and workplaces. While they would be compensated for the loss of their homes, they'd receive less than fair-market price and most likely wouldn't be able to relocate close to their work—if their jobs remained afterwards. There were violent debates also going on as to how wide the expansion would need to be to be effective and how uniform it could be without taking out basic support structures like major roadways, power stations, and utility rights-of-way.

Those members, though, tended to be the most levelheaded ones as they'd spent years dealing with having a hole into another universe in their backyard.

The FBI said that the most dangerous members were the ones who had been forced to move from Pittsburgh during the Shutdown. The treaty had specified that the elves would not have to deal with insane, criminal, or orphaned humans. The terms had been extended out to the more general definitions. People who had received treatment for mild depression, eating disorders, and controllable bipolar disorder were lumped in with dangerous psychotics. Drunk drivers were exiled with murderers. Shamed and driven out, they held a great deal of resentment against the elves.

Since the bombing, the details of Vance Roycroft's life had been put on public display. It was a long, disjointed story of disasters and bad choices. Roycroft's childhood home had been squarely on the Rim. The first Startup had leveled the house; his father's body had never been found. It had been assumed that his father had been shattered down to atoms when Pittsburgh had been transferred to Elfhome. His mother had suffered a nervous breakdown and been deported. Vance had been put into foster care on Earth. Roycroft's life never recovered from that first Startup. Early brushes with the law exchanged foster care for juvenile detention centers. When he turned eighteen, he was given a clean slate. Shortly after that he'd joined Earth for Humans.

It must have been then that he was chosen to be a tool. He "started" a business importing and exporting goods from Pittsburgh. The media took it at face value since, as a native Pittsburgher, Roycroft had the privilege of being able to come and go without having to constantly go through the visa process. Louise suspected that Ming had set Roycroft up with a strong line of credit and a list of customers. There was no other way someone could go from absolute nothing to being able to lease trucks, fill them with gas, and drive them to another world.

The authorities claimed that all the explosives had been purchased on Earth and taken to Elfhome, where Roycroft assembled the bomb inside the packing crate for a large ironwood chest. Because of the nature of traffic out of Pittsburgh, the terrorists would have been unable to predict the exact time of delivery. For some reason, Roycroft didn't use a cell phone as a simple trigger. Instead he'd used a fairly sophisticated AI-driven trigger that had been programmed to do detailed safety checks prior to the explosion. If it had worked properly, it wouldn't have obeyed the command to explode before being delivered to the correct location. No wonder the authorities hadn't considered the terrorists "dangerous" enough to try and lock down the city.

There had been a flaw, however, in the range of GPS coordinates that the device used to check to see if it was properly delivered. What the designer thought was several inches in any direction actually translated to dozens of feet. A simple stupid mistake had cost people's lives.

Roycroft had been a high school dropout with no real aptitude for technology. He couldn't have created the trigger.

No one at Perelman fit the FBI profile. Assuming that Roycroft's accomplices had designed the trigger, then Tristan's choices made sense. Everyone he ran background checks on could have possibly created the device. He focused mostly on the teachers who had military backgrounds. Tristan, though, was unfamiliar with the school. He didn't realize that there was only one person with unlimited access to the one piece of equipment necessary to make the trigger: the 3D printer in the technology annex. When Louise had checked the print history a few days after the bombing, Mr. Kessler was the only teacher who had printed anything for weeks prior to her creating the magic generator.

"No. No. This is wrong. What could have happened?"

On the day of the bombing, Mr. Kessler had dashed up twelve flights, in a rush to start a program running on his desk computer. Of all the teachers, only he had been overcome with horror, unable to react. Was it because he was responsible for all the carnage he could so clearly see from the annex window? He'd carefully designed a humane bomb, one that was careful not to kill anyone, and instead he'd unleashed it on children.

If he had made the trigger, then the record should be in the print history.

Louise logged into the school's administrative system via their back door and accessed the printer. It had been wiped clean. Nothing remained. The lack of evidence was just as damning.

Louise felt Tristan's stare. She made the mistake of glancing up and meeting his eyes. He looked puzzled. She realized that her reactions to what she'd found must have shown on her face.

She ducked her head, heart pounding. Mr. Kessler was a horrible, self-centered man but she didn't want to be responsible for getting him killed. What were they going to do?

First period, they had their final in Math. Louise raced through the questions, scribbling out the work with her stylus. She turned in the test slickie ten minutes into class.

"What? No artwork this time?" Mr. Nakagawa asked. Normally she spent the entire class doodling in the margins when they had a test; it amused her that the software allowed an array of colors and line thicknesses.

"Can we use our tablets?" Jillian joined her at his desk. For some weird reason they weren't allowed to use their phones at school, but tablets supported the same texting software.

Mr. Nakagawa flicked his fingers, indicating that they could sit down. "No talking."

Tristan watched them with eyes narrowed, stylus poised over the questions. Surely he was just making a show at struggling with the test. He was old enough to get a doctorate degree. Why was he even taking the test? He'd only been in class for a day!

Mr. Nakagawa tapped on his desk loudly. "Eyes on paper."

Tristan focused back on his test, answering faster than before.

The twins sat down and Louise texted Jillian what she had figured out.

"Obviously we turn Kessler over to the authorities and let them deal with him," Jillian texted.

"We need evidence," Louise texted back.

"We could restore the data and then send it to the police," Nikola offered.

Louise eyed her tablet. She hadn't thought it was possible for someone to "overhear" text messages between two people, but the babies were bored. They'd obviously figured it out. "Yes, do that."

Jillian *eep*ed in surprise, earning a loud knock from Mr. Nakagawa. She pressed her mouth tightly shut on any other exclamations and texted furiously, "If you restore the data, the plans for the magic generator and the decoy Tinker Bell spotlight will also be restored."

"We need to know if he made more than one trigger," Louise typed. "There could be a second bomb."

Jillian flinched as if hit. "Okay, okay, restore the data but don't send to police!"

"We could delete our stuff back off," the babies offered.

It seemed like a simple fix, but most likely the FBI would seize the printer and examine it every possible way including under a microscope, because they would need evidence to convict Mr. Kessler. If the twins turned Mr. Kessler in, then the magic generator would be found. Erasing the info would only make them look guilty—guiltier.

Louise shook her head. "We need something else as evidence. Something that ties him to Roycroft or the bomb."

Jillian leaned back in her chair and stared at the ceiling a moment before texting, "Maybe we could get him to confess. If he tells the police that he was involved, they don't need evidence."

"He'll never confess," Louise texted. "He'd be facing the death penalty."

"New York doesn't have the death penalty," Nikola stated.

"It's an act of terrorism," Louise texted, while Jillian replied with, "It's a federal case."

But perhaps Jillian had the right idea.

"We could send Kessler an anonymous letter saying that if he didn't confess to creating the trigger to the bomb on his 3D printer, that we—"

Her tablet was suddenly jerked out of her hands. She yelped in surprise as Tristan glanced at the screen and his eyebrow rose.

"Kessler?" He said it like he was only mildly surprised.

Mr. Nakagawa knocked loudly.

Tristan handed back her tablet and went back to his seat.

Flying Monkey knew.

He'd only glanced at her tablet for a moment. Nikola's text had scrolled out of view. The babies were safe from him, but Mr. Kessler was a walking dead man.

Maybe. Assuming that Ming didn't want him to make another bomb.

They had to act faster than Louise wanted to. Tristan had taken his own tablet out and was typing something.

"We need to restore the data on the printer," Louise texted.

"We're doing it," Nikola replied.

"As soon as we get a copy, we need to send it to the FBI so they'll act now."

"He got the printer's memory deep-scrubbed, but the programs were automatically copied to the administration system."

Louise had assumed that he'd deleted those, too. "He didn't wipe those?"

"No. He doesn't have clearance to do that."

Neither did the twins, but that didn't stop them. Was Mr. Kessler really so stupid that he couldn't hack the school's system? Or did he think that the school board simply wouldn't understand the code that they were looking at?

She gasped as the log showed that he'd printed three triggers, one day after another, during the first week of March. According to the media, Roycroft's business had promised to deliver all packages during the next Shutdown. He could only make the guarantee because of a well-exploited loophole in the treaty that let US customs prescreen shipments and then keep them in guarded storage areas prior to Shutdown. The EIA then would do a cursory check on the seals and pass the shipments quickly through the quarantine zone. Using Roycroft's records, the FBI had tracked all the thinly disguised bomb components to Elfhome. None of them should have gotten past the US customs, as the treaty banned them. In addition to the quarantine zone expansion, the UN was also debating closing the loophole so that all goods would pass through EIA. Since Ming controlled the EIA, he would effectively control everything in and out of Pittsburgh.

What wasn't clear was how many bombs had been made with the goods sent to Elfhome. The EIA paperwork claimed that Roycroft only transported one crate, but it also claimed that the crate contained a large ironwood chest. Had there been more than one bomb? Where were the other two triggers?

Louise created a temporary e-mail account, making sure it couldn't be traced back to them. She composed a short message that stated simply that Mr. Kevin Kessler of Perelman School for the Gifted had printed the enclosed program on a 3D printer at the school to create the trigger. She hated that she hesitated at sending the message once she was done; the lives of hundreds of people might be at stake. Still, it was putting Jillian and Nikola and Joy at risk, and it scared her.

Was she doing the right thing? There was no sense of right or wrong. Pure logic said that she had to act, and quickly. Steeling herself, she hit "send." The message vanished into the Internet and she felt nothing but continued unease.

Mr. Kessler vanished that afternoon. He'd left his phone on his desk in the annex, rushed down twelve flights of stairs, careened through the seventh-graders returning from lunch, and bolted out of the building. The FBI arrived an hour later with warrants. They started to dismantle the technology annex with frightening thoroughness. When they discovered the triggers in the storage room, school was hastily dismissed.

It was chaos on the street. The bomb squad was assembling outside as teachers herded out the students. Louise kept a firm hold on Tesla's leash as the twins headed toward the subway. She hoped that they could slip away unnoticed by Tristan, but he fell into step with her before they reached the station. The platform display had Mr. Kessler's photo; it was captioned: *Police search for teacher bomber; bombs found at private school.*

What should Louise say if Tristan asked how they knew that the bomber was Mr. Kessler? Should she admit she contacted the FBI? Did he think that she knew where Mr. Kessler went? Why was he still following them? What did he want?

They rode in strained silence to their station and got off.

As they walked down the steps to the street level, Louise realized there was nothing keeping Tristan from following them the whole way home. That they couldn't go into their house and keep him out. It scared her, and that made her angry. If he wanted to pretend he was nine years old, she'd act like he was nine years old.

She spun to face him. "Listen, you stupid booger head! You're making me mad! Are you some kind of pervert?"

"Booger head?" He took a step back, surprised by the attack. "What? I'm not a pervert!"

"Liar, liar, pants on fire!" She gave him a hard push. "You know what they call nasty old men who follow little girls around? Perverts! Just because you're a little boy doesn't mean it's any different when you do it, too! You're a sick little booger head!"

Jillian gazed at them both in wide-eyed amazement.

"I'm not a pedophile!" Tristan cried.

"Neener, neener, boo, boo, stick your head in doo-doo!" Louise gave him a hard push. "Just go away. Cootie breath! Didn't your mother teach you not to be mean to little girls? Your mother would be ashamed of you."

Judging by the way he flinched, Anna would have been upset. Which meant that Anna didn't know that he was there.

"I'm trying to protect you!" Tristan snapped.

"From what?" Louise cried.

Tristan pointed toward Manhattan and their school. "If you didn't notice, there was a bomb at school!"

"And you were going to protect us how?" she shouted. "Poop on it?"

"I would have taken care of it!" Did that mean he hadn't been the one who warned Mr. Kessler?

"By pooping and peeing on it?" Jillian realized what Louise was doing and joined in.

"Don't be so stupid." Tristan sounded his forty-some years. "I know you're smarter than that. How did you know it was Kessler?"

Louise clamped shut her mouth, not sure how to answer.

Luckily, Jillian had something prepared. "Mr. Kessler hates us because we keep blowing his curve; he used to tease us during class. When we started working on the play, we had to go through him to use the printer in the annex."

"Through?" Tristan mimed a ramming motion. "Like a plow through a snowbank?"

"Somewhat," Jillian admitted. "He slipped once or twice and ranted in class about how much he hated elves. Once the FBI released the news about the trigger, Mr. Kessler was the first person we thought of."

All mostly the truth. Convincing Tristan that they were still just normal fifth-graders was probably the wisest thing to do. Louise took up the thread and started to weave out a more elaborate fabrication. "I was in the annex on the morning of the bombing. I saw him come in and trigger the bomb; I just didn't realize it until later. After the bombing, he was really nice to us. Super nice. It made us suspicious."

Jillian tied off the loose ends. "Then we found out he'd scrubbed the memory of the printer."

"So you told the FBI."

"No, that wasn't us," Jillian lied. "We think it was Mr. Howe. We've been dropping hints to all our teachers over the last week and a half, but we didn't think any of them took us seriously."

Louise wrapped up the story in a neat bow. "That's what we were debating this morning: what to do since no one seemed to believe us."

And he believed it. Tristan's eyes widened as he calculated the vectors of their made-up activities. Homeroom. Art. Music. Library. French. Math. In the course of a week, they had over a dozen teachers. Any of them knew Mr. Kessler well enough to make the leap that Tristan had failed to make.

Of course that left the question of how Mr. Kessler had known that he had to flee.

30: CURTAIN OPENS

"Are they here yet?" Jillian whispered as Louise checked her video screens.

"No." Louise could see the two empty seats beside Nikola. Aunt Kitty hadn't been able to change her business meeting in California when the date of the play had been moved. The babies desperately wanted to see the play, so the twins used Aunt Kitty's ticket for Nikola. Louise had settled him into the seat next to Zahara's little brother and explained to Zahara's mother that their nanny-bot was going to film everything for their aunt. They'd spent dinner break stuffing Joy with tuna fish sandwiches. Last Louise checked, the baby dragon was deep asleep in Nikola's storage chamber.

The babies seemed fine, but where were Mom and Dad?

Louise scanned the crowd filtering in through the doors at the back of the theater. Their parents were driving in to the city so that they wouldn't have to brave the subway after the play and the celebratory dinner. Their mother hadn't been able to get off work early but promised to be there well before the curtain went up. Anything could be holding them up, from their mother's boss wanting "one more minute" of her time to them running into a talkative parent in the lobby.

The sense that everything was about to go horribly wrong echoed through Louise, making her focus tightly on the control board. Between the large sets needing to be lowered from the ceiling, four of the cast members on flying wires, and a sword fight, there was so much that could go wrong. The FBI still hadn't found Mr. Kessler, but Louise wasn't sure that he was still alive.

The clock on Louise's console indicated that it was nearly time to cue the overture music. She scanned her sound levels, and made sure everything was reset back to base. She moved her finger to the play button and waited for the time to change.

"I wish they had gotten front seats." Jillian bit her bottom lip to keep it from quivering. "I hope they don't come in so late that they end up standing in the back."

Louise glanced at Jillian, surprised. Jillian had never cared before where their parents sat. She supposed it was because this was the first time that Jillian was playing the hero instead of the villain. "They'll be able to see more of the stage. If they're right up front, they might miss something you do because they're looking at Elle or Iggy."

Jillian gave her the little frown that said she knew full well that Louise was trying to cheer her up.

The clock hit start time, and Louise tapped the play button and clicked her first timer to start the countdown. The overture started with the upbeat "To Neverland" song that Louise had written for the production. The rustle of people finding their seats grew louder. Louise started to slowly dim the house lights and bringing up the curtain lights. There was a gasp from all the other kids as they realized it was time.

"Jillian!" Mr. Howe whispered loudly and waved at Jillian to come get into the flying harness.

Jillian flung her arms around Louise.

The fear that had been echoing faintly leapt forward, and Louise clung hard to her twin, suddenly afraid. "Be careful."

Jillian laughed nervously. "What could possibly happen? It's not like I'm going to be flying around twenty feet above—ow!"

Louise had pulled Jillian's hair hard enough to hurt. "I'm serious." She considered adding that she had a bad feeling but decided that Jillian was already nervous enough. "Just be careful."

"Jillian!" Mr. Howe hissed louder.

Jillian squeezed her once and then darted away.

The seats beside Nikola stayed empty. The rustle from the audience died to an expectant hush. The overture ran five minutes and three seconds. At a minute and a half, Louise killed the house lights completely. Where were their parents?

Louise watched everyone scurry into place, her hands over the keys of the console as her timer counted down. Giselle and Renata in a two-person dog suit were sprawled out in the middle of the Darling nursery floor. They were jointly playing the nanny dog, Nana. Carlos and Darius, who played the Darling boys, jittered beside Louise. Elle stood poised as Wendy, no nerves showing. Across the stage, Ava waited in the wings. She looked nearly adult in Mrs. Darling's evening dress and high heels, wringing her hands in nervousness.

Flying harness hooked up, Jillian bounded from the wings to the nursery window stage-center and stepped through to the back of the set.

Everyone in place. Louise spared another glance at the monitor on the now darkened theater. Had their parents slipped in after she dimmed down the lights? She couldn't make out Nikola to check the empty seats beside him.

Louise tensed as the timer counted down the last few moments of music and, at zero she danced her fingers over the console, opening up the curtains, bringing up the spotlight on Nana, and hitting the sound effect of the nursery clock chiming nine o'clock.

Nana leapt up and the play was officially started. Louise took a deep breath. It felt like she'd started a massive boulder rolling and now had to watch it trundle forward, too large to be safely stopped. She waited with her hands poised over the control panel. Onstage, Mr. and Mrs. Darling tucked their children in, happy despite the fact they were poor and struggling. In a few minutes, they would leave for a rare evening out, thinking their children were safe in bed, but they would be wrong. A powerful stranger had been watching from a distance, jealous of what they had. He was about to swoop in and steal away the Darlings' happiness for his own selfish gain. Blind to the danger, the children wouldn't even understand enough to fight their abduction.

Louise grew aware of someone on her right, watching her, not the play. She spared a glance. Tristan stood beside her in his Lost Boy costume. He had an odd stunned look on his face, like someone had just told him bad news and he wasn't sure how to react to it.

Louise's stomach churned sickeningly. What did he know? All afternoon she had felt as though something horrible was going to happen. Had something happened with Mr. Kessler? It had been over a week and the police hadn't found any trace of him after he fled the school.

Louise realized that the next section of play was about to begin, and she needed to focus. Mrs. Darling was turning off the nursery's lamps, leaving on only dim night-lights. An earlier glimpse of Peter Pan at the window, though, had filled Mrs. Darling with fear for her children. Louise felt the trembling echo of that unease.

"Dear night-lights that protect my sleeping babes." Mrs. Darling spoke her last line before her children flew away from their safe little house. "Burn clear and steadfast to-night."

And then Mrs. Darling was gone, exiting stage right, disappearing into the darkness. Louise felt the burn of tears suddenly and blinked rapidly. Why was she crying?

Act One ended with Peter and the Darling children flying out the nursery window to thunderous applause.

Louise closed the curtains as she dimmed the lights and cued the intermission music. Tapping her timer, she sent the walls of the nursery up into the rafters and brought the forests of Neverland down. "Get the beds offstage," she whispered once she stopped moving the big sets around. "Move the rocks on."

A square of light in the back of the darkened theater caught her attention. For a moment, the figure of a man in uniform stood there, outlined in brilliance from the lobby. Was that a police officer?

She brought up the house lights slightly to verify that it was a policeman in blue, cap on his head.

Principal Wiley had noticed the lights go up and glanced about in confusion and spotted the officer. He hurried over to the policeman, and the two exchanged greetings. The officer said something and Principal Wiley reacted with visible shock and dismay. Hand over mouth, he looked toward the stage.

Louise whimpered. She'd never seen an adult look so distraught. It was terrifying. What could have caused Principal Wiley to look that way?

"Louise!" Mr. Howe murmured. "The music ended."

She lowered the house lights. Just as the theater went dark, the back doors opened again, highlighting that the police officer and principal were leaving together.

✧   ✧   ✧

Something had happened. Something horrible. Something related to the play or someone in the play.

She took out her phone and typed in a text with shaking hands. "Are Mom and Dad with you?"

"No." Nikola responded. "They never showed up."

She dialed her mother. After six rings, the phone went to voice mail. Her father's phone simply stated that the user couldn't be reached. What did that mean? She tried her mother again, but it went straight to voice mail.

"Louise! The act is ending!" Mr. Howe paused with his fingers over the console, obviously wanting to push buttons but not sure which ones. "Close the curtain!"

"Yes, I'm getting it." She tucked away her phone and stabbed the correct button. As the wall of curtains rolled shut, she triggered the intermission music. What else? What was she supposed to do? Everyone was offstage, waiting for the big backdrop of the mermaid lagoon to be lowered from the rafters. She used the sliders to carefully set them into place and then flicked on the holographic projectors, covering the stage with rolling surf.

Jillian was across the stage, helping to move Marooner's Rock into place, watching her with worry. "What?" Jillian mouthed.

"Later." Louise motioned for her to focus on the play. She could barely think past the flood of worry. One of them had to stay clearheaded. Why weren't their parents answering their phones? Why hadn't they texted to say why they were late? Why was the policeman here? What had the cop told Principal Wiley?

The timer on the intermission music was nearly over.

She triggered the holograph of the mermaid perched on the rock and opened the curtains back up. Her duties fulfilled, she pulled her phone back out.

She couldn't bring up her father's location. His phone had to be dead for nothing to register. She checked the GPS on her mother's phone. It gave an address Louise didn't recognize. As she zoomed in tight on the map, she gasped. It was a hospital. "Oh, no. No."

What should she do? Was that why the policeman was here? Because their parents were in an accident and had been taken to a hospital?

The rest of the play was a blur. The massive boulder rolled on, crushing her underneath it. And then the play was over and whatever was coming next was sweeping toward them. The applause was loud and warm, but Louise felt hollow and that the sound was echoing through her. Zahara pulled her out onto the stage for the bow, and Jillian caught her hand and squeezed it tight. Jillian was shimmering with the excitement of being the star. Louise wanted to protect Jillian from the looming disaster, but she also wanted someone to lean on, to be strong.

Everyone poured down into the audience to be claimed by their parents.

Out of the crowd of adults came Principal Wiley, the policeman, and Miss Hamilton. Tears were streaming down Miss Hamilton's face.

Jillian looked up at the adults and caught Louise's hand like a lifeline. "What's going on?"

"Oh!" Miss Hamilton cried. "Oh girls!"

She dropped to her knees in front of them and gathered them into her arms. Her lilac perfume was overpoweringly sweet.

"What's wrong?" Jillian shouted.

"You're scaring us." Louise tried to push Miss Hamilton back. She wanted someone to cling to, someone to be strong for both her and Jillian, not this weeping person who mistook weakness for comforting.

The police officer crouched down beside them. He was big and scary, but at least he wasn't crying. "I'm afraid your mommy and daddy were in a really bad accident. Their car was hit by a big truck."

Jillian started to wail.

Louise reached for the police officer and caught tight to his shirt. "Are—are they—are they dead?"

"No!" Jillian howled. "No!"

The officer flinched at Jillian's cry but nodded solemnly. Louise pulled Jillian between them and clung to his strength. Jillian burrowed tight into Louise, wailing, refusing to take comfort from the man.

Principal Wiley said something about going to the office and pulling their records to call their emergency contact. "Your grandmother is on her way. She was at a charity event nearby."

"We don't have..." Louise started to say that they didn't have a grandmother and then remembered that they did. "What?"

"Here she is now." Principal Wiley beckoned to someone at the lobby doors.

And like something out of a nightmare, Anna Desmarais came sweeping down the center aisle, tall and regal as a queen. She wore a black cocktail dress and diamonds at her neck.

Louise clung tighter to the officer against the flood of impossibility that was about to sweep them away from everything they knew. "Aunt Kitty is our emergency contact."

Principal Wiley shook his head. "According to your records, Kitty Kennedy is a family friend. We needed to call an actual relative."

Louise whimpered and looked to Jillian. She wanted Jillian to stop crying; her twin was so much better at explaining.

"Oh, you poor babies." Anna sunk down and opened her arms. "Yes, I know, it hurts so bad. Come here, ladybug."

Jillian unwrapped from Louise to let herself be coaxed into the woman's embrace. Louise stood feeling like she would collapse.

"We'll get Jillian's street clothes from the changing room." Principal Wiley tapped Miss Hamilton's shoulder and pointed toward the hallway.

Louise could only whimper as he led away the only person they knew in the room, leaving them alone with strangers.

31: LOST IN DARKNESS

There was a sleek black limo parked in the school-bus lane outside the school. It had rained sometime during the play, and the night gleamed wet and dangerous. A tall driver in a black suit got out as they approached and opened the back doors.

All the warnings to not get into cars with strangers played through Louise's mind.

Louise glanced at the police officer and Principal Wiley watching, letting them be taken. They couldn't see the wrongness of this. They knew nothing about Esme's warnings.

She kept a firm hold on Nikola, who seemed to be stumbling through the same grief that she was feeling. There had been no chance to check to see if Joy was still asleep in Tesla's storage bin or if the baby dragon had woken up and gone in search of food. "We'll get in first."

Louise pretended to struggle with getting Nikola into the limo, praying that Jillian was coherent enough to delay Anna. She cracked the top of the storage chamber, and Joy peered up at her, nearly vibrating with nervousness.

"Stay." She used Tesla's command, knowing that if she were overheard, the adults would assume she was talking to the nanny-bot. She fished a handful of jawbreakers out of her pocket and poured them in with Joy and hurriedly closed the lid.

The need for distraction, though, had broken what little control Jillian might have had. Wailing, she needed to be lifted into the car.

✧   ✧   ✧

Louise knew that Esme's family was crazy rich, but it was another thing to drive up to a mansion larger than their school and spill out of the limo into a foyer that was all polished marble, gleaming gold leaf, and sparkling crystal.

Their footsteps echoed through vast empty areas as they made their way through the house to a second-floor bedroom.

"This is Esme's old room." Anna moved through the large room, flicking on lights. It was a great cave of a room with a twenty-foot ceiling. At one time it had been decorated in the same tween princess-style as Elle's bedroom. Apparently it was the set of furniture that rich people bought their little girls. In the Pondwaters' case, it was an effort to mold their daughter into a demure princess. Whatever reason had moved Anna to purchase the furniture, it obviously had been a complete failure. Every piece had been attacked, defiled, and remodeled by someone who was as whimsical as she was angry.

The four-poster bed had been sprayed high-gloss lacquer black and fitted in what looked like a steampunk elevator cage so it could be raised up to a loft area. The other pieces had also been sprayed black and trimmed with silver, and random gears and cogs had been added. The mirrored vanity had been merged with obscure antique electronics so it looked like the control console of an ancient spacecraft. One wall was floor-to-ceiling bookcases with a tall library ladder on a brass rail. Another wall had faux windows installed and painted so they seemed like they were looking out over eighteenth-century Paris with airships drifting past a half-built Eiffel Tower. There was no sign of real windows, as if Esme had drywalled over them. An odd assortment of furniture crowded the room, from a half-disassembled pinball machine to model airships strung from the ceiling.

"You'll have to share Esme's bedroom tonight." Anna opened a door and turned on another light, revealing a Jack and Jill bathroom that had been spared the steampunk makeover. "Lain's bedroom is connected through here, but it's empty. Lain moved all her things to Elfhome, but Esme just walked away from everything."

"Everything" included old paper books and toys and gadgets crowding the bookcase shelves.

Anna threw a huge wall-mounted knife switch, and the bed lowered down to the ground. "We'll get some furniture for the other room and—which one of you is the oldest?"

"We're twins," Louise said. "We're the same age."

"One of you was born first." Anna started to strip the comforter and sheets from the bed. Dust scented the air as if no one had touched the bed for nearly twenty years.

Louise welcomed the flare of anger. "Mom and Dad said that there isn't an 'oldest' and 'youngest' for us." Since their father had fainted during the delivery, there had been a lot of confusion in the birthing room, and it was possible that their parents simply hadn't known.

"We've always shared a bedroom," Jillian whispered and clung to Louise as if Anna was about to force them apart.

Anna sighed, dropping the comforter and sheets onto the floor. "I suppose, for now, it won't hurt for you to share a room."

There was a knock on the door. It opened, and a tall, elegant woman swept into the room with fresh linens in her hands. She had that same hidden elf look that Ming had, as if everything that said "elf" had been carefully erased, and yet nothing could hide the tall, willowy build and the unearthly beauty.

"I'm sorry," the non-elf said. "I only had time to dust and run a mop around the room. The vacuum cleaner threw another hissy fit. I wish we could find a good old-fashioned one without any sensors or filters or computers."

"This is Celine." Anna dipped a hand toward the female. "She's been our housekeeper since she was very young."

Louise eyed the female. If Tristan was nearly forty and looked ten, then how old was Celine? The housekeeper seemed unaware of the twins' stares. She unfurled the bottom sheet and then expertly tucked the corners around the ends of the mattress.

Anna stripped the pillowcase from one of the pillows and gave it a tentative sniff. "These are too musty." She gazed about the room. "I don't know why I left everything this way. Esme's not coming back. Even if she could, she wouldn't. She hated this house."

Celine took the pillows, carefully keeping whatever she thought of Esme off her face. "I have good goose down ones stored in plastic for guests. They'll be good for tonight—unless the girls are allergic to down."

Louise flinched under the women's joint gaze. "No. At least, I don't think so. Our father was allergic to them, so we never had them in the house."

"George Mayer was allergic?" Anna asked to clarify whom Louise meant by "father."

"Yes, our father!" Louise snapped.

Anna pursed her lips against whatever she wanted to say in reply. "Are you allergic to anything? Are there any medicines you should be taking?"

"No. No," Louise said.

Celine gathered up the dusty bedding. "I'll get the pillows and a blanket."

"I can't sleep without Fritz," Jillian mumbled, leaning against Louise.

Louise whimpered in dismay. Jillian had never slept without her security blanket. Even when they stayed over at their Aunt Kitty's, they took it with them. If they forgot it, Jillian *couldn't* get to sleep. "Fritz is her blanket. Our Grandma Mayer made him for her. He's at our house. Can—can we go get him?"

"I'll have someone go get it. What does it look like? Where does she normally keep it?"

Louise stared at her for a minute in confusion. Surely Anna didn't mean that a stranger would walk into their house and go through their things. And then in a wave of horror Louise realized that soon strangers were going to go through all their stuff. "Can't we just go ourselves?"

"No, you're both too upset. Just tell me where it is."

Jillian pressed against Louise and whispered, "I want Fritz."

"On her bed." Louise fought not to cry as she gave up. "It's inside the blue flannel pillowcase."

"I'll send a driver to go get it."

Within an hour, Fritz had been fetched from their house. In the meantime, the twins had been fed a dinner of hot oatmeal and given a hot bath. They were dressed in long white nightgowns, obviously brand-new and still warm from the dryer.

Every moment of Anna or Celine fussing at them was like sandpaper against Louise's nerves. Finally she could take no more. She pushed Anna toward the door, crying, "We just want to be alone!"

Louise got Jillian into the bed with Nikola and fiddled with the controls she found in the headboard to close the elevator doors and raise the bed up to the loft. In the small fortress, she undid the storage lid and let Joy out.

The baby dragon whimpered in distress and cuddled against Louise's chin.

"We're all together," Louise whispered the only comfort that they had. "We have each other."

She found the light switch and turned off the lights. In the darkness, familiar stars spread across the ceiling. Strangely, some forty years earlier, Esme had painted her ceiling with glow-in-the-dark paint, a low-tech equivalent of their holographic star field.

Between the familiar constellations were words visible only to someone who knew which dots were out of place.

"Don't give up hope."

Louise had felt weirdly hollow, like she'd been filled nearly to bursting with burning grief and then slowly drained. The residue of unbearable pain coated her, but every thought and action now dropped into a vast, echoing pit. Jillian could not stop crying. Joy sat on the pillows and stroked Jillian's hair. Jillian wept even in her sleep.

Nikola lay beside Louise. "What is happening? Why are we here? Why didn't we go home?"

"Something happened to Mom and Dad." Louise felt the words tumble through her, burning as they struck sides, to vanish into the emptiness. The darkness swallowed everything up, leaving nothing but the remembrance of pain.

"What does that mean?"

"It means they're gone away and they're never coming back." Louise had been little when Grandma Johnson and Grandma Mayer had died, but it set a pattern. Each time there had been a tiny funeral, sparsely attended by Aunt Kitty and old people that Louise didn't know. They would clean out the house, taking first the treasures. The old photographs. The family Bible. The beloved Christmas ornaments. Then there would be the mountain of unwanted things to be given away to Goodwill.

After that—nothing. No calls. No visits. No cards in the mail. A painful emptiness that at first was constantly tripped over but slowly healed to nothing.

As much as Louise wanted to go home, she dreaded it. It would be another step along the familiar road. The house would be too still. Too silent. They would gather up what they wanted, constrained by common sense, and be forced to throw out everything else. Their mother's beloved shoes. Their father's wine cork collection. The everyday dishes.

The house would be emptied, and then it would be gone and there would be nothing left at all of their parents.

The grief came flooding back, surging up through her throat, hot and burning, to spill out as fiery tears.

Nikola gave a raw whimper of pain. "Why do we feel so bad? What's wrong with us? Are we going to die?"

She scrubbed away her tears and hugged him tight. "No, no, you're just sad. You're okay. It will go away."

"This is sad? Sad is horrible."

"Yes, it is."

"How do you stop being sad?"

"You think of something happy."

"Like being real and able to hug back? And being able to smell flowers? And eat cake?"

Louise hugged him tighter. "Yes, think of being real."

She tried to sleep. She knew that she did a little, in that she became aware that she had been dreaming, and thus must have been asleep. Alexander haunted her dreams, pursued by monsters. At four in the morning, she gave up and cautiously lowered the bed.

"What are you doing?" Nikola whispered as she stripped off the long white nightgown and dressed in her stage ninja clothes.

"Joy is going to wake up hungry. I'm going to find her something to eat." She pulled the pillowcase off her pillow.

"Okay." Nikola padded to the door and waited expectantly for her. Much as Louise didn't want to creep around the big scary house alone, she knew that there was less of a chance of her getting caught if she didn't take Nikola. He just wasn't built with sneaking in mind.

"Stay here," she said.

"We want to come with you."

"You need to stay here and keep Jillian and Joy safe."

"Joy never listens to us. She says we're just a dumb babies."

"You're not dumb." Louise responded to the part she could positively address. "There are things about the world that you know a lot more about than she does. Like the Internet and robotics."

"Hmm." Nikola sounded unconvinced.

"I don't want Jillian to be alone while she's asleep, so please, just stay here with her."

"Okay."

Louise was filled with sudden certainty that Jillian would try to come looking for her and get caught. "And don't let her come looking for me! Sit on her."

The house was huge and dark and quiet. She used her stage manager flashlight to pick her way through the seemingly endless halls, trying to quietly find the kitchen. Downstairs, every room she peered into could swallow her parents' entire home. They were vast Cinderella palace rooms with marble and crystal that echoed the slightest sounds.

The kitchen was tucked in the corner, behind a great dining room with a table that could sit dozens of people. There were two massive gas ranges, a granite countertop island nearly fifteen feet long, and an entire wall of cabinets.

The far door led to a service entrance facing the massive detached garage. Since no one seemed awake in the house and she would be able to see a car drive up, the kitchen seemed safe to ransack at will.

Louise opened a door to what she thought might be the pantry and discovered an entire room of dried beans, sacks of flour, sugar, and cartons of salt. A locked door in the back of the pantry suggested a way down to a wine cellar. Bins along bottom shelves held three types of potatoes and four types of onions. The elves apparently were preparing for nuclear winter. Despite the abundance, there was little she could carry back to the room and feed Joy. She loaded one of each potato into the pillowcase just in case she found nothing else. Did these people not have anything that could be eaten instantly?

She moved through the kitchen, opening and closing doors as quietly as she could. Finally she discovered a cabinet full of sardines, smoked oysters, herrings, mackerels, kippers, cod liver, and something called tonno all in flat little cans. Luckily the hockey puck cans featured pull-tab lids. It meant that she wouldn't have to take a can opener, but Joy would be able to open the cans and gorge. They would also have to figure out a way to dispose of the smelly cans afterwards.

How were they going to keep Joy hidden and fed?

There was a huge freezer and a big walk-in refrigerator. The latter was a jackpot of fresh fruit, from oranges to pineapples. Louise took one of each. One shelf held wheels of cheeses. She found a knife and cut thin slices from every single block. When she was done, she washed the knife and returned it to its drawer. Another shelf had jars of opened jellies of types she'd never heard of before. Lingonberry. Black Currant. Cloudberry. Wild Choke-cherry. Confit of Violet Petals. Rose hip Jam. Lilikoi Jelly. She eyed them with intense curiosity, but they were small single jars and would probably be missed. There were also several jars of more mundane strawberry and grape. She took a large jar of Smucker's strawberry jam plus the thing of honey and tracked down a stack of fresh baked breads on the counter and stole a loaf. Her pillowcase was now bulging with food, but how long would it last?

Somewhere in the house, she heard a door close. Someone was awake and moving around, and she was suddenly sure they were coming to the kitchen. Louise scanned the room for a hiding place. It was all cabinets and stainless steel appliances; a gleaming trap. She hurried back to the dining room and pulled out one of the center chairs. As she hoped, the table was wide enough that underneath there was a tunnel of space down the middle.

She ducked under the table and turned off her flashlight. She was just pulling the chair back into place behind her when she heard the voices and footsteps of people coming down the hall.

The lights went on in the room.

"I brought an orchid for my mother. I wanted to give it to her on Mother's Day, but he had me searching for crows."

"Sire is not happy that you only located Shoji." Celine went into the kitchen, the door swinging back and forth behind her.

"They're very clever birds." Tristan raised his voice so that Celine could continue hearing him in the kitchen. There was a thump on the table as he apparently put the flowerpot down. "No one else was able to find him. Did Yves manage to capture Shoji after I found him?"

"You don't need to know that," Celine called.

Apparently Tristan was used to this type of answer. He only huffed and pulled out a chair. He sat down, swinging his legs as his feet didn't touch the floor. "I'm really not good with plants. It nearly died once." And then in a quiet voice, he asked, "Do you think she'll like it?"

"It's pitiful." Celine set a dish on the table with the clink of china and silverware. By the smell, she'd made him toast.

"Can I have something else?" he asked.

"What is wrong with this?" Celine asked.

"I'm sick of toast and cereal for breakfast. I've tried to make kippers and eggs like Nattie makes it, but I can't figure out what I'm doing wrong."

"I am not a cook," Celine stated flatly. "You will have to wait until Nattie rises."

"She won't show me how to cook them." Tristan kicked the leg of the table.

"You should be able to find a place that cooks that kind of thing in the morning. He gives you money enough to buy breakfast at a restaurant. You should be getting proper amounts of protein."

"I hate eating out alone." Tristan slumped down onto the table. "Always getting the same questions. Where are my parents? Why am I there alone? Don't I have someone to take care of me?"

"The monkeys are too damn curious," Celine muttered.

"Why can't I have a cook? I could say that they're my guardian."

"We can't afford for the monkeys to learn our secrets," Celine stated.

"I mean one of us!"

"To live away from the manor is a slow death sentence. You are young enough that you do not suffer from the lack of magic. The rest of us grow sick without it."

"I know, I know, supposedly I will grow up faster. I wish it would just hurry up and happen already. Everyone else grew up already. Lain. Esme. Adele. Bethany. Chloe. Felicie. Danni."

"Shh!" Celine hissed loudly. "You're not to mention the inbreeds in this house."

"You said my mother was still asleep." He was unrepentant.

"You must always be vigilant with our secrets. It is the only way for us to stay safe."

"Why can't one of them be with me? They all grew up."

Celine went to the door and glanced down the hall before whispering. "Your half sisters are all wholly human, and they will die before you are even adult. In a very short period of time, you will be the caregiver, not them. You will grow up. You must be patient."

"I'm tired of waiting." He kicked at the table leg again.

Half sisters? He'd named at least six or seven girls. Louise only recognized Lain and Esme. Who were the others? How were they related? Lain and Esme were his half sisters because they shared the same mother. Ming was Tristan's father, and he was an elf. If the girls were true humans, it meant that the other girls couldn't be Ming's children, so the parent that they all shared had to be Anna. But at the gala, Anna had said that she had two daughters. Did this mean that somehow she wasn't aware that the others existed? And who was their human father? Why had Celine called them "inbreeds?"

He kicked the leg again. "Where is Bethany? No one talks about her anymore."

"I told you, do not mention them in this house."

A clock chimed somewhere in the house. Someone was walking through the house in long, solid strides.

"When does mother come down for breakfast?" He sounded slightly afraid.

"She has been sleeping heavily lately."

"He's been giving her *saijin* to make her dream more?"

"Her visions are vital to our success."

Tristan growled slightly.

Celine scolded him for his anger. "For thousands of years we've had to hide ourselves among these savages, huddling over fissures in the earth. We who were gods of paradise were forced to this. But it soon ends."

The footsteps grew louder. Louise huddled under the table, growing more afraid. It was Ming. She was sure of this. Celine turned toward the door and Tristan stood up.

"Sire," Celine murmured, her voice full of reverence.

"Father," Tristan said.

"You were not to come here today." Ming's voice was deep and menacing.

"I want to see her. I haven't seen her for over a year."

Ming continued as if he hadn't spoken. "You're to go to Cranberry."

"Cranberry?" Tristan cried as if it were a death sentence. "Why?"

"There are some more crows for you to find. I want them found before the next Shutdown. Once you've done that, you're to go to Elfhome."

"For how long?"

"You will not be coming back."

"Ever?"

"We have what we need to pull the bastard's teeth. More importantly, the Eyes have seen that Feng's people have a dragon."

"Malice?"

"No, not one of the ones Feng cobbled together out of pieces of the Stone Clan's holy dogs. A true dragon. With it, they can preempt our strike. I need you with Lucien on Elfhome."

Tristan panted harshly, as if he had taken a deadly wound. Louise ached for him; to love his mother enough to desperately want just a few minutes with her and to be told he would never see her again.

"Shutdown is not for another week or so." He scrambled for a delay. "There is no reason for me to rush away. Can I at least have a few hours? Just this morning?"

"She is too distracted after seeing you."

"Please." It was a horrible, heartfelt plea.

"No. Here is a list of our people in Cranberry. Here is money. Go now."

He went, slow and dejected.

Ming took the orchid from the table and handed it to Celine. "Throw this away."

Nikola was sitting on Jillian in the middle of the floor when Louise returned to the bedroom.

"Where have you been?" Jillian cried. "What did you tell Nikola to do?"

"She said I shouldn't let you go!" Nikola stated.

"Food!" Joy scampered across the carpeting to climb up Louise's leg. "So hungry! Smells wonderful!" She danced across Louise's shoulders, patting her on her head. "Gimme!"

"I almost got caught by Ming." Louise tugged at Nikola's scruff to get him off Jillian. "He's horrible. I hate him!"

"That doesn't sound like almost," Jillian said. "And did you have to tell Nikola to sit on me? He's heavy!"

"Would you rather be tasered?" Louise said.

"Gimme!" Joy caught Louise by both ears and pulled.

"Ow! Wait!" She dug through the bag to find a slice of cheese and handed it to Joy to give her time to think about rationing out the rest of the food.

"A note would have worked," Jillian grumbled. "What happened? Why do you hate Ming?"

"Because he's horrible!" Louise moved Joy from her shoulder to the desktop; she didn't want the baby dragon to see into the pillowcase. Joy probably could and definitely would open all the cans of fish and gorge on them.

Having gobbled down the slice of cheddar, Joy twiddled her fingers. "Yummy yellow stuff!"

"It's cheese." Nikola sounded slightly smug for being able to name the food but ruined the image by adding, "Right?"

"Yes, it's cheese." Louise fed a wedge of smelly blue cheese to Joy, who sniffed it experimentally and eyed the blue-green lumps. "That's blue cheese. I think."

"Stinky!" Joy cried as if this was a wonderful quality and then crammed the entire wedge into her mouth. "Nom, nom, nom."

"Lou!" Jillian cried. "What happened with Ming?"

While feeding more cheese to Joy, Louise explained what she had heard. "Because half-elves grow up slower than humans, he's just as much a kid as we are, and they've been making him live all alone for years. They won't get him a nanny and they won't leave here to take care of him because they think this place has magic."

"It does," Jillian said.

Louise gave Jillian a puzzled look. Had Jillian been experimenting with magic while Louise was gone?

"I noticed last night downstairs." Jillian only got more confusing.

"What are you talking about?" Louise said.

"I could see magic downstairs." Jillian pointed toward the foyer.

Louise stared at her twin.

"You can't see it?" Jillian asked.

"No!" What's more, Louise had never heard of anyone being able to "see" magic. "What does it look like?"

"It's purplish and misty and it's warm," Jillian said.

"How do you know it's magic?" Louise asked.

Jillian pointed at Nikola. "Because it's the same as the magic generator."

"You can see magic?" Louise barely kept from shouting. It felt like a betrayal that Jillian had some weird special ability and she didn't. That Jillian hadn't even mentioned it up to now.

"I thought you could, too." Jillian started to cry.

Louise stared at her twin in dismay. Once again Jillian had bested her without even trying; so why was she crying?

32: FLAYED

One good thing about Joy stuffing herself was that she was asleep before Anna knocked on the door and walked in before they could answer. Jillian was in her Peter Pan costume and obviously hiding deep within the character.

"Jillian, where are your clothes?" Anna asked.

"I want to keep them clean," Jillian stated. "If we eat something like pancakes for breakfast, they might get messy."

"She's a very messy eater," Louise said because it might be useful for one of them to constantly be dropping food. It would be easier to sneak out food if some of it was always rolling under the table. "When can we go home and get everything we want to keep?"

"This is your home now." Anna waved to take in Esme's steampunk bedroom. "The house is part of your parents' estate. It's up to the executor of their will to go through things and decide what is to be done with them."

"Who is that?" Louise hated the idea of a stranger going through their things.

"I don't know. I have my lawyers looking into it."

"We should be able to get our stuff," Jillian said. "Our clothes and everything in our bedroom are ours."

"In these kind of things, it's best to follow protocols; otherwise things get messy."

There was a protocol for kidnapping your grandchildren? "What are we going to do for clothes?"

"We'll go out shopping later." She waved them toward the door. "Come downstairs for breakfast."

Would the cook notice the missing food? Would she tell anyone? Would Ming realize Louise had heard everything? Louise wished she could turn to someone for comfort, but she was afraid that if she leaned on Jillian, her twin would break under the pressure.

Nikola was leaning against her, obviously not wanting to be left alone. It would be better, though, that he never come to Ming's attention. Besides, Joy probably wouldn't stay hidden if there was a table full of food just above her head. Louise patted him reassuringly but commanded firmly, "Stay."

They didn't eat breakfast in the grand dining room with the massive table. Instead, Anna led them to a tiled sunroom. Louise recognized it as the place where Ming's photograph had been taken eighteen years earlier. It seemed as though time had stopped in the room. Ming sat in the same wooden thronelike chair. He wore a dove-gray suit of linen and a purple shirt without a tie. It could have been the same suit that he'd been wearing when his picture was taken. The pale fabric made his white hair, ashen skin, and strange amber eyes less striking.

"This is my husband, Edmond." She touched them each on the shoulder as she introduced them. "This is Jillian and Louise."

He studied each of them without so much as a nod to acknowledge the introduction. "What do you know of your real parents?"

"Our real parents are George and Mackenzie Mayer," Jillian stated with Peter Pan's bravado.

Ming frowned slightly. "Your genetic donors."

"Our parents never told us who donated the stuff they used to make us," Jillian stated firmly since it was true.

"They didn't tell us anything. We figured it out," Louise added cautiously. "Our blood types are wrong to be their naturally conceived children."

"The paperwork only has lot numbers on it," Anna murmured as if it were something the twins shouldn't hear. "I suspect Esme pulled material from a sperm bank."

"I am interested in who she selected to father her children." Ming didn't lower his voice; he acted as if the twins weren't present. "The DNA scans were interesting. I'm having more detailed tests run on them."

"I can't imagine what Esme was thinking. Why go through all that pain and angst if she wasn't going to stay on Earth? Was she afraid she was going to have an accident like Lain and be stuck on Earth, unable to bear children? It breaks my heart that she never told me that she was afraid. And to think, that she sat right here, a week before she went into orbit and never breathed a word about what she'd done." Anna gave a sad little laugh. "After she left home for that last time, I had several vivid dreams about her hiding babies in a cabbage patch. Every night, a different woman would come to the garden and steal away a baby."

Ming looked at her sharply. "You did not tell me about those dreams."

"I thought it was utter nonsense."

Ming breathed out what might have been anger. Whatever it was, it didn't touch his face, but his eyes were ice-cold. He motioned to Celine, who was hovering by the door. "We'll eat now."

They sat at a round table with exactly four seats. Even if Tristan had stayed for breakfast, there wouldn't have been room for him. A female that Louise hadn't seen before rolled a cart into the sunroom and produced plates out from under silver covers. She had lush red hair woven into a long braid. Like Celine, her beauty marked her as an elf even though there was no sign of elf ears.

"This is Nattie, our cook," Anna introduced the female.

The dishes were identical in content. Each had a split-grilled fish with a poached egg, a small mound of cooked spinach, a dark slab of bread, a wedge of lemon, and a yellow flower of something. The skin and head were still on the fish, and it stared up at Louise with reproach.

"This is breakfast?" Jillian didn't like runny eggs, and the yolk glistened like a drop of honey in the morning sun, ready to burst open.

"Yes, dear." Anna picked up her silverware and started to dissect the grilled fish. "The skin comes off easily and the filet is exposed. But be careful—there are bones underneath."

The yellow flower proved to be a very nice buttercream. The dark bread had a strong sweet flavor to it, some odd cross of rye and molasses, which was acceptable, but Louise would have liked toasted wheat instead.

"The lemon is for the spinach." Anna demonstrated, squeezing the juice onto the mound of rich green. "It's very good for you. It's a very balanced breakfast."

Was this a typical elf breakfast or some kind of weird take on breakfast for immortals? Every part of it was well-cooked and tasted fine but was just too strange after a night in an unfamiliar bedroom. Louise nibbled at it, thinking of the contents of the pantry. Everything in the kitchen had been strange and unappealing. It did not bode well for future meals. They might starve to death here.

In the end, it had been smart to leave Nikola in their room. Anna took them straight from the table to clothes shopping. Louise felt he'd be safer and happier in their room than dragged through dozens of new places, unable to ask questions or comment on their surroundings.

"I want to change into my regular clothes first!" Jillian obviously wanted to warn Nikola that they were going to be gone for a long time.

"You both can change into the first dresses that you like." Anna had a hold of Jillian's wrist when she announced her plan. She used her hold to gently but firmly tow Jillian toward the front door. "It will make it easier to deal with the sales staff if you're wearing something better than your normal clothes."

Celine appeared in the foyer, blocking the stairs back to their room. Louise had little choice but to follow behind Anna.

It was still raining outside, a downpour that well reflected Louise's state of mind. The limo waited under the shelter of the portico with two elves in black suits pretending to be men. Considering that the car could drive itself, two drivers was extreme overkill.

Louise tried to get a better idea of the neighborhood where the mansion was located, but the rain smeared the windows.

Anna outlined her shopping plans, ending with, "Until we can get things settled out, you'll need dresses, socks, and underwear."

"We like T-shirts and pants," Jillian stated firmly in Peter's voice. "Dresses are sissy."

"We will get those, too," Anna said as if she'd won some point. "If we have time, we can look at furniture for your bedrooms. We'll remodel Esme's room and then Lain's, so you both can have your own space."

"We like being together." Jillian leaned forcibly against Louise to underscore her point.

"And we like the room we're in." Louise liked to imagine Esme was protecting them in her old bedroom, even though she knew that was impossible.

Anna breathed out a small sigh. "I indulged Esme's grief after her father was killed and Lain had her accident. I let her make that room into a cave and fill it up with so much escapist whimsy. I thought it was good for her, hammering nails instead of heads, but looking back it seems exactly the wrong thing. It was the beginning of the end."

Anna spoke as if Esme was dead instead of just in another star system billions of miles away. The colony sent audio updates on a regular schedule, delayed by nearly five years. Esme's ship would have arrived nearly eighteen years ago; had she not sent messages home?

"She's not dead," Louise said.

"To me, she died the day she jumped out of Earth's orbit. She's lost to me. That damn gate has stolen all my baby girls from me. I hate it."

"What about—" Louise caught herself. She and Jillian shouldn't know anything about the rest of the family. How could she salvage her question? "Were Lain and Esme your only kids?"

"No." Anna didn't seem to notice how horribly the question was cobbled together. She sighed and looked out the window, although it was so hazed by rain it was unlikely she could see anything but her own blurred reflection. "I wanted rafts of children, and Edmond was more than willing to indulge me. After several— failures—we had two little boys. The doctors said I wouldn't be able to safely have any more. We talked about using surrogate mothers; India had a booming business in it at the time. We went so far as to take the first steps, and have some eggs harvested and fertilized. I still dream of the little girls they might have been; the grown women they would be now. The doctors said, though, that the genetic testing showed that all the girls had inherited the same genetic illness as our little boys.

"Our two little boys were so ill. They didn't sit up until they were nearly one and didn't start to walk until they were three. They were always so small for their age. When they were twenty, they were smaller than you are now. I couldn't bear to subject more children to that, and Edmond agreed. I had the embryos disposed of."

Louise stared at her. Bitter sorrow and self-blame were obvious in her voice. Anna didn't know. She didn't realize that her sons were half-elves. It took a hundred years for elves to reach "adult," so it was probably no surprise to Edmond that the boys had grown so slowly. He had left his wife believing that somehow she was responsible for their lack. How had he fooled Anna for so many years? Had she never considered it because when the boys were born, elves were still mythical on Earth?

Louise glanced at Jillian, who shrugged. She scrambled to come up with more questions. "Do—do they live at the house?"

"No. They might look like little boys, but they're full-grown men. They moved out years ago."

But they weren't really adults. They were still children.

And who were Tristan's fully human half-sisters? The missing Bethany and the otherwise unmentionable Adele, Chloe, Felicie, and Danni? Had they been the embryos that Anna thought destroyed? Had the DNA tests been a lie so Edmond could do what he wanted with the unborn children? Louise remembered the loathing in Celine's voice as she called the girls "inbreeds." What had Edmond done to the girls?

The next few hours were a whirlwind of shopping. Anna seemed to want to compact nine missed years into a single day. First stop was a hair salon for three-hundred-dollar haircuts. Then they had their nails done. Deeming Macy's too common, Anna took them to Les Petits Chapelais, Kisan, Half Pint Citizens, and Julian & Sara. They shopped for dresses along with a sprinkling of shirts and jeans as promised, each piece of clothing over a hundred dollars. Then their shoes were deemed too worn and new ones were bought.

Louise felt like she was being flayed, everything familiar and safe being torn away. Finally, as they were "slumming" in Neiman Marcus, Louise locked herself in the cell-like fitting room and called their Aunt Kitty. Jillian was serving as a distraction, doing a full-blown version of the song "Tomorrow" from the musical *Annie*.

Aunt Kitty answered with a frantic "Louise! Where are you? Is Jilly with you? Are you two okay? Where are you?"

"Shopping." Louise eyed the fitting room's mirrors. She barely recognized herself. She hated how little and scared and fashionable she looked. She turned around to face the blank door. Four black dresses hung from a hook, waiting to be tried on, just in case Anna "deemed them stable enough to attend the funerals." By the way she phrased it, Louise wasn't sure Anna would actually allow them to go to the funeral home, let alone the burial. "The school called Anna Desmarais, because she's our grandmother. She got her name on our records as emergency contact. She's taken us clothes shopping."

Apparently Aunt Kitty knew some of this because she didn't ask how Anna was their grandmother. "Are you okay? What's wrong?"

My mommy and daddy are dead! Louise closed her eyes tight on the tears that wanted to come. "I'm scared. I don't like her, even if she's our grandmother. She's not letting us go home. She says we have to wait for someone called an executor to go through everything first."

"I'm your parents' executor," Aunt Kitty said. "I'm at the house now. I'm trying—I'm trying—God, I don't know what I'm doing. I can't believe this is happening."

Aunt Kitty seemed close to crying.

Louise huddled in a ball in the corner of the changing room, trying to be brave. At least it wasn't some stranger going through all her parents' things. "Can we come live with you?"

"Oh, oh, honey bear, you're going to have to be patient. I'm trying to get hold of my lawyer. It's a holiday. And—and I need to set up the funerals."

Louise whimpered. It hadn't seemed completely real until Aunt Kitty mentioned funerals.

"Oh, honey, I'm so sorry."

"Can she really just keep us?"

Aunt Kitty was silent for a minute and then said reluctantly, "Lou, I know this is hard for you. I'm going to do everything I can so you two can come and live with me, but that doesn't mean that your grandmother is a horrible person or that you shouldn't love her. She wants you because she loves her daughter so much, and she wants to love you, too."

"You don't think you can get custody."

"I might not be able to." Their mother had always loved Aunt Kitty for her honesty. It wasn't, however, what Louise needed right now. She really wished her aunt would lie to her, paint everything as something less frightening.

"After Grandma Mayer died, our parents changed their will. They made you our guardian if something happened to them. It's in their will!"

"I know, but Anna has DNA test results proving that you're her granddaughters. The clinic doesn't have any paperwork showing that Esme donated her embryos. It means your father used his position to steal you and Jillian. Her lawyers can make what your parents did seem as if they snatched babies out of the hospital."

"It's not the same! It was just a few little frozen cells. We would have gotten thrown away if they hadn't used our embryos. We were leftovers that only our parents wanted."

"I know, but it's up to the courts to decide who you'll live with."

"Why do we have to live with her until they decide? Her husband is scary. We don't like him."

"What did he do?" Aunt Kitty growled, her voice suddenly full of fear and anger.

It would be an easy card to play to say that Edmond had somehow molested them. Aunt Kitty would come down on him like a she-bear protecting cubs. But what would he do in response? These were people that casually discussed killing people.

"He's albino." Louise tried to make her fear sound stupid. "He's scary-looking. His hair is white and he's really pale, like a vampire, and his eyes are weird."

"That's it?"

"And they eat weird food. We had a fish with its head and tail on it for breakfast. You had to peel the skin off it before you could eat it. It's creepy. We're going to starve to death."

Aunt Kitty breathed out. "Oh, Louise, I'm sorry. I know you two have to be scared. I really wish that you didn't have to go through this, but you're going to have to be patient. Since I'm not your aunt by blood, I can't do anything until a judge settles it. In the meantime, promise me you'll try to be good."

"We will."

"Don't run away. That will make things worse. And don't blow anything up."

33: FORTRESS OF EVIL

❖❖❖

"I feel like I'm trapped in Dracula's castle." Jillian sprawled in the loft bed, high above the bedroom floor. They'd been living at the mansion for ten days now, held by Louise's promise to Aunt Kitty.

Although they bought the black dresses, in the end Anna refused to let them attend the funeral. She thought it would be too much for the twins to bear, and Louise was starting to wonder if Anna was right. Every time she fell asleep, she had vivid nightmares. Jillian rarely left the bed and had slept almost endlessly. Louise was worried that something might be wrong with her twin. Even Joy sensed that Jillian was somehow broken and kept her constant company.

"It seems more like Frankenstein's castle than Dracula's." Louise paced the room full of steampunk furniture that could easily pass as the set to the legendary horror movie. The one filmed in black and white with Boris Karloff as the monster. The images were combining weirdly in her dreams: Edmond in a white lab coat, making little Anna-Bride monsters. Instead of two eyes, the miniature Annas had only one in the center of their foreheads.

"This place is full of them!" Jillian meant the hidden elves. "Haven't you noticed? All tall and pale and beautiful and sparkling."

Louise had counted two dozen secret elves moving quietly through the mansion, all of them looking like Paris models. She found a spyglass on Esme's crowded bookcases. She used it to furtively study the estate's extensive grounds from the windows of Lain's empty bedroom. Entire herds of elf gardeners took care of the pristine gardens while armed guards patrolled the shadows. She'd been making lists of names and habits. She hadn't thought Jillian had noticed the elves; all of Louise's careful spying missions had been alone. Nor had she thought it wise to actually tell her twin how outnumbered they were. It was comforting, though, to know that Jillian wasn't being as completely oblivious to her surroundings as she seemed. "I don't think Dracula sparkled."

"Ming does."

After thinking of the male as Ming the Merciless for so long, it was nearly impossible to refer to him as "Edmond," especially knowing that wasn't his real name either.

Jillian rolled to peer down over the edge of the loft bed. "What does Anna see in him?"

Louise had been wondering herself. At breakfast, there was never a hint of warmth between the two. "I'm not sure if she loves him, or if she only likes that he gives her everything she wants. She likes being rich. Think about it: she comes to the breakfast table all made up even when she's not going out. Mom always said she was a perfectionist. It's like she defines her worth on being flawless. His money lets her be as perfect as she wants."

"But what does he get out of it? She's old, and he's got all these beautiful secret elves."

"He married her to make her loyal. He let her have his children so they would have common bonds. But I think that's also why he won't let Tristan stay here—she stops thinking about 'the family' as some nebulous whole and starts to think of only Tristan as an individual."

"Why would it matter?"

"Because what Tristan wants isn't the same as his father. Not deep down inside."

Jillian retreated, and silence came from overhead for a long time.

They needed to come up with a plan to get them out of this mess. At first Louise didn't ask Jillian what she thought they should do, because Louise had promised Aunt Kitty that they would be good. It was becoming obvious that Aunt Kitty wasn't going to win custody of the twins. A small mountain of belongings arrived from their house without a promised visit. Jillian crumbled into a crying heap within minutes, leaving Louise to deal with the painful treasures.

Someday Louise would want it all; every little fragment of her parents that she could cling to. Each box, though, was filled with almost too much pain for her to bear. Even their toys were unexpected landmines of hurt. She culled out the things they could not live without—all their various printers, the tools they'd adapted to spell-casting, and their video-production equipment. The rest she stacked into the back of the bedroom's big walk-in closet. She would deal with it later. Somehow.

She had to stay focused on what was important: protecting Joy and the babies.

She'd been sure Jillian would have a plan; asking would only start them barreling toward breaking her vow. Now she was afraid that Jillian didn't have a plan.

They had to do something. Joy had plowed through the food that Louise had stolen from the kitchen, and it was nearly gone. Every time that Louise had tried to bring food back from breakfast or lunch, Anna caught her. Sooner or later, hunger would drive Joy out into the open.

Humans might believe that Joy was some kind of exotic lizard. Even if humans understood what Joy truly was, they probably wouldn't be able to hurt the baby dragon. At least, not while she had access to magic. But Edmond was an elf. He might be the very person that had trapped Joy in the *nactka*. Of all the treasures found on Earth, the only one that Yves truly wanted was the box with the eleven other baby dragons. What had the secret elves planned to do with them?

And what would Edmond do to Nikola? Louise was fairly sure her parents wouldn't have believed that Nikola was a magical merger between the babies and the nanny robot. They would have insisted that they dispose of the embryos as a biohazard in one of their maddening "we know what's best because we're adults" moves. It was the main reason that the twins had kept him secret. Edmond would probably believe Nikola existed, but then what? Would he care? Would he see the embryos as biological waste or, worse, something to use to his advantage? He'd done something to Anna's unborn daughters, Louise was sure of that, although she couldn't prove it.

And what had happened to their older sister?

Had April's cousin warned Alexander before the secret elves figured out that she used the name Tinker? Had the NSA secretly escorted her out of Pittsburgh during the last Shutdown? Was Alexander already enrolled in some kind of witness-protection program here on Earth? Or had the secret elves captured her and given her to "that idiot cat" which had killed the other scientists?

Louise shuddered at the thought. The next Shutdown was in two days. If they left in a few hours, they could get to Monroeville in time to sneak across the border while Pittsburgh was on Earth. Somehow. They could find Alexander or hide with Orville. Maybe. But if Alexander had been kidnapped and brought to Earth, the twins would be the only ones who had any hope of finding and saving her.

The only positive note in their life was that their video had influenced enough people that the UN vote was blocked long enough to render it moot. The world was holding its breath, waiting to find out if Windwolf had survived the attack, instead of blindly accepting that he'd been killed. If the viceroy had been killed, how could they hope to stop Ming again with a video?

There was no one the twins could turn to without endangering the person. They were all alone in this Fortress of Evil. The babies. Alexander. Windwolf. Elfhome. The sheer magnitude of responsibilities overwhelmed Louise.

"Jilly, what do we do?"

"I don't know." Jillian seemed too small, too young to be her twin. Somehow during the last few days, she'd become so much less than her real self. "Do you think they had anything to do with Mom and Dad's accident?"

"I don't think so," Louise said with more confidence than she felt. The accident had been splashed across all the newsfeeds; a dozen people had been killed when a tractor-trailer truck had plowed through downtown traffic. The driver had been drunk and asleep in the back of the cab when the auto-drive failed. The truck had plowed through a crowded crosswalk before striking her parents' car on the driver's side, pushing it into the path of an oncoming bus. "If Anna killed someone, it would be neat and clean, like laser surgery. She wouldn't be that messy." She shuddered, thinking of the one victim that had been wedged up under the truck's undercarriage and only discovered hours later. "Edmond might go for wholesale slaughter, but he sent his own son away so Anna wouldn't be distracted."

Despite all that, she had a small niggle of doubt. Jillian, though, wasn't strong enough to hear anything else. Not now.

Louise wondered if Edmond would send them away, too, if they were a big enough distraction. A shiver went down her spine. No, that had "would not end well" written all over it. On the heels of the fear came a wash of anger. She was braver than this, wasn't she? Yet the idea of having to do another pantry raid terrified her. She hated the fact that now that she knew what evil the house held, she didn't want to leave their room by herself.

She felt safe in the bedroom. Esme had planned for them to search out April. She'd guessed that they would be entangled with Edmond and Anna. Louise was sure that Esme had known that they'd end up in her room. Surely she'd left them something; breadcrumbs to follow while lost in this dark place.

The problem was that the room was stuffed to the brim with Esme's childhood. The bookcases alone spanned thirty feet of the bedroom, floor to twenty-foot-high ceiling. Esme apparently deemed them sacred, as the cherry built-ins were the only furniture in the room that hadn't been spray-painted black. The ladder connected to a rail via a wheel mechanism that let it glide back and forth the entire length of the bookcase. When the twins first arrived it had been pushed to the far end, and there it had stayed.

Every morning, while they were at breakfast, a team of maids descended on the room to clean. The dust vanished like entropy in reverse. Despite the bric-a-brac, all the lower shelves had been carefully dusted.

The bookcases held everything from obviously beloved picture books like *Harold and the Purple Crayon* to all fourteen of the Oz books to high school textbooks. (Esme must have left home to go to college and never come back, for there was no sign of anything past the age of eighteen.) On low shelves there were worn toys and on a shelf only reachable by the ladder were seemingly new and apparently unwanted toys. Between the two were random machine parts, interesting rocks, a scattering of seashells, and an animal skull or two. Esme had to have been one odd kid.

Louise paced the length of the bookcases, studying them. Thousands of hiding places, yes, but Esme would have known that the bookcases would be systematically cleaned by the maids the moment her children arrived. Louise pulled out a worn paperback version of *Escape to Witch Mountain* and flipped through it. Nothing was written on the blank inside covers. There was no scrap of paper tucked between the pages. No, Esme wouldn't have trusted something so easily found. She would want something like the box she'd left with April, a puzzle to be solved before unlocking its secrets.

Louise slowly turned, studying the entire room. To hide something you wanted found but only by your clever children and no one else. It would be something that would draw the curious person to it, but defeat anyone not smart enough to figure it out. Her gaze fell on the princess vanity that had been spray-painted black and remodeled with an old video screen and dozens of antique knobs and switches into a steampunk spaceship console. She'd tried a few of the controls and nothing seemed to happen, so she'd assumed that they were simply for display. What if Esme had made the controls functional? They could require a combination of settings to get results.

Louise sat down at the vanity and considered all the dials, knobs, buttons, and switches. The number of combinations was daunting. She memorized the initial settings of all the controls. Cautiously, she started to experiment.

There were three banks of controls. A set of simple on-off switches across the top monitor frame activated a Jacob's Ladder, a hidden mirror-ball light, three of the airships suspended from the ceiling, and finally the monitor itself. There was a webcam built into the frame so that the monitor essentially acted as the vanity's "mirror."

The webcam suggested that there was a computer linked to the monitor. The rightmost set of controls was a number keypad from some vintage machine and beside it the keys from a manual typewriter labeled *A* through *F*. At a glance they would seem like two separate sets of controls, but a dull black line had been painted around them. It was nearly invisible, but it definitely paired up the keys. They combined to form a hexadecimal keypad. Progress, but it just made the possible combinations go astronomical.

The third set of controls was on the left and was a toggle control and two buttons that Louise guessed to be a stand-in for a mouse.

Assuming that the computer had booted up after so many years of being idle, what was the password to unlock Esme's secrets?

If Esme thought that Alexander might end up stuck here, then maybe she'd keyed the password to her.

Louise used the hexadecimal keypad to type in "Alexander."

The monitor flickered, and Esme gazed steadfastly at Louise. Judging by the background, the footage had been filmed with Esme sitting at the vanity. Esme looked too old, however, for the video to be something recorded while she lived in the room. Her hair was cut short and dyed purple, exactly how it was just before she left Earth. Esme looked worriedly into the camera, yet it seemed as though she were looking beyond the lens and seeing Louise.

"Hi, kiddo. I really hope you're not watching this, but if you are, I'm so sorry this is how this all turned out. I'm recording this on what will be my last time in this house. I just..." She paused and glanced over her shoulder, as if she realized that she might be overheard. "I just put my affairs in order. In Manhattan." She meant having the embryos created that would be Alexander, Jillian, Louise, and Nikola. "Tomorrow I go back to China, and in a few months I'll pass through the orbital gate and leave Earth forever.

"On Elfhome, my dreams are so clear and sure. Here, I have dreams but also nightmares, and sometimes it's hard to tell which is which. I don't know if it's because the magic here is screwy, as if leaking through the cracks in reality messed it up, or what. I just woke up from a doozy that I really hope is just a nightmare. You need to get out of this house. Get as far away as possible. Now. Before it's too late. In my dream, he found you when you were much too young. Too small. Too helpless."

Tears filled Esme's eyes. "God, I wish I could stay now. I know I've never laid eyes on you, but I do love you. I've seen reflections of you in my dreams; heard the echoes of your laughter. But I have to go and do what I need to do." Esme pressed her hand to the glass. "Oh, baby, I hope you never see this. You need to find a way out of here and go. Quickly. Be safe."

Esme had dreamed of them. She'd known that they were going to be here.

Louise stared at the screen, barely able to breathe. She was seeing the future. Her dreams had started when they got the magic generator and had gotten stranger since coming to the mansion.

✧   ✧   ✧

"That's it?" Jillian cried when Louise replayed the video for her. Jillian dropped her pitch to parrot Esme. "I have to go and do what I need to do. And do what? Go to a colony a zillion million miles away? What so freaking important about that?"

"I don't know." Louise studied the image closely. "She's afraid that this recording might be found, so she's trying to be as careful as possible. If Ming had found this, there's not much to lead him to us or betray anything else she's trying to keep secret."

Now that Louise examined the video carefully, she noticed that the angle was off. Instead of showing the middle of the bookcase, it was showing the far end and one corner of the false window looking out at the fantasy Paris landscape. Esme sat off-center, so that the window's edge dominated the screen.

Had Esme hidden something in the window frame? Louise walked across the room to examine the window. The mural had been painted on a panel that was inset into the wall. The trim covered the seam, but as she peered closely, she could tell that there was a small gap on all four sides.

"I think this is a door," Louise whispered. She gave it an experimental push, but nothing happened.

Joy bounded over and phased through the mural. Louise pressed her hand against the painted wood. It was solid. No wonder they couldn't keep Joy trapped anywhere; she could walk through walls!

The baby dragon bounced back through the solid panel a moment later. She had clutched in her hands a foil-wrapped packet. "It says cookie! Is it food?"

Jillian took the packet and squinted at it. "Peach cookie crumble? It's freeze-dried emergency food. Oh, I think it's expired. Shelf life is only seven years, and Esme left eighteen years ago."

"Open it!" Joy clapped her tiny hands together. "I'm so hungry! Gimme! Gimme! Nom, nom, nom!"

Jillian gave Louise a questioning look. Louise wasn't sure when she got to be the one that decided everything. Had it always been this way and she hadn't noticed before? She shrugged.

"I think it should be okay. I think when it's freeze-dried that shelf life means that it's still at the same nutrient level."

"I can check." Nikola sounded eager to help. The last few days had been hard on him.

"Yes, could you?" Louise searched the mural for how the door opened as Jillian dealt with the hungry baby dragon. "There must be some kind of room behind this panel. Esme wanted us to find it. She must have left some kind of clue as to how to open it."

"You're right, Lou," Nikola said. "The food loses its nutrient value after it expires, but it continues to be eatable in an emergency as long as it's stored correctly and the package isn't compromised."

"Wait!" Jillian cried as she tried to keep the packet out of Joy's reach. "It needs water."

There didn't seem to be any type of keyhole. It was possible that the lock was operated from a switch hidden elsewhere. Louise scanned the room. If she were going to hide a switch or a key, where would she put it? She wouldn't use anything like a light switch. With the mansion's cleaning staff poking around, someone was sure to notice it eventually. Certainly she could understand not putting in a straightforward lock—a keyhole invited lockpicks.

Actually a magnetic lock would make sense. Esme could keep the key with her and yet the lock would stay hidden from search. Unfortunately, Joy wouldn't be able to open a magnetically locked door from the other side. Esme created the secret room when she remodeled her bedroom. Esme would have hidden the card somewhere in the room before leaving Earth. She knew that they were going to be trapped here.

"Oh, you little monkey!" Jillian cried as Joy shoved fistfuls of the now wet dessert into her mouth. "You better wash your hands before getting into our bed!"

"Mish nummy." Joy looked like a squirrel, her cheeks puffed out with food.

"Wish I could eat," Nikola said wistfully. "It looks fun."

"You'll be able to eat after you're born." Jillian patted Nikola on the head. "You just have to be patient."

Okay, so maybe Esme hadn't known *they* were going to be there. She had obviously been expecting one kid, not twin girls and four unborn children inside a robotic dog. Apparently she'd thought Alexander would be her only child.

Where would she hide something for Alexander? The room presented a mind-bogglingly large number of hiding places.

"You're about to leave Earth." Louise slowly turned in circle, scanning the room. "You're never coming back. You're only here because you want to keep up appearances; you don't want your evil stepfather to guess you have some grand scheme. It's natural to say good-bye to your mother, so you're here, saying good-bye.

But then you have a glimpse of the future—your daughter is going to be dragged to this mansion and locked up by the man you fear the most."

"We're not locked up."

Yet, Louise thought but didn't say. "Your ace in the hole is a secret room that you've stocked with food and God knows what. Where do you hide the key?"

Jillian snorted as she attempted to keep Joy from stuffing all the food into her mouth. "Chew first! Nobody is going to take the rest." Once Joy actually paused to chew, Jillian glanced around the room. "Considering Esme's 'clues' so far, it's not going to be anywhere sane. I say we just forget about finding it and pick the lock."

There was the possibility that Esme would have made the hiding place too obscure, going on some weird trust that they'd be able to figure out the clues in time.

Jillian continued, "If I was going to leave a key for a kid I'd never met but was fairly sure they were going to be smart, I'd put it someplace famous. Someplace literary. I'd put it in a bottle labeled 'drink me' like *Alice in Wonderland.* Or inside a seaman's chest, like *Treasure Island.*" Jillian pointed at the steamer trunk that served as a dresser.

They searched the trunk while trying to think of other famous hiding spots.

"This is Esme. It's not going to be obvious," Louise said once they had pulled out drawers and checked the lining. "Still, she was under a time restraint. She couldn't get too elaborate and still expect us to find it."

"April, Tim Bell, and Lain all were on Elfhome, so she couldn't give anything to them," Jillian said.

"She didn't trust her mother or Ming or anyone that we know of."

The only clue she seemed to have left regarding the secret door was the video, which showed the mural. Louise went back to examine it closely again. Obviously the mural had been painted ages prior to Esme filming her warning, so whatever clue she would have left would have been added. The mural was a busy landscape of a Paris that never existed. Odd steam machines labored through a Victorian-period city landscape while great airships drifted overhead.

Was there anything added? Louise peered at all the tiny little details. The little windows of the houses. The storefronts. The people in Victorian dress.

"The *Dahe Hao*." She read the name written on the gondola of one of the airships. "That was Esme's spaceship, wasn't it?"

Louise frowned at the mural for a minute, thinking. "Let's go with the assumption that this is one of Esme's stupid clues. She realized that we were going to be here and would need to get through this door. She shifted the vanity so the door would be in the video she left and then she wrote this name here. She couldn't have written it when she was a teenager because she wouldn't have known it was the name of her ship." Scratch that if Esme was a precog; magic skewed the normal odds. "Probably didn't know."

"The models!" Jillian cried. "I bet it's one of the airship models."

They looked up at the models hung from the twenty-foot ceiling.

"Oh, she has to be nuts," Louise murmured.

"How would she even get up to them without everyone in the mansion knowing?"

"She's an astronaut. She has to be smart."

"And how are we going to get it down?"

Louise studied the models. "Same way." She pointed to the one that most closely matched the *Dahe Hao* in the mural. It nearly touched the bookcases. "She used the library ladder."

The twins rolled the ladder to under the model airship, and Louise climbed up to the top. The maids hadn't started on the top shelves yet; they were thick with dust. There was one faint smudge in the dust, as if someone had put out their hand to balance themselves after a first layer of dust had settled. Had it been Esme? Or someone searching for the key?

Louise turned to study the nearest airship model that was still two feet from the bookcase. Like most of the room, the airship was steampunk in design, a cobbling of improbable and might-have-been. A brightly striped balloon held up a wooden pirate ship complete with five small bronze cannons. It had been crafted with amazing detail. The balloon was stiffened so it looked plump with hydrogen. Hemp ropes like sailing ships' rigging wove a net around it and fastened it to the wooden hull with dozens of miniature knots. Tiny sandbags and an anchor dangled over the sides. Instead of a wooden rudder there was a massive airplane prop. The original name had been scratched off the bow and "Dahe Hao" had been printed in its place with a Sharpie.

If this was indeed where Esme hidden the key, she'd done a good job for something seemingly spur of the moment. Louise couldn't see anything resembling a key on the ship.

"Well?" Jillian had lost patience. She stood with her hand on the ladder like her curiosity was going to overwhelm her common sense.

"It's well hidden, but I'm sure this is it." Louise couldn't shake that feeling even as she stared at the model. Since they couldn't find a keyhole, she was fairly positive that the key had to be to a magnetic lock. How well hidden it was depended on when Esme started to use the airship as a hiding spot. Had she originally carried the card with her or kept it stashed someplace lower? No, that would be too dangerous. Esme had no more privacy than they did. The model was a perfect long-term storage area. The location wasn't improvised, but the clues pointing to it were.

So there was probably a hidden trigger or switch that opened up the airship. There were all the little sandbags and such dangling from the side, but pulling on one seemed risky. It would be too easy to pull the entire model down. So a switch or a knob. The five cannons seemed the most obvious choice. Of course if she was wrong, she might be snapping off delicate pieces. It occurred to Louise that as far as Esme knew, there were five children in her family, thus the nicknames for the flying monkeys. Esme was number three or the middle cannon.

Louise carefully twisted the center barrel. It turned easily. There was a small click and the floor of the quarterdeck flipped up, revealing a small compartment built into the stern of the ship. Inside was a key card.

The method to Esme's madness was revealed in the secret room beyond the door. By covering the windows and creating the framed steampunk cityscapes, she'd been able to disguise the fact that she had actually created a fake wall four feet out from the real wall. It created a long, tall, narrow treasure room stuffed full of things that Esme wanted to keep hidden from Edmond and his staff. Louise couldn't imagine, however, how Esme had managed to get everything past the elves unnoticed. There was a huge supply of freeze-dried food, both in packets like Joy had carried out and in large cans.

"Food?" Joy danced on the shelf in front of the large cans.

Jillian picked up one. "Turkey tetrazzini. Yes, it's food. Twenty-five-year shelf life—and it's still good. Makes ten one-cup servings. It's a lot of food. Diced turkey, asparagus, and gourmet pasta noodles in a flavorful sauce. I wonder what kind of sauce is tetrazzini."

"Is it yummy?"

"I'm not sure." Jillian sorted through the cans. "There might be something more familiar. Spaghetti with meat and sauce. Chicken teriyaki with rice. Blueberry cheesecake."

Joy squealed, making them all wince. "Cake! Cake! Cake!"

Louise laughed, suddenly giddy with the sense of relief. Esme's spirit was here in this secret room, strong and protective. They weren't totally alone.

34: SHUTDOWN

The secret room and all that it promised lifted Jillian's spirits. For the first time since the play, she almost seemed normal. They spent the day inventorying everything the room held, killing the hours before Shutdown. Some of it was extremely logical, like lockpicks and Swiss army knives, some more eccentric, like sharpened wooden stakes and a mallet.

Jillian held up one of the stakes. "See, we're not the only ones that see them as vampires."

"That's probably from before the first Startup. I'm fairly sure Esme knew they were elves after that." Maybe.

Joy held out something wrapped in foil. "Candy?"

Louise took it and eyed the item. "No, this is a glow stick. It's not food. I'm not sure if it's even any good." She unwrapped it, snapped it in the middle, and shook it. The chemicals had degraded to the point where the glow stick barely gleamed, but it was enough to impress the baby dragon.

"Ooohhh." Joy murmured at the glow. "Pretty."

"It just makes light." Louise handed it back to her. "It's not good to eat."

Joy disappeared into the upper shelves, a faint gleam of green marking her passage.

Louise crouched to check the bottom shelf. There were plastic storage boxes with airtight lids. She opened the first one and found old newspaper clippings. Louise actually had never seen a newspaper before. She spent a few minutes in awe of the feel of the paper and how thin it was. She puzzled over the section of text on one side, talking about two airplanes colliding in midair. Then she flipped over the clipping. Neil Shenske in full spacesuit gazed up her. The headline read "Astronaut Killed in Shooting." It was the same photograph that Esme had included in the Chinese puzzle box, only that picture had identified him as the King of Denmark. The newspaper gave all the pertinent details. Why had Esme left them the mislabeled photograph and not this article?

Almost as if in answer to her question, she noticed that the words "police have no leads" had been underlined in red.

In *Hamlet*, the King of Denmark was killed by Claudius, who then married Queen Gertrude and became Hamlet's stepfather. Esme had labeled Anna's photo as Queen Gertrude. If the roles continued to pair up, then Ming was the king's murderer. Esme must have believed that Ming had killed Neil Shenske so he could marry Anna.

Louise flipped through the clippings. They were all on the shooting. Three people had been killed and five more wounded when a lone shooter opened fired at a high school science fair. In an age before cell phones, the person had evaded the handful of surveillance cameras on the school grounds. Witnesses stated that the shooter was tall and slender, but that was the end of the agreement. Follow-up stories spoke of candlelight vigils and angst-filled funerals, but there was never more evidence that led to a killer.

"Joy!" Jillian cried from the other side of the narrow room. "Oh, oh, don't get that on the paper!"

Louise glanced up and groaned. Empty glow sticks lay on the floor, snapped in two after being activated. There were little gleaming paw prints all over the shelves and walls. Joy perched on Jillian's shoulder, holding on to her hair while trying to finger-paint on the paper that Jillian was studying.

"No, no, this may be important." Jillian tried to hold the paper farther away from the baby dragon. "Here, let me find something else."

"What is it?" Louise quickly tucked away the box of newspaper clippings. Jillian probably would see Neil's murder as proof that Ming had killed their parents. The possibility still rocked Louise, but like Esme she'd found no evidence. At least not yet. Jillian couldn't take another hit. Until Louise found something more than a niggling fear, she couldn't let Jillian know.

"Esme has dozens of maps of caves." Jillian held up a blank sheet of paper for Joy to finger-paint. "Here, play with this instead. If Esme was just into spelunking, I don't think she'd have the maps in here. I think they're important."

Louise eyed the crowded shelves of the long, tall, secret room. It was going to take them days to dig through it. In a few hours, though, Shutdown would start. "We should go to bed early. We're going to get up at midnight and try to reach Orville."

At first, every attempt to dial through to their cousin resulted in "All circuits are busy, please try again later." At six in the morning, the phone clicked and Orville's voice mail picked up on the first ring. "Hi, I'm not on Earth with the rest of Pittsburgh. I got permission from the EIA to ride out Shutdown at one of the enclaves. I got this feeling Tinker might come back from Aum Renau, find everyone had gone to Earth without her and just freak. You know the drill; I'll be back after Startup."

Louise stared at her phone. "What is Alexander doing at Aum Renau?"

"Where is Aum Renau?" Nikola asked.

"It's Windwolf's palace on the Palisades." Louise pointed east out of habit. She winced as she remembered the Desmarais mansion was very near to the cliffs. "Aum Renau is hundreds of miles from Pittsburgh. But the only humans that are allowed beyond the city limits are a handful of biologists and the railroad employees."

The railroad didn't lead the entire way to the Elfhome equivalent of the Hudson River but instead stopped at an elf settlement roughly in the same location as Philadelphia. There the cargo was off-loaded to ships that would travel downriver to the Delaware Bay and across the Western Ocean to the Easternlands. Humans only knew of the palace by name; no one had ever actually visited it. How did Alexander even get to Aum Renau?

Nikola tilted his head back and forth as he searched out data. "Oh, she's married Windwolf."

"What?" both the twins cried.

Nikola read the news story aloud. "Derek Maynard, director of the EIA, has issued a statement saying that Tinker has agreed to become the viceroy's *domi*. She should now be considered his

wife and vicereine of the Westernlands. She is now the joint head
of the Wind Clan in Pittsburgh."

"You're kidding!" Jillian cried.

Nikola shrank back, ears dropping. "No. Windwolf had been
summoned to Aum Renau to meet with Queen Soulful Ember.
His gossamer returned with a Hand of Wyverns for Tinker; the
queen wanted to meet the new vicereine."

Windwolf was alive and safe at his palace? And married to
Alexander?

"How did that happen?" Jillian voiced the exact confusion that
Louise was feeling. "When did it happen? Obviously during the
last thirty days—but—but—huh?"

"We're looking!" Nikola cried.

Louise couldn't get her newsreader to acknowledge any updates
beyond "Viceroy Lives!" The news flooded out of Pittsburgh from
three television stations and one newspaper. Affiliate networks
would vet the hours and hours of video and choose what to release,
if anything. The twins had found that much of what came out
of Pittsburgh was quickly buried in film vaults. They'd assumed
in the past it was because they were the only ones interested in
Elfhome. But the popularity of their videos could only mean that
humans were hungry for information on elves.

Anna had been at the NBC gala like a ruling queen. Did the
secret elves have a stranglehold on the news media? Were they
vetting all the information to keep the humans in the dark
about what was going on in Pittsburgh? It was one thing to keep
their activities hidden from sixty thousand humans with limited
resources, and another to blind several billion. Even if only one
percent of the Earth's population was obsessed with Elfhome, it
would equal millions of people analyzing all information flowing
out of Pittsburgh.

A filter was slowly releasing stories onto the Associated Press
site in chronological order. The day after last Startup, Windwolf
had been reported wounded but recovering quickly at the elf
hospice. EIA was detaining two people, at the time unnamed,
for questioning. Growling with frustration, she circumvented the
filter to see what was sitting in the buffer.

Within days of the attack, Pittsburgh was fully aware that there
was a hostile force at work on Elfhome. They quickly learned
even more than what the twins knew.

"A third mirror planet!" Jillian gasped as she hit the news at nearly the same time as Louise.

"Onihida. World of the oni," Louise murmured to let her twin know that they were on the same page. Onihida lay in a parallel universe to the two known worlds, mirroring the landmasses of Earth and Elfhome. Its inhabitants were close enough to human that they could live undetected by anyone. As she read, hurt started to burn deep inside of her. The elves had known about the third world for centuries; they'd simply never told the humans. "The elves not only already knew about Onihida, they'd had a war with the oni. How could they not tell us?"

Jillian snorted in disgust. "Because they didn't know if they could trust us—and they couldn't. Ming and Yves and Ambassador Feng: they're hiding here on Earth, pretending to be humans. They've been fooling everyone for hundreds of years."

"I don't understand." Nikola cocked one eyebrow and ear to show his confusion. "Is Edmond Desmarais an elf or an oni?"

Louise and Jillian exchanged a glance.

"Elf," Louise said after some thought. "Feng had said something about pathways between the worlds being closed. I thought at the time that he meant Elfhome and Earth, but there must have been a way to Onihida, too. When Desmarais—Ming—whatever his name really is—was emperor, the elves traveled between all three planets. What I saw at the museum was a meeting between the three factions of elves. They'd lost contact with each other when the pathways were closed. The people on Onihida don't fully see Ming as their ruler anymore, but they want to go home to Elfhome and regain what they lost. For that, they need to work with the elves in exile on Earth and the elves like Sparrow, who are secretly loyal to Ming."

"Then the oni are elves?" Nikola cocked his other eyebrow and ear in confusion.

"I think oni were the people living on Onihida before the elves arrived." Louise shivered, remembering how Sparrow talked about creating an army of monsters. "The secret elves are using them as weapons."

"Queen Soulful Ember is probably at Aum Renau because of the 'oni' attack on Windwolf." Jillian used her fingers to denote the assumed identity of the attackers.

"Ming and his people have had thousands of years to breed

armies of monsters. There may not be any real oni left on Onihida." Jillian eyes went wide as her own statement dawned fully
on her. "Oh my God, we could meet Queen Soulful Ember. That
would be so cool. And Sword Strike!"

Hopefully no one had ever shown the queen the Lemon-Lime
videos. Soulful Ember didn't have a sense of humor—at least not
the way they always wrote her.

Louise was torn between joy and dismay to discover that because
it was Shutdown, Ming did not eat breakfast with them as usual.
She was happy that he wasn't there, quietly radiating scientific interest toward her and Jillian. Nattie the cook had been persuaded to
scramble the eggs and toast plain white bread and provide a small
dish of Welch's grape jelly. It meant, however, that Ming could be
planning horrible things for Windwolf and Alexander.

"We're going out," Anna stated as the dishes were being cleared,
signaling the end of breakfast.

"Where to?" They shrank away from her, earning a sad, unhappy
look.

"We need to buy new furniture for the bedrooms. I could just
buy whatever I thought would suit you, but I thought you would
like a say in the matter."

Jillian pouted and leaned against Louise.

"We like Esme's bedroom—our bedroom just the way it is,"
Louise said for them both.

Anna pressed her lips together and took a deep breath, as if
there were dozens of things she was leaving unsaid.

Louise could feel the unspoken words rise up, looming over
them, threatening to do harm. If they balked too much, Anna
would plow through their protests. Louise understood now why
she'd felt that they were so much alike when she first saw Anna
at the gala; the twins had apparently inherited the trait from her.
"Can we—can we just do Lain's bedroom—the other room—first?"
Louise picked her way cautiously through the landmines of silent
arguments. "We can stay in the one room while the work is done."

Jillian shot her a look of dismay, but Anna sighed again and
nodded.

"Come along." Anna held out her hand.

Nikola bumped into Louise's other side and looked pleadingly
up at her. Despite the danger of bringing him to Ming's notice,

they had deemed it safer for the babies to come with them instead of being in the room while the maids cleaned. Louise hated the idea of leaving him in a house full of dangerous people as they traveled miles and miles away.

"Can Tesla come?" Louise patted Nikola on the head so Anna knew who she meant since they had never introduced him to her before.

Anna gave a startled laugh. "Nikola Tesla?" The question made Louise flinch in fear. "Esme loved Tesla; he was her favorite scientist. She also had a toy dog named after him. She just loved it to pieces."

"Oh!" Louise looked down to cover her alarm. Had Esme known about the babies? Was that who Esme had seen in her dreams? Or was it just a weird coincidence that Esme had named a dog the same name?

"He's too big, Louise," Anna continued. "He'll take up too much room in the car."

"He can sit on the floor!" Louise stepped forward to take Anna's hand. It was an old woman's hand, veins a vivid blue under the pale, tight dry skin. It was like their Grandma Mayer's hands, but she had been all sweetness and forgetfulness and prone to sudden naps. She would hold their nut-brown hands in hers and try to guess which twin they were. Anna had always gotten their names right.

Tristan had said his mother was a fortune-teller. Did Anna see the future just like Esme? How had Esme kept her mother from knowing everything? Anna hadn't known anything until Esme came to see her, and then she had the dreams of the cabbage patch. Had Esme avoided her mother because contact exposed each one's secrets to the other?

Louise stared at her hand caught tight in Anna's. If that were true, then every moment with her was dangerous. But jerking her hand free might seem as insulting as a slap to the face. She forced herself to squeeze Anna's hand tighter. "Please?"

Anna sighed. "Oh, all right. You can bring your toy."

They rode in the limo to a furniture store in Manhattan, two different male drivers than last time but both unmistakably elves. Where did Ming keep them all hidden? Was there a separate house stuffed to the rafters with them? Nikola had his nose pressed against the window, staring in fascination at the parts of the city he'd never seen before. Jillian hunched over her phone, answering his silent questions.

The salesman at the furniture store caught sight of the limo and was waiting at the door with badly hidden excitement. He didn't glance at Jillian or Louise, staying locked on to Anna as if laser-guided. "How can I help you, madame?"

"I need bedroom sets for my granddaughters." Anna waved toward the twins. "You do sell furniture for children?"

He deflated and eyed the girls for the first time. Obviously children's beds didn't fetch as big a commission as adult furniture. "Yes. We do. An entire floor of it. Let me show you!"

He led them to an elevator, and they went up to the topmost floor. The first large room was a vast sea of cribs and toddler beds. The room beyond was devoted to furniture fit for princesses. Most of it was pink. Even the white-painted pieces were accented with ribbons and bows of pink. There was a Hello Kitty set and a coach straight out of Cinderella.

"Gag me," Jillian muttered darkly.

"We don't like pink," Louise stated. "Do you have anything less girly-girl?"

The salesman looked to Anna.

Anna considered Louise and Jillian as if with X-ray eyes. "Do you have anything more exotic?"

"Exotic? Y-y-yes!" The word started as an automatic statement as the salesman thought frantically and then became a solid confirmation as he thought of something appropriate. "In our adult bedroom section. We just got it in this morning."

Anna flicked her hand, indicating that he should show the way.

They went back downstairs, through a room so crowded with leather sofas that the air was thick with the scent of cured hides. Jillian gasped when they came around the corner to the first bedroom set. It looked like a room lifted out of an Elvish home. All the pieces were intricately carved from ironwood and stained the color of dark honey, bringing out the luminescent gold grain. The canopied bed was draped in white fairy silk that looked magical even under the showroom spotlights. The lamps on the marble-topped nightstands looked like gnarled branches holding small round LED bulbs like elf shines. The price tag discreetly displayed on the end table gave a staggering amount for the set and noted "special order" with no estimate of delivery time. It was totally and utterly perfect.

"All the pieces are solid ironwood and are nearly unbreakable despite their delicate appearance. It's handcrafted on Elfhome using spells and magically sharp tools. It's one of a kind and unique on this world."

"Oh, Grandma," Jillian breathed, only partially faking her enchantment. "Can we have this one?"

Anna obviously melted, just as Jillian had intended. "Of course you can."

Louise bumped Jillian slightly. The logical tactic would have been to only vaguely like the furniture and extend out the shopping for as many days as possible.

"Our floor will need to be redone," Jillian pointed out. "This hardwood has been stained black. The white flokati rug is just stunning against it."

Anna frowned slightly. "Louise, what do you think?"

"I love the bed," Louise said with all honesty. The more changes they could demand to Lain's room, the longer they could delay moving into it. "And I love this rug!" She bent down to run her hand over the thick shag. It was like petting a sheep. "It's so soft and warm. And I really like how everything looks on the dark wood."

"The black seems too depressive to me," Anna said.

"Please!" Jillian cried.

Anna didn't seem swayed by Jillian's cuteness on the color. She was probably thinking of Esme and all the black-painted furniture.

Louise sought to appeal to Anna's intelligence. "The floor needs to be assertive to counterbalance the size of the bed. If the two are too close in tone, they'll clash, and if they match, they'll wash each other out."

Anna's eyebrows went up in surprise, and then she smiled. "All right. At least the rug will cover most of the black. I'll want the largest one you stock."

Louise waited uneasily as the salesman wrote up the order.

"This is a custom piece," the salesman explained. "We got the display in a few hours ago, straight from Elfhome. You're the first ones to see it. We expect it to be popular with the upcoming royal wedding." He paused in the middle of filling out the order form. "You did hear the news this morning? About the wedding?"

"No," Anne said in a tone that stated firmly that she didn't care.

Jillian, however, fed him a line to keep him going. "What royal wedding?"

"Prince Windwolf is alive, and he's getting married. Total *The Queen's Salvage.*"

"Pardon?" Anna said coldly.

"L-lemon-Lime?" he stuttered. "Videos? Pop culture? A human girl saved the viceroy and they've fallen in love. Her name is Tinker, and she's a hoverbike racer! There haven't been any pictures of her yet; everyone expects her to look like the video, but what are the odds?"

Zero. Louise had stolen the heroine in the videos from her dream of Nigel; she was Valkyrie-tall, blond and seemingly able to produce guns from thin air. At least Louise had the comfort of knowing that Nigel would find a heavily armed ally on Elfhome.

Louise tried to push the conversation past the videos. "How long will it take to get our order in? Today? Next Shutdown?"

"We phoned the manufacturer as soon as we heard about the news this morning. People always go gaga over royal weddings; every woman in the city has fantasized about Prince Windwolf at least once. It's a small furniture company, but they assured us that they could have another set ready in two months."

Jillian ducked her head to hide her grin. Louise felt her stomach drop. Two months for anyone else, but Anna had the family trait of plowing through everything in her way to get what she wanted. She wanted to get them out of Esme's bedroom as quickly as possible. She wasn't going to let anything slow her down.

"I'll take the display model then," Anna stated firmly.

The salesman visibly jerked to a full halt. "What?"

"I came to this store to buy quality furniture, not wait for two months for a knockoff copy."

"This furniture is handmade on Elfhome."

"It's made in Pittsburgh by a human, whom you called on the phone. You implied that it's made by elves. 'Spells and magically sharp tools.' I have no way of knowing if the set that the human is capable of creating in two months is anywhere near this level of quality."

"I-I-I never said that elves..." The salesman flailed as Anna plowed through him.

"We want this set," Anna said firmly. "Now. I would suggest you don't offer anything else or I'll have my lawyers draw up a bait-and-switch lawsuit."

The salesman blinked at her for a minute and a half, gears spinning wildly as he considered all the ramifications. Without a sample, he couldn't sell more sets, but there was a chance that no one else would be willing to pay for such expensive furniture. Or that another salesperson might close the future sales. His eyes went to the confirmation of payment from Anna's bank. The amount could have bought their house in Astoria. He winced, obviously thinking of the commission he would lose if Anna backed out of the sale.

Anna relented and sweetened the deal. "Deliver it within the week and we'll take a second identical set."

"Identical?" the salesman's voice broke. "Okay. How does tomorrow sound?"

35: OF COURSE YOU REALIZE
THIS MEANS WAR

Another night, another nightmare.

Louise jerked awake, breaking free of the bad dream. She'd gone to sleep feeling safe in the high loft bed, but the nightmare had stripped away all sense of being protected by Esme's spirit. Panting with fear, Louise touched each of her family members to make sure they were all safely huddled around her. Jillian was curled into a tight ball, her back pressing against Louise. Joy slept tucked between them. Nikola lay carefully beside her so his weight wouldn't crush them.

Nikola lifted his head as she sat up. "What's wrong?"

"I had a bad dream. Bad, bad dream!" She hugged him tight, using his solid presence to drive away the horrible visions. Since arriving at the mansion, every night she'd had a nightmare, but this one was the worst. Ming had locked the twins in a birdcage, deep in caves under the mansion. All the babies had been killed when Nikola tried to free the twins. "Promise me you won't fight. Please, whatever happens, don't ever try to protect me or Jillian."

"But—but—but that's my function."

"No, that was Tesla's function, but you're not Tesla. You're Nikola and I love you so much and I couldn't stand to lose you. You have to be made into real babies and get to do everything real people do. You need to laugh and eat and sleep."

"I don't know. Sleep doesn't seem to be very interesting. You just lie there."

"Please promise me. You're really just a little fragile egg inside of Tesla. If that egg breaks, you'll die. Tesla has to protect you."

"If someone is hurting you..."

"Jillian and I can get ourselves out of any problem we get into. We've been doing it for a long, long time. If someone grabs one or both of us, or locks us up, or even if they seem to hurt us, you can't do anything to try and save us. Promise me that you won't."

"Lou!" he whimpered.

"You have to trust us, Nikola. We can take care of ourselves. You need to trust us to do that."

"Sometimes I feel so useless."

"If things go bad, the most useful thing you can do is to just pretend you're a robot that anyone can order around."

"Just do nothing while someone is hurting—"

"You'll be doing something. You'll be acting. Just like Jillian was Peter Pan in the play. Your character is the robot dog, Tesla, and nothing more."

He made a soft whimpering noise. Louise suspected that if he were a real little boy, he'd be crying. It was so sad that all he could do was little half vocalizations so it sounded like he was mumbling "Ow...ow...ow...ow." She was sure that the pain was real, but he had no way to shed tears.

"It's okay. It's okay." She stroked his head. "It was just a dream."

Only she knew it wasn't.

How ironic that she'd discovered that she actually had a special magical gift, only to have it scare the shit out of her. This *knowing* was confusing and horrifying. She could see the future, and it was the stuff of nightmares. Obviously there had to be a way to use her ability to pick a future she wanted; Ming wouldn't hold Anna so dear if he couldn't use her gift for his own gain. Louise felt like she was trapped in a maze with dozens of literal "dead" ends.

She'd been keeping her promise to Aunt Kitty, unconsciously waiting for her to pull off some legal miracle so that they could live with her. Louise had been too scared to be honest with herself. Jillian might have spent the last ten days curled up in bed, but Louise truthfully hadn't been much better. She'd limited herself to spying on the secret elves and being overwhelmed by everything.

The awful truth was that Aunt Kitty wasn't going to win custody of the twins. She didn't have the money to win a legal battle against Anna. The only way the girls could live with her was if she took them and ran. To stay hidden, Aunt Kitty would have to abandon her songwriting career, something she'd worked her entire life to create. If they were found, Aunt Kitty could be arrested for kidnapping. The best their aunt could hope for was simply going bankrupt, and the worst was spending the rest of her life in prison.

Her dreams were full of danger. Dark caves. Cages. Dark wings. Fire. Things falling out of the sky. Jillian falling from great heights. Nikola battered and broken and dying.

Only one thing was clear. The moment they tried to flee, Ming would bring to bear all his massive resources to recapture them.

Obviously she had to take away all his assets before they fled.

The next morning a work crew invaded Lain's old bedroom. Tall, lean, and beautiful, they looked more like movie stars than construction workers. They spoke French to each other loudly, but when they were talking quietly, a word or two of Elvish would slip in. Louise sat against the door of the connecting bathroom, keeping track of the workers' progress. She had wanted to use a spy camera, but she was afraid the elves would find it as they remodeled the room.

While they worked with the slow, deliberate care of craftsmen, there were several of them, they worked without taking breaks, and the room wasn't that large. In a day they had sanded down the floor by hand, swept it clean, wiped it down with mineral spirits, applied a dark stain and then several coats of sealer. The next day the secret elves returned to paint. Slowly. Carefully.

She felt like she was in a race against them. When they were finished, Anna would want to move on to Esme's bedroom. If Ming found the secret room, everything would unravel. The secret elves would search Tesla and find the babies. They would trap Joy. And if the twins lost the rest of their family, Jillian would break so completely, there would be no fixing her.

Before that happened, they had to cripple Ming and flee the mansion. She and the babies studied Desmarais' sprawling empire, trying to figure out how to wreak the greatest havoc.

It quickly became apparent how dependent Ming was on Anna for his wealth. His oldest surviving company bred champion-quality animals. There had been other companies that had done well and then failed as he refused to change his business plan to cope with changes in technology and cultural ideals. He'd been a plantation owner in Huntsville, Alabama, prior to the Civil War. All that had survived the war was a company that built quality horse coaches, but that died as cars took over. He'd had a large distillery that hadn't survived Prohibition. Toward the end of the last century, he'd been rich but not impressively so, for as many mouths he had to feed. Immediately after marrying Anna, a series of successful high-risk investments skyrocketed his wealth to a level comparable with that of small countries. Judging by the current financial newsfeeds, Anna continued to make huge gambles with their wealth.

No wonder Ming had banished Tristan from the mansion; billions of dollars were at risk. Tristan had said his mother was a fortune-teller, and Ming didn't want Anna distracted, so both of the males knew that Anna had a magically enhanced gift. How had Ming found Anna in the first place?

Their paths apparently crossed in Huntsville, where Ming still had an estate, and astronaut Neil Shenske was training at the Marshall Space Flight Center. Anna worked as an investment banker at a small firm. Within weeks of Ming's meeting her, Neil was dead, and a few months later, besieged by a series of disasters like her house burning down and her car being stolen, Anna married Ming.

Was Esme right? Had Ming killed her father in order to claim Anna's ability for himself? If he had, he'd been careful not to leave any evidence behind. Esme only had nightmares as proof.

Which raised the question: Why wasn't Anna plagued by the same dreams as Esme? Did Ming use some kind of magic spell to keep Anna unaware of his more questionable activities?

Proof of his invasion plans of Elfhome was everywhere as long as you understood the shape of his ambitions. Tracking the money, Louise could practically roadmap his activities. He did own a controlling interest in several of the television networks and news agencies, so he could filter information coming from Elfhome. He also owned three of the largest companies legally shipping goods into Pittsburgh. Through holding companies, he controlled dozens of others, creating a vast network of possibly illegal transportation. Two of which were under investigation. One had funded the Earth for Humans bomber Roycroft. The other company had been involved in the June Shutdown shoot-out on Veterans Bridge.

What didn't make sense was that he was also funneling massive amounts of food, medicine, and weapons to a tiny island in the South China Sea. While Google Maps showed only a sparsely inhabited circle of land, redirected military satellites revealed a beehive of activity. Cargo ships sat at a big dock that nearly dwarfed the island while shipping containers were unloaded via cranes. According to the manifest of one ship pulling away from the dock, it was leaving empty. Material was flowing in but nothing was being shipped out. Where was it all going? Onihida? A quick check confirmed that the island was directly below the hyperphase gate in geostationary orbit. Apparently the same effect that caused Pittsburgh to shift universes to Elfhome also made this island go to Onihida. During Shutdown, everything that had been stockpiled would have been loaded onto boats on Onihida.

Ming's people had created an army of monsters on Onihida to invade Elfhome, but they were going to be armed with weapons from Earth. While the *domana*-caste could go toe-to-toe with tanks, they were few and far between. Most elves had nothing more sophisticated than bows and arrows. What elves survived the slaughter, Ming was going to enslave.

So how could Louise throw this operation into mayhem? What she really wanted to do was bomb it out of existence. She eyed the port with its growing stockpile. Ironically, bombs were currently being off-loaded. Specifically, ammo for a shoulder-launched multipurpose assault weapon. A fire would work well enough, if she could cause one big enough. What did she have to work with? Four ships, all with diesel engines, mostly controlled by computers. Several container cranes that appeared about fifteen stories tall—also computer controlled. An entire shipyard filled with chemicals and fuel. She should be able to create a small disaster that would lead to something bigger.

Technically, she'd only promised Aunt Kitty that they would try to be good. Aunt Kitty had tacked on the "don't blow anything up" afterwards, so that really didn't count. And "be good" was subjective. Stopping an invasion was being good—wasn't it?

Louise focused on one of the ships that had a ridiculous amount of ammonium nitrate fertilizer. What was Ming going to do with that much? The volume nearly guaranteed that the blast would reach munitions. How to ignite it? She ran through the manifest to see what else was on the ship. At the center of the ship was a shipping container filled with potassium. She had no idea what idiots would ship potassium on a boat when the material exploded on contact with water. But there it was, all but gift-wrapped. She merely had to release the shipping container while it was nine stories up. Gravity and the ocean would take care of the rest.

She felt like a stage manager again as she reached out and took hold of the various computers on the other side of the world. The curtain was about to rise on a new act. Cue the war drums. Bring up the lights. Set the actors into motion.

Annoyingly, she lost control of the distant computers immediately after the first explosion. She took it as a good sign, but it was annoying that she couldn't be sure that the entire daisy chain of explosions would actually reach the munitions.

Hopefully it would draw Ming's attention and resources to the other side of the planet. It was a big flashy disaster to draw his attention from the more quiet attacks that she had planned. Now to start the more local damage.

She did a quick search and found a Canadian website that worked with governments of certain countries to set up shell corporations. She wanted the companies she used to be as legal as possible to make it harder for Ming to take back his money, just in case he ever managed to track it all down. For a small fee for each transaction, the Canadian legal firm created dozens of shell companies scattered around the world. Another small fee, and she had a matching number of perfectly legal Singapore bank accounts, owned by the companies in such privacy-minded countries as Belize and Malta. It took her less than a half hour. It was a lot easier to set up bank accounts when you weren't concerned about breaking the law. If she were caught, being taken away from her guardian would be the least of her worries.

The offshore accounts set up, she turned her attention to the massive sprawl of Ming's holdings. He kept them isolated from each other to make it harder for anyone to realize the extent of his wealth. Hopefully, it would also make it harder for Ming to realize someone was systematically cleaning them all out. Still, once he noticed, every transfer increased the likelihood of him intercepting her. How long before the explosion distracted him?

In the next room, the painters finished up painting. During the last two days, Louise had come to recognize individual voices. The workers' supervisor was a female that Anna believed to be named Cosette, but whom the other elves called Dovetail. As Louise listened, Dovetail announced that she would install the lighting, but she wanted to wait on hanging curtains and moving in the furniture. Louise breathed out in relief; another day of work before Dovetail could call the room finished.

The workers gathered up their painting equipment and trooped out. Dovetail remained to install the lights. Her footsteps echoed in the empty, high-ceilinged room. She sang as she worked. The song seemed to be Low Elvish, full of puns that Louise suspected were sexual in nature.

Dovetail suddenly stopped in mid-word. "Oh! *Husepavua!* I'm so sorry! I wasn't thinking."

Husepavua? Was Sparrow here?

"Finish what you're doing," a familiar male voice answered in French.

Louise smothered a gasp as she recognized Yves. The twins hadn't officially met the male. According to Anna, he had been away on business since they had arrived. When had he returned?

Dovetail's sigh of relief echoed loudly in the empty bedroom. "Yes, *husepavua.*"

"Black and gray?" Yves snorted. "They're just like their mother; she was a moody little bitch. It's ironic that Sire felt that he couldn't safely lock Esme up and use her as a brood mare. Yet she turned around and made herself one."

"Do you think there are more than these two?"

"Assuredly," Yves said. "Finding them is the problem. Damn these monkeys with their mechanical idiocy. Every twenty years, they're changing how the world works. Just as you're starting to understand how to run their machines, they change everything. Nothing new works with anything old."

Dovetail made a sound of disgust. "I know. Every fifty years I've had to completely redo all the damn lighting because they've changed the lightbulbs again. You can't get one of these to save your soul." She apparently held up the old bulb. There had been an antique crystal chandler hanging in Lain's bedroom with large flame-shaped bulbs. "What is it you need, *husepavua?*"

"I need you to supervise uncrating our prize."

"Ha! I heard about your adventure! So we're going to take it apart here? I thought you'd ship it to Elfhome with the others."

"I don't want the others to know I have it. They've been saying that the beast doesn't exist. I'm not sure if they were being naïve or deceitful."

"Or just plain stupid."

"Possibly. Still, you're right. This is not the best of places for spell-working, so I need your expertise."

"Understood."

Footsteps echoed, moving away.

"*Husepavua?*" Dovetail called before Yves left the room. "Will we follow Sire soon?"

Follow? Follow Ming where? The twins hadn't seen Ming since before Shutdown. Had he return to Elfhome without any fanfare?

"What are a few months to the thousands of years that we've waited?" Yves said.

"I'm so sick of this world," Dovetail whispered fiercely. "I'll be glad when we can go home. Reclaim all that was taken from us. I hate huddling around little pools of magic, praying that it will be enough to sustain us. I hate the monkeys with their stupid hidebound mores that keep changing according to some illogical male whim. Don't bathe together. Don't go out without a veil. Don't go out without your breast covered up like it's something indecent instead of a simple mammary gland. Don't sleep with the slaves! Don't own slaves. Treat everyone equally. They're imbeciles."

"*Oui, oui.*" Yves laughed in agreement. "We will follow soon. The monkeys found us that damned box with the loaded *nactka*. Sire now has everything in hand that he needs to crush the rebel slaves underfoot. We will continue to funnel weapons to Pittsburgh for as long as we can and then destroy the gate. A year or two at most."

"Tomorrow would not be soon enough."

Yves snickered at Dovetail's impatience. "Patience. We want the first blow to be crippling."

Jillian was in character. Louise wasn't sure if this was a good thing or bad. Her twin had found an Air Force officer's peaked cap, a baseball and glove. She strutted around the card table, tossing up the ball and catching it. She had placed an enlisted man's garrison cap on Nikola's head; judging by the beat of his thumping tail, this made him one happy puppy. Even Joy had a little paper hat that she was currently taste-testing.

"Private Dufae!" Jillian flung the baseball so it hit the floor, bounced off the side of the desk, and rebounded to her glove. "Cue *The Great Escape* theme song."

"Aye, aye, sir!" Nikola saluted, paw cocked up to his ear. The trumpet and drum military music started to play on Jillian's tablet.

"Now to break out from *Stalag Luft Drei*, we face the following difficulties." Jillian used a broad Midwest accent that gave a nod toward Missouri.

Nikola cocked his head. "*Stalag Luft Drei?*"

"Prison for Air Force Three," Louise translated the German and then explained. "She means here. Just go with it."

Louise decided that Jillian being in character was a good thing. She was patterning after Steve McQueen as Hilts, the most defiant of the Allied prisoners. Unfortunately, Hilts was recaptured in the movie.

"The Stalag is isolated deep in the German province of Lower Silesia." Jillian nodded to the card table and flung the baseball again. The ball *thud-thunked* as it hit the floor at an angle and rebounded off the side of the vanity. It smacked back into the glove.

Blueprints covered the card table. The title block identified them as the original plans for the mansion as it was built in 1905. As Louise had suspected, several outbuildings that served as servants' quarters flanked the mansion, hidden from view. The detached garage had originally been a large carriage house. Further out was a stable for the estate's horses. Someone had noted that the stable had been converted to a dormitory in 1930s. "Where did you get these?"

"Esme." Jillian gestured toward the secret room as if their genetic donor was hidden within it, handing out secret documentation like the French Resistance. "As we can see, the estate is mindboggling large for this close to New York City. Ming must have bought the land from Native Americans with glass beads, as there's no evidence that it ever changed hands on the county records." Jillian pointed to a satellite map on her tablet. It showed a paved walking trail through a public park. "We'll need at least fifteen minutes to get from this bedroom to this trail." She slid her finger several inches down the winding path line to the park's parking lot and then across a busy street to a small collection of buildings. "This small strip mall is the nearest public building. I figure it would take us an hour to walk there. We could arguably call a taxi to pick us up there and take us into town. It's ten miles as the crow flies to the nearest train station, River Edge, but that's up and down fairly steep hillsides and across the Hackensack River. We'll have to stick to the sidewalk, and that adds another four to five miles to our hike."

So half a day to walk to the nearest train station since Louise didn't think she could walk fifteen miles without breaks. They would need to cover the distance before the secret elves noticed that they were gone. If the twins left immediately after breakfast, however, they would just be reaching the train station at lunchtime, which they normally ate with Anna. They'd be missed, and the elves would probably check all logical points of transportation. Leaving after lunch created the same scenario, only dinner being the trigger. If they left in the evening, they might miss the last train. Two little girls out in the middle of the night would draw instant attention. Even the hour's walk to get a taxi was full of danger. This would all be so much easier if they were just adults!

They probably would have to figure out alternate transportation. Something clever and unexpected. In prison movies they used laundry trucks, but the secret elves washed their own linens. Louise started a checklist of things they would need. It seemed massively overwhelming, but at least Jillian wasn't huddled in bed, crying.

"I've devised four exit routes from this room to the sidewalk, depending on time of day." Jillian poured out M&Ms onto the blueprint. "In the mornings, Nattie is in the kitchen along with Celine. Ming and Anna are in their suites in the east wing." She slid red M&Ms to mark the locations of the adults. "And the rest are scattered among the outbuildings." She placed four green M&Ms in the west wing. "And we're here."

She flicked a 3D-rendered model to Louise's tablet. "These are the four exits. That door." She pointed at the hallway door. "The bathroom into Lain's bedroom and then out into the hallway again. I've discovered that Esme actually hinged the plywood over the real windows." She pointed at the false wall of the secret room. "There's climbing equipment that we can—"

"Candy!" Joy abandoned nibbling on the paper hat to frantically snatch up the M&Ms. "Nom, nom, nom!"

"Joy!" Jillian cried. "That's mine! I was saving those!"

Escape planning was paused while Jillian and Joy frantically ate the candy until both looked like chipmunks with stuffed cheeks.

"What's the other ways out?" Louise asked once the M&Ms were gone.

"Mmm." Jillian pointed at Joy while chewing. The baby dragon pulled the paper hat onto her head and saluted. "Mmmhm." Jillian swallowed. "She's phased at least twice her mass through the false wall. I'm not sure of her limit. We could experiment."

"Let's keep that as Backup Plan B or maybe even C or D." Louise gazed at the blueprint, feeling uneasy. If they could wait the twenty-seven days to the next Shutdown, fleeing to Pittsburgh would be simple. But she *knew* they couldn't wait that long. They had to go soon. "Who the hell came up with the stupid idea of having Shutdown once a month? Why not days on Elfhome and nights on Earth, or something sane like that?"

Nikola took it as a serious question. He tilted his head as he announced, "That was actually one suggested schedule, but the elves rejected it. They proposed that Pittsburgh would visit Elfhome only once a year. Pittsburghers advocated that the city would go through Startup and Shutdown once a month, staying on Elfhome for forty-eight hours every thirty days. The UN chose the current schedule as a compromise."

Compromise? The UN must be using some new definition of the word where neither party got anything they wanted.

If the UN "arbitrarily" set the cycle of Pittsburgh being stranded for a whole month, then it meant Ming really chose the timing. If Louise had to guess, he wanted to drive away the two million humans living in the metropolitan area. It was one thing to live in a city that occasionally visited another world, and quite another to be stuck there three hundred and fifty-three days out of the year. With one manipulation of the treaty terms, Ming made it so the humans fled Pittsburgh, leaving the city short of skilled manpower. People chosen by Ming could then be positioned on Elfhome.

For a moment, the scale of what was against them overwhelmed Louise. So much stood against them. Ming and all his people here at the mansion. His people in the EIA. The oni hidden among the humans. Elves like Sparrow. She wanted to reach out and take Jillian's hand, but she *knew* that her twin wouldn't be able to take her leaning on her. Not yet. Jillian was getting her feet under her, but she couldn't be strong for Louise. In the very same way, Louise *knew* that she couldn't go to Anna and tell her all the things she suspected of Ming. Esme, no doubt, had tried. When her mother wouldn't listen, Esme had painted all her furniture black, built her secret lair, and woven complex plans.

"In my dream, he found you when you were much too young. Too small. Too helpless."

Louise clung to memory. Esme knew that they would be caught and had left a secret hoard of weapons. They weren't completely alone. If they could get to Elfhome, then they would have Alexander and Windwolf.

"They'll finish the work on Lain's bedroom tomorrow." Louise circled back to the real threat. "All they really have to do is put up curtains and move in furniture."

"How does it look?" Jillian asked.

Louise threw up her hands. "I don't know. It doesn't matter."

"I want to see." Jillian headed for the bathroom that connected the two bedrooms.

"Why?"

"It's like a movie set that we had built." Jillian opened the door and gasped. "Oh, Lou, it's going to be beautiful."

She walked to the center of Lain's bedroom and spun slowly, arms outstretched.

The floor was now a deep warm black and the walls were a rich creamy gray. Dovetail had hung a new chandelier that was a wonderful cascade of silver branches and crystals.

"It's going to be done," Louise grumbled. "When they finish, Anna will want to redo Esme's room. If they start tearing out everything, they'll find the secret room."

Louise had had uneasy dreams all week of Esme frantically giving orders as workers dismantled her spaceship around her. While Louise believed that the nightmare had actually been her own fear that Esme's bedroom would be torn apart, she felt more and more sure that something horrible had happened to Esme in the cold darkness of space. While Louise still couldn't think of Esme as "mother," she'd begun to think of her as something like an aunt or a much older sister. It made her sad to think that Esme might have died painfully years before they were even born.

The question remained, though, why. What was Esme trying to do, arranging for children to be born and then leaving Earth? Whatever Esme had been attempting, it had been important enough that Esme had been willing to die trying to succeed. Had she succeeded or failed? Certainly lives had been at stake. Maybe even worlds.

But they didn't have the luxury to worry about worlds right now. They had to protect the babies and Joy.

"We won't let them remodel." Jillian sounded like her normal self for once. "We'll tell Anna that if she changes the bedroom, we'll lose the only thing we have of Esme."

It might work. It was probably why Anna hadn't changed the room in the first place. But if Ming had already left for Elfhome, how soon would he want Anna and the twins to join him? How much time did they really have? It felt like a very short time.

The bugging software that Louise had on the mansion's phone indicated an incoming call. Since she'd set it up, there hadn't been any calls, which made her think she'd bugged an inactive line. After careful checking, though, she'd discovered that the secret elves avoided most lines of communication. It put the meeting at the museum in a new light: the secret elves didn't call someone when they wanted to talk.

She tapped an icon so they could listen to the rare conversation. Rapid-fire High Elvish spilled out of her tablet. She only recognized a handful of English words thrown in, referencing technology that elves normally didn't have access to. Cargo ship. Overhead crane. Ammo. Someone had the unfortunate job of telling Yves about the fire in the South China Sea. The news was not being taken well. There was a thunderous noise and then silence.

"I think we got their attention," Louise said. "Let's take everything they have while they're trying to put out that fire."

36: MISCHIEF OF MICE

⋘══❍═══⋙

"What we need are mice," Jillian *thud-thunked* the baseball against the floor and vanity instead of helping Louise. "A whole bunch of mice. A herd? A flock? Whatever they call a lot of mice."

"Huh?" Louise wasn't sure she had heard her twin correctly. It was proving harder than she thought to raid Ming's many bank accounts. Most of his liquid capital was well hidden in offshore accounts. She had to track all large transfers of cash and then determine who actually owned the destination company. Once she found the accounts, however, it was fairly simple to trigger another transfer to one of theirs. She bounced the money between shell companies, like a pea under a set of cups, and then dropped it into one of their super-secret accounts.

"A mischief of mice," Nikola answered Jillian's question, head cocked in confusion. "That doesn't make any sense."

"That's so cool." Jillian laughed evilly. "And utterly perfect. Then what we need is a mischief of mice. Robotic mice. Exploding robotic mice. A couple hundred of them. Maybe several thousand."

Louise sighed out her anger. Dovetail and the others had already finished moving all the furniture into Lain's old bedroom. Luckily the chaos that they were creating had distracted Anna along with the elves. Louise could feel that they were running out of time. Still, she couldn't insist on Jillian focusing on looting Ming's finances because it would make her twin more aware of their danger. Even now, Jillian was barely coping with their

363

situation; they'd been playing WWII prisoner of war for two days now. Louise comforted herself with the knowledge that Jillian probably was making important progress in their actual escape. Hopefully. "Mice? What are you talking about?"

"Getting across the border on the next Shutdown. There's a pedestrian-only gate between the North Side and the North Hills. Only Pittsburgh residents can use it to visit Earth; they're given a bracelet that allows them to quickly cross back through the gate later without the hassle of checking visa paperwork." Jillian put aside the baseball and glove to pull up a map on her tablet. "See, Pittsburghers park in this lot here, walk through this gate, and they're on this dead-end street. They can walk down to this corner and catch a bus that only runs during Shutdown that loops from this bus stop to these local malls. The setup only works because none of the roads on either side actually connects to the four highways that link Pittsburgh to Earth. The normal traffic jams that happen at Shutdown don't affect this area."

If they could get to one of the North Hills malls, then they could take the bus to the gate. It was easy to see why April had ignored the option; the parking lot was in the middle of nowhere. Still, they could conceivably walk to Orville's. "Why the mice?"

"We need something to distract the guards," Jillian said. "It probably should be something small enough that they don't call for reinforcements, but unwieldy enough that they can't easily deal with it. Even a dozen people would be overwhelmed by a tidal wave of mice."

"Why do they have to be robotic? Real mice would work just as well."

"Real mice would probably just run and hide. Robotic mice could be programmed to 'play' and thus actively seek out humans and attempt to be chased."

"And exploding?"

"Well—they don't all have to explode. Just in case the EIA decided to ignore them, one or two should be able to blow up."

It had the benefit that no one had probably tried it before; thus the EIA probably had no standard protocol for a mischief of exploding robotic mice. The biggest problem with the plan, however, was sheer lack of time.

"Where are we going to get that many robotic mice in twenty-six days? And have them modified to explode?"

"It's a work in progress." Jillian *thud-thunked* the baseball and caught it in her glove. "Maybe they could just have tasers."

Louise had her doubts about the entire plan, but she kept them to herself. Jillian was starting to sound like herself; there was no reason to poke holes in her plan.

They ate at the dinner table alone—if "alone" meant they had an army of servants watching their every move. Said servants could not be coaxed into giving up any useful information on where Ming and Anna were beyond "not currently home." Was Ming even on the planet? Yves had been at the mansion to take the call about the explosion. So far, though, they had not met him face-to-face. Where was Yves? Was he personally going to oversee dealing with the disaster? Or was he in some computer center, chasing down bank transactions? According to Louise's last check, they had stolen over nine hundred million dollars from the secret elves. Getting caught now would be very, very bad.

Unlike the breakfast they'd eaten "alone" with Anna, the menu hadn't been altered.

The "meat" was something that Louise chose to pretend was small lobsters. (They looked more like insects than crustaceans.) She also pretended to eat it by breaking it into tiny little bits with her fork and knife. No wonder Esme had stashed so much freeze-dried food in the secret room; she must have known that they would be in danger of starving to death on the elves' weird diet. Louise comforted herself with knowing that they could have lukewarm mac and cheese back in their room later.

Jillian had taken the baseball and peaked cap with her. She spent the meal arranging accidents with the ball. Louise was glad for the little acts of courage and rebellion, but she could feel Celine slipping toward breaking. They were speeding toward a vast array of possibilities, none of them leading to happy endings. Louise kicked Jillian before Celine could start down any of the paths. Jillian gave Louise an innocent look but stopped.

Nine hundred million dollars bought a lot of robotic mice. The twins could download modified schematics straight to the Indonesian manufacturer that used a mixture of high-end 3D printers and cheap hand laborers to create the "toys." While the factory could quickly mass-produce a limited run of robotic rodents,

US Customs, however, took a dim view of all things that went boom. While there probably were ways around import laws, the red tape would delay shipments to Monroeville.

So they went with mice armed with tasers. They needed a working prototype prior to the start of production. Luckily they had ordered lots of exotic printing supplies while working on the museum heist and Aunt Kitty had dutifully packed it. The design work seemed to help keep Jillian distracted from her grief; the ball and glove sat idle until she sent the job to their 3D printer. Louise had created a pattern for the mouse "skin" and started to deconstruct the rabbit fur muffs that Anna had gotten with the winter coats that she insisted on buying for them. (*Really, it was the middle of July! What was Anna thinking? Hopefully nothing to do with a mischief of mice...*)

Nine hundred million dollars also rented a warehouse in Monroeville and hired on a small staff that believed they worked for a Belizean importing company. They would take delivery of the mice and whatever else the twins needed for crossing the Pittsburgh border.

"With all this money, we could just buy a small island and hire someone to be the babies' mother," Jillian pointed out. "It would simpler."

"No, it wouldn't." Louise shivered slightly when she saw that the total was now over a billion dollars stolen and climbing slowly. How much more did they have to take until Ming was unable to act? Had they already crippled him and were now wasting valuable time? Or was this just the tip of the iceberg and leaving now would be too soon? Thoughts of staying and leaving both filled her with unease. Was she going to *know* when the time was right?

Jillian *thud-thunked* her baseball. "Just saying we could make it so no adults can tell us what to do."

"Mary Poppins is not going to fly down out of the sky with her talking umbrella!" Although, in one dream, she had; but Louise was willing to bet that was a normal kind of dream and not a prophetic one. "If we hired someone, unless they're complete idiots, they're going to notice there's no one taking care of us and that we have gobs of money. How long do you think it will take them to figure out that they could easily hurt us until we gave them everything?"

"We would hire nice people and do background checks."

"Oh, grow up. The only people we could risk hiring are the type that wouldn't call the police the moment they realized we were orphans living by ourselves. And someone like that would also be ones that steal us blind, first chance they got."

"It always works out in the movies." Jillian mumbled and *thud-thunked* her baseball again.

Louise opened her mouth to say, "Not in horror films," but realized that Jillian had lifted up the WWII escapee persona like a shield to protect herself. Making Jillian see the truth would only hurt her now. They couldn't afford, though, to chase after an impossible dream. "Babies need a real mother. Not a woman who had poverty or some disaster that forced her into giving birth to children she doesn't want. They need someone like our mom. Someone that wants children. Someone that can love them completely. Someone that can be patient and strong and wise..."

"They'll have us."

Louise hunched against a scream of denial. She felt so close to crumbling. She couldn't bear the idea of being responsible for four real babies, each one as hungry as Joy, and as inquisitive as Nikola. Four Joy/Nikolas all with poopy diapers? Louise couldn't be their mother. The babies needed someone that wasn't teetering on the edge. They deserved someone that didn't feel so eggshell fragile that they were starting to wonder when, not if, they would break under the stress.

The twins needed to save the babies. It would destroy them both to lose the babies now. But be the babies' parents? No, they couldn't do that.

Louise woke up to a mischief of singing mice. Four of them stood on her pillow; one tapped her on the nose. When she opened her eyes, they began to sing in four-part harmony.

"*Blue Moon,*" the four mice sang. "*You saw me standing alone. Without a dream in my heart, without a love of my own.*"

"Nikola?" Louise rubbed at her eyes, wondering if she were dreaming. When she'd fallen asleep, there had been only one naked mouse robot. She had been struggling to fit fur onto it. Her sewing skills weren't matching up to the task of creating the form-fitting skin.

No, she was awake, and there were definitely four white-furred mice sitting on her pillow. They each had a tiny scarf of different colored fabric wrapped about their neck. The one with a blue muffler waved its hand, identifying itself as her baby brother while the other three clapped their tiny paws. It was very cute in a slightly creepy kind of way.

She sat up, careful not to knock them from the pillow. "How did you...? There was only one... And it was naked." She cautiously picked up Nikola mouse to peer closely at its skin. The rabbit fur had been perfectly joined together so she could barely see the seams.

The babies all started to talk at once.

"Joy fitted the skins," Pink Scarf said.

"We printed more mice!" Red Gingham said.

"She used magic!" Green Velvet said.

"It was boring waiting to take turns!" Pink cried.

"They're kind of cramped, even just for one," Nikola squeaked. It was still Christopher Robin's Welsh lilt but sonic high, thin, and fast.

"So we made one for each of us!" the girls chorused.

"Vroom! Vroom!" Pink cried. "We can run really fast!"

"And climb!" Green added.

"We can race!" Pink cried.

And the girls took off running in a lap around Tesla, making high-pitched motor noises. Tesla lay unearthly still. Louise had gotten used to the babies moving the dog's body. It was even creepier to see the big robot sitting idle.

The mice finished their lap with Pink winning.

"Joy made us racing scarfs." Nikola showed off his blue muffler. "Mine is Wind Clan blue!"

"Mine's wonderful amazing pink!" Pink cried. "I want goggles, too! Just like Tinker and Oilcan!"

It took Louise a moment to recognize the nicknames of their sister and cousin. It also made Louise realize that she'd been thinking of all of the babies as Nikola Tesla when only one of them was a boy. The three girls still were unnamed.

"Have you thought about names?" Louise asked.

"I want to be Jawbreaker," Red Gingham stated.

"Jawbreaker?" Louise echoed, mystified.

"It's Joy's favorite candy," Jawbreaker explained.

"Maybe..." Louise hesitated in suggesting "Candy" as a name. It was one of those weak, sexist female names that always appalled her mother. *"Girls should have names that allow them to be Supreme Court judges if they wanted. Sissy and Candy would have an uphill battle just because of their names."* Still, Candy had to be better than Jawbreaker...right?

"I want to be Chuck Norris," Pink announced as Louise struggled on with the whole "strong name" issue.

"Chuck Norris is a boy," Nikola pointed out.

"I can be a boy if I want to be," Pink stated firmly and then turned to Louise. "You get to pick your gender, don't you?"

Before Louise could answer, Green Velvet squeaked, "I want to be Jawbreaker, too."

"No! I said it first!" Red Gingham cried.

They collapsed into a ball of squirming fur as they wrestled for use of the name.

"Careful!" Louise caught them in her cupped hands before they could roll off the edge of the bed. "Hey, no fighting."

They were so tiny and light. The two of them barely weighed anything at all as they squirmed about, all soft rabbit fur and plastic bones. They felt so fragile that it took her breath away. She could crush them by accident.

This isn't really them, she reassured herself. *They're still safe within Tesla.*

"What's wrong with names like Jane Goodall, Dian Fossey or Rachel Carson?"

"We want names like Tinker and Oilcan!" the babies squeaked in chorus. "They're so cool! You should see them race! They're awesome!"

"Race?" Louise wondered if she was mistaken about the whole "awake" thing.

Sometime during the night, the babies had visited the Jello Shot forum and discovered a vast treasure trove of pictures and video of Alexander. All of them had to do with hoverbike racing. The still shots were all after winning a race, covered with mud except where goggles protected her eyes, grinning triumphantly. In many of the photos, Orville was within arm's reach, smiling just as brilliantly.

The Jello Shot people were divided in several camps. The haters were disappointed that Alexander didn't look like the valkyrie from *The Queen's Salvage*. What did Prince Yardstick see in such a short, dirty, wild thing? With so many beautiful female elves to choose from, why had he married her?

The romantics decided that the blonde in the video was a clear reference to Disney's Cinderella and that Lemon-Lime had merely presented an iconic princess with a Pittsburgh twist. Clearly the masses weren't ready for the truth, which was "Love is indeed blind."

A growing number of fans, however, were entranced by Alexander. They wanted to know everything about her, hence the unearthed videos. The sources were Pittsburghers in college on Earth, people who had studied at the University of Pittsburgh, and the small but rabid niche fandom of hoverbike racing.

The Jello Shots had found an amateur documentary made during last year's blistering hot summer. The filmmaker was Charles Wyatt, a grad student in history attending the University of Pittsburgh. Apparently it was his only effort at making a documentary, and it showed. All the scenes were horribly framed, badly scripted, and lacked anything in terms of editing. At least he had a rich, deep voice. He saw the hoverbike as the first integration of elf magic and human machine. It might turn out to be like the Jacquard loom, which could be "programmed" via paper tape, arguably the great-grandfather of the modern computer. "A chance to record history as it's being made by the people actually making it," Wyatt announced at the start of the video. He'd conceived of the documentary with only a few months left on Elfhome to film it. Almost immediately, he ran into an unexpected reluctance of those involved to talk to anyone with a camera.

Wyatt started with the president of a company that made hoverbikes.

The man laughed and shook his head. "I don't really know how they work. I could rebuild the gearbox for the spell chain blindfolded, but explain how it actually makes the bikes move forward? No."

There was a long surprised pause that hadn't been edited out. "I was told you've made *all* the hoverbikes in Pittsburgh."

"Mostly. There are a handful of custom jobs that we didn't do. Deltas. The next generation. They're faster."

"How can you be the only manufacturer of hoverbikes and not know how they work?"

"We're mostly just modifying motorcycles. We order in superbike racers with twin four-stroke twelve-hundred-cc engines. Hoverbikes need powerful engines for the lift drives. We strip them down for the engine, the transmission, and the entire electrical system, including the headlights—just about everything but the frames and the wheels. We discovered it was easier to carve the frame out of ironwood. The flexibility of the wood allows for more vibration damping and better impact tolerance."

"Vibration? Like what you get while riding a bicycle on a rough road? Is it really that much of a problem in a flying vehicle?"

"No, not that. The spell chain is sensitive to some sound resonance..." The president paused and considered the camera with a slight widening of his eyes, as if he realized everything he was saying was being recorded. "I'd rather not discuss specifics. Company secrets and all that."

"But-but-but where do you get the spell chains?" Wyatt asked. "Who makes them? Are they actual chains?"

The president considered for a moment before admitting. "Yes, there's a chain. The design is under patent, but we're trying to keep it a literal black box. We have an exclusive licensing agreement with the inventor. Like I said, except for a handful of custom models, we're sole producer of hoverbikes in Pittsburgh, and we would like to stay that way. It's a small niche market, and we have to sink a lot of money into parts and labor before we can make a profit."

"I understand. Historically, it's the mass supply and demand that fuels innovation. When only a handful of companies could afford computers, the rate of improvement in the technology was minuscule compared to the leaps in advances when they became tools of the masses."

"Pittsburgh doesn't have masses. It's still an expensive, nearly handmade piece of equipment with a very narrow profit margin."

"But if you could find some way to translate them to Earth..."

Suspicion filled the Pittsburgher's face, and the segment ended with president gesturing that the camera should be turned off. "I think I've answered enough questions."

Wyatt then proceeded to stop random people who owned hoverbikes and ask how they worked. The riders could explain that the lift drive took power from the gasoline engine and "somehow generated the vertical motion." The more power into the lift drive, the higher the bike would hover, at the sacrifice of speed to the horizontal motion. That much they all knew.

One college student leaned against his hoverbike, shaking his head. "It hurts my brain when I try to understand it. The lift you can actually see if you're like over a mud puddle. See. There's a force pushing downwards, and it's creating an equal and opposite reaction. But the forward motion? I really don't know how it possibly works. Especially the fact that you can brake. Logically the bikes should be like boats in water; in a frictionless state, things in motion stay in motion. It's not stopping on a dime, but you can brake—only I have not a clue how. It's not like you throw out an anchor."

Louise could guess which spell Alexander had used to create the lift. She wondered about the possible combinations of spells that could have created the forward motion of the hoverbike.

It took Wyatt weeks before he managed to catch Alexander on-camera. Even then, he wasn't aware that he'd found the person that he was looking for. He'd cornered Team Tinker at the racetrack, packing up to leave for the day. Heavy steel toolboxes and a mud-covered hoverbike were being strapped down onto the back of a big flatbed truck with "Pittsburgh Salvage" painted onto the door. Two massive elfhounds came to their feet as Wyatt walked up to the team, their growls as deep and menacing as a grizzly bear's.

"Bruno. Pete." A man in a Team Tinker T-shirt called to the dogs, silencing them. "We don't allow photographing of our riders except during the races. We do sell publicity photos. If you want pictures, come by our table in the concession area next week."

There was a jump in time as Wyatt negotiated the right to continue filming. During the interval, Alexander appeared on the back of the flatbed. Hair damp from a shower, she wore a Team Tinker T-shirt, cargo shorts, and hiking boots. She stomped in and out of the shoot, checking gear and complaining about the heat. Either Wyatt had been banned from photographing her or he missed the subtle body language of the people arrayed around him. Alexander might have been the youngest member of the team, but her teammates rotated around her like planets about a star. Instead, Wyatt kept the camera trained on the team's business manager, who was only identified by the name of "Roach." (Everyone in Pittsburgh apparently used weird nicknames.)

"Everyone I've talked to says that the Chang family might have built the race track but it was Team Tinker that started the sport."

"I suppose," Roach admitted cautiously. "Most of us went to high school together." This generated a rude noise from Alexander. "Those of us that went to high school. The statistical outliers we met through business." Another rude noise. "Roach Refuse." He tapped his chest. "Pittsburgh Salvage." He waved vaguely toward the truck. "Even people with brains the size of a planet need help with how to successfully run a business when they're first starting out, and I learned it at my grandfather's knee."

"How did you start the sport? Where did you get the hover-bikes? Were they already invented or was that part of coming up with the sport?"

Roach's eyes widened slightly and the corner of his mouth twitched with what might have been a nervous laugh. He started to turn toward Alexander, but she cut him short with, "Ah-uh! You're the one that agreed to this!" He winced and ducked his head to kick at the ground for a moment.

Orville came onto camera, freshly showered, carrying his muddy riding leathers and a cherry ice pop. With a wary look at Wyatt, he handed the ice pop to Alexander. He asked a silent question with the jerk of his head and Alexander snorted with utter disgust. The cousins sat side by side on the edge of the truck's bed as Alexander sucked on the ice pop and listened to Roach trying to explain.

"It's not like we don't have money," Roach said. "But in Pittsburgh, we use barter a lot instead of cash. It's a simple way to cut out the middleman who would normally take a big chunk of the profit to collect and redistribute goods. I've got a puppy. The guy who wants an elfhound has a half dozen old snowmobiles that are useless eight months out of the year. I know how to set up accounting books so the county won't hassle you." He jerked his head in the direction of the cousins. "They know how to cannibalize snowmobiles into something more all-weather. The thing nobody has a lot of are tires, especially ones for ATVs. Harder than sin to come by. We're sitting around, drinking beer, having a bull session on where we could scrounge up tires, and the little mad scientist starts to giggle."

A woman walked into camera range, carrying gear that she dropped beside Alexander. "Usually a very terrifying thing, and you want to get out of blast range as quickly as possible, but still be in viewing distance, because it *will* be worth watching."

Alexander glared at the woman, who danced away from a halfhearted kick.

Roach took a couple of steps out of reach, too. "A week later, we all had hoverbikes. And of course, the most natural thing in the world is to race them."

There was a long silence after Roach came to the end of his story. Wyatt waited for more but none was coming. Judging by the looks Roach was giving Alexander, he was vaguely afraid of saying anything else.

"You're Team Tinker," Wyatt broke the silence. "Is Tinker the one that invented the hoverbikes? I've heard all sorts of wild rumors about Tinker."

The racing team all froze in place at the question.

"What wild rumors?" Alexander had been in the middle of licking melted ice pop off her fingers.

"Umm." The camera bobbed as Wyatt accessed his notes. "Umm. The half-elf that runs the general store in McKees Rocks said that Tinker lives in the middle of the river and hands out magical swords to future kings."

"What?" the entire team half-shouted, half-laughed.

"Yeah, it sounded really Arthurian to me," Wyatt said. "I talked to a few elves, and they all said that Tinker is a baby wood sprite, which apparently is a race of very clever but dangerous elves or a very clever but dangerous raccoon. My Elvish isn't that good."

Roach was making little snorts as he tried to hold in his laughter.

Orville scooped up Alexander as she started to sputter and carried her off-camera.

"One person, an EMT, by the name of Johnnie Be Good, claimed that Tinker fathered most of the half-elves in Pittsburgh and is Blue Sky Montana's real father."

Roach lost control of his laughter. After a full minute of laughing, he wiped tears out of his eyes and stated, "That one is utterly true."

There was a howl of anger and the video went black. Captions explained that Roach had ducked a helmet thrown at him, and it hit the unsuspecting Wyatt instead. His only camera broken, he was unable to continue filming. The team reimbursed him for his camera. There was no indication, however, that they ever told him the truth.

Louise played the interview with Team Tinker over and over again. This was her older twin sister. Their cousin Orville, who obviously was loving and protective and caring. Their close friends that they could count on. A warm and bright happy moment that Louise wanted for herself.

The babies, however, quickly grew bored of it and started to add mini-windows to the screen to show off clips of Alexander and Orville racing on hoverbikes. The mice stood on her shoulders, tugging at her hair and pointing, squeaking excitedly.

"Maybe we can make mini-hoverbikes!" Nikola stated. "They use a gasoline engine only because they need to lift the weight of an adult. If we can figure out what spells Alexander used, we could just stand on top of a magic generator and fly."

The thought of the four mice zipping around the bedroom like hyper bats felt dangerous. Louise knew that the mice bodies were merely remotely run puppets for the babies, but mini-hoverbikes just seemed to have "will not end well" written all over it. (Even though she had to admit—quietly to herself—that she didn't *know* it would. Surely common sense overruled precognition.)

At least they had a completely tested prototype of the robotic mouse. While the babies were still focused on some newly added racing videos, Louise ordered ten thousand mice from the Indonesia factory. Not that they needed that many; it was the smallest number that the manufacturer would take on rush order.

"Lou!" Chuck Norris tugged on Louise's hair to get her attention. "What does this mean?"

The babies had found a new video. Someone had splintered down the documentary and picked out only the frames of Alexander sucking on the cherry ice pop. They looped the few seconds to prolong the action for two minutes and then ended with her licking her fingers. The title of video was "Why Prince Yardstick loves Tinker."

She winced. "I'm not sure, but it probably has to do with sex."

"What's sex?" the babies asked in chorus.

Louise blushed hotly. "It's icky stuff that adults do."

"What kind of icky stuff?" The babies started into a barrage of questions. "If it's icky, why do they want to do it? Is it like eating Brussels sprouts?"

Brussels sprouts? "I don't want to have to explain it. It's icky. Don't ask."

The babies were working systematically through the postings. Louise noticed that one post further down was generating thousands of shares per second. It was titled "Announcing Prince

Windwolf and Princess Tinker." She clicked it and discovered someone had used the documentary to do a 3D rendering of Alexander and then paired her with a scale model of Windwolf. The animator had dressed the male elf in a white tuxedo with his long black hair falling loosely over his shoulders. Alexander wore a skin-tight elfin gown of fairy silk in Wind Clan blue. They stood holding hands, looking like two teenagers about to go to the prom. They bowed to the camera and then turned to look into each other's eyes. Music started and the two started to waltz. During the documentary, Alexander hadn't gotten down off the truck bed, so she never seemed overly short. But if the render was correct, Louise and Jillian weren't going to get much taller.

Louise realized that the animation on the waltz was very good quality. She checked the credits and squeaked with surprise. A real animation studio had created the piece.

With sudden foreboding, Louise closed the Jello Shots forum and did a general search on the title. There were a hundred pages of hits. Apparently frustrated by the lack of pictures of Alexander and Windwolf together, one of the tabloid new feeds had paid for the animation. "What is a Wood Sprite?" had also become a meme with various odd animals PhotoShopped onto the flat bed, licking the cherry ice pop. Red pandas. Koala bears. Gibson monkeys. And most alarming, one featuring Disney's version of Tinker Bell. Whimpering, Louise typed in "Princess Alexander Graham Bell" and Alexander's picture came up complete with a small bio explaining that she was the daughter of Leonardo da Vinci Dufae. The information apparently had been supplied by the EIA Director, Derek Maynard. Unlike all the pictures of Alexander covered in mud, the bio had frames from the documentary. The family resemblance between Alexander and the twins was unmistakable.

Yves was going to find the photos. Yves was going to see the family resemblance and realize what Esme had done. He was going to know what the twins were.

"We need to go." Louise told Jillian when she woke her twin. She fought to keep her voice calm and level even though the enormity of what was ahead of them scared her. They still hadn't figured out how they were going to get away from the mansion without getting caught or where they were going to go or how they were going to stay hidden. "Let's get packed to leave."

"Huh?" Jillian sat up, rubbing at her eyes. "Now? What happened?"

"The Jello Shots dug up a bunch of videos of Alexander and they're getting plastered everywhere. Sooner or later, Yves is going to figure everything out. We've got to go before he does."

Jillian squinted at her, apparently still half-asleep, stepping through the logic. "Videos?"

"Of Tinker and Oilcan!" Chuck Norris squeaked.

"Racing!" Red Gingham Jawbreaker cried.

"But we can't get to Elfhome now!" Nikola cried. "It's twenty-five days to Shutdown. We haven't moved all the money yet…"

"…and we don't have all the mice!" the girls chorused with Nikola.

"I know." Louise waved them all to be calm, even though fear skittered about inside her. "Everything can go as planned—just someplace else—not here—as far away from here as possible."

The babies rapid-fired questions in excited squeaks. "Where are we going? How are we going to get there? Can we make the mini-hoverbikes first? We can use the magic generators. Oh, we'll need to make more generators to make one for each of us. We're taking the mice, too, aren't we? What are we taking with us?"

"Holy hell!" Jillian cried. "Where did the mice come from?"

Louise let the babies explain in a confusing four-part narrative. She could only think of all the things tucked into the back of the walk-in closet. Their favorite Christmas ornaments. The family tree that had hung over the fireplace in living room. Their mom's wedding rings. Everything so precious that it hurt to look at them. Too painful for Jillian to even deal with. Were they going to have to abandon it all?

If we can rob a museum without getting caught, we can sneak back later and get our stuff.

Even as she tried to comfort herself, she knew it wasn't true. The future that was hurtling toward them was dark and full of pain, and there would be no coming back.

"We have to leave today," Louise made herself say while trying to think of what they had to take. Other than the babies and Joy, what did they really need? Their tablets and phones and the flash drive of the codex. Louise found her backpack and set it down in the middle of the floor.

They had money. Lots of money. In theory they could buy anything they needed. In truth, kids normally didn't buy anything alone. Not real food like frozen vegetables and raw fish. Not real clothes like underwear and jeans. Children always followed behind their parents who pushed carts in supermarkets. They were supposed to stand quietly behind the adult paying the cashier at department stores. And children never checked into hotels alone.

We'll figure it out, Louise thought firmly to hold back the fear. They probably should take a change of clothes until they worked out basic life necessities. One shirt, a pair of jeans, and a single set of clean underwear, however, took up most of her backpack. They probably should take all of their socks and underwear, not just one set. Louise raided their underwear drawer and struggled to pack it all into the space remaining in her backpack. Nothing else would fit, even if they desperately needed it. Should she take the blue jeans out?

Panic surged up through Louise, like a shout that wanted to be let out. She covered her mouth, trying to keep it all in. How much could someone take before they broke?

"We may not have to wait," Jillian said.

Louise stared at her for a minute. She'd lost track of what they were talking about. She'd never said anything about waiting, had she? "What?"

"We might not have to wait for Shutdown to get to Pittsburgh." Jillian ducked into the secret room. Her muffled voice came through the open door. "Remember that in the codex, Dufae talked about the pathways between Elfhome and Earth."

"Yes, but after his wife died, he tried to take his son back to Elfhome and all the pathways had been deliberately destroyed. He didn't find one that was still intact."

"In Europe he couldn't find one intact!" Jillian came back out carrying an armful of papers that she spilled out onto the card table. "Dufae died in 1791. Windwolf was the first elf to land on the Westernlands in 1910. In the 1700s, North America was still largely unexplored. Even if Windwolf had access to the maps created by the humans, most of the cave systems wouldn't have been marked. There are only a few thousand elves in the Westernlands even now, so they couldn't have checked out all the cave systems."

The papers were dozens of cave maps. Some of them were real geological surveys and others were brochures by tour companies that owned the cavern. Jillian sorted through the papers. The babies climbed up the table's wooden legs and complicated the process by trying to study the maps themselves.

"Ming married Anna before the first Startup," Jillian said. "If he was relying on the pathways in Europe to get to Elfhome, and they were destroyed, he would have had to search out a new way."

Louise followed her logic. "Which is why Esme was collecting the maps."

"Collected them and kept them hidden. If she just had some weird love of caves, they'd be on her bookcases, not stashed in the secret room."

Louise looked down at the dozens of maps. "If there's this many choices, then he was still looking. He didn't find a way."

Jillian whimpered slightly, shrinking with disappointment. She looked as if she was in danger of collapsing back to the stranger that had huddled in the bed the last few weeks. "That's true."

"But your reasoning is sound." Louise rushed to repair the damage. "It proves that the pathways are natural formations and that the elves didn't destroy the ones in the Westernlands. Ming has been seeking a pathway, so he believes it's there, but he doesn't really know how to find it."

"How could it be so hard? He found this place." Jillian gasped. "Wait! This place has magic, so it's linked to Elfhome. Maybe this is like stately Wayne Manor with bat caves all under it."

"There are caves!" Chuck Norris stated firmly.

"But there aren't any bats," Nikola added with some uncertainty.

"Not that we noticed!" the Jawbreakers finished.

"When were you in caves?" both twins shouted.

The babies cringed.

"Two days after we arrived," Nikola volunteered.

"It was boring watching you sleep!" Chuck Norris cried. "So we went exploring!"

"We didn't get into any trouble!" Green Jawbreaker stated.

"You never said that we couldn't," Red Jawbreaker stated.

"And why do we have to do what you tell us?" Chuck Norris asked. "Don't we get to vote? We outnumber you!"

"Yeah!" her two sisters cried.

"No, you don't get a vote!" Jillian shouted, throwing her hands up in the air. "Don't ever leave the bedroom again without us!"

"Unless it's important—like the mansion is on fire." Louise earned an annoyed look from her twin. She was more worried, though, about the future than the past. The damage was already done. She couldn't figure out how the babies even got Tesla out of the bed without them noticing. They always slept with the bed in the raised position.

"We didn't actually leave," Nikola said.

His sisters nodded. "We didn't."

"You said you left," Jillian growled.

"We did, but we didn't," they cried.

"Oh, that's perfectly clear," Jillian grumbled.

"Tesla didn't leave the room, but we did." Nikola attempted to clarify. "We just didn't have any bodies."

"Huh?" Jillian looked utterly confused.

"Oh." Louise realized what Nikola meant. It was like when she dreamed of the babies. They existed somehow separate of Tesla as well as integrated with him. If they could enter her dreams, then moving through the house like ghosts wasn't completely impossible, just very weird. "I understand."

"You do?" Jillian cried. "I don't."

"The babies dream-walked," Louise said.

Nikola nodded vigorously and then pointed toward Louise's feet. "Joy showed us how."

Joy was pulling the clean underwear from Louise's backpack and tossing them over her shoulder. She had cans of freeze-dried blueberry cheesecake stacked beside her. She looked up, wide-eyed with surprise at being the center of attention.

"Joy!" Louise cried. Their underwear was scattered all across the bedroom floor.

"Must take yummies!" Joy shoved the cans into the emptied bag. "Not stupid panties."

"No, junk food is the one thing we can get easily!" Louise gathered up the underwear.

"Wait!" Jillian shouted. "Dream-walked? What the hell does that mean?"

"Shhh!" Louise bent down, trying to unload enough of the cans to fit the clothes back into the bag. "The secret elves might hear."

"What does it mean?" Jillian whispered fiercely.

"They astral-projected. That's how the babies are talking to us through Tesla. It's their spirits. Their souls." Louise sighed at the disbelieving look Jillian was giving her. "They're sitting on top of a magic generator. And they're elves. Maybe all elves can dream-walk."

Joy made a raspberry and jerked the can out of Louise's hand. "Not elf. Dragon, silly!"

"What?" both twins cried.

"Joy says that we're related to two dragons: Brilliance and Clarity. That's why we can dream-walk."

Surely that couldn't be right. Still, Dufae's Elvish name had been Unbounded Brilliance. There were certainly lots of myths about dragons having children that were very humanlike. Louise struggled not to get distracted by the possibility. "So there are caves under the mansion?"

Nikola nodded. "Caves, but we didn't notice any bats."

Jillian disappeared back into the secret room, mumbling about billionaires with secret identities and their propensity for secret lairs. She returned with a fat roll of papers nearly four feet long, and unrolled to be nearly four feet wide. Esme had provided them—somehow—with a copy of the blueprints of the mansion. Judging by the frayed edges marked on the copies as jagged lines, they were scans of the original as-built prints. "Ming has to know the caves are there. I'm sure he picked this place because of the magic." Jillian flipped through the pages until she hit the last one that showed an entire warren of rough-shaped rooms under the mansion. According to the title block, the cave systems had been labeled as sub-basement. "Holy bat caves!"

"No bats!" the babies all squeaked.

Louise studied the maze. It seemed too easy to be true. Surely they couldn't just slip through the mansion's cellars and come out on Elfhome. The magic, though, was coming from somewhere. Dufae had written about leakage from his world to Earth. If there were a pathway, surely Ming would claim it for himself and keep it well hidden from the eyes of mankind.

As she studied the blueprint, though, nothing seemed to suggest that there was a pathway to another world. "There's no way to get a car or even a horse down into the caves easily." She pointed out what seemed to be the only staircase into the area through the mansion's large walk-in pantry. "According to this, the mansion was built in 1890. It was another twenty years before Windwolf came to the Westernlands, and he might have settled anywhere on the East Coast, or even gone to—whatever they call South America. Ming wouldn't have had to hide moving people and supplies to Elfhome from Earth, because there weren't any elves to see."

Jillian pouted and reached for her ball and glove. "But if we could get to Elfhome here in Hudson Valley, we would be at Aum Renau."

"Windwolf probably picked this area for the same reason Ming chose it. First thing Dufae did was find places on Earth opposite massive pools of magic so he could cast spells with what leaked across. On Elfhome, right here, there's probably the strongest source of magic on the continent."

Which reminded Louise that they should take some of their most portable spell-casting supplies. It looped her back to the realization that they would have to abandon everything left of their parents.

37: MOUSE CAGE

An hour later, everything came crashing down on them.

There was a knock after someone tried the door and found it locked.

"Hide!" Louise whispered to the babies, waving the mice to take cover. She could feel the danger looming outside the door. They had run out of time. The mice darted under the furniture.

What should I do? A dozen possibilities flashed through Louise's mind, followed by dozens of possible outcomes, some horrifying. She glanced frantically around the room. Between the babies and Joy "helping," the twins had barely started with packing. Jillian had insisted that they scan the cave maps and the mansion's blueprints before returning them to the secret room. It meant that everything that Louise didn't want the elves to see was sitting out, waiting to be packed.

Tesla stood up; the babies had fled out of the mice robots to inhabit him again.

"Sit!" Louise hissed as one possibility became terrifyingly probable. "Do not fight! You promised!"

"Why do we have to listen to you?" Chuck Norris Pink grumbled in Nikola's Christopher Robin lilt, but this time Louise recognized the true speaker.

"We won't fight," Nikola stated and Tesla sat. "Because we promised."

"But we don't like it," one or both of the Jawbreakers complained.

The person knocked again. Louder. Impatient.

Joy wasn't anywhere in sight. Hopefully she was inside Tesla or the secret room. There was no more time left to look for her. Louise snatched up items blindly from the "to pack" pile and started to shove them into her pockets. No, they were going to check her pockets. She pulled up her left pant leg and slid what would fit into her socks. At least their tablets had secure passwords; there was no way to take them with them and keep them hidden. The babies, though, were vulnerable inside of Tesla's storage compartment.

There was a murmur of voices beyond the door and soon someone was going to be breaking down the door if they didn't unlock it. Louise rushed across the room, turned the lock and flung open the door.

Louise had expected Anna. It was Celine, gazing down at Louise with dark suspicion. Behind her was a small herd of the male drivers who doubled as bodyguards. Louise managed a look of surprise on her face even as she realized that the fact Anna wasn't there meant real danger for the twins. There were too many adults for the children to put up a fight and have any hope of winning.

"Where's our grandmother?" Louise hated that she couldn't keep fear out of her voice. Jillian could have done it.

"Why did you lock the door?" Celine attempted to brush past her.

Louise held her ground the best she could since the female was nearly two feet taller than her. She wanted to keep the door between the secret elves and everything dear to her. "Where's Anna?"

Celine put a hand on Louise's shoulder and shoved her back. "She's in the hospital."

"What?" the twins and the babies all cried.

"She was fine yesterday!" Louise shouted to cover the babies' slip. "What did you do to her?"

"Humans get old and die," Celine snapped and then alarm flashed across her face as she realized that she had all but admitted she wasn't human. "She collapsed yesterday afternoon while she was at a business meeting. Someone there called an ambulance instead of her drivers."

And what did Celine think the drivers would have done? Brought Anna back to the house to die instead of to the hospital?

Louise clung to her anger despite the fact she knew that Ming needed Anna. If she let her rage slip away, all Louise would be left with was the knowledge that they were alone in the house, surrounded by powerful enemies.

"Come with me." Celine reached for Louise seconds after the girl slid backwards, leaving the female snatching at air.

"Where to?" Louise asked in as steady a voice as she could muster.

"We don't have to listen to you." Jillian thumped her baseball into her ball glove.

"No!" Louise cried out as everything unraveled. She jumped forward and took the slap that Celine aimed at Jillian, turning with the force so it looked more real, just like Mr. Howe taught them in the stage-fighting classes. Even then, the hit was hard enough to make everything go black for a moment.

When Louise could see again, Jillian was pulling her backwards, shouting, "Don't hurt her! Don't hurt her, you witch!"

Tesla was standing a foot closer than before, whimpering softly.

"Shhh." Louise tried to calm all her siblings, making a "sit" motion with one hand at the babies while holding the other up to keep Celine's attention. She could feel blood trickling warmly down from her nose and taste it her mouth. "I'm okay. Don't cry."

Celine watched them closely with a slight pleased smile. "Hurt one, hurt them both. Good to know."

"We'll go with you," Louise stated as calmly as she could. She pressed the back of her left hand to her nose to hide the blood from her siblings. Her hand was shaking and she couldn't stop it. When she sniffed, the hot metal taste of blood filled her mouth. Every word, every motion, seemed tied to infinite possible outcomes. To cry. To fight. They all tumbled into dark destruction. She had to stay calm. She had to do what Celine wanted. It was the only path that led toward escape for all of them. "Please. We'll do what you want us to do. Just don't hurt us."

Celine nodded smugly. "Good. Come with me." She headed toward the open door. She pointed at two of the bodyguards and indicated that they were to follow. The others she directed toward the walk-in closet. "Start in there."

Jillian whimpered and clutched Louise in a death grip.

"It's okay," Louise said, even though she wasn't sure. She had to keep the babies from doing anything to draw attention to themselves. "Don't be scared. We'll be fine. Just wait and see."

Tesla sat down, trusting that they'd return. Louise could only hope that she could keep her promise that she and Jillian would figure a way out to save them all before the secret elves realized what the robot held inside it.

Yves and a dozen of the male bodyguard drivers were in the foyer. Two of the guards stood on ladders, carefully lowering a large painting they had just taken down off the wall. The males worked in near-reverent silence. Yves' rich voice filled the echoing foyer like an actor on a stage.

"Make sure they understand I want a cashier's check, not money wired to an account. If you need to, tell them the truth: I don't trust electronic transactions. I never understood how the Knights Templar sold the idea of banking."

He glanced up the sweeping staircase as Celine herded the twins down them. "Have you checked their pockets? Wood sprites are like pack rats; they always have some nasty surprise hidden away."

"No, *husepavua*. Forgiveness." Celine stopped them at the foot of the stairs and turned out their pockets. Louise's heart hammered in her chest, trying to pretend that she was only confused by what was happening as the female tugged and pulled at Louise's jeans. The taste of blood still filled her mouth as it dripped from her bloody nose.

Celine frowned at the scraps of white rabbit fur, thimble, and spool of thread left over from making the mouse skins. "They're making something."

"Of course they are," Yves said. "It's in their blood."

"We're making designer clothes for our dolls," Jillian snapped, anger in her voice. Her eyes, though, were on the blood leaking through Louise's fingers as Louise kept her hand pressed against her nose. Tears started to shimmer in Jillian's eyes.

If Jillian started to cry, Louise was sure she would break too. She took her hand from her nose and smeared the blood like war paint on her cheeks.

Yves shook his head. "Wood sprites. Always so ridiculously brave for how stupidly small they are. I could never decide if they were our greatest success or our worse failure. Certainly, they are the most dangerous of our rebellious creations."

Louise stared at him, trying for brave but achieving only fearful confusion. What did he mean by rebellious creation? Did this mean that Leonardo Dufae wasn't their male genetic donor?

Yves laughed dryly. "You don't even know what you are, do you?"

"We're nine years old?" Louise said it before she remembered that Esme had warned her not to be snarky. She was sure that Yves was going to tell her; he thought their helplessness and ignorance was funny.

"All you see. The electricity. The light bulbs. The horseless carriages that drive themselves. All the trinkets of human civilization are the results of a handful of genetic mutants that humans call geniuses. It's so purely random that anyone who attempts to influence it via breeding is called immoral. God's touch alone elevates the great thinker from the common human.

"But we are the gods of elves, and we made you."

"I'm fairly sure Esme had us made from her genetic material," Jillian muttered.

Yves laughed. "Oh, she only combined together what we wrought several thousand years ago. Two of our greatest achievements in three little females." He was counting Alexander in with the twins. "And surely there are more than just three..."

The bodyguard nearest the door lifted his hand to his ear, and cocked his head to listen to some report over an earbud. "*Husepavua*, Feng's car just pulled into the driveway."

Yves growled. "That idiot. I didn't send for him."

"Should we turn him away?" Several of the bodyguards moved toward the door, placing themselves between the entryway and Yves.

Yves glanced toward the twins, apparently hoping that they could give him a clue. Louise could only sense onrushing disaster in every direction. "No," Yves said finally. "Let him come. Perhaps he has some useful news." He turned from the door to point at a set of Elvish wyvern armor standing in an alcove. "Pack that." He pointed at a Van Gogh oil painting beside the armor. "Sell that."

The front door swung open and Ambassador Feng walked through. He checked at the sight of Yves and all the bodyguards in the foyer.

"Yves?" Feng said in confusion.

"What are you doing here?" Yves snapped in English, putting lie to his claim at the museum that Feng couldn't speak English.

"Where is Aumvoutui? A force from the MSS just landed at Newark..."

"Have you gone native?" Yves interrupted him. "Use words, not letters."

"The Ministry of State Security for the People's Republic of China," Feng growled out. "They have the authority to arrest me and my entire staff and most likely that's why they're in New York. The people of the Republic have realized that they've shouldered the funding for the hyperphase gate, five spaceships to a mythical colony that doesn't exist, and the settlement to the United States for the loss of Pittsburgh. Trillions of yuan. All so our people can return to Elfhome. They are not happy. Riots have broken out in Beijing. They make your Americans look like misbehaving children. They're calling for blood."

"Another century, another witch hunt," Yves stated coolly. "We have taught you the song. Now dance to it."

"It's not as simple as Aumvoutui said. They now have cameras everywhere. There is no more anonymity. I can't just disappear and resurface someplace else."

"We warned you of that danger when you came to this world."

"The bank account you gave me for such emergencies is empty. Aumvoutui must—"

Yves pressed his hand against the ambassador's chest and spoke a word that sounded Elvish. The ambassador went to his knees with a cry of pain. A spell glyph appeared on his forehead, gleaming brilliantly. "You must remember your place. You were my little pet project. I alone made you. I am your god." Yves cupped the male's chin in his hand and whispered menacingly as tears ran down the ambassador's cheeks. "The pure black of your hair. The raven wings of your eyebrows. The strength of your chin. Every line on your face, I picked for you. I planted you into a female's womb and gave you life. I made you, and I can unmake you with a word."

"Forgiveness," Feng cried, his voice breaking from pain. "I was afraid—"

"Humans are lowly beasts, products of random chance, barely above monkeys. You are a masterpiece of spell-working."

"Even lions fear large packs of monkeys," Feng whispered.

Yves growled another word, and Feng screamed as his veins suddenly blazed under his skin as if his blood had turned to liquid fire. The ambassador convulsed into a tight knot, shrieking.

Louise bit hard on her lower lip, trying to keep in an answering scream of pure fear. She had never heard an adult male cry out in pain before; she had never heard a sound so raw and terrifying. Jillian clung tight to Louise, burying her face in Louise's shoulder, sobbing with terror.

Yves spoke a word and Feng slumped to the floor, panting hoarsely as his skin faded back to normal.

Yves stepped back from the male. "You will bring the dogs sniffing at my heels if you try to hide at my feet. You will go and be the warrior I made you and draw them off my scent."

"Yes, *husepavua*," Feng whispered.

"Follow the plan as you were told to do in emergencies like this. Use one of your alternate identities to go to the island and cross to Onihida. Someone has to keep rein on the oni until the Dufae heir can be caught and harnessed—or we find someone else to open a gate for us."

"Yes, *husepavua*."

Yves turned away, not bothering to watch the male stagger to his feet and stumble out of the mansion. He walked down the hall to stop at the next painting and pointed to it. "Sell that." He pointed to a small statue. "Pack that." He turned and gazed at the twins. "It's a shame they're not true identical twins. I'll have to be more careful with them. Take them down to the casting chamber and put them into a spell cage. I'm sure they would figure out how to escape anything mechanical."

Louise tried to tell herself that the spell cage was a fascinating awesome thing. In almost any other instance, it would be. Being carried down into a maze of dimly lit caves, shackled to the floor, and locked inside one, however, was really, really scary.

"Right," Jillian muttered after the elves had trooped back upstairs. "This is a sticky wicket."

"Could be worse." Louise knew it could be much worse. She had at least kept the elves from discovering what she had shoved into her socks as they snapped the manacle about her right ankle. By luck or that weird sense of knowing what was coming, she had pushed the Swiss army knife painfully deep into her shoe.

The electric lights went out, leaving only the gleam of the active spell encaging them. They sat at the center of the spell inscribed into the stone floor.

"I say." Jillian used a thick British accent. Louise wasn't sure who Jillian was channeling but she was glad that her twin wasn't freaking because at the moment Louise was slipping toward totally losing it. "Let's not give fate any more ideas."

"Uh-huh," Louise forced out as she fumbled in the deep shadows. Light suddenly flared out from Jillian.

"What's that?"

"Spell light. I made it." Jillian held up a brightly gleaming orb.

"Awesome!" More heartfelt words were never uttered. Louise unfolded the various blades of the Swiss army knife, trying to figure out which she could use on the shackle. Luckily the thick iron cuffs were probably over a hundred years old and fashioned when tolerances were in the fractions of an inch, not microns. "We need to get out of here. Get the babies. And—"

"Burn the house down."

"Yes. Somehow. I doubt they have a closet full of high explosives that we can use."

"We can improvise. We're good at that."

"Yes, we are." Louise breathed out relief as her manacle clicked open. She bent over the cuff on Jillian's leg, glad that Jillian was embracing anger to keep out fear. Her twin was trembling from one or both of the emotions flooding her. When Jillian's manacle unlocked, she threw the hunk of metal as far as the chain would allow. They hugged each other tight, just for a moment, trying to draw strength without weakening the other.

Jillian pulled away first and stood, hands on her hips, looking very much like Peter Pan. "So, what do you think? How do we take down this spell?"

The cage was a weird mix of things that they'd never seen and spells from the codex. It had the familiar design of concentric rings, the outer rings triggering first and cascading inward. The inner layer shimmered in the deep shadows of the cave, weaving like the mad vines around Sleeping Beauty's castle. The scrollwork seemed no more substantial than a hologram. When Louise reached out to tap it quickly—triggering a gasp of alarm from Jillian—the bars proved to be solid and cold as steel. They arched overhead, creating a sphere. Since the inner shell was tightly woven, they wouldn't be able to reach the more vulnerable parts of the spell.

When Celine activated the cage, she hadn't used a typical trigger word but a series of phonemes, much like those used in spell locks. Louise focused the light onto the spell engraved into the floor. The first ring contained elements from a lock. It was inscribed on an inlaid piece of marble that most likely hid the actual keywords that switched the cage on and off. If they had their tablets...

If wishes were fishes.

"Without magic, it will collapse," Louise said. "Do you think we can burn all the magic in this area?"

"No," Jillian said after glancing around them. "There's too much magic here. The sunroom is a mud puddle compared to this. This is a lake. Look over there."

Louise turned to see what Jillian was pointing at. The narrow beam of the spell light picked out details across the large room. The floor was several large slabs of marble fitted together to make one large block. A spell had been marked onto the floor with a combination of wax and metal filings. It was a massive spell with a Celtic-knot complexity of subroutines and processes. She could identify all the pieces, but how they worked together she couldn't even guess.

"I'm drawing a blank on how to get out of here," Jillian whimpered.

"It's okay. I managed to keep these." Louise pulled out the two metal-ink pens she'd tucked into her sock. They were designed to draw functional circuits for electronics but it worked just as well for magic. "We can do a force-strike spell."

"Will it be strong enough?"

"We can ramp it up with a series of focusing rings."

Jillian considered it and nodded, but added a warning. "There might be a rebound effect. It could be bad."

"We could do a simple shield, like the ones that the *sekasha* use, to protect us."

"I'll do the shield!" Jillian cried and snatched one of the pens out of Louise's hand. She crouched on the floor and carefully marked a circle just big enough for both of them to stand in. "You do remember force strike well enough?" she whispered. "Because I don't think I do—not all of it."

They both had drawn the *sekasha* protective spell countless times for their videos, both for the Wind Clan and the Fire Clan, and had discussed at length the differences in the tattoos and the information they'd found in the codex. Louise took a deep breath, looking down at the bare floor. If she screwed up, there wouldn't be any way to fix the mistake.

"I can do this," she said more to herself than to Jillian. "It's a fairly simple spell. I just have to take my time and do it right."

It was odd that she realized that the few times that they'd gone to church with their Grandma Mayer had sunk deep roots into her psychic. She wanted to believe in God because she wanted to believe he would hear her earnest prayer that she would actually draw the spell correctly. The consequences for failing were all too easy to imagine, and she was afraid that meant she would fail.

She clicked out the pen and knelt on the floor. *Dear God, please. Please.*

She was just finishing when she realized someone was calling her name.

"Lou! Lou!"

She looked up to find one of the mice was standing beyond the edge of the cage, waving to get her attention. "What are you doing here? I told you to stay!"

"They're loading all our stuff onto a truck. They've taken Tesla to the garage and put him in a giant box. We don't know what to do! We can't get him out. The Jawbreakers are watching over Tesla, and Chuck Norris is looking for Joy."

Where the hell had Joy gone? Last Louise had seen, the baby dragon was in their bedroom. Joy had been trying to pack the cans of freeze-dried food and complaining that she was hungry.

"Oh! Oh! I bet she went to the kitchen. Did Chuck look there?"

"There are people in the kitchen!"

Louise felt a flare of panic at the idea of the babies trying to search the big gleaming kitchen. It was so brightly lit and sparsely decorated that a moving mouse would stand out. "Tell her to stay away from the kitchen. We're almost out of this and we'll...we'll get the gossamer call. Joy will answer it."

Behind her, Jillian hissed out a swear word. "Oh, I'm so stupid! I have the gossamer call! Joy can get us out of here."

Jillian took the small whistle out of her shoe and blew it. Most of the sound it produced was inaudible to humans, but the lowest frequency notes echoed through the caves.

"Jilly!" Louise cried. She thought she heard something rustle in response to the sound but it was gone before she could identify it.

"Sorry! Sorry! I forgot that it isn't totally ultrasonic."

"What's this?" Joy appeared beside Nikola with a big tub of ice cream that she could barely carry. Her face and both front paws were smeared with white cream and little blots of chocolate. Joy held the nearly empty container out for inspection. The label stated "Stracciatella Gelato." It explained why the babies couldn't find Joy; she'd been sealed in the massive walk-in freezer. It also confirmed that the monster call traveled on a magical wavelength beyond normal sound. "What is it? What is yummy cold stuff?"

Louise rubbed her face to stop the scream of frustration and anger from coming out. Joy was a baby and didn't understand the danger they were in.

Jillian, though, didn't muffle her scream. "It's ice cream, you greedy little—"

Louise slapped her hand over her twin's mouth. "Shhh, shhh, we don't want anyone to hear!"

Jillian continued for another minute, muttering angrily against Louise's hand.

Louise ignored her sister. "Joy, can you get us out of this spell?"

Joy eyed the gleaming cage of power. "Oooh. Nasty cage spell. No."

Jillian mumbled, "Mm mm mmm mmm."

Louise translated. "Can you at least try?"

"There is no try." Joy pointed at the shimmering bars with a crème-covered paw.

Jillian growled with frustration and pulled Louise's hand from her mouth. "I'm done with the shield. What about you?"

Louise eyed the spell nervously. It looked right. "Yes, let's do this." She waved at Nikola. "Get back. We're going to try blasting our way out."

Nikola scurried back into the shadows. Joy waddled away, carrying her tub of gelato. Jillian spoke the command word and then "oohhh" in surprise.

"What?"

"I can see it. It's like . . . black glow . . . all around us."

"Good." Louise took a deep breath. She spoke the command word.

With a loud crack, the spell activated and arrowed force along the directional arrow drawn in the runes. It plowed through the glyphs of the cage spell, instantly reducing part of the floor into rubble. The sudden trench continued to plow forward, into the distant casting room. The cage vanished as if it had never existed, and they were plunged into darkness. Dust and pieces of the ceiling rained down around them, the *sekasha* shield protecting the twins.

"Whoo-hoo!" Jillian shouted and cancelled the shield.

They did the dance of joy, jumping up and down, screaming with excitement until Louise remembered that they might be heard.

"Shhh!" Louise smacked her twin.

"If they didn't hear that, they're not going to hear me!" Jillian cried. "And how did you hit me? I can't see anything."

"I could hear you!" Louise took the spell light out of her pocket and panned it across the room. First thing she spotted was the now empty gelato container lying abandoned on the ground. Then she spotlighted Joy licking her fingers. There was no sign of the little white mouse. "Where's Nikola?"

Joy looked around and then shrugged.

"Nikola?" Louise called as Jillian picked up Joy, muttering darkly about the baby dragon's eating habits.

Louise thought she heard a distant squeak. She caught hold of Jillian's hand and headed toward the noise. How far could Nikola have gotten? She didn't think a mouse could run so far in such a short time. Had he been hurt by the explosion? There didn't seem to be any rubble in the direction of his voice, but had she really heard him? "Nikola?"

"Lou!" came the faint answer from the darkness.

"That way!" Jillian whispered.

Around a rough corner and down a narrow hallway and they entered another casting room. The light picked out the glyphs of a spell marked out on the marble in wax and iron. She didn't recognize any of the components but something about it made her skin crawl.

"Nikola?" Louise whispered.

She jumped when the mouse robot suddenly scurried up her leg so Nikola could perch on her shoulder.

"Lou, something is inside the sphere." Nikola huddled against her neck, a small, fearful ball of fur.

She panned the light upwards. A massive orb hung from a chain at the center of the spell. The bars were solid metal wrought into elaborate circles and glyphs. Four legs jutted out of the bottom where it would connect to runes on the floor, acting like jumper cables on a circuit board. While she didn't recognize the spell, she could tell that the magic all focused inward to the four points, and thus funneled into the orb.

And there was something trapped inside.

The creature shifted with a quiet rustle. Louise gasped as the light shone on glossy black feathers. There was some kind of bird in the orb. A massive bird as the beam of light revealed dozens of long flight feathers, each broader than her hand. It was too big to be a turkey vulture or a bald eagle. Why would anyone lock a bird up in this dark, cold place? Was Yves experimenting on the poor thing? Did it even have food and water or was Yves letting it suffer since he planned to kill it anyhow?

"What kind of bird is it?" Jillian whispered.

"I don't know." Louise cautiously moved closer to the orb to get a better look. "The feathers remind me of a crow, but it's too big. Maybe a condor. Maybe something from Elfhome."

"Like a roc?"

"The elves haven't verified that rocs exist—"

With a loud rustle of feathers, the wings shifted to reveal a boy's face. He had short unruly black hair sticking out in all directions, thick dark eyebrows, surprisingly blue eyes, and a large hooked nose. For some reason, he looked familiar even though Louise was sure that she didn't know him. He tilted his head this way and that, like a bird would, trying to peer past the glare of the spell light.

"That's not a bird!" Jillian cried. "It's a—It's a—What the hell is it?"

"I don't know," Louise whispered.

The bird boy wasn't wearing a shirt. While they couldn't see how everything connected to his back, it was obvious that he had wings and not just a feathered cloak. He looked like a high school gymnast, lean but strongly built, all his shoulder and chest muscles sharply defined. His wings were raven black, shifting just like a nervous bird's. He wore dark fabric pants but his feet were bare.

"He has bird feet!" Jillian cried.

Why were bird feet more stunning than wings? Louise didn't know, but she couldn't stop staring. His shin and ankle looked human, but his foot split into three long toes with sharp talons at the end of them.

"Do you think he's—he's intelligent?" Jillian asked.

Was he in the orb simply because he was more bird than boy? He felt at once pitiful and dangerous. She took a step back.

He lunged and caught hold of Jillian.

The twins both screamed. Louise grabbed the boy's wrists and tried to free Jillian.

Joy appeared on his arm, hissing angrily. "Bad! Bad! Let go!"

He let go with a cry of dismay, spilling the twins onto the floor. "I'm sorry!" he shouted as they scrambled backward. "Please! Wait! I'm sorry!"

Louise was across the room and halfway up a flight of stairs that she hadn't noticed before when she realized that Jillian wasn't following. Nikola was clinging to Louise's shirt collar, squeaking frantically, "Go! Go!"

"Jilly?" Louise shouted.

"Listen!" Jillian called from somewhere in the darkness.

"Please!" the caged winged creature cried. "Forgive me! I'm sorry!"

"He could be just parroting the words." Louise dashed back to take Jillian's hand and tug her toward the steps.

"If he's intelligent enough to talk, we can't leave him in the cage!" Jillian resisted being pulled away. "We're going to burn this place down, remember?"

They were probably going to need a distraction to get cleanly away from the mansion. A fire would work well. To leave any animal trapped in a cage, intelligent or not, while the place filled with flames was unthinkable. Still, Louise didn't want to risk her twin. Without Louise's precognition power, Jillian couldn't sidestep danger. It was probably why Jillian was often caught when Louise had always managed to stay one step out of trouble. "What if he's dangerous? How do we let him out without getting hurt?"

"We'll talk to him!" Jillian cried. "The enemy of my enemy—"

"Is a circus freak," Louise muttered darkly.

"Well, yes. But if he's intelligent, then he'll probably see the benefit of cooperating with us. He's bigger than us; we could use some added muscle. Besides, you dropped the spell light and you'll need it to find our way out of here."

Louise hadn't even realized that she'd dropped it; she'd run through the darkness without noticing it. She might be able to continue safely, but she didn't like the idea of blindly trusting some vague spider-sense instead of just seeing where they were going. "Okay, we'll get it."

As they neared the light, Louise realized that Joy was perched on Jillian's shoulders. The baby dragon was smacking Jillian on the head, muttering "Other way! Other way, stupid!" as they crept back to the cage.

The creature fell silent as they neared. He had shifted so he was crouched on all fours. He bowed, touching his forehead to the cage's floor. His wings half-unfurled, showing the bone and muscle structure of his back needed for flight.

"I'm sorry." He remained bowed low. "I thought you were one of them. I'm sorry I scared you."

"Okay, we get it." Jillian obviously didn't like him begging any more than Louise did.

The boy kept his head bowed to the floor of the cage. "You are her Chosen?"

"Yup! All mine!" Joy hugged Jillian's face.

"Mmm!" Jillian struggled to pry the baby dragon off her face even as Joy stuck out her tongue at the boy.

"What's a Chosen?" Louise studied the giant birdcage. If he wasn't dangerous, how were they going to get him free? Where was the lock? "Is that like being an elf? Are you—were you an elf?"

Jillian managed to pry Joy free. "I don't think he's an elf."

"He's a tengu," Joy stated. "Stupid poopy face." She muttered other things that sounded like curses that the tengu seemed to understand. Hurt and dismay showed on his face.

"He said he was sorry." Jillian held Joy in her arms so the baby dragon couldn't plaster herself to Jillian's face again.

"Who are you?" The boy sat up, moving slowly so he wouldn't scare them. The circular metal cage didn't allow for him to stand. "What are you doing here?"

"We're trying to escape from Yves," Louise said.

"Yves?"

"Crown Prince Kiss Butt. The son of the exiled emperor of the elves. Yves Desmarais. *Husepavua.* Whatever his real name is."

"Ah, Okami Shiroikage," he whispered. "The Unmaker. I thought he was just a legend made up to frighten our people. I was wrong."

"He locked us up in a magical cage so he could study us," Louise said.

"But we broke free," Jillian added. "What did he do to you?"

"Nothing yet," the winged boy said.

"Nothing?" the twins both cried. "But you have wings!"

Despite everything, he grinned. "Yes, I have wings. I was given them on my sixth hatching day. It was like having Christmas and New Years and Halloween all at once. My people are part human, part crow. Not that you can usually tell when we're on Earth."

Louise completed a full circle around the spherical cage without seeing anything that looked like a door. Maybe if they raised the orb. She panned the light up the chain and across to the winch controls. To her dismay, there was an arc-welding machine sitting on the floor. One of the elves had sealed the orb shut after they'd put the tengu into it. The finality of it shocked her. Yves didn't intend for the crow boy to come out of the orb alive.

Jillian was right. They couldn't leave him here. It would haunt them the rest of their lives.

But how could they free him? Even if they could figure out the welding machine, they didn't have time. They had to save the babies. They couldn't use the force-strike spell; a blow hard enough to break the orb open would probably kill the crow boy.

She scanned the room, quickly considering what she had to work with.

"Oh, be nice!" Jillian cried as Joy wiggled her butt at the boy.

They had called the baby dragon down to the caves to phase them out of their cage. "Joy, can you get him out of that?"

The baby dragon turned up her nose like an offended princess. "No."

"No?" Louise echoed in dismay.

"Tengu belong to Providence," Joy explained.

"Who is Providence?" Jillian asked.

"He's the guardian spirit of the tengu," Crow Boy said.

"Five Claw Dragon." Joy lifted her front right leg and showed off the fact that she had five claws on her paw. "Double stupid poopy face."

"A dragon?" Jillian cried as Louise asked, "Like you?"

Joy blew a raspberry. "Completely different but mostly the same."

Louise guessed that meant that the dragons were about the same as humans were to one another. She and Elle were both nine-year-old girls, but after that everything was different about them.

"So you can't get him out because of Providence?" Jillian asked.

Joy nodded her head energetically. "Tengu belong to Providence."

Perhaps Joy wouldn't be so insistent if Crow Boy hadn't grabbed

Jillian. They couldn't stand there endlessly debating with the little dragon.

Louise reached out to pet Joy on the head. "You can't touch him, but can you move the cage?"

Joy stared at her with suspicion. "Move cage: free tengu."

"He stays where he is," Louise pointed out. "You leave him where you found him."

"Please, Joy," Jillian added, "I'll get you candy!"

"Jawbreakers!" Joy cried.

"Whatever. Just phase the cage, please!"

"Okay."

They swung the cage side to side on the heavy chain. When it was at its farthest point, Joy shifted it and the tengu was left in midair. He landed lightly and leapt forward to get out of the way of the swinging orb.

The twins backed nervously away from the tengu.

Crow Boy knelt down before them and bowed his head. "Thank you."

"We're not out of the doo-doo yet," Jillian muttered darkly.

They found their way to an extensive wine cellar. Judging by the boxing supplies, the staff would be packing up the wine after the art. Yves was truly abandoning the mansion at full speed. They picked their way through the racks until they found the dimly lit spiral staircase leading up. Louise stopped at the bottom step. She could smell fried onions, cumin, and coriander. She thought she could hear voices.

She reached up to pet Nikola where he was riding her shoulder. He'd been quiet since they found Crow Boy. "Nikola, are there still people in the kitchen?"

"Yes. Nattie is cleaning up from dinner, and there are six others with her. They're fighting about money; the mansion's general operating fund is empty."

On the house blueprints, it had been clear that this stairwell was the only way down into the sub-basements. It spiralled down two stories, past the basement level without connecting, from the large walk-in pantry off the kitchen. There had been no other way out. Obviously they would need a very large distraction somewhere else in the house to lure off the elves.

Louise started ticking through available resources when Crow

Boy brushed past her. He'd picked up a long bar of steel from somewhere that he carried like a spear.

"Hide," he whispered and ran silently up the stairs.

"What's he doing?" Jillian whispered fiercely.

"Getting into a mess!" Louise ran after him. She couldn't even shout after him to stop him; they were too close to the elves. What was he thinking? For them to hide and then sneak out when the elves dragged him back down into the basement? It wasn't going to go that way. The elves were going to kill him, and they'd be trapped as the secret elves searched the basement. What could she do to stop the oncoming disaster? Have the babies call 911? No, the police wouldn't be here in time to save Crow Boy. No one would get there in time. Turn off the lights? No, the mansion electrical system was still last century. Blow something up? Yes, that would work!

"Is Tesla still in the truck?" Louise cried to Nikola clinging to her collar.

"Yes. The Jawbreakers are with him."

"Tell Chuck to get to the garage! We're leaving now!"

"We are?"

"Yes!"

At the top of the steps, Louise nearly tripped over unconscious elves sprawled on the pantry floor. It was Celine with a big ring of keys and one of the males that acted as drivers. Were they the reason Crow Boy had run upstairs? Had he heard them coming and realized that the elves were about to check on the caged prisoners?

And this was the best plan he could come up with?

Granted he had mowed these two down easily enough, but her spider-sense was screaming "this will not end well." Louise stepped over Celine and grabbed a large sack of flour from the pantry shelf. She had only seconds before everything toppled to complete disaster.

As if on cue, someone shouted, "We need help! The *yamabushi* is loose!"

Louise ran into the kitchen, carrying the bag of flour.

After the cave dark of the dank sub-basement, the kitchen was a sudden assault of light and smell. Every light was on, reflecting off the gleaming granite counters and stainless-steel appliances. The coppery scent of fresh blood mixed with hot spices and fried onions. Dirty pots and pans beside the sink with steaming water still running was proof that Crow Boy had taken the elves off guard. The fight had spilled to the other side of the kitchen, where he leaped and kicked and spun, fending off Nattie and three males armed with butcher knives. Shouts of "The *yamabushi* is loose" rang deeper within the house, and Louise could hear reinforcements racing toward the kitchen. Crow Boy was about to be overwhelmed by sheer numbers.

Louise put the flour bag on the granite counter and quickly sketched a disperse spell onto the wrapper.

Nattie snatched up one of the kitchen chairs and swung it hard at Crow Boy. It caught him mid-leap and smashed him down to the floor. The elves leapt to pin the boy to the floor.

"Don't kill him," one of the males warned. "We need him breathing."

"Breathing, yes." Nattie stomped down on Crow Boy's left leg, and there was a sickening crack. "In one piece, no. Give me that knife."

Louise gave the flour bag a hard shove, sending it skidding across the polished stone. She shouted the trigger word. The bag exploded as all the particles blossomed in all directions like an instant dry blizzard.

In the whiteout, Nattie cursed loudly. "Oh, shit! The wood sprites!"

Flour was drifting down. When it settled it would be useless. Louise needed a spark to cause a dust explosion!

Jillian screamed as Celine suddenly caught her from behind.

"I've got one of them!" Celine cried. "The other one is here—"

"Let her go!" Louise snatched up a skillet from the sink and swung as hard as she could at the female's knee. The elf screamed and lunged toward her. Louise backhanded her with the skillet like a tennis racket. There was a satisfying *clang* as the stainless-steel pan connected with Celine's face.

Celine lost her grip on Jillian. Louise caught her twin by the wrist and dragged her away from the elf. Celine staggered backwards, glaring at Louise as blood seeped from her mouth.

"You little breeding bitch," the elf snarled and picked up a meat cleaver. "We only need one of you."

Joy reared up on Jillian's shoulder. Her mane flared out, and the baby dragon breathed a blast of fire at Celine's face.

Celine's scream was drowned out by a massive fireball as the flour hazing the air exploded.

Louise felt the explosion quake the floor under her feet, but the flames rushed past, a swirl of orange and reds, not touching the twins.

"Mine, stupid poopy face, all mine!" Joy stood on Jillian's shoulder, mane bristling, muttering in anger as the firestorm raged around them.

The entire kitchen was on fire. Flames crawled up the walls and raced across the ceiling. The stove erupted in a secondary blast.

"We have to get out of here!" Jillian cried.

Celine seemed dead, curled into a tight ball of burnt flesh. Her body, though, reminded Louise that Crow Boy was somewhere in the kitchen.

"We need to find Crow Boy first!"

They found him halfway across the room, crawling toward them instead of toward the blown-open door.

"I was afraid you would be trapped." He coughed as they got him up. Using his wings and a hand on either of their shoulders, he managed to balance and then half-hop, half-fly toward the door.

"That was stupid!" Louise cried. "There were dozens of ways we could have gotten out of there without them even knowing we were free. Next time, wait until we tell you what to do."

He grimaced in pain. "I sincerely hope there isn't a next time."

The three of them couldn't fit through the shattered doorway at the same time, so Louise stepped through first. It took her outside the protection of Joy's shields, and the sudden flare of intense heat and thick smoke made her stumble forward, coughing.

She saw the gunman just as he saw her. She stared unbelieving as he raised his rifle and took aim at her.

But then the male fell over, twitching.

"Hooyah!" Chuck Norris squeaked as she fist-pumped. "Taser is in the mouse!"

"Chuck!"

Chuck waved her tiny hands. "I totally saved you!"

Louise scooped up the mouse robot. "Yes, you did. Thank you."

The detached garage had obviously been built to hold horse carriages. It was a massive, dimly lit building with heavy timbers supporting its barnlike roof. It housed a dozen sleek modern cars.

The light of the growing house fire flickered through celestial windows over the bay doors. From deep pools of darkness, the light gleamed off polished chrome in pinpoints like demonic eyes.

A box truck sat in the oversized end bay. Louise's heart sank as she envisioned trying to find Tesla in a tightly packed truck. As they rounded the back end, however, she was relieved to see that the elves hadn't started to load it yet. Carefully labeled boxes sat in stacks, obviously organized into groups. The Jawbreakers stood on one of the larger cardboard boxes, waving.

"That was so scary!" The two broke into excited squeaking. "We were so scared. And Lou! Bang! That was awesome. And then boom! Better than fireworks!"

"Are you in here?" Jillian asked.

"Yup! Yup! We're right here!"

The box had been labeled: "Wood Sprites' toys, possibly dangerous." It had been sealed shut with strapping tape. Louise pulled out her Swiss army knife. While the mice all sang "Boom, boom, fireworks bloom" in four-part harmony, Louise cut open the box and folded back the flaps to reveal Tesla.

The mice fell silent as Louise snapped open the storage hatch. The *nactka* was still safely inside. The twins breathed out with relief, and all the mice cheered. The elves must not have realized that Tesla had a hidden compartment.

"What is that?" Crow Boy looked like he was going to fall over.

"The most important thing in the world." Louise closed up the hatch. "We need to get out of here. Fast."

"Lou." Nikola tugged at her hair. "Put this mouse someplace safe and I'll drive Tesla."

She tucked the little bundle of fur into her carpenter pants leg pocket. Tesla shook awake and wagged his tail. She hugged him tightly.

"Awesome!" Jillian cried as she lunged into the box to pull out their tablets from deep inside it. "They're still password locked. And our phones! Yay!" She dove into another box that was labeled: "Wood Sprites' objects, unidentified, possibly dangerous."

"What is so dangerous about a soldering gun?" Jillian muttered, still half inside the box.

"We need to go!" Louise scanned the cars around them. "We'll take one of the cars and send the rest out to random addresses to muddy the trail."

"I say we take the Lamborghini." Jillian pointed at the dangerous-looking sports car.

None of the cars blended in with normal traffic. All the other vehicles were the tanklike limousines. The Lamborghini could outrun anything short of a helicopter and maybe even that. At the moment, speed and maneuverability outweighed everything.

"Does it have self-driving?" She scooped up the Jawbreakers. "It is a Lamborghini."

Nikola tilted his head, which usually meant he was accessing another computer. "Yes, it has a self-drive option. It's recommended to be used when the driver has been drinking. What does taking in fluids have to do with driving?"

"We'll explain later," Jillian said. "Can you disarm its security and unlock it?"

The Lamborghini chirped and its doors opened. The garage doors all started upwards, gliding slightly on well-oiled tracks, preparing for a mass exodus of cars.

Crow Boy wavered in place, looking like he was upright on sheer willpower alone. There were a dozen thin cuts on his arms, seeping blood. If he fainted, Louise doubted that she and Jillian could get him into a car. It took several tense minutes to get him across the large garage to the Lamborghini and into the passenger seat, wings and all.

Only then did Louise realize that the sports car was much smaller inside than she had expected. There was no backseat and there was a stick shift between the two front ones.

Nikola hopped into the driver's seat and put his paws on the steering wheel. "Where are we going?"

"River Edge Station." Jillian scrambled into the car and straddled the divider between the seats. "Yves can track us via the anti-theft GPS on this."

"No." Louise vetoed that. "We need to get Crow Boy to a hospital quickly."

Crow Boy murmured something about no hospital and flying under the radar.

Louise ignored him as she eyed the crowded interior. The only place for her was on Crow Boy's lap. She eased carefully in, making sure that she didn't put weight on his broken leg. "The trains don't come often enough to River Edge; we'll be stranded at the station for too long." She tried not to be scared when he wrapped his arms around her. Joy sat on Louise's lap and *glared* up at the boy. "We'll go into the city and have the car make a bunch of stops. They won't know where we actually got out."

"Okay, the city," Nikola said. The engine suddenly rumbled loudly to life.

"Oh shit, it's a combustion engine?" Louise thought only big construction vehicles were still run by gasoline.

Nikola tilted his head. "To go we do this?"

The sports car leapt forward with a roar and squeal of tires. They slid sideways through the turn of the driveway and raced toward the far road. Louise and Jillian both shrieked in surprise and fear.

"Oh. Sorry." The car started to slow.

"No, don't slow down now! Go!"

"Okay!" Nikola bounced in his seat with excitement and they flew into the night. "Mapping quickest route to Manhattan."

Third star to the right, Louise thought, *straight on toward dawn.*

It was twenty miles to Times Square. They did it in nearly ten minutes, leaving black contrails of tire marks at every turn. They slowed down—slightly—for the Lincoln Tunnel while Nikola explained that he'd avoided the George Washington Bridge because it was congested despite the 3:00 a.m. time.

Louise gripped tight the armrest built into the door, trying not to scream as they zipped past slower cars. "I thought that self-driven cars couldn't speed."

"Speed limit is set by the road, not the car." Nikola tilted his head back and forth as he communicated with outside computers. "Snow or ice or something could change the speed that the road can be traveled safely, so the car is told the speed limit along with all the other traffic data. We're filtering the information as it's coming from the road, leaving all the other factors constant but changing the speed limit upwards by sixty miles per hour."

Louise glanced at the dashboard, read their speed, and whimpered slightly.

They slewed sideways into an impossibly rare parking space within view of the Times Square subway station entrance. They sat there panting as the car rumbled in idle.

"So, where do we go?" Jillian whispered.

"We need to go to a hospital for—for—Crow Boy." Louise

winced as she realized that they'd spent the last hour fleeing and not asking the most basic of questions, like "What is your name?"

"We need to take him to a hospital."

"Which one?" Jillian made it sound like there might be several hospitals that specialized in boys with wings.

Louise decided to focus on "boy" instead of "wings." "Morgan Stanley Children's Hospital."

Nikola took that as a plan, and the car roared as it leapt out of the parking space.

38: MORGAN STANLEY CHILDREN'S HOSPITAL

The automatic door opened for them as they helped Crow Boy into the emergency room. He barely seemed aware of what was happening, and it took all their strength to get him out of the low-slung car, upright and moving. There was a woman at the admittance desk intently working at a computer while fielding phone calls. She chewed gum while listening to the other side of the conversation, shaking her head and saying "No. No. No" as she stabbed computer keys. She glanced at them, focused back on her computer screen, and then, with confusion spreading across her face, looked back up. She sat there, jaw dropped, piece of gum showing, as they limped up to her desk. Her name tag read "Martha."

The woman's stunned expression gave Louise courage to swallow down her fear and say in Elvish, "Please, we need help. His leg is broken."

The woman blinked rapidly. "Um, please hold." She stabbed a button on her phone and leaned back to call, "Gerri! Gerri!"

An older woman appeared, summoned by the shouting. "Oh, that's new."

Louise used Elvish to plead for help and then made a show of pointing at Crow Boy's obviously broken leg.

"They're elves!" Martha claimed.

Gerri frowned at Crow's black wings and then at the bug antennae that the twins were wearing. As they hoped, the wings won out for close inspection, which was good because the antennae were just wires attached to bobby pins.

"He's not an elf." Gerri didn't bother to qualify the twins.

"She's speaking Elvish." Martha pointed at Louise.

"You understand what she's saying?"

"I only recognize the one line from *The Queen's Puddin' Cake*. The Lemon-Lime JEL-Lo video. She's asking for help. I'm not sure what the rest is. His leg looks broken."

"Do you speak English?" Gerri spoke slowly and loudly. After a moment, she tried Spanish, which was easier to ignore. "Shit. Okay, we need a patient advocate. Also try to find some kind of translator; we're going to need one."

Louise half-expected to be told to wait in the waiting room but they were all shepherded into the examination area. It was only when she glanced at Jillian that she realized why: the twins were covered in bruises, soot, dirt, and blood. Celine might have broken Louise's nose when she slapped her; certainly it had bled for a long time afterwards.

The staff's focus was on Crow Boy once they determined that the girls weren't showing any signs of shock. They hooked him up to an IV and monitors. A security guard appeared and swept them with a metal detector and collected the Swiss army knife, to Louise's dismay.

After several intense minutes, they were left alone as various trauma nurses conferred on the other side of the curtain. They spoke in a fast mix of medical terms and possible legal ramifications. In addition to being children without parental permission for medical treatment, the nurses were debating the wording of the treaty with the elves.

"But we really don't know if they're elves or not," one nurse complained.

Another one answered with, "We have to assume that their baseline might not be normal to humans and work from there."

In the examining area's bright light, Louise could also see Crow Boy clearly for the first time. He eyed their surroundings with confusion. He hadn't been fully conscious throughout the whole discussion of where to go and the drive to the hospital. The IV was working and he was growing aware of where they were. Despite the fact that he was much taller than them, he looked only three or four years older. The idea that he was a ninth-grader triggered a memory, and she realized why he looked so familiar.

"What?" Jillian asked in Elvish. "You just got a 'Oh my God' look on your face."

"We've met Crow Boy before," Louise whispered. "The day after the explosion, he was at the..." Elvish didn't have a word for "museum" and she didn't want to use any English around the hospital staff. "He was at the gift shop with the girls who were going to buy that snow ball."

"Snow ball?" Jillian clearly wasn't following.

"The snow thing." Louise mimed shaking the snow globe. There might have been a word for "globe" in Elvish, but she didn't know it. "*Tianlong Hao.*"

"Oh! Yeah! He was there with all the kids."

They turned to look at him.

"But he didn't have wings then," Jillian pointed out.

No, he hadn't.

"I-I-I remember you now." Crow Boy spoke in fluent Elvish. He frowned at the twins. "You were with a beautiful black woman and you had your dog with you. I couldn't figure out how you got the robot past security."

They both squeaked with surprise.

"But where were your wings?" Jillian asked.

"I can dismiss them—if there's magic. On Earth, we need to pass as human."

"Were all those other kids tengu, too?"

"Yes, I was escorting them to Pittsburgh. We've been sneaking our people to Elfhome where they could live free of the oni. We started within days of the first Startup, before even the oni realized the opportunity that Pittsburgh gave them. Years and years, carefully moving our entire race across three worlds. And then everything came crumbling down this spring. Shiroikage's spy ferreted out where the *yamabushi* had hidden the Chosen line."

Shiroikage was what Crow Boy called Yves. By "spy" did he mean Tristan? The half-elf had said he'd been bird-watching in California before coming to New York. "Clever crows," Tristan had complained. Had Tristan really been searching for tengu? "In Pasadena?"

"Yes. We thought we could hide the Chosen line among the masses in Los Angeles. I was guarding Keiko and Mickey as they attended school. I managed to get them to safety, but their parents..." He took a deep breath, as if he were fighting off tears. "You should go. Leave me."

That was what Tristan was doing? Or did he not know what happened after he found the tengu? He had asked Celine if Yves had captured Shoji; he'd left before the fighting started. Louise wanted to believe that Ming kept the slaughter from the half-elf. That Tristan was innocent by way of ignorance.

The curtain rustled back to admit a tall man in blue scrubs, ending all conversation. According to the ID badge clipped to his shirt pocket, he was Dr. Stefan Harmeling. He had a black Afro cropped short into stubs, dark brown skin, and tattoos tracing up his arms. "*Jesús santisimo*," he whispered. He cautiously canted to the side so he could eye Crow Boy's back. "Wings. Now I've seen everything."

The children jumped slightly when the curtain rustled open again. It was only a nurse joining the doctor in the area.

"It's okay. No one is going to harm you." Doctor Harmeling smiled reassuringly and cautiously closed the distance between him and Crow Boy. "Let's take a look at you and see how badly you're hurt."

Crow Boy scowled at him and then focused back on the twins. "Do you have someplace safe to go? You should leave now. Protect yourself."

Jillian gave Peter Pan's fearless laugh. "We, at least, have clothes on! You're going to be naked when they're done with you."

And he'd need them to dismiss his wings, but when the hospital staff wasn't paying close attention.

"They will follow," Crow Boy said. "They are relentless."

"First they're going to have to put out the fire and track down the vehicles. We sent all the vehicles away from the mansion."

"Well...actually...the truck is still there," Nikola interrupted in Elvish. "It's quite durable, so we've been using it as a battering ram. The rest we drove into the river; so it's going to take them quite a long time to get them back."

The doctor swung around to stare down at Nikola. "*Jesús santisimo*! Elfhome dogs can talk?"

The nurse carefully eyed Nikola. "It's not a real dog. It's one of those new very realistic nanny robots."

"Perfect!" the doctor cried. "If it's from Earth, it probably can translate for us."

Louise winced. Nikola had never had to lie before. She wasn't sure he knew how. He shrank back with a whimper as everyone in the room focused on him.

The doctor crouched down to Nikola's level. "Hey, boy, do you speak English?"

Nikola whimpered again and looked to the twins and then looked at the doctor and then back to the twins.

"Dog, what's your name?" the doctor said.

"*Konnichiwa.*" Nikola slowly stumbled over the Japanese, using his deep male samurai voice. "*Boku wa Akita da.*"

Strictly speaking, he was an Akita.

The doctor sighed and scrubbed his face. "Okay, we need a translator here as soon as possible and a child advocate. The fibula is fractured and this bruise has a tread pattern on it. Someone stomped on his leg to break it. If I remember my history correctly, the treaty forbids children from being removed from Elfhome, so I'm thinking that someone might be slave-trading them."

He wasn't that far from wrong.

Luckily the hospital didn't have a translation device equipped to handle Elvish. They cycled a dozen human languages past the twins, three of which they were fluent in, but they pretended not to understand. The child advocate arrived and signed release forms so that Crow Boy could be X-rayed and MRI scanned. The test results triggered a phone call to the city zoo to summon a vet.

"This is so wild!" the vet murmured as the adults all eyed the test results.

Dr. Harmeling shook his head. "I'm not sure what the girls are. Their vitals are fine, so we don't really have a reason to test them. But he's definitely not human."

"Yes, I agree," the vet said. "His anatomy is very birdlike. His bones are hollow and thin-walled but dense. These masses resemble a crop and gizzard, and these look like the air sacs that play an important part in respiration in birds. These bony hooks on the ribs support the anchorage of the muscles that move the wings. He has three toes in front and one in back, not five facing forward. These are claws on his toes, not nails. It's just mind-blowing.

"That said," the vet added, "he's displaying a lot more under-standing of his situation and surroundings than any animal I've worked with, and that includes gorillas. I believe he's equal to human in intelligence. I don't think he's an elf, but what do I know about elves?"

"What does anyone know? We'll just put him down as a black-winged elf." Dr. Harmeling tapped the MRI of Crow Boy's leg. "Some bastard deliberately broke this boy's leg. All these knife cuts on the arm? This is clearly torture."

"Setting bird bones is similar to a mammal but occasionally it's harder to keep the thinner bones lined up. We'll have to take X-rays after the cast is on to make sure nothing shifted after we set it."

"Think we can give him anything for pain?" Dr. Harmeling asked. "We'll need to get these leg muscles to relax to line the bones up."

"There are some things that we use in birds that are also used with humans. What I tend to use with birds is inhalant anesthesia. It's pretty safe. As you know, it is gotten out of the system by breathing, so you can wake the birds up pretty quickly."

A police officer arrived armed with a machine translator. Apparently the New York City Police Department had to deal daily with people speaking one of the nearly seven thousand different languages on Earth. He was unruffled at the prospect of interviewing victims in Elvish.

The wings, though, freaked him out.

"He's definitely half-bird," Dr. Harmeling stated after he reassured them that the wings were attached via bones and muscles and not just some clever costume. "He's not from Earth. They seem to be communicating in Elvish. At least, my staff has picked up a handful of words that they recognize from some videos."

Crow Boy had his face set to an unemotional stare, but the nervous flutter of his wings showed his fear.

"And no one came in with them?" the officer asked.

"They were dropped off by a sports car. We checked the video, but all our cameras went haywire about ten minutes before they showed up. They're still down."

The twins had nuked the hospital's security system while en route so the police couldn't backtrack them to Yves.

"I'm police officer Jayden Cohen." The man paused, waiting for the translating machine, which decided "laedin-caste Fire clan royal marine" was as close as it could get to "police officer." His given name came out as "God will judge priest." Obviously the translator wasn't the most sophisticated piece of hardware. "What is your name?"

Crow Boy stared. His face stayed neutral but his quickly tracking eyes betrayed that he was trying to think of a safe answer and failing.

Louise hadn't considered what they would tell the staff if a translator showed up.

Luckily, Jillian had. "He is Crow Warrior Boy of Wind." Crow Boy's eyes widened and he gave Jillian a panicked look, which she ignored. "I'm Sweet Lemon Scent on Wind and this is my twin sister, Flowering Lime Tree Swaying in Wind."

The police frowned at the machine as it butchered their names to "Child Boy Fighter Crow, Candy Stink Lemon, and Tree Waving Limbs Madly Lime," and after a moment of thought added "Facilitating Outcrossing."

The police officer then eyed Jillian and Louise. He reached out and tugged one of the antenna out of Jillian's hair. "What exactly are you?"

Jillian raised her arm—covered with a blood-soaked sleeve—to wipe at her eyes. Life lesson number five kicked in: adults will believe the stupidest things when you're covered in blood. "Those that kidnapped us put those into our hair and then laughed at us and told us that if we took them off, they'd cut off one of our fingers. Please put it back."

Louise acted out comforting Jillian. "We don't understand. Why did they do that? What is that? What does it mean?"

Suspicion bled off of the officer's face as the machine translated their lies.

"I don't know, sweetheart, but you don't have to be scared." Officer Cohen produced an evidence bag and dropped the antenna into it. "We're not going to let anyone hurt you." He collected the other three antennae. "Are you elves? From Elfhome?"

Jillian used the time it took the machine to translate out the questions to launch into a series of distraction questions, just to muddle things. "This box that talks? Magic speaker voice thrower? Ham loaf? Pickle questions?"

Crow Boy looked confused as the machine faithfully attempted to put the garbled Elvish into some reasonable English translation.

"This box that talks? Fling voice orator magic? Bread of smoked pork? Questions preserved by anaerobic fermentation in brine?"

Jillian obviously was hoping that if she garbled the replies enough, the policeman would assume any holes in their story were from bad translation and not because they were fabricating almost everything.

The policeman frowned and replayed her answer. A very good sign. "Yes, this is a translator. It translates what I'm saying in English to Elvish." And then obviously not trusting the machine now, he pointed to his mouth and said "English" and then pointed at the machine. "Elvish." And then muttered quietly, "I hope."

The twins waited for the translation, which was perfect.

"Oh! How clever!" Jillian stated.

"Yes, it is wonderful!" Louise cried.

"Please help us!" Jillian cried. "Madly galloping into the night, we transfix. Please help Crow Warrior. His leg is broken! They put us in cages and fed us zombie donkeys. Pickle questions? They stomped on his leg and broke it and they had knives and they were going to cut him up!" Jillian mimed the elves attacking with the butcher knives. "Dirty dog! Train biscuit train! If they find us, they'll kill everyone and put us back into the cage!"

"You're safe," the police officer stated after the machine struggled to translate the mix of good and purposely garbled Elvish.

"They have a hidden army here on Earth!" Louise warned. "The EIA has been infiltrated. The ambassador to China is one of them. Ambassador Feng!"

"Female dog breath yelping," Jillian added quickly.

"Purple!" Louise stated firmly, nodding.

Crow Boy stared at them as if they'd both grown two heads.

"The ambassador of China?" The policeman latched onto the first clear lead they had given him.

"Purple!" the twins cried in unison.

"He came to the mansion asking for help..." Louise started.

Jillian continued, "He needed help because royal marines from his country were coming to arrest him. They found out he's oni."

Louise added. "Crown Prince Kiss Butt of the oni told him to run and hide and not come back!"

Jillian held up her right hand and smashed thumb and pointer finger together. "Dokadokadokadoka."

"Purple," Louise breathed. "The hidden prince tortured him with magic before telling him to run away. It was scary."

Jillian nodded. "They put us into a cage, but we managed to escape! They caught us again and broke Crow Warrior's leg. They said they were going to cut off his feet. But then there was big explosion. Boom! Everything was burning, and we got away."

They had to wait a long time for the machine to translate and then Officer Cohen to puzzle out the basic gist of their night.

"How did you get here?" Cohen asked.

Good question. Louise frowned at the translator as if it had said something strange. Intermixing babble with actual real information was harder than she'd thought.

"The box that moves on wheels," Jillian made a motor noise while indicating spinning tires by twirling both pointer fingers in circles.

"Automobile!" Louise provided the term that the elves used for cars.

Jillian clapped with excitement. "Purple! Purple! Automobile! We came in an automobile!"

The police officer looked to Crow Boy.

"Purple," Crow Boy confirmed faintly. "Automobile."

The police officer frowned at the machine with frustration. He obviously wanted to ask all sorts of questions, but they had him on the ropes.

"They're going to kidnap Tinker *domi*..." Louise started and faltered.

"She invented hoverbikes." Jillian launched into an elaborate mime that seemed to involve weaving cloth. "They are full of eels!"

"Her father made the gate that the oni created in space." Louise pointed up at the sky.

"The oni thinks that the apple never falls far from the raccoon." Jillian stood up, picked up one of the hospital gowns stacked nearby, and tossed it over Louise's head.

Luckily Louise had realized what Jillian intended to do. She did not startle at being blindfolded. As the world vanished, she was filled with a sense of calm. She knew exactly what to say. "Black wings murdered time and now wait in timeless darkness. The dream crow stirs. She will cry out and the blood of her beloved will answer. The promised time is at hand. Let the flock be gathered and stand strong against those who enslaved them. Providence will provide. His child returns, bringing forth all that is needed for salvation. Impatience will—"

There was a loud outcry as Crow Boy suddenly lunged off the table and landed at her feet. Catching hold of her hands, he gripped them painfully tight. "Jin is alive?"

"No, no, no!" the doctor shouted. "Orderly!"

"Is Jin alive?" Crow Boy cried.

Louise squeezed close her eyes, trying to hold on to the sense of calm knowing. "His prison is about to be broken and he will be set free to fly again. The door is closing, but evil has taken root on Elfhome. All can be lost—"

The blindfold was torn away as Crow Boy was muscled back into his bed, gently but firmly, by two large male orderlies.

"He tore out his IV," someone cried, and Louise realized that her hands were covered with blood. Louise stared at her bloody fingers. How did this keep happening? Up to today, blood was something that she half-expected after a great deal of planning and debate and risk assessment. It never came as a surprise. Other than Jillian's, she had never even seen someone else's blood, and here it was, all over her, again and again.

Jillian started to whimper, a prelude to real crying. Fake crying would have been loud and instant. With her sniffles, the day proved too much for Louise, and she felt hot tears filling her eyes.

"Oookay." The police officer was shaking his head. "I have not a clue what the hell that was all about."

"We need to put the boy under," the doctor murmured as he pressed his hand over the machine's microphone. "None of our translators are loaded with Elvish. Can you help us explain to the children what's about to happen?"

It was stressful to watch them apply the anesthesia and see Crow Boy become totally helpless. Louise hugged Nikola tight, trying to find the inner calm that she'd experienced just moments before. It had been as if she'd stepped out of herself, shedding all fears and worries along the way.

After they wheeled Crow Boy away, she realized that Joy was rummaging through medical supplies, tearing open plastic wrappings to taste the contents. The girls were out, scurrying about in their mice robot bodies.

"What are you doing?"

"Hungry!" Joy cried. "Candy! You promised!"

"Bored," Chuck Norris said.

"Scared," the Jawbreakers squeaked.

Nikola pressed up against Louise, nodding silently in agreement with the Jawbreakers.

"We need to feed her now." Jillian went to the door and peeked out. "They said it would be hours for them to set the leg and him to fully wake up from the anesthesia."

In other words, if they waited, Joy would only get more uncontrollable.

"I thought I saw some vending machines near the waiting room." Louise scooped up Joy with one hand and plucked up the mice one at a time with her other, depositing them on her shoulder. "We're getting something!" she cried as Joy squirmed. "Just be patient."

They waited until the nurses at the station across the hall were distracted and then slipped out. The other rooms were all dark; the patients asleep. The twins walked quickly through the deserted hallways to the waiting room. There was an entire wall of machines. The first offered hot coffee. The second was water and chilled juice and milk. The third was fruit and veggies.

"Oh God," Jillian whispered. "Of course a hospital would only have healthy snacks. What about grapes? You like grapes."

"Feh," Joy muttered from Louise's arms. Then she spotted what was in the next machine. "Oooooh!" She leaned far out of Louise's hold to press her paws against the glass. "Candy!"

Jillian sighed and pointed out the ones they knew the baby dragon liked the most. "Gummy worms? Snickers? Kit Kat? M&Ms?"

Joy gazed up them with pure delight on her face and nodded.

"Which ones?" Jillian asked.

"Candy!"

"I think she wants one of each," Louise said. "She's been really good so far. We owe her."

"All this can't be good for her." Nevertheless, Jillian used her phone to buy one of each type of candy. "We're lousy mothers, you know. Our mom would never give in to us. She'd give us that look and we knew we'd better behave and we would."

Louise felt a sudden floodwater of sorrow rise up. "I know."

"What are we going to do about the babies?" Jillian whispered. "Joy is good at taking care of herself, but what are we going to do with real babies?"

Louise steeled herself against wanting to cry. "I don't know. We don't have any way for the babies to be born yet, so let's not worry about it now."

"When they're born, we'll work hard and be the best mothers ever."

"How can you be our mothers when you're our sisters?" the babies asked.

"Oh!" Jillian used one of their parents' distraction tricks. "We're going to have to get new phones."

Louise gasped as she realized that they would need phones to purchase everything from Joy's candy to new clothes. (They hadn't been stripped down like Crow Boy, but their clothes were blood-soaked and reeked of smoke.) Ming would be able to track every purchase and chart their movements through the city via their old phones.

"We can order replacement phones and pick them up at an automated kiosk." It would mean severing ties with everyone they knew as they changed phone numbers. Should they call their Aunt Kitty and warn her? Her last text had her on a plane heading back to California; she needed to keep working if she had any hope of gaining custody.

Louise took out her phone and turned it on to check for recent text messages from Aunt Kitty. There were five hundred and six new texts. The last dozen all from their classmates.

Louise had gotten a handful of texts after their parents were killed. Their friends had wanted to know if they were okay. She hadn't answered any of them. She didn't know how, because the true and obvious response was "no." After a few days, the incoming texts trickled to nothing.

Why had she gotten over five hundred since this morning? As she stared at her phone, it vibrated with a new text.

It was the middle of the night. Why would anyone be texting this late?

The text was "Where are you?" from Iggy. The one before was from him, too. "Are you okay?" And before that was "Call me!"

A quick scroll downward showed that all five hundred were from her classmates.

What in the world had happened?

She scrolled down and found the first text.

It was from Elle Pondwater, and all in capital letters. "OMG! OMG! I DIDN'T DO IT! I SWEAR!"

Oh, this did not bode well.

The next one was from Iggy. "Someone leaked your names to the press. The world knows you're Lemon-Lime."

"Oh no," Louise whispered.

Zahara pointed the finger at Elle with: "That witch sold your pictures to the tabloids!"

And then another from Elle. "That horrible photographer from my party figured out who you were! He's sold the picture of you two made up as elves!" And then a minute later, a second text. "YOU'RE PRINCESS TINKER'S SISTERS?" Followed by a series of "?" and "!" marks.

"No, no, no," Louise whispered, scrolling down. How did anyone know that?

Iggy texted again. "They're just making wild guesses by saying that you know all that stuff about Elfhome because you're Princess Tinker's little sisters. Right? Yeah, you look a lot like her, but that's not because you're related. Right?" And then an hour later. "How did you know that Princess Tinker saved Windwolf?"

Zahara reported more damage. "Elle says she didn't do it, but her mother had her photographer film the play. He recognized your music. He started a bidding war for the video."

Louise groaned. She'd been so stupid. Pressed for time, she'd used all their normal music-composing tools that included the digital recreations of the Elfhome instruments. Any claims that they were the creators of the Lemon-Lime videos might have been discounted if not for the corroborating evidence of their signature music.

Zahara had reported more bad news while they were locked in Yves' magical cage. The Jello Shots had waded into battle, a hundred thousand strong, determined to find out the truth. Like data locusts, they'd swarmed the school computer, found the student list for the twins' class, and gone after home computers looking for evidence. Unlike the twins' personal systems, the other students' were easy prey.

Louise called up the Jello Shot forum and winced at what their fans had stolen. Everything from the anti-mermaid music video to set designs to costume sketches were mined, shared, compared to existing Lemon-Lime work, and debated in detail. In Giselle's computer, the Jello Shots had found the ultimate proof. While the twins were working on their response to Nigel's shout-out, they hadn't noticed Giselle filming them. She sat behind them in class and managed to get a clear shot of Louise animating the first act while Jillian wrote dialogue. Louise always thought that she crawled through the process, but removed by time and place, she realized that she worked at an amazing speed. She pulled up old sets from previous videos, worked camera angles, blocked in characters, did special effects, and fiddled with lighting angles. And then, proving to be a ninjalike stalker, Giselle managed to film them recording the lines in the girls' restroom.

"Lemon-Lime is so super amazing awesome cute!" The Jello Shots mostly agreed (there were still hold-outs that didn't believe the evidence), and then tore into the twins' life. In the course of an hour, they knew everything that could be known about the girls. The dust explosion in their playhouse. The bomb outside their school. Their connection to the bomber. Their parents' death. The custody battle.

The Jello Shots reeled at what they found and poured out their sympathy. To Louise's alarm, their attention moved from what the twins had done in the past to where they were now. "They're only nine years old! Has anyone seen them since the play? They weren't at the funeral! Why didn't they go? Where are they? Did something happen to them?"

How did the Jello Shots find out that they weren't at the funeral? She discovered there was an entire thread of the fans calling the funeral home and grilling the staff as to who attended.

Louise's phone vibrated.

It was Iggy texting again: "Please let me know you're okay!"

Was it really Iggy texting her? Or was Yves using Iggy to find the twins? Was Iggy in danger, too? If Yves wasn't using Iggy, then contacting him directly might make him a target.

She took out her tablet and found an unsecured network and tapped into it.

"Who are you calling?" Jillian asked.

"Iggy. Something's wrong."

He picked up on the first ring with a cautious, "Hello?"

"Say 'Who is this' if there's someone threatening you."

"What?"

"Is someone looking for us?"

"Huh? I am. And half the free world. Where are you?"

Louise considered possible answers. "We're safe. For now."

"You weren't hurt in the explosion?"

"Which one?" She winced. People normally didn't have multiple explosions in their lives.

"The one in Alpine! Your grandmother's house blew up! Lemon-Lime Love just broke the news a few minutes ago."

Louise groaned. She'd forgotten that they had more than one website of rabid fans.

Iggy continued, apparently assuming that she knew nothing about the fire. "Neighbors heard an explosion and called 911. They think that there was a gas leak in the kitchen. By the time the fire department got there, though, the whole house had caught on fire. They're still fighting it."

Which was why Iggy was frantically texting them.

"Yeah. We blew it up before we left."

"What?" Iggy shouted.

"Our grandmother is married to a very evil family. She got sick and went to the hospital and her stepson locked us up in the basement. In a cage. And he had a boy locked up in the next room. So we blew up the house and ran away. He's probably looking for us, so it's not safe for us to tell anyone where we are."

There was a long silence from the other end, and then Iggy said, "You're totally serious. You're not making that up?"

"Completely totally serious."

"Louise, your grandmother died today."

Louise felt tears burning in her eyes. She rubbed them away, surprised that she actually hadn't seen the news coming. Yves wouldn't have dared to lock them up without being sure that there was no chance of Anna ever finding out.

"Everyone is saying how you don't have any family left," Iggy said. "You don't have any place to go, do you? Come to my house. You'll be safe here."

"No. No, we won't." There was no way Louise was going to be responsible for getting Iggy or his protective sisters hurt. It would kill her to bring harm down on the close-knit family. "If the Jello Shots can find all our friends, so can Desmarais."

"Just come to our house and my mom and dad will find a place you'll be safe."

"We have family. Princess Tinker is our older sister."

"She is? I thought the tabloids were just making that up?"

"No, they're not making it up. She's our sister." Not that Alexander knew it. There were Orville and Lain, who were also complete strangers. Louise shivered at the knowledge that they were putting all their hope on people that they would barely recognize in person, who didn't even know they existed. "We're going to Elfhome. Windwolf will protect us there."

"Are you sure?"

Louise closed her eyes tight and took a deep breath. And another. She sought that mysterious calm of knowing. Would Windwolf protect them? "The shards of the fallen have slipped from our fingers. With Joy, the darkness will strike at the heart of the wolf's greatest strength and his greatest weakness. The wolf must gather the children to him. From oldest to unborn, Brilliance must hold the door."

"Huh?"

She opened her eyes. "It means he'll protect us. He has to. He has no choice. He needs us if his world is going to survive."

39: WALDORF ASTORIA

They were deep in the planning of their next move when Crow Boy hobbled out of his bedroom and stared out the penthouse window in confusion. The sun was setting over New Jersey, and the canyons between the tall buildings were filling with darkness. He had discovered the blue jeans shorts and crutches but had ignored the T-shirt. The only sign of his wings was the mysterious complex spell tattooed onto his back.

"Where are we?" he asked without turning.

"Midtown East." Louise pointed toward the kitchen. "We ordered Thai takeout for dinner. There's shrimp pad thai and chicken satay and vegan fried rice." The last because they weren't sure he could eat shrimp, and chicken felt a little cannibalistic. There had been all the makings of banana splits, but Joy had gorged herself on them. The baby dragon was asleep in the twins' bedroom, sprawled on the unmade king-size bed.

Crow Boy turned awkwardly on his crutches, eyeing the lush luxury of the sprawling sitting room. It was done all in soft blue, butter cream, and highlights of gold: a grown-up version of a fairytale castle. According to the literature, kings and queens, movie stars, and dozens of presidents had stayed in the suite.

Crow Boy startled slightly when he got to them and registered the change in their appearance. Jillian had wanted to bleach their hair blond, but it turned out that the dye had turned Jillian's hair carrot orange. (Louise had told her that it was a bad idea.)

Jillian waved it off, saying they looked less like twins this way. They dyed Louise's hair jet black and got her a pair of cosplay glasses. They were dressed in mismatched baggy T-shirts and pants, hoping that they would read as "male" to a casual observer. Louise secretly thought they'd only achieved looking like Harry Potter and Ron Weasley.

Crow Boy gestured at the cityscape outside the window. "Midtown East as in Manhattan?" Getting a nod, he waved his hand to take in the richly appointed room. "And we're where?"

"The penthouse suite at the Waldorf Astoria." Jillian took the freshly printed magic generator out of the industrial 3D printer. It was proving to be ten times faster than the printer at school.

"Also known as the Elvish embassy." Louise double-checked the fake ID she was working on. One would think the state's computer system would be more secure.

"How did we get here?" He obviously remembered nothing of his kidnapping despite the fact he'd been conscious enough to dismiss his great black wings.

"Garbage truck," Jillian explained. "No one really ever pays close attention to them. We overrode its auto-drive program. It picked us up at the hospital and dropped us at the Waldorf Astoria's loading dock."

Louise took up the narrative of their escape. "We hacked the hotel's computers in June to open up a meeting room so we could talk privately with Nigel Reid. So all we really needed to do was to use the back door we left to fabricate a wealthy but mostly absent parent who managed to pick up a card key without anyone remembering actually checking him in. As long as the credit card clears, the hotel doesn't really care."

"At ten thousand dollars a night, they really, really don't care," Jillian said. "They've been trotting up packages from the front desk and leaving them by the door without a single question asked."

Crow Boy's blue eyes had widened at the cost of the room. "How are you paying for it?"

"Stolen money." Jillian waved her new phone over her head. "Money is the one thing we have lots of."

"Oh, you should step back a little." Louise motioned him to back up.

He did and a moment later the babies raced into the sitting room in their little mini-hovercarts. Chuck Norris was still in the lead; she was quite fearless compared to the other three. They popped up to the end table and again to the back of the couch and along the gilded wood at speeds that they'd clocked at thirty miles per hour. At the other end, the babies bounced down to the end table, to the seat of the wing chair, and then to the floor.

Crow Boy glanced again around the suite and then frowned at the marbled foyer where they'd set up a scale-model mock-up of the quarantine zone, complete with ten-foot-tall chain-link fence. "Am I really awake?"

"Asks the Crow Boy." At some point, Jillian had decided "Crow Boy" was more fitting than "Crow Warrior" as a name for him.

"Yes, life currently is this odd." Louise realized that they really should discuss basics. "What's your name? We can't keep calling you Crow Boy."

"Crow Boy is fine," he said. "I don't like my real name."

"Which is?" Jillian asked ruthlessly.

"Haruka Sessai."

"What's so horrible about that?" Louise asked.

"Haruka is a girl's name. It means Spring Flower."

"What do your friends call you?" Jillian asked.

He blushed and looked away as he murmured, "Daffodil."

Jillian burst into laughter. Louise snorted as she tried to keep from laughing.

"What happened to my wings?" he asked.

"You made them go away after we woke you up the first time," Louise explained.

He'd kept falling asleep as they escaped, so it wasn't surprising that he didn't have a clear memory.

"But..." He turned to look out the window again. "This is Earth. There's only pockets of magic and certainly none in Manhattan."

"Step back!" Louise motioned him backwards again.

The babies lapped through the room. Nikola and Chuck Norris were tied. Green Jawbreaker had the lead on her sister, Red Jawbreaker.

"We really need to come up with better names for the girls," Jillian murmured quietly.

Louise nodded. "We have generators that produce magic. We're mass-producing them."

"We're going to fly into Pittsburgh next Shutdown." Jillian glanced toward the foyer. "Was that four laps?"

Louise paused to count. "Yes."

Jillian picked up the checkered flag and waited for the racers to return.

"I need to get to Monroeville," Crow Boy said. "As soon as possible. Before Shutdown."

"That's the plan," Jillian said.

"Why?" Louise asked.

"I need to free the nestlings." He saw their confusion. "Nestlings are children without tattoos. They can't fly. You saw me with them at that museum. Since the Shoji household was raided, we pushed ahead getting all our flock to Elfhome. My group of nestlings was the last. Since they can't fly, we needed to take them across in a shipping container instead of just flying in at night. We were supposed to cross into Pittsburgh in June, but those idiots had that gunfight on Veterans Bridge with the police. Inbound traffic stopped before we managed to cross the border."

Louise gasped. She'd never considered what his imprisonment had meant beyond him. "Oh no, they didn't get to Pittsburgh?"

He shook his head. "I didn't know what to do. Most of our people had gone ahead, so there was no one to call for help. There were rumors that the Veterans Bridge was damaged and that the road would be closed next Shutdown, so I took them to a safe house in Monroeville. Three days ago . . ." He glanced toward the setting sun. "Maybe four—I've lost track of time—Shiroikage hit the house with a full squad of oni."

Shiroikage was what he called Yves. It didn't sound Elvish either, so Louise doubted it was Yves' real name. It was becoming clearer and clearer why Esme hadn't used the names she knew her stepfamily by.

Crow Boy fell silent, right hand tight in a fist, eyes closed as if in pain. "Shiroikage must have found us days earlier and planned the attack, knowing we wouldn't move until Shutdown. They had flash bangs and nets and dart guns." He shook his head. "The worst part of being in that cage was knowing that Shiroikage has those kids and I'm the only one that can do anything. The only one that knows. I have to get back to Monroeville and save them before the oni takes them to Elfhome and uses them."

Louise wasn't sure she wanted to know what "uses them" meant. The words filled her with unease. "What will Yves do to them?"

"I heard him discussing their plans after they captured me. The greater bloods suspect what we've been doing, so they've developed a new spell. Since they captured the Chosen line, Yutakajodo has been experimenting on how we exist as a flock. It's a magical power that Providence gave to us, not the greater blood that transformed us to half-crow. Yutakajodo has discovered that"—he closed his eyes tightly in pain—"that at the moment of death, a child's soul calls to the flock. He's developed a spell to trace the direction. It's not a fine-tuned spell; they'll have to kill all the children to triangulate the position of our village. And once they do, the hundreds of children already there won't be strong enough to flee. Their parents won't abandon them. It will be a slaughter."

Louise couldn't help but remember the kindergartener Lai Yee Zhao; how gentle and kind Crow Boy had been with the little girl. The two girls in the gift shop—one was about to loan all her money to the other girl to pay for the snow globe. The children had been quiet, well-behaved, and graceful.

It had been horrible to know that the oni planned to kill Windwolf, but he was never within touching distance of the twins. To have heard the children's excited conversation, to brush against them in the crowded gift shop, to step into the place they stood and buy the toy that they treasured. To have them be that real, and then to know that each and every one of them was about to be killed...

The babies came flying in from the foyer, and Jillian waved them over the finish line. It required a photo finish. Nikola won by the literal nose, having leaned far out over the front of his hovercart. Chuck Norris was a sore loser and launched herself at her brother, squeaking furiously.

"No fighting!" Louise plucked up Chuck Norris. So small. So fragile. It seemed unthinkable to risk the babies—but with the lives of other children in the balance, what real choice did they have? "We don't have time for this. We need to change the plan."

"We do?" Jillian and the babies all cried.

"Yes, we need to find the tengu children and figure out how to save them."

The babies surprised her by all cheering. "It will be like *The Great Escape*!" they cried in chorus and then started to whistle the theme song.

Jillian sighed at the babies, who obviously didn't understand the danger. "Are you sure they didn't take the kids across the last Shutdown?"

"Shiroikage tried to take all of us across the border, but the EIA had realized that they had been infiltrated and weeded out all the oni in its ranks. What with the gunfight delaying shipments from the Shutdown before and the change in the guard, Shiroikage had acted too late. He thought he could use his influence to jump the queue, and luckily he couldn't.

"So they're in Monroeville, at least until the queue starts to form at the border."

"We've got a week then," Jillian said.

Louise pointed firmly at Crow Boy. "But you have to listen to us. You might be bigger than us and stronger, but we're a whole lot smarter than you. We're not going to risk everything if you're going to charge in without even asking us what we think."

Crow Boy glanced about the suite, nodding slowly. "Yes, I see that you're resourceful. And there was the explosion that saved us in the kitchen. And you got us to the hospital. And back out of the hospital. And yes, perhaps I leapt to battle too quickly..." He fell silent a moment and then came to carefully lower himself into a kneeling position. "Thank you for all you have done. You could have left me in the cage and fared well without me. To be truthful, I would be hard-pressed to get myself to Monroeville with little more than the clothes you've provided. There is no one I can trust in this, except you. I need your help to save my people. I will do anything you ask, just please, help me rescue them."

"We'll help." Louise picked up her new phone and snapped a picture of him. "The Pennsylvanian runs once a day. It leaves New York around eleven in the morning. We have to have IDs and a battle plan by then."

40: TEAM MISCHIEF

This can't possibly work, Louise thought.

"Do you see them?" Jillian was hopping up and down as she tried to peer through the crowds. The new Penn Station might be an airy, light-filled building, but it still contained thousands of people, all intent on their own journies. All of them taller than the twins.

"Are you sure about this?" Crow Boy murmured.

No, Louise thought. It was a patented crazy plan. There was a full-out manhunt for the mysterious trio of children who had disappeared from Morgan Stanley Children's Hospital. Taking the train was full of hurdles, but so was every other way of getting to Monroeville.

"They're here." Nikola's little-boy voice came over the ear-buds that they were all wearing. "Northeast, fifty-seven feet, at a standstill." There was a pause and a very Chuck Norris-like "Team Mischief move out" followed in the same Welsh lilt. Odd how Tesla now seemed very much like four little people. He felt much more like a tank operated by a crew instead of just one person in a puppy outfit.

"Which way is north?" Jillian hopped up and down more.

"This way." Crow Boy headed toward the right.

The Amber Alert for the three "elf" children scrolled across the large monitors even as Crow Boy plowed through the crowds. The twins had managed to keep any cameras from recording their pictures, but the alert featured long detailed descriptions. A winged boy with a broken leg, twin brown-haired girls, and a large dog nanny-bot were entirely impossible to forget.

They'd done what they could to change their appearances. They'd found a healing spell for broken bones in the codex and cast it on Crow Boy's leg. He'd muffled whimpers of pain but refused to let them cancel the spell. Twelve hours later, hurt had etched a dark glower onto his face, but he was walking without a limp. Without wings or the cast, he started out well disguised, but they took the precaution of spiking his hair and bleaching the tips. He looked like an angry porcupine. Even New Yorkers were veering out of his path.

Louise and Jillian were pretending to be boys. Harry P. Johnson and Ron W. Johnson, to be specific; as long as Jillian didn't slip too far into character and use a British accent, no one should catch the allusion. They were young enough that in T-shirts and jeans they really didn't need anything more.

Tesla was the most problematic to disguise. Most nanny-bots were smaller dogs, leaving Louise to wonder at her parents' choice. They had discussed very briefly buying a different nanny-bot and shipping Tesla on ahead. The outcry from everyone killed that idea. In the end, they printed out the invisibility spell and affixed it on a large cardboard box that covered him. The babies had practiced keeping Tesla behind Crow Boy and between the twins as "Team Mischief" moved like a wedge through the hotel suite.

In the busy train station, Crow Boy was having no problem blocking people. The twins, however, needed to throw their arms wide to stop people from tripping over Tesla in his invisibility box.

"Maybe we should split up." Louise scanned the area for a quiet corner for Tesla to stand. "You and Crow Boy look for—"

"There they are!" Jillian cried.

Amtrak had a rule that children under twelve couldn't ride unescorted. Crow Boy was old enough to be an unaccompanied minor, but he would still need an adult to check him in with station personnel and undergo an interview apparently designed to keep loose cannons from traveling alone. Since they couldn't travel alone, the twins had simply found a family to travel with.

Brian and Helen Johnson and their three young children were traveling to Monroeville. They had a nice bland name and came with three chaos generators. As Team Mischief neared the West

Thirty-Fourth Street entrance, Louise could hear one of the generators screaming over the roar of the crowd.

The Johnsons were gathered beside a minivan taxi, trying to juggle three children, a car seat, and a heavily loaded luggage mule. The screamer was three-year-old Jayne on a harness and leash. He was stretched to the end of his tether and shrieking.

Helen had the leash in her right hand and was holding onto five-year-old Malcolm, who was attempting to lie down, with her left. She had the infant Alleyne in a sling on her chest.

Neither parent noticed Team Mischief staring, but Alleyne did. The baby raised her hand and waved. Louise twiddled her fingers in a covert reply. This was what the babies would be like if the twins could find some way to have them be born. Nearly hairless, toothless, and grinning happily at dangerous strangers. Louise felt guilty. They'd chosen the Johnsons because it was the second most common surname in the United States. There were two other passengers and a crewmember with the same last name. Even if someone discovered Team Mischief had traveled to Monroeville under the name, it was unlikely they would connect the four to Brian and Helen. Still, Yves and his people were ruthless and relentless.

"The meter is still running on the taxi." Helen pointed a key fob at the car seat and it unfolded into a stroller.

"I know!" Brian snapped. "I think the doorman did something to the luggage mule when he put it in. I can't get it to move."

"Did you flip the thingy?" Helen mimed flipping something with one finger while still holding onto Jayne's leash.

Brian glanced at her, eyebrow cocked. "What thingy?"

"The thingy! The thingy! Oh, Jayne, please!" This was with a slight tug on the leash of the screaming three-year-old. "The thingy that locks the wheels!"

The luggage mule whined and stepped out of the taxi hatch and lowered its wheels. Brian trotted to the front and thumbed the release pad that had been flashing red. All the doors thumped shut and the taxi rolled away.

Claiming Alleyne, Brian put the infant into the stroller. As the family hurried away, Alleyne leaned out to watch Team Mischief follow slowly.

The Johnsons weren't frequent travelers; they needed to stop at the check-in kiosk to pick up tap cards. Afterwards they took the escalators down to the tracks where the train waited. The engines were idling with a deep, throbbing growl.

"Look! Look! It's a train!" Brian cried for the boys' sake.

The family ground to a halt in a spasm of train love. Team Mischief veered out of the path of people coming down the escalator, and the twins' party killed time consulting Jillian's tablet about things that arguably were more interesting to tweens than the big engine at the head of the line of cars.

"No, no, Malcolm, don't put that into your mouth. It was on the ground." Helen pinned Jayne's leash to the ground so she could use both hands to keep the five-year-old from eating his discovery.

"Nine hours," Brian murmured with mild reproach.

"I'm not flying to an area that has a city popping in and out of existence," Helen sang in the manner adults used when not wanting to frighten children overhearing them. "I want to keep my feet on the ground. Besides, the boys will love the chance to ride on a real train!"

The last sentence was addressed more directly to the boys, who leapt up and down and cried, "Yay, trains!"

After a few minutes, Helen steered the boys to the steps with, "Let's go see what's inside the coaches!"

There was a conductor waiting with a reader. Brian fumbled through the cards, accidently feeding one through twice before getting the four tapped correctly into the reader. (The baby apparently rode for free.) They did a small circus act to get the three children and the stroller up the steps. As a closing act, the luggage mule picked up two dropped toys and then negotiated the steep stairs with surprising grace. While everyone was suitably distracted, Team Mischief slid into position. Normally the twins would use a phone app instead of tap cards, but they wanted to match themselves to the Johnsons.

The conductor noticed them standing waiting with tap cards in hand. He glanced past the children, obviously looking for accompanying adults. "Where's your parents?"

"They just got on." Louise pointed up the steps where the Johnson family had just vanished out of sight.

"Mom and Dad said we could do our own cards and luggage since they had the babies to take care of." Jillian turned slightly to show that she had a full backpack as well as a large rolling carry-on. It worked as an excuse as to why "their parents" weren't expecting "the older kids" to help juggle babies and luggage.

"We take the N train every day to school." Louise made a show of shifting her backpack as if it was nearly too heavy for her to carry.

"You just checked our parents in." Crow Boy glared at the man. "Brian and Helen Johnson." He pointed at the reader in the conductor's hand. "Can't you call their names up on your machine?"

The conductor tapped on his console, checked their names against the Johnson family, and then nodded, "Ah, I see. Okay, you can go."

The real Johnsons were mid-coach, still settling into a row of seats, two on either side of the aisle. Team Mischief claimed the next row. Crow Boy lifted the twins' luggage into overheads as Tesla took the window seat on the left. Jillian and Louise took the seats on the right.

It had worked. They were on their way to Monroeville. They had nine hours of relative safety. Louise didn't even want to think of what lay beyond them.

"Where are your parents?" Helen Johnson asked when she passed them the second time on her way to the bathroom with one of the boys.

Louise had been focused on ordering supplies for the rescue mission. Beside her Jillian was working with the babies to find out where Yves might be holding the tengu children. Assuming that they found and saved the nestlings, they would still need to figure out how to reunite the children with their families. Crow Boy had never been to the tengu village; he couldn't give them clear directions beyond "someplace north of the city, flying to the point of near exhaustion." There were safe resting sites—"cotes," he called them—but they were tree houses high above the ground, and none of the tengu children would be able to fly. They would be blindly stumbling through an endless virgin forest. Except for one horrible trip to Vermont, the twins had never been outside the New York metropolitan area. Central Park was the limit of their exposure to "nature."

"Where's your parents?" Helen Johnson repeated. "You're not alone, are you?"

Totally blindsided by the question, Louise blinked at the woman. Louise had never thought a stranger would actually talk to them on the train. The woman must not be a true New Yorker. Crow Boy was curled up in the aisle seat opposite to Louise, sound asleep. A side effect of the healing spell they had used on him seemed to be exhaustion. To a casual observer, the twins were alone.

"We couldn't find seats all together as a family." Jillian had a lie prepared. "Mom and our little sister are in the next car."

"We've got our older brother." Louise pointed at Crow Boy.

Helen eyed the tengu boy with the spiked hair with suspicion. Her five-year-old whimpered and tugged on her hand. "It's wonderful when older siblings take care of their little brothers and sisters." And she let herself be dragged away.

After that the twins took turns getting up every couple of hours to "check in with their mother." But otherwise the trip on the train went without a hitch.

41: THE EDGE OF TWO WORLDS

During the first Startup, Monroeville had been one finger of urban sprawl extending along I-376 to where the artery led out of the heart of Pittsburgh to connect up with the Pennsylvania Turnpike. Businesses extended only a block or two from the main roads and few buildings were taller than one story. Its largest claim to fame up to that point had been a 1978 horror movie filmed in its shopping mall.

Reporters during the first Startup repeated that point often when a mated pair of sauruses went on a rampage in the parking lot. The twins had studied the hours of videos taken from that time, and Louise thought she would be able to recognize landmarks. Over the years, though, Monroeville had grown as a gateway to Elfhome, taking over neighboring towns as it expanded. The road edged with low-slung businesses was gone. In its place were dozens of thirty-story skyscrapers and skeletons of even taller buildings still under construction.

Their hotel was one of the newer buildings, and the presidential suite proved to be a penthouse apartment. From the living room, they could see for miles. The hotel had been built with views of the Rim in mind; it stood on the last hilltop before the quarantine zone. Even in the deepening shadows of twilight, it was easy to spot the curving line where Monroeville stopped and the Rim started. It arched from horizon to horizon, sweeping close to the hotel as it passed.

Louise peered downward and spotted the tall border fence just a block away, edging a 7-Eleven parking lot. She was surprised that Monroeville pressed up so tight against it. In all the news reports she'd ever seen, the video showed the fence bordered by desolate fields. Beyond it lay a mile of burned sterile land, a no-man's-land to isolate Elfhome flora and fauna and make it easy for the EIA border guard to spot illegal immigrants. Far in the distance, the tall ironwood trees rose as a solid, unbroken wall.

"So close," Jillian whispered with forehead and hands pressed to the glass.

They had less than a week to rescue the tengu children, and then the forest beyond the fence would be swapped for Pittsburgh. If Team Mischief hadn't succeeded by then, the fight would be moved to Elfhome as the secret elves transported the nestlings across the border. Yves would have thousands of oni warriors at his command. Last anyone heard, Windwolf had been hundreds of miles away at Aum Renau. And one by one, the tengu children would be murdered.

Louise turned away from the window, trying to focus. They'd spent the nine hours on the train verifying that the children weren't in the safe house anymore, nor at any of the other safe houses that Crow Boy knew that his people used while seeking the freedom of Pittsburgh. Logic suggested that Yves would have kept the children close to the quarantine zone, but it was nearly a hundred and sixty miles in circumference.

Less than a week and hundreds of square miles.

"Pft, nuts!" Joy muttered from the minibar, and a can went flying across the hotel room. "Oh! Candy!"

The cans of nuts landed beside the babies, who were ransacking the luggage, looking for the mini-hovercarts. Nikola was operating Tesla to move the heavy things and the girls were in the mice, darting here and there, squeaking excitedly. Like the Johnsons' children, eventually they'd found their first train ride unbearably long and boring. Taking their cues from the real children, the babies had repeatedly asked how much longer the trip would be and fought with each other. At least the Team Mischief babies did not vomit, poop, pee, or scream—something that the Johnson kids did with alarming frequency. The three children had been an education on how difficult parenting really was. After five hours, Louise had been really wishing the Johnsons had off switches.

The hotel room door opened and Crow Boy came in carrying bags of takeout.

"The house is empty." His voice was wooden. He set the bags on the suite's dinette table. "Empty and clean."

Louise breathed out in mixed relief. They'd tapped spy satellites on the train, pinpointed the safe house, and examined it remotely by every means they could think of. Crow Boy had insisted on going and checking it alone. The twins agreed because the only thing they couldn't discount were the children being dead inside.

He collapsed into one of the chairs. "I feel so useless."

"We'll find them." She opened the bags. "Indian?" There had been a Chinese restaurant just on the corner.

"I don't know who I can trust." He laid his head on the table. "Not everyone who is Chinese is an oni, but the human-looking oni are all traveling with Chinese visas. The oni need to have people close to both sides of the quarantine zones to get their people in and out unseen. The EIA have weeded out the moles in their agency, but there are plenty of others on Earth. We need to be careful not to be seen."

She nodded, her stomach flipping at the thought of being captured again. Yves had been careless once, mostly because Feng had been there, distracting him. Yves wouldn't underestimate the twins again. This time he'd know all about the babies and Joy.

Her hands trembled slightly as she opened up the containers of palak paneer, vegetable korma, chicken tikka masala, samosa, and naan bread.

Crow Boy reached out and took her hand; his was large and calloused compared to hers. "You only need to find them. I'll deal with the guard." For a moment he seemed like an adult man, and then the moment was gone, and he was an exhausted, battered fourteen-year-old boy with the world on his shoulders.

"I told you: no charging in." She smacked him on the top of his head. "We're smarter than Yves. He'll never see us coming."

Crow Boy's shoulders shook with silent laughter.

"Promise!" Louise smacked him again.

"I will do anything you ask of me, but I won't let you put yourself in danger. If it comes to a fight, you must let me do what I've been trained to do. Alone."

At the mansion, he had taken on half a dozen adults by himself. He taken out two and held his own for several minutes against four. Those he was fighting had been worried enough to call for help.

"Are you like some kind of super ninja warrior?" Louise asked.

"Yes."

"Really?"

His shoulders shook again with silent laughter. "It is a long story of love and honor and loyalty, but the simple answer is yes."

"Oh, come on!" Louise cried. "I know you're tired, but we need to know everything we can about what's going on. If we'd known what was going on right after our first visit to the museum, we could have stopped—stopped everything. As it was, we didn't even get a message to our sister warning her or Windwolf."

He laughed tiredly. "Geez, where do I even start?" He sighed and was silent for a little while. "My people were human once. We lived in what is now China during the time of the Warring States, over two thousand years ago. The first Wong Jin was a wise sage who had fallen out of favor with the Flame Emperor. He and his seven loyal and brave servants became bandits, kind of like Robin Hood and his merry men, if Robin Hood had a secret cave hideout that led to another world. Over time, they gathered hundreds of poor people to them in a remote mountain village on Onihida. Then one day—" He laughed. "You have to understand, we love to tell stories about Wong Jin. It gives us hope that someday—if we're clever—we'll outsmart our enemies and find freedom."

"One day—" Louise prompted him.

"One day Wong Jin and his servants were out on one of their many adventures—which mostly involved stealing something and then escaping in a clever way—when they discovered Elfhome. And there, basically on the doorstep to that world, was Providence. Most men would have been frightened—and certainly Wong Jin's men wanted to flee the dragon—but Wong Jin saw that Providence was an intelligent creature and so engaged him in conversation.

"The dragons had put Elfhome under edict. By the laws of his people, Providence could not travel to Elfhome, but he'd lost his daughter on that world. Fearing the worst, he pleaded with Wong Jin to find his child and bring her to him. He promised to reward Wong Jin richly if he succeeded. Wong Jin accepted the challenge. Providence marked Wong Jin so his daughter would know that Wong Jin was his Chosen. To make a long, long story short, Wong Jin carefully made his way through the elves' defenses to find where Providence's child had been entrapped. Only he arrived too late. The elves had already shattered the child to pieces."

Louise thought of Joy and the eleven baby dragons all still inside Dufae's chest. She and Jillian had been so focused on saving their siblings that they hadn't stopped to consider where the baby dragons had came from. Dufae had known that the *nactka* were "loaded," but had he understood that meant that each one had an intelligent creature locked inside?

"What did Wong Jin do?" Louise asked.

"He was about to return with bits and pieces of the daughter when he discovered that the elves had also created a hybrid, a dragon-elf child. Assuming that Providence wanted anything related to his daughter, Wong Jin stole the child and carried her back to Onihida. Somewhere along the way, things got complicated."

"Complicated?"

"They fell in love." Crow Boy said this like a typical boy; that love was weird and possibly icky. "By the time they reached Onihida, Wong Jin did not want to hand her over to Providence, nor did she want to leave Wong Jin. While his men were fearful of Providence, they pledged that they would protect her with their lives."

"So Wong Jin brought to Providence all the shattered pieces of his child, including the female dragon-elf. He reminded Providence that he had promised Wong Jin a rich reward. For his prize, Wong Jin wanted the female, and only her. They braced themselves for a fight, but Providence knew that this would happen; it was why he picked Wong Jin to be his Chosen. He gave his blessing to their marriage and promised to watch over their people as their guardian. And to Wong Jin's seven loyal servants, Providence gave magical powers so that they could guard his daughter."

"So Wong Jin became your king and you're one of the knights?"

"When you give thieves magical powers you don't get knights in shining armor, you get super ninjas."

"Wait, if you were humans, where did all the crow stuff come from?" Jillian joined them at the table. She picked up one of the samosas and started to eat it.

"For hundreds of years, life was good. The land was rich, our neighbors were distant, and we had our guardian, Providence.

We had all that we needed, and Earth became a place of legend for us. But then about a thousand years ago, the oni came to our valley and captured Providence. Dragons have a dual existence. Their minds and their bodies can exist separately. His spirit came to our dream crow and begged for us to kill his body. If the oni intended just to kill Providence, it would be one thing, for it would have freed his soul. What they intended, though, was to shatter him down and remake him into a weapon of war. It would have been worse than what the elves had done to his daughter. He could not allow it."

"But—but—why kill him? Why not save him?"

"What he asked was for the blood guard to sacrifice themselves. The oni had Providence in a magical trap. The blood guard would need to fight to his side. There would be no time to free him, only time enough to strike a killing blow before they would be overwhelmed. They were a thousand against an army. It was a slaughter on both sides. The Chosen One and all of the blood guard that fought that day died. But our people succeeded at what Providence had asked; we killed him, freeing his soul."

"A thousand lives for one?" Jillian cried. "That was a win?"

"If the oni had kept control of his soul, the damage would have been worse. They had caught other dragons and shattered them and experimented. They wanted Providence to craft what would be basically a global living spell. It could reach for thousands of miles, affect millions of people, guided by his soul. It would be like an intelligent nuclear bomb, programmed to seek and destroy, and having no will of its own to resist its orders. As it was, they gathered my people together and experimented with just his body. They locked the survivors within one massive cage and cast one spell. Everyone was transformed; merged with crows that—that..." He trailed off, his eyes widening slightly, and then he blushed and looked down. "You don't need to hear all the gross parts. One spell and we were forever changed as a race. Providence shielded us from the worst that could have happened. Because of him, we still function as humans. Mostly. We have bird feet and we lay eggs. But we couldn't fly. We didn't have wings at first. Providence provided the spell for our wings."

Dufae's chest had contained twelve "loaded" *nactka*. The twins exchanged glances and shivered. Dufae had opened the box and instantly known that he had to flee with it to Earth where it was harmless, lest it fall into the wrong hands. According to Yves, Ming had it now on Elfhome.

"The dragons had tried to isolate Onihida. Keep the evil that had taken root from spreading. But they missed one pathway. The oni guessed of its existence, but they couldn't find it. Somehow they tricked the elves into finding it. As the oni started to flood their people through it to China, we got out the newborn Chosen One and all of the blood-guard children that survived our enslavement. We fled to Japan and took refuge in a mountainous temple with a sect of warrior monks known as the *yamabushi*."

That explained his Japanese name. Louise wondered what kind of magical powers he had. She also wondered what exactly Joy could do. If Providence could give out magical powers, what did it mean for the baby dragon?

Crow Boy lifted his head and gave Louise a desperate look. "We thought Jin Wong had sacrificed himself on the chance of finding us a new home, one where we could live free. We've been waiting for the mark of Providence to appear on a new Chosen. So many of the bloodline have been killed, and now the oni has the baby in their control, and because of that, Riki let himself fall into their power. At the hospital, though, you said that Jin's returning. Does that mean he's not dead?"

He wanted it to be true. Considering all that he'd been through—and what could lay ahead—it seemed cruel to tell him that she had no idea what she had babbled out.

"I-I-I don't know..." She couldn't crush his hope. "I don't know how he'll return. Or when."

"Please, can you try to do another prophecy?"

The word shocked Louise. Prophecy? Her?

"I don't know what I'm doing," Louise said. "I don't even remember what I said. It sounded like nonsense to me. Jillian covered my eyes." Louise unfolded one of the napkins that had come with the takeout and pressed it to her face to illustrate. "And it just happened."

"We could get an Ouija board," Jillian grumbled. "Would make as much sense."

Louise blushed and started to drop her hands, but Crow Boy caught her wrist.

"Please. Just try." His voice sounded husky, like he was about to cry.

She took a deep breath. Just try? Try what? If she did have a magical power, so far she had only done the equivalent of randomly changing channels on a television. What she needed was meaningful search terms to pull up what she wanted. Captain Jin Wong. The *Tainlong Hao.* Providence's Chosen One. What had she been thinking of at the hospital? They were trying to feed the police information on Alexander being in danger...

"Brilliance strikes into the darkness!" It was like plugging into an electrical outlet: power came sure and strong. "The attack is true, and the dark pathway is torn asunder! All that were trapped are free! Providence Child spreads his wings as he falls. He falls!"

Louise found herself on her feet, pointing toward the window. Something streaked past, a fiery comet in the dark night.

"What the hell?" Jillian ran across the room to lean against the glass. "What is that?"

"It's Esme!" Louise cried. "She's trying to save Providence's Child."

42: PLAN B

"They say something has happened to the gate!" Nikola reported as he joined them at the window. They'd been watching a continuous storm of burning debris rain down through the night sky. "They think something hit it. They've lost contact with the crew that maintained it, and there's a huge debris field where it should be and where it shouldn't be. Though I'm not sure what that means."

"It probably means that there is debris that they can't account for." Louise couldn't tear herself away from the window. "The wrong orbital plane. The wrong trajectory."

"Like from a colony ship?" Nikola asked.

Louise shook her head. "No. It couldn't have been a ship that hit it. Earth's gate can only jump spaceships *to* Alpha Centauri Bb; the ships can't return back through it. Even if the colonists somehow built their own hyperphase gate to return to Earth, it would be astronomically improbable that the exit point would be the same exact position as the Earth's gate."

"But you said Providence's Child was falling!" Crow Boy leaned against the glass, staring up at the night sky. "You said Jin Wong was returning to us!"

She had? When she tried to recall the exact words, though, they slipped through her memory like elusive minnows, darting this way and that. It was as if even as she tried to catch hold of the words, they changed as the future changed.

"Esme did say that she had to leave Earth to do something important. Maybe she was going to get Jin Wong." For some odd reason, Jillian stared downwards toward the street instead of up at the sky.

Did it mean that Jin Wong was tumbling through space, falling to Earth, with Esme desperately trying to catch him? Try as she might, Louise couldn't force that scenario onto the facts she knew. The colony ships couldn't jump back to Earth. Even if they could, "debris" indicated that neither ship remained intact. Did the elusive nature of what Louise foretold mean that Esme had probably failed at her attempt to save Jin Wong?

"If the gate is gone," Jillian said slowly as if trying to work out a difficult logic problem, "why hasn't Pittsburgh returned?" She pointed at the quarantine zone just a block from the hotel's parking lot. "Shouldn't it be right there?"

They stared at the dark Elfhome forest in silence.

Jillian chanted a litany of, "This is bad. Badbadbad. Really bad. We're totally screwed."

"Don't say 'screwed.'" Louise murmured as she struggled to be calm and find a satellite that had caught the accident.

"There's nothing we can do!" Jillian cried. "Nothing. There's huge ginormous hunks of stuff falling out of the sky that we can't change or stop or anything."

Louise locked down on a scream until she could say calmly, "We will find a way to deal with this. First, we need to know what exactly we're facing."

Within a few minutes, she found a Russian spy satellite that had been launched while the Chinese started the construction of the hyperphase gate. Over thirty years of silent observation with nothing more to report than occasional spaceships jumping to another star system. The spy satellite showed a confusion of metal pieces drifting where the gate had been. Louise scanned backwards through the satellite's memory, watching the accident in reverse. The debris coalesced down then vanished, replaced by the gate, wreathed in violent greens and reds.

"It's never looked like that before." Crow Boy leaned over her shoulder. "Is that Rim fire?"

"Maybe," Louise said. There had been no explosion, just one moment the large round gate had been there, and the next debris, all seemingly too straight to ever have been part of the circular structure.

Jillian snorted with contempt, despite the fact she didn't know any better than Louise. "Rim fire is simply an aurora effect caused by the collision of energetic charged particles in the field that holds Pittsburgh on Elfhome."

But normally Rim fire only appeared on Elfhome. Why was it suddenly wreathing the gate? And was the debris even from the gate?

"The crew on the gate sent out a distress call." Jillian reported on the results of her research. "They reported strong vibrations before Earth lost contact with them."

Louise stepped back through time and gasped as the gate flickered in and out of existence. There. Gone. There again. Gone again. While the gate winked in and out, the Rim fire continued to mark the gate's location. "I don't think anything hit the gate. I think something went wrong with the field."

Louise scanned the footage to check her theory. Nothing seemed to interact with the gate until the last moment, when the mystery debris appeared. Nor did the debris seem to come from the gate but just flickered into existence as the gate vanished. The Rim fire appeared first and then, detected only by zooming in tightly, the reported vibrations started. The aurora grew for several minutes before the gate started to blink in and out. The question was: In and out of where?

She locked on to the falling debris. It looked like a jigsaw puzzle thrown into the air and caught on film before raining onto the ground. Judging by the speed it flashed out of camera range, it had a vastly different orbit than the gate. It appeared only in a dozen frames of film.

Space limited the number of possible sources. It wasn't like Earth where "machine" could run from anything airplane to mining equipment to submarine. She linked a recognition program to the "known space objects" database and fed it the dozen frames of film that showed the debris.

"I don't understand," Crow Boy said. "The gate in orbit generated the field that kept Pittsburgh on Elfhome. If the gate is gone, what happened to the city?"

"We don't know!" the twins and Nikola cried.

The recognition program found a match. The largest piece of debris was an odd glittering mass that looked like an iceberg growing out of a medusa of silvery tubing. The iceberg was spinning as it rocketed away. In frame number nine, it showed its smooth underbelly. There were three small ports and the start of a Chinese letter in red. The recognition software filled in missing pieces and the ghostly outline of the colony ship *Minghe Hao* took shape. Part of the ship's hull had been peeled back by some unknown collision, laying bare the water-treatment plant. The ship's vast store of water formed the glimmering iceberg blooming out of the shattered remains. The constellation of smaller debris was identified as pieces of the ship's orbital maneuvering system. Burn marks indicated that the rocket engines had been fired prior to the ship's destruction. It would explain the speed and angle of the wreckage. But *Minghe Hao* had jumped out of Earth's orbit six years ago.

Crow Boy made a small hurt sound. "I had family on the *Minghe Hao*."

"Maybe Esme saved them." Louise offered what little comfort she could. "The colony ships are massive. We're looking at only a small section of the *Minghe Hao*."

It was enough, though, to wreak havoc on Earth. The television was showing complete panic as the pieces rained down. No one else had yet identified the debris. The news was still calling it "the gate." The *Minghe Hao*'s missing engines had aimed the ship at American's heartland prior to being sheared off. Remains of the water-treatment system struck the town of Bellbrook, Ohio, with such force that the reporters were stating "possible nuclear weapon" to describe the destruction.

"The gate is gone!" Jillian tossed her tablet aside and began to pace around the room in long, man-length strides. She was fleeing into the character of Captain Hilts as fast as she could. "Even if the gate wasn't what fell, it's not in Earth-space anymore. It's probably wherever the rest of the *Minghe Hao* is, and that can't be a good thing. The *Minghe Hao* hit *something*!"

Jillian was desperately trying to be strong. Now that Louise knew the signs, it was all so clear. Her twin was trying to press her lips into Hilts' thin, confident sneer, but they kept trembling. She threw herself onto the couch, trying for the soldier's seemingly carefree slouch. "We're not talking rush hour on the George Washington Bridge here. There's not a lot of shit to hit in space."

All completely true.

Statistically, whatever accident shattered the *Minghe Hao* most likely had also claimed the gate. The structure had been built in space, spiderweb-delicate and carefully balanced. It hadn't been designed to take a hard blow and recover. The gate had small positioning-correction thrusters but it wouldn't be able to save itself if it had been smashed out of its orbit.

If something had gone horribly wrong over Elfhome—and all evidence pointed that way—the gate had been lost. Without it, the magic that linked the two worlds was broken. The great ironwood forest would forever be on Earth and Pittsburgh was lost.

It was frighteningly huge, and Louise didn't know what they could do. All her hopes had been pinned on the idea that they would find the tengu children, free them, fly over the quarantine zone next Shutdown in hovercarts, and in short order be with Alexander and Windwolf. She had found a great deal of comfort thinking that powerful, unflappable Prince Yardstick would be protecting them. All they had to do was to get to his side and all would be over.

Now she had no idea what they should do.

But Louise did know that they couldn't do nothing. They were standing out in the middle of a freeway. They had to move or be mowed down by everything hurtling at them with murderous speed.

Or more correctly, Louise had to do something.

At the mansion, right after their parents had died, Jillian had been too broken to pretend anything. She'd pasted all her broken bits back together, but the cracks were all still there. The promise of escape to Elfhome was the only glue that was keeping Jillian in one piece.

With that promise gone, the cracks were coming undone.

Jillian covered her mouth to hide the betraying tremble of lips and stood back up. The hurt lost look was filling her eyes as her control crumbled more. "Where—where's my ball?"

Crow Boy staggered back to the window like someone had hit him with a sledgehammer. Super ninja or not, he was still just a fourteen-year-old boy, stranded on a world full of enemies. "What are we going to do?"

"We fall back to Plan B," Louise stated as calmly as she could.

"We have a Plan B?" Crow Boy asked.

"We don't, but the elves will have one. They probably knew

that the gate could be damaged in an accident at any time—or the Chinese might be forced to actually abandon the colony program—or Queen Soulful Ember might figure out what they were doing and somehow blast the gate out of orbit. Feng was told years ago what to do in case of emergency. They have plans. Long-thought-out plans."

"Okay." Jillian breathed like she was willing to grab hold of any lifeline thrown to her.

"Yves is finding out right now that Shutdown isn't going to happen." Louise ignored the fact that Jillian whimpered and Crow Boy gasped as if she'd hit him. "He'll switch to Plan B, and that involves getting to Elfhome another way."

"No, no, no!" Jillian cried, her voice breaking. She covered her face with her hands, hiding her weakness as logic tore away hope. "If they had another way, they wouldn't be trying to kidnap Alexander."

"They want Alexander because there isn't another way to Onihida," Louise lied quickly to cut that fear off but then realized that she was right. "The tengu were isolated because the pathways from Onihida to Earth had been blocked."

"By the dragons," Crow Boy explained, "to try and isolate Onihida, but it didn't work. They missed one path, but after the war, the elves pulled down all the pathways, even the ones between Earth and Elfhome."

"See! See! Ming's army is on Onihida! The island we blew up was the only way for his army to get to Earth. He would still need to get his soldiers from the China Sea to Monroeville first."

"You blew up Pejamu Island?" Crow Boy cried in surprise.

"Parts of it." Louise waved him away from distracting her argument. "The elves only blocked the pathways that they knew—"

"The caves!" Jillian cried.

"Yes," Crow Boy said. "The pathway was in a cave."

"No!" Jillian waved her arms frantically. "Remember all the maps of caves that Esme had? I bet Plan B is to go to Elfhome via caves."

They'd ruled that out. Louise didn't want to crush Jillian, though, not when she was so fragile.

"It would be difficult," Crow Boy stated. "But they could do it."

The twins turned to look at him with surprise. "What?"

"They found several cave systems in Westernlands that lead to

Elfhome, only all the pathways were much too small to be useful. They took the worst and tried to expand the passages. It turns out that any construction destroys the pathway; the connection between the worlds is cut completely." They stared at him in silence until he added, "The ones they attempted to expand had been too small for even a child to use. The ones that remain, you can squeeze a person through."

"Child" made Louise think of the tengu children. Yves had been calmly sorting through the mansion's treasures, keeping what would be useful for the takeover of Elfhome. He'd keep the children alive if he could still get them to Elfhome.

"Where are these pathways?" Jillian asked.

Crow Boy deflated, shaking his head. "I don't know. We only know of their failures. They otherwise kept the natural pathways secret from us."

Louise could almost see the cracks in Jillian's composure widening. "Yves would want to stay as close to Pittsburgh as possible. That's where all their resources are centered." Louise did a quick search. There were fewer than a dozen caves listed for Pennsylvania, most of them more than a hundred miles from the quarantine zone. Only one was close. "Laurel Caverns. Was that one of the caves that Esme had a map to?"

"Yes, it was." Nikola tilted his head, searching out data. "Desmarais bought it from Randolph Humbert in 1861, when it was known as Dulaney's Cave, and he changed the name. Desmarais opened it as a show cave in 1961."

"If they didn't sell the cave after exploring it carefully, then there's a pathway," Crow Boy said. "It most likely is only big enough for a person to crawl through. They could send scouts through and some camping gear, but nothing larger."

Between predators like wyverns and wargs, man-eating plants and rivers full of sharks, Elfhome's wilderness wasn't someplace you could live with just a tent and sleeping bag. "They wanted to take over the Eastern Hemisphere of Elfhome. A pup tent in the middle of the Western Hemisphere would seem to be wasted effort. At least, until the first Startup. Afterwards, though, they could have used it as a secret back door to Pittsburgh. They could have a fortress built over the cave on the other side."

"A back door only stays secret if you don't advertise it." When the twins stared at him in surprise again, Crow Boy elaborated.

"The oni do not play well with others, even other oni. I have not heard of there being a pathway near Pittsburgh, so it is possible that they have kept it for emergencies only. Plan B."

That was good news at least: a way to Elfhome that wasn't heavily guarded.

In a matter of minutes they had everything to be known about Laurel Caverns spread across the dozen monitors and their two tablets.

Nikola tilted his head back and forth. "Their website says that they host fieldtrips, caving tours, Girl Scout events, gemstone panning, and something called Kavernputt." He tilted his head a couple more times in confusion. "Oh, it's miniature golf in a cave, entirely handicap-accessible."

For a secret back door, it sounded overrun with humans. Maybe Crow Boy was wrong. Maybe Ming had kept the caverns just because they made him money.

"Putt-putt?" Jillian obviously was trying to link miniature golf with plans of global conquest. "There's something very twisted about a bad guy hiding out at a putt-putt course."

"Oh!" Nikola cried. "Their website just posted that they will be closed to the public. It says they're going to be renovating the gift shops and lighting systems."

Louise breathed out in relief. "Yves just fell back to Plan B."

43: HIGHJACKING PLAN B

"You didn't say anything about ostriches," Crow Boy said.

In the scramble to implement "Highjack Plan B," Louise had left finding transportation to the babies. At first glance the box truck, painted fire-engine red, had seemed a bit flashy, but it did match the specifications she'd given them. She'd assumed that the tall, matching red, livestock box on the back was empty.

Crow Boy's puzzled look after he'd climbed up into the high cab warned her that she was wrong.

"Ostriches?" Louise scrambled up beside him. To her dismay, the back window of the truck afforded a view of eight ostriches. They studied Louise back with large soft brown eyes and thick eyelashes. They were the most beautiful eyes Louise had ever seen. "Oh no!"

"Chuck!" Jillian cried. Louise wasn't sure how Jillian decided it was Chuck's fault.

Nikola cringed, but it was Chuck who defended the choice. "You said we needed a self-driven truck with combination locks on cargo pods, fully fueled."

"Someone is going to notice it's missing!" Jillian cried.

"They haven't yet. And we wanted to see the ostriches. We've never seen one before! We haven't seen any animals."

Louise sighed. The babies didn't have enough experience to understand cause and effect. It worried Louise, not just because of what they might do, but because of what *she* might miss. She might be smart as a rocket scientist, but she didn't have twenty years of learning how the world really worked. She was gambling all their lives that she understood things enough to see a way to safety.

"What do we do?" Crow Boy asked.

Louise took a deep breath and swung the door closed. "We need to get moving; we're running on a time table."

Nikola pressed his nose to the window and stared in fascination at the ostriches. They stared back, seemingly equally fascinated.

Jillian eyed the ostriches with open suspicion. "What are we going to do with eight ostriches?"

"Play with them?" Nikola suggested.

Louise knew that was impossible, although a tiny part of her wished they could. "If we don't need the cages, we'll set the truck back on its original course with the pride."

"Pride?" Jillian echoed in confusion.

"Groups of ostriches are called prides," Louise said.

"Like lions?" Jillian said.

One of the Jawbreakers said, "Evidence has been found to show lions in Africa have been kicked in the head by ostriches and had their jaws broken and starved to death."

Jillian gave Louise a dark look. "We're in a truck filled with lion killers?"

It didn't seem nearly as fun when Jillian put it that way.

"Hello!" Joy pressed against the glass to look up at the big birds. "Who's there?" She tilted her head back and forth. "Oh, no one's home."

Jillian snorted.

"That's not nice," Louise said. "They're just not as smart as you."

The cavern's entrance was marked with a low split-rail fence and a giant arrow sitting on a rough stone slab. There had been a barrier with a "closed" sign attached to it, but that had been run over. Louise wished they could have stopped and reconsidered, but they were already committed. Crow Boy had flown ahead, and their first attack was already underway. The truck's auto-drive put on turn signals, slowed, and gracefully turned into the driveway. Their truck thumped over the fallen barrier. Her heart started to race. She wished she could take Jillian's hand and hold it tight, but she didn't want her twin to know how scared she was. Louise gripped her hands together.

The two-mile-long driveway climbed up the steep ridge and crested in a large parking lot. Their two other trucks sat near the low-slung stone and wood-planked visitor center. The ten thousand robotic mice were still pouring endlessly out of the back of the mouse truck. Unlike the prototypes, the factory-built mice were dark brown. There were two people on the ground, twitching, and one running for the visitor center with a thousand mice on his heels.

"Get him!" Louise pointed at the last fleeing elf. "Get him."

"We're working on it!" Nikola cried.

"Hooyah!" Chuck Norris cried as the male tumbled to the ground. "Score!"

Three down, Louise thought, *how many to go?*

Crow Boy suddenly appeared in the sky, swooping down onto the fallen elves. For a moment, Louise's heart stopped, thinking he was going to strike them with the machete they'd bought at Home Depot. When he landed, though, he whipped out a handful of the twenty-four-inch zip ties and used them to hogtie the male.

"Pull over by Crow Boy," Louise instructed. They'd specified a locking cargo section on the truck so they could hold and transport prisoners if they needed to. If the tengu children weren't here, they might have to question prisoners at length.

The truck stopped next to the fallen elves. The twins scrambled down out of the cab.

"Nikola, you stay with Tesla; keep him out of danger." Louise took three of the white mice from her pocket and placed them on the ground. "Girls, you three control the brown mice, but keep them close. If they get out of range of Tesla, their own AI will take over and we might not get them back."

Each mouse had a seek-and-neutralize program that would have them taser any humanoid object that wasn't wearing a "friend" transponder. Their programming also allowed them to be linked into large groups acting as one unit. With the babies herding them, the mice would actually end up in the caverns instead of wandering the neighboring woods, tasering hapless hikers.

"Roger!" Chuck snapped. "Team Mischief, go!"

"Jillian, unload the luggage mules." Louise pointed Jillian toward the truck that had the rest of their gear. Away from the elves. Away from the violence. Jillian nodded, trying to look anywhere but at the bound males.

Only once Jillian was out of earshot did Louise ask quietly, "Are there any other elves in the area?"

Crow Boy shook his head. "The one outbuilding is an equipment shed and the other is a picnic shelter. There's no one in either one. If there's more elves, they're inside the caverns."

"Any sign of the nestlings?"

Hurt flashed across his face. He took something out of his pocket and held it out to her. It was a small plushie of a black bird. "This is Lai Yee's. It was on the ground in the equipment shed, but it could have simply fallen out of a truck."

It only meant that the little girl had been moved in a vehicle that then came to the caverns. Lai Yee, though, might have been taken out of the truck someplace else.

"We'll find them," Louise promised.

While he hogtied and gagged the other fallen elves, Louise sorted through the spells they'd preprinted. They'd made copies of every spell that might be useful, from shields to detection to healing ones like the ones they'd cast on Crow Boy. She found the scry spell and laid it on the warm asphalt of the parking lot. Taking out four magic generators, she connected them to the spell via the power leads. With the increased power input, the scry spell would reach further.

With a word, she activated the spell. With the extra power, a massive dome gleamed to life over the paper. The parking lot flared on the surface, a brilliant dot of confusion as the spell attempted to highlight all the living objects from the ostriches down to the twins. The gift shop was a tangle of metal, rending the building unreadable to the spell. The magic poured down through the caves, though, painting the deep maze hidden under the rolling hills around them. With the parking lot to mark the scale, the sheer size of the cave system was intimidating.

"There they are!" Jillian cried, pointing not at the spell but to a point somewhere to the right.

"What?" Louise couldn't see anything.

Jillian dashed over to study the spell. "There! See!" She pointed to a bright knot within the largest cavern space. "That's them."

"How can you tell?" Louise peered closely at the point. There seemed too many motes of light shifting around to be just the children; if it was the nestlings, then they had several guards.

Jillian gave her a startled look. "They feel like Crow Boy."

She said it as if Louise should understand. "We all felt different when you triggered the spell. The ostriches. Us. Crow Boy. The elves. Even Tesla. What's down there felt mostly like Crow Boy."

Louise compared the gleaming three-dimensional maze to the map they'd downloaded from the caverns' website. The paper-based version of the caves failed to indicate the slope; the deepest point was easily hundreds of feet underground. She estimated that the nestlings were nearly a hundred feet deep. "Mostly?"

Jillian considered the mysterious feeling. Slowly, she shrank inward and whispered, "There's a bunch of elves with them."

Louise steeled herself against the fear that went through her. They had the upper hand; the elves couldn't possibly guess the nature of their attack. "Find the signal repeaters; we'll need them first."

Louise cancelled the spell. The heat of the spell had singed the paper slightly. As she disconnected the power leads, the brittle and browned sections crumbled. She whispered a curse; they had a limited number of printouts for each spell.

"Joy, no!" Jillian cried.

Louise turned to see Joy fling open the cage door on the livestock carrier.

"Cage bad!" Joy cried. "Be free!"

The big birds spilled out and headed toward the twins.

The ostriches suddenly seemed a lot bigger as they headed toward her. Dealing with the small heads on the slender necks was much different from being surrounded by tall muscular legs and wicked-looking feet. The big bodies were at shoulder height to the twins while the birds looked down at them from another foot up.

"Eep!" Jillian backed up until she was pressed against Louise's right side.

"They are friendly, right?" Nikola pressed against Louise's left side.

"Probably." Louise wished she felt surer of that. She moved in front of Tesla. The ostriches were probably hand-raised and gentle with humans, but there was no telling how they'd react to the robotic dog. "I think they probably imprinted on the people that raised them. They're looking for their 'mother,' and we're the only humans in sight."

"Or they might kick us to death," Jillian grumbled. "We shouldn't have taken them in the first place."

"We're sorry!" Nikola cried. "We didn't think Joy would let them out!"

"It's okay." Louise hadn't factored ostriches into her attack plans. They didn't have time, though, to mess around with the giant birds. Crow Boy brushed past the big birds to shove the first hogtied elf into the livestock cage. "Let's just ignore them, and hopefully they'll wonder off to graze. Make sure Joy stays out of sight of them though: they're omnivores. They will eat small lizards."

"At this point in time," Jillian growled, "I'd be happy to feed her to them."

Louise didn't agree with the sentiment but was glad that Jillian sounded more angry than scared. "We need to move quickly. If the elves call for reinforcements, we'll be caught between two groups." She took the case that Jillian handed her. "Chuck, start the mice toward the gift shop. Nikola, keep Tesla with me."

The visitor center for the caverns was perched on the first ridge of the Allegheny Mountains. Louise had only been vaguely aware of that fact when they'd climbed the driveway. As she headed toward the gift shop, the reality of the landscape hit Louise hard. They were a thousand feet or more above the rest of southwestern Pennsylvania. The land rolled out to the horizon, fifty or sixty miles in the clear morning sunlight. The ironwood forest transplanted from Elfhome loomed far in the distance, the curving edge of the Rim and the quarantine zone encircling it. As the crow flies, it looked miles away. Ten? Twenty? Louise couldn't judge. When they crossed over to Elfhome, the rolling farmland would be replaced by virgin forest. No roads. No bridges. Man-eating plants, spiders the size of lapdogs, wolves the size of ponies, and a distant cousin to the T. rex.

"Don't think about it," she whispered to herself. "All that will do is scare you. You've got to be the strong one."

She forced herself to focus on the gift-shop entrance. Glass double doors, just like pictures on the Internet. Unlocked.

"Nikola, keep Tesla at the door with me. Girls, take in the mice and get me a feed of what's inside the gift shop. Take down anyone inside, but don't move down into the caves."

"Roger!" the three white mice beside her right foot squeaked.

Louise cracked the right door wide enough for the mice to pour through it. Once the flood was past, she let the door close and pulled out her phone. The screen flickered dozens of confusing images. "Just pick one." The image fixated on a closeup of a trilobite fossil. "No, of the whole room beyond the door!"

"It's two hundred and fifty million years old!" Nikola said with awe.

The view changed to the dim interior of the gift shop. Light streamed in through windows on the far side of the long room. The contrast between the dark foreground and brilliant background made it difficult to see what was in the room, but there didn't appear to be anyone inside.

Where were all the elves? She had counted forty-three individuals between those at the mansion and the others scattered worldwide. They had to be the tip of the iceberg, as she suspected the far-flung operations had more than one elf running each.

Crow Boy appeared beside her, making her jump.

"Nothing so far," she whispered as she showed him the screen.

He nodded and ghosted silently inside. Jillian came down the walkway with a caravan of ostriches and luggage mules.

"I can't get them to stop following me." Jillian had obviously moved past fear of the birds and was now just annoyed. "And they keep—ow—pecking at my head."

One of the birds had lowered its head to rap Jillian on her carrot-orange pixie-cut.

"Maybe they think you're a something to eat." Louise propped open the door. "Get inside with the luggage mules and I'll try to keep them—no, no—oh geez."

Something inside had caught the ostriches' attention, and in they marched into the visitor center.

"Ugh!" Jillian flailed her arms in frustration.

"At least they're not interested in you anymore."

It was very odd to watch the pride of ostriches stalk through the gift shop, randomly eyeing items and then pecking at them.

"You know, I don't think they're actually ostriches," Jillian muttered. "They don't have wings. Don't ostriches have wings?"

"What?" Louise stared hard at the birds. Jillian was right: they didn't have wings.

"Maybe they're emus," Jillian said.

Louise was fairly sure that emus were a good deal smaller than ostriches, but it might be a matter of scale. Maybe all flightless birds would seem giant to the twins. "Emu. Ostrich. Whatever." She took out one of the repeaters and set it down by the door. When one the birds stalked over to eye the signal booster, she tucked it under the edge of the counter.

"This leads down to the cave," Crow Boy whispered from a doorway across the room.

Louise nodded, taking a deep breath. It felt like they were careening toward disaster. She couldn't tell, though, if it was her magical *knowing* sense or just fear mixed with logic. They were three kids (seven if she counted the babies) going against heavily armed adults who wouldn't hesitate to kill them.

Yet, if they were to be truly safe, they needed to get through the cave ahead of the elves.

Jillian had found a hardhat and strapped it onto her head. She held out one to Louise. They would only need one if they went deep into the caves, past the normal tour areas, but obviously Jillian wanted a costume to hide behind.

And maybe some head protection from the ostriches.

Louise left the door propped open so the birds could get back out.

The hallway sloped steeply downhill; the walls seemed chiseled out of the stone hillside. Crystal chandeliers dimly lit the rough corridor. The air felt cold and damp and smelled of moist earth. Names and dates had been etched into the rock over centuries. One stated "1891 H. N. Mose" and another proclaimed "1953 R. D." It was "2013 A. G. Bell" and an arrow pointing inward that caught Louise's eye and made her heart leap. That was the year that Alexander had been born. Had Esme been here? Did the arrow pointing inward mean they were doing the right thing? She hurried forward down the ramp, sweeping her flashlight into the dark corners of the cave, searching for more clues.

The ramp became a series of steps down and then an elevated walkway with iron banisters to keep visitors from falling into the shadows below. The crystal chandeliers continued, a few feet apart, for as far as the eye could see, like a strand of Christmas lights. This was the Hall of the Mountain King, with the massive Dining Room at the far end. After that point, the caverns became a sprawling maze, much of it undeveloped. So far there was no sign of the tengu children or their captors. Had the elves taken the children through already?

Jillian whispered loudly, "There's magic here."

"Really?"

"It's not as strong here as at the mansion, but I can feel it."

"Strong enough to do spells?"

Jillian shrugged. "I guess. Maybe."

Louise placed a signal repeater on the edge of the walkway and then hurried on. Crow Boy had disappeared into the darkness ahead of her. She was afraid that despite his promise, he'd try to take on all the guards by himself.

"Girls, stay with Crow Boy," Louise whispered.

"They are," Nikola said. "The rock is making it difficult. The signal between Tesla and the mice keeps dropping. At least a hundred have gone rogue."

"Running on their AI alone?" Louise asked to clarify.

"Yes," Nikola said.

Louise double-checked her "friendly" transponder. "Get them back if you can. We don't want them tasering the nestlings."

"Roger!" Nikola saluted with his right paw. While she wasn't paying attention, he'd put on a private airman's cap. She had no idea where he'd gotten it. It made her feel completely out of control of the situation. Careening.

They stopped short of the Dining Hall. The area was full of shadows and primary-color lights shining on the sandstone, as if the tour operators had thought people would find the caves boring without added color.

They gathered together, a thousand brown mice in the lead and the ostriches somewhere in the back.

"Ten guards," Crow Boy whispered.

Louise's heart leapt at the number. Three or four would have been difficult. Ten? She nodded despite her fear. It was going to be up to the mice. She wanted to protect the babies, but her only choice was to use them as weapons. As long as Tesla stayed out of the fray, the babies would be safe.

"Girls, on my signal, take all the mice and rush them. Chuck, take the four elves to the right. Jawbreakers. Green, take the three to the left. Red, take the middle three. Try not to taser the nestlings. Okay?"

"Roger!" the three girls squeaked.

"What's the signal?" Chuck asked.

"She'll say 'On your mark, set, go!'" Red stated.

"No, that's for races," Green disagreed. "I think she'll hoot like an owl."

"Shh! When I tell you, you'll know." She held out her hand to Crow Boy. "Give me some zip ties."

"What?" Alarm filled his face.

"You can't do all ten before they recover from being tasered." She held out her hand.

He didn't like the idea; it showed on his face. He handed her a dozen. "You don't have the strength to move their arms behind their back, so just bind them the way you find them."

She nodded. "Nikola, keep watch on the gift shop and warn us if anyone else enters the cave. Jillian, try and keep the ostriches out of this mess."

"Like I can actually control them!" Jillian whispered fiercely.

Louise waved her to be quiet. She took a deep breath. Fear jangled through her. She took another deep breath, trying to steel herself against the feeling of its tingling through her like electricity. "Ready?"

"Um, is that the signal?" Green asked.

"Go!" She waved them toward the elves. "Go!"

"*That's* the signal!" Chuck cried. "Charge!"

The swarm of mice flooded away. Crow Boy bounded after them. Louise followed.

The narrow Mountain King's Hall opened into the huge Dining Room cavern. The rocks were highlighted with colored spotlights. Most of the cave, however, was cloaked in darkness, its true size hidden. The tengu children were all bound, hands and feet, in a long line. Boxes of gear sat in stacks, evidence that the elves were planning a well-stocked, orderly retreat. The brown robotic mice scurried forward with a rustle that sounded like running water.

"What is that sound?" one of the elves said.

"What are those?" another cried as she spotted the mice and pointed.

"Look out!" a third shouted.

They went down, stomping and flailing, under the wave of mice.

Crow Boy leapt on the nearest elf. He flipped the male onto his face and jerked the elf's arms around behind his back.

"Get that one!" Crow Boy indicated a female elf twitching a few feet from him.

Louise hesitated, clutching tight the zip tie in her hand. She hadn't actually thought about the fact that she'd have to touch the elves to bind them. She'd never hit anyone in her life. Movement caught her eyes and she saw one of the older tengu girls trying to wriggle her way toward one of the fallen elves. The girl knew that they had to win this battle and, helpless as she was, was trying to fight.

Louise swallowed down her fear and caught hold of the elf's wrists. She fumbled through pushing the rigid limbs through the wire loops and pulling the plastic ties tight. The female elf groaned, obviously trying to struggle, as the mice kept her pinned with repeated shocks. She glared at Louise with hate-filled eyes and lips curled back in a snarl.

"You started this!" Louise shouted at her. "We're just children! You should never have treated us this way!"

"Louise!" Crow Boy called to her. "She's thousands of years old. Nothing you say will change her mind. We're nothing but tools to push her own agenda."

The second elf was easier to bind. Louise was securing the fourth when Crow Boy pushed a wire clipper into her hands.

"Free the nestlings. I'll get the others."

To bind the children, the elves had used zip ties identical to the ones that the twins had bought at Home Depot. The kids had blackened eyes, broken noses, bruises and cuts on their arms. They'd obviously been sitting tied up for hours wearing nothing but T-shirts and blue jeans; they were shivering from the cold fifty-two-degree cave. When she cut them free, they scrambled fearfully away from her and snatched up anything that could be used as a weapon. Even the kindergartener Lai Yee found a small knife. The elves had tortured two of the older children by drenching them in water; they lay on the ground in a hypothermia-induced stupor.

They weren't going to be able to force-march these kids through virgin forest twenty miles to the edge of Pittsburgh where they might find safe shelter.

"Jillian! We need the mules in here!" Louise called to her twin.

"Stupid birds!" Jillian grumbled, earning hard looks from the nestlings. She waved toward the ostriches, which trooped in behind her, inspecting everything as they slowly followed the luggage mules. "Them! Them!"

The hostility turned to confusion and slight fear as the huge birds strutted over to eye the nestlings closely.

"I sent some mice out to the gift shop to keep watch!" Nikola reported and saluted.

"Good work." Louise indicated the two unresponsive nestlings.

"We need dry clothes and blankets for them, and see if you can find a healing spell that might help."

Jillian's eyes widened, and she saluted, too. "Yes, Commander."

Louise returned the salute. If that was what Jillian needed to keep it together, then that's what she'd get.

Crow Boy moved to freeing the last of the nestlings. It was the English-speaking girl, Arisu, who had tried to buy the snow globe for a fellow nestling. Once freed, Arisu hugged him tightly.

"I knew you'd get free and save us!" Arisu cried. "I knew you'd come!"

Crow Boy glanced to Louise, guilt on his face. He obviously felt that the twins should be given credit for the rescue. All of the nestlings, though, were cringing away from the twins—and the mice and ostriches and the big robotic dog wearing a hat. Not that Louise blamed them; it was a bit much even for her.

He pulled free of Arisu to fumble with his belt pack. "I have candy," he announced loudly.

Instantly Joy, who had been God knows where, appeared on his shoulder. "Oh, candy! Gimme!"

The nestlings went wide-eyed and still with amazement.

Crow Boy gave the baby dragon a large jawbreaker. "This is Joy," he said in Mandarin. "And these two girls are her Chosen. They are as clever and wise as Wong Jin. You're to listen to them closely and do what they say."

The nestlings eyed the twins with awe and curiosity, but at least not now with fear.

Louise swallowed down on the automatic desire to hide from strangers' gazes. Now was not the time to be shy. "We took out three guards outside," Louise said in Mandarin, earning a surprised look from Crow Boy. "Are there more? Where are they?"

The nestlings eyed the hogtied prisoners and counted on their fingers.

"That should be all that have been guarding us since we were captured." Arisu kicked two of the bound male elves. "Those two went through the pathway earlier and set up a shield spell on the Elfhome side. Nothing to keep a determined force out, but something strong enough to deter a stray saurus or black willow."

"So it's safe to cross through?" Louise asked.

"They made sure there were no strangle vines or steel spinners or anything," Arisu stated. "There are no oni in the immediate area, either. They wanted to avoid oni encampments until they could connect with Kajo and find out what has happened since the last Shutdown."

"They're waiting for the Unmaker," one of the male nestlings added. "He's to arrive soon."

Louise's breath caught in her chest. None of the guards so far looked familiar; they weren't from the mansion. If Yves brought everyone from Alpine, it could be a virtual army. She closed her eyes, focusing on the future. *How can I keep my family and the nestlings safe?*

"We'll seal the entrance." Louise pointed back toward the gift shop. Toward danger. Toward disaster. "There's no other way into these caves."

"Doesn't that mean there's no other way out?" Jillian slowly asked as if doubting the logic of the move.

"There's the pathway to Elfhome." Louise pointed deeper into the caves and knew it was the right way to go. "Once we seal the entrance, we'll have time to do whatever we need to succeed."

While two of the older nestlings worked with Jillian at applying magical and nonmagical first aid to the wounded, Louise put the others to work unloading the luggage mules.

"Get dressed in something warm first," she instructed as she found the black hoodies. One of the warehouse employees had written "midget ninja outfits" in marker on the outside of the package. Obviously their employees—soon to be ex-employees—had been mystified by the weird assortment of items the twins had shipped. "You're all on the verge of hypothermia."

She followed her own instructions, putting on one of the hoodies and handing one to Jillian. "Drink some water and eat something." She pointed at the case of water and boxes of power bars. "Then get one of the backpacks and fill it with as much food and water and camping gear as you can carry."

After the luggage mules were quickly unloaded, Louise pointed at the bound elves. "We'll use the mules to carry the prisoners back to the gift shop."

"We could just kill them," Crow Boy whispered to her.

"No." Louise glared at him. "I'm not turning my siblings into killers. It's bad enough the babies are acting like a bunch of storm troopers. It will take time for me to set up the spell. Take them to the gift shop."

Crow Boy bowed slightly to her. "As you wish."

Jillian realized that Louise intended to leave her behind. She gave Louise a betrayed look. "I want to go with you."

"You can see magic," Louise stated firmly. "It stands to reason that the greatest concentration of magic will be where the two worlds connect. It has to be hard to spot. If it was easy to find, then all the tourists visiting this cave would be popping over to Elfhome all the time."

Jillian huffed at the inarguable logic. She flung her arms about Louise and clung tightly to her for several minutes, taking deep breaths.

Louise twisted a line from *The Great Escape*: "I haven't seen Pittsburgh yet, not from the ground or from the air, and I plan on doing both before the war is over."

Jillian snorted and pulled away. "Put a fence in front of these girls... and they'll climb it." That was the tagline for the movie when it was released.

"Climb it? We'd run a bulldozer through it!"

Jillian laughed in surprise. She snapped a salute and sauntered away, whistling the movie's theme song.

While Crow Boy took the luggage mules on to the gift shop, Louise stopped at the entrance to the Hall of the Mountain King. She eyed the graffiti etched into the stone that might have been left by Esme. Bell was number sixty-seven in the list of the most common surnames in the United States; any number of Bells could have etched a date and an arrow into the wall. Was this really one of Esme's cryptic clues? When Louise first saw it, she was sure it meant that they were supposed to follow it to Elfhome. Now she was wondering if it meant this was the best place to collapse the passageway.

Certainly it was a logical spot. The ceiling was at its lowest point. Trying to ignore her doubts and fears, she set up a scry spell. The sandstone formed a solid ceiling for twenty feet before giving way to a thin layer of dirt at the surface far above.

I'm going to bury us. This could be our grave if I'm wrong.

Louise pressed her hands to her eyes. Was she right? Was this the best action? Jillian was her control; without *knowing*, her twin operated on logic. The doubt on her twin's face had been easy to read. They weren't on Elfhome proper yet and they didn't understand the delicate forces that created the pathway. Even though she was nearly a quarter-mile from the Dining Hall cave, she could trigger a shift in the entire area and break the connection between the worlds. They had no idea when Yves would arrive; she could wait until they were safely on Elfhome.

All her instincts, though, were screaming that she had to act. *Now. Quickly.*

She dug through the printed-out spells. They had three force strikes printed out. The paper trembled as she held them, trying to decide if she should use them in combination or just take the time to ramp up the power of one.

Crow Boy returned with empty luggage mules. "I locked all the prisoners in the ostrich truck."

"They can't get out, can they?" Louise asked. "We could."

He grinned. "Yes, you could, but I doubt they can. They're not that clever. I also programmed the truck to take them to the Miami-Dade police department."

"Miami?"

"It will take about a day to get there."

Long enough to keep the elves out of their hair but short enough that the elves wouldn't die from lack of water.

"I locked down the gift shop," Crow Boy said. "They will have to break their way in."

Louise nodded her understanding. "Okay, head to the pathway."

Crow Boy surprised her by hugging her. "Be safe," he murmured like a blessing.

44: THE UNMAKER

Louise considered the printed spells again. The slips of paper represented their only true attack spell. If she used all three, they would be helpless later on—unless of course she and Jillian could cast spells like Queen Soulful Ember. Dufae had stated that setting up a resonance with the Spell Stones was unreliable through the pathway and charted his attempts in the codex. His failure rate was so high that they'd kept to the surefire success of printed spells.

On Elfhome, things would be different. If they could cast spells like *domana*, then they wouldn't need the preprinted spells.

She closed her eyes and tried for the calm knowing. One or three? Use or keep? *Use. Quickly.*

She pulled out a plastic painter's drop cloth and unfolded it to spread out over the damp floor. She carefully taped the printed spells onto the sheet. There was a railing along the uneven path; she could drape the plastic over the railing to aim the force of the spell at the ceiling. Which would it be: a direct blow or glancing? If she made it too glancing, it wouldn't shear off enough stone to fill the passage, but the impact of a straight-up blow might not be enough to bring down the roof even with the combined power of all three spells.

Should she choose a different target for each spell? A series of hits with slightly different vectors might create a large collapse. She sat back and tugged at her hair with both hands. She was overthinking it, wasn't she? She didn't have time to debate choices.

She quickly taped blank paper between the spells and took out a metal ink pen. She desperately hoped that she was as clever as she thought she was. This was so going to suck if the spell didn't work like she wanted it to. She would need to use all four magic generators, but that much power would quickly char the paper. She would have one shot to bring down the cave ceiling.

Maybe she should just do one spell at a time—

"Lou!" Nikola's voice came out of a brown mouse that crouched by her foot. "A truck just pulled into the parking lot."

"What?" She jerked up the pen to keep from misdrawing the timing circle.

"A box truck. It's backing up to the gift shop."

Her heart started to hammer into overdrive. "Stay calm. You can do this."

"Can you?"

"Yes! I can!" Louise really hoped that she wasn't lying now.

"What should I do?"

"I need to concentrate. Please don't talk to me."

She quickly finished drawing the ramping section and shifted the plastic up onto the railing. There was a distant crashing noise in the direction of the gift shop—glass shattering. She connected the magic generators as fast as she could and then said the trigger word.

Nothing happened.

"Oh no!" she cried. "Why isn't it working?"

"Lou! Lou! They're coming! It's Yves and twenty of the people from the mansion and a dozen people we don't know! Oh no, another truck just pulled up!"

She gripped her hair with both hands. What was wrong? The spell hadn't powered up at all. It meant power wasn't getting from the generators to the timing ring... She cried as she spotted the point where she hadn't drawn in the full line.

"I can't stop them, Lou!" Nikola cried.

"There's one of the damn Wood Sprites!" Yves shouted as a wave of elves ran toward her, the sounds of their boots thundering in the tight space.

Louise drew in the missing trace and shouted the trigger word.

The world roared into darkness. She sensed tons of broken rock dropping down all around her, and she dodged to the side. Rubble thundered down beside her, tearing the bag from her grip and knocking her down. Whimpering with fear, she scrambled on all fours, not even sure in which direction she was blindly heading. She hit some kind of shallow hollow in the wall and tucked herself into it.

After the deafening roar of falling rock, the silence afterwards was strange and unreal. It was like she had accidently muted the universe. She huddled in her tiny shelter, panting in the dusty air. Was it over? Had it worked? Was the hallway completely blocked? She was too scared to even move.

Somewhere nearby, there was a deep male grunt and then the scrape of boot on rock.

Louise pressed her hands to her mouth. Crow Boy had metal fighting spars on his crowlike feet, so it wasn't him. An elf was on her side of the rockslide! What if there was more than one? What should she do? What could she do?

Most of her things had been in her backpack. She groped in the darkness, trying to find it. The floor of the cave was covered with a confusion of pebbles and larger stones.

There was another boot scrape. Louder. Closer.

She froze, fingers deep in the mix of sand and rocks. Even if she found the bag, what could she do? What spell would get her out of this mess? She didn't have a box for invisibility, nor would it matter in this utter darkness.

A small light flared in the dark. The elf stood only six or seven feet from her, a small flashlight in his hand. Louise didn't dare move, lest her motion betray her. From her low, protected hollow in the wall, Louise could see that the male wore high boots, tailored canvas slacks, and a wool pea coat. A sword and a pistol hung from his hips as though he were a soldier from hundreds of years out of the past. She couldn't see his face, but she *knew* that it was Yves.

The male slowly examined the cave around him. Thick dust hazed the beam of the flashlight as it swept over the broken wall that was the rockslide. Surely he was wondering the same thing Louise was. What had happened to the other elves? Were they trapped under the rubble or were they safely on the other side? Were they digging through even now? Was there a way through? How thick was the blockage? A few feet or several yards? They had been nearly fifty feet from the gift shop.

The light swung around and pointed down the hall. The floor

was strewn with random boulders and a carpet of rubble but was otherwise clear. Something gleamed, reflecting the light, and it caught Yves' attention. He knelt down and picked it up.

Louise stifled a gasp. It was a crushed signal repeater. It meant that she was out of range for Tesla. The others wouldn't know that Yves was on their side of the collapse, armed and dangerous. The babies would have lost control of all the mice from the gift shop to another hundred feet back in the caves. They'd have to move Tesla closer in order to find out what happened to Louise. The babies had asked what they should do and she had shushed them! She should have made sure they told Crow Boy what was happening!

Would they have sense to move all the mice with Tesla? Would they think to tell Crow Boy before they moved? They were just babies! They wouldn't know how to fight Yves except by using Tesla's automated defense programs.

Yves took something from his coat pocket, stepped back, and pressed it to the wall. Brilliance lit the hallway, blinding Louise. "Ah, there you are, annoying little mouse. Sire wanted you two alive." He pulled his pistol out of its holster. "But you're not worth the bother of keeping."

"Warning!" Tesla came running down the hall, barking in his deep Japanese-man voice. "Primary target under attack! Response code one!"

"Nikola!" Louise cried. "You promised!"

The pistol thundered in the narrow space, horrifyingly loud. Yves fired again and again. Tesla staggered and fell.

Louise put her hand to her mouth, bent her fingers, and called the Spell Stones. Instantly she felt a deep vibration in her bones as she plugged into potential. She changed her finger position to a force strike.

Yves shouted in alarm and swung the pistol toward her. She shouted the spell command and pointed at him even as the muzzle flared. The light vanished. The world thundered noise. Something struck Louise and knocked her from her feet.

Yves had shot her! She lay in the sudden silent dark. She could smell the blood. Her left arm hurt like her humerus was broken. She could feel something hot and sticky tricking down her arm, and she was fairly sure it was blood. Her blood.

Think! Think! She might faint from shock and blood loss; everything already felt a little swimmy in her head. She had to get this right. She needed light to stop the bleeding, but if Yves were still conscious, then it would allow him to shoot her again.

"Lou?" Nikola's voice came out of the darkness, banishing all thought.

"Nikola!" She sat up, and the swimmy feeling got stronger. Yves' flashlight lay a few feet away, pointing to Tesla's front paws. One paw raked the air in an endless sideways run.

"Louise?" Nikola called. "Lou!"

Louise managed to stand and stagger to the flashlight and pick it up.

A bullet had caught Tesla in the head, shattering his right eye and clipping off his ear. The fur had been torn away, exposing metal and circuitry.

"Oh, babies!" Louise sobbed as fear tore through her.

"Something is wrong. We don't feel right. We're scared."

"It's okay. I'm here." Her hands didn't want to work right. She fumbled with the flashlight and the catches of Tesla's storage compartment while blood ran down her fingers.

There was a fine line etched in frost across the surface of the *nactka*.

"Oh no!" Louise gasped. A bullet had scratched the magical device. The spell holding the embryos in stasis had failed. The frozen nitrogen that they were stored in was leaking out, and once it was gone, they'd die. She had to keep it cold. How could she do that?

She ran the narrow beam of the flashlight through the dusty air. A solid wall of fallen rocks blocked the way back to the gift shop and any possible freezers in that direction. Nor would any standard freezer be cold enough. The embryos needed to stay far below what even a commercial-grade freezer could produce. There was a reason that the clinic kept the material in special tanks.

There had been the one freezing spell in the codex. They'd experimented with it, but it created a big block of immobile ice. When the information on the *nactka* came to light, they had abandoned the spell.

Louise searched through her pockets. Had she tucked the pen into her pants? Yes. And two sheets of spare paper. And the plastic bag from the hoodies. She drew out the spell, leaving bloody fingerprints on the paper. "I need to take you out of Tesla."

"Why? What's wrong?"

"Tesla is too damaged to move," she lied as the world blurred at the edges. She couldn't bring herself to tell them that they would die if she couldn't save them. She didn't want their last minutes to be in terror of what was about to happen. If she failed, she wanted their deaths to be quick and painless. "Try to go to sleep. When you wake up—When you wake up—you'll be real. I promise."

45: LET'S GO FLY A KITE

Time was lost in a haze. She remembered only vaguely being woken up, carried about in the dark, buried under blankets, forced to drink countless cups of what seemed to be giblet gravy, and Jillian clinging to her, sobbing. She had long odd dreams about Mary Poppins and a horde of tengu chimney sweeps and giant penguins doing tap-dance routines. Later she was lucid enough to understand the others had done what little they could to keep her from dying from massive blood loss. Sitting up had the alarming tendency to make everything go swimmy and occasionally dark. At first her left arm felt like it was on fire, but later it was only annoyingly itchy. Worse than the fainting was the fear plain on her twin's face. It reminded Louise that she had left much undone before losing consciousness.

Louise tried to list them out to Jillian. "I don't know how much of the cave I blocked..."

Jillian pointed at a nearby patch of brightness. "We're on Elf-home. Joy collapsed the pathway days ago. We're safe."

Louise sat up. "The babies!"

"Joy moved them!" Jillian pushed her back down. "I don't know how. I don't know when. But she did. She's got them in something that seems just like your spell, but I don't recognize any of the glyphs. It's huge, but it works. Crow Boy says it's dragon magic. I'm trying to get her to teach it to me, but you know how she is—a senile grandmother on a sugar rush."

Louise wished she could laugh. Jillian was so fragile she couldn't even weave a mask to hide behind. Laughter would have soothed her twin.

"I have no idea how we're going to get you and the babies to Pittsburgh." Jillian gripped Louise's hand tightly. "We ran the luggage mules out of power getting all the gear through the caves, and there's no way to recharge them. Crow Boy says there's lots of oni moving through the woods around us; he's afraid if we don't travel fast and quietly, we won't be able to avoid them. I don't know what we're going to do."

"We'll figure it out." Louise squeezed Jillian's hands, trying to summon courage that she didn't have anymore. It had all bled out when she was shot. It left a hollow space inside her, coated with a sick, cold dread that the babies were already dead and they were just moving icy remains around.

She'd lost track of time and, when she felt well enough to walk shakily out of the small cave they'd been camping in, was shocked. The leaves on the trees were tinged with fall oranges and yellows. Somehow, while she was too weak to notice, September had raced up to meet them.

The egglike *nactka* sat on a section of rock that had been polished to a mirrored surface and a large complex spell etched into the glass. The *nactka* sat at the center, wreathed in frost and mist. A small hut of wicker had been woven over both.

"How did Joy . . . ?" Louise trailed off, confounded by every part of the structure.

"I don't know." Jillian held on to her arm like she was afraid that Louise might fall over. It wasn't a completely unreasonable fear. "And I don't know how we're going to move it."

"Joy moved them once." Louise clung to that idea. "She can move them again."

"I don't think even she can move them the whole way to the tengu village."

"I mean onto something more portable. Like a shipping pallet."

Jillian gave her a look that said she wasn't sure that Louise was fully lucid.

"I'm brainstorming," Louise said. "Work with me."

Jillian sighed. "Okay. If we could get it onto the pallet, then we'd need wheels or something. Maybe use the ostriches—"

"We still have those?"

"God, yes. Joy dragged them through the caves." Jillian glanced around. "They're around here somewhere. They actually make good guard dogs against things like spiders and strangle vines. This would be so much easier if we'd been able to fit the hovercarts into the caves or we could make the ostriches fly..." She paused, squinting. "Do you think we could do that?"

"We could steal something that flies," Louise said.

Jillian looked at her puzzled a moment, and then her eyes widened. "The gossamer call!"

They climbed up to the rocky outcrop at the top of the ridge. It was a clear summer afternoon and Pittsburgh was a break in the dense forest canopy on the horizon. The one thing they hadn't packed was a powerful telescope. There was no way to tell if one of the massive living airships was docked over the airfield next to the enclaves. If there was, the whistle should be able to reach it. Everything the twins knew about Elfhome, however, suggested that the airships rarely traveled to the city. The common elves traveled via train. Only Windwolf and Sparrow ever arrived via gossamer.

Last the twins heard, the viceroy was at Aum Renau.

It was possible that the whistle could reach as far as the East Coast, but Louise doubted it.

Nor was there any guarantee that the gossamer would be unattended.

Louise pressed her hands together and prayed to any god that might be willing to listen. *Please.*

The whistle seemed dangerously loud and shrill when she blew the "come" command. A flock of birds flew up and something large crashed at the foot of the cliff, screened by the foliage. The twins squeaked and crouched down.

"What was that?" Jillian whispered.

Louise shrugged, heart hammering. Minutes passed and nothing emerged out of the forest. Cautiously, she stood up and blew a second "come."

Crow Boy ghosted down beside them. One moment the sky had been empty and then he was settling silently on the rocky outcrop. Louise wondered how he did it; was it one of the ninja powers that Providence had given the *yamabushi*? There wasn't even a noise from his metal fighting spurs on the bare rock. "How long before we know it isn't coming?"

Louise winced. "An hour if there's one in Pittsburgh. If we're pulling one from the East Coast, it could take almost a day."

"I'll get the others ready." Crow Boy sprang up into the air, black wings rustling as he unfurled them.

His confidence in her was at once calming and embarrassing.

An hour later, they spotted a gossamer floating toward them. The body glittered in the sun like a thousand diamonds. The sight of it took Louise's breath away. None of the videos did justice to its massive size. It dwarfed any airplane she'd ever seen. The long wooden gondola slung under the beast was a comforting solid Wind Clan blue. Mooring ropes trailed down from the gondola's underside.

"How are we going to anchor it?" Jillian asked quietly.

Louise breathed out a curse. "I'll deal with the gossamer." Louise gestured to the rocks and trees around them. "You set up temporary anchors."

As Louise watched the gossamer approach, she tried to determine what else she might have forgotten. She planned to take the gossamer to the tengu village—probably scaring the daylights out of them—so probably sending Crow Boy on ahead would be wise.

As its massive shadow started to eclipse her, Louise played "hover" on the whistle.

Suddenly she was scooped off her feet in a fury of black wings. She squeaked in surprise as Crow Boy leapt backwards with her in his arms.

"What?"

"Back off!" Crow Boy growled, warding off an adult tengu male with his spar-sheathed feet.

"*Yamabushi*?"

"She is under my protection."

"A human?" The male cocked his head to study Louise. "Wait— Tinker *domi*?"

"That isn't *domi*." A woman came floating down out of the sun. Hidden by the brilliance, she was only a warm voice and shadow of a female figure with wings arching like an umbrella above her.

Crow Boy gasped as if struck and lowered Louise to the ground. "Wai Sze!"

Louise gasped with recognition. She had seen this before. "You're Mary Poppins!"

The female landed silently before them, black-winged and almond-eyed. She didn't look at all like a British nanny. And yet, there was something very much like Louise's dream. The female laughed with surprise and delight, "I am?"

"I dreamed of you. You are—were Mary Poppins."

The female knelt down in front of Louise. "I'm Gracie Wong. Gracie Wong Dufae." She took Louise's hands in hers and gazed at them with wonder. "And you're one of my beloved Leo's babies. They said that there was just one of you, but I kept dreaming that there was a whole nest of you, still so young, needing me."

Something inside of Louise released. She crumbled into Gracie's arms and felt completely safe for the first time in months. Grief long buried deep inside her—too dangerous to release until now—roared out of her. The sorrow tore through her, hot and huge. She felt as if she would choke on it as it burst out of her chest, her throat far too tight and small to release it all. She clung to the safety she had glimpsed again and again in her dreams, desperately wanting to believe it was real.

"You're safe, my little one, you're safe."

"I don't know what to do!" Louise cried. Between painful sobs that tore through her, she tried to explain the whole horrible mess. Of the babies in danger of being thrown out and magical *nactka* and the nestlings and how their siblings were now trapped within the protective spell on the polished stone.

"I would bear them if I could. I loved Leo so much. Nothing would bring me greater joy than to have his children."

With a loud rustle of wings, another tengu female came flying in from the southwest. "There's a major force of oni not far from here. They've spotted the gossamer and are coming to investigate. If they have human weapons, the ship is too big a target to miss."

"Get the children onto the airship," Crow Boy ordered. He scooped up Jillian and launched himself up into the air. Jillian's yelp of surprise trailed after them as he flapped upwards.

There was a thunder of wings as the tengu adults swooped down, snatched up the children, and carried them upwards to the waiting ship.

"We need to move the babies!" Louise stepped back to avoid being carried off. "Joy! Joy!"

The baby dragon appeared on Gracie's shoulder. "Hello, who's there? Oh! Providence!"

"Be nice!" Louise carefully took Joy from Gracie's shoulder, mindful of Joy's claws. "She's here to help us. We need to move the babies."

"Move?" Joy said doubtfully.

"Oni are coming!" Louise pointed to the east where birds rose up, scattered by something moving unseen in the dense forest. "We have to leave. You need to move the babies."

Joy eyed Louise for a long moment, as if totally confounded by the request.

"Please, Joy. The babies love you so much, and they're totally helpless right now. You need to help them or the oni will find them and..." The possibilities were too awful to say.

Joy sat back on her haunches, mane bristling out like it was filled with static electricity. She puffed up like a balloon and then howled. The sound rushed up the scale from a low rumble to a sonic shrill shriek. For a mile in all directions, startled birds flew up into the air. Overhead, the gossamer shied away.

Louise stuck her fingers into her ears, but she could still feel the sound in her bones. All the hairs on her arms raised up, and her hair felt like it was trying to stand on end. "Joy! What are you—?"

The rest of the sentence caught in Louise's throat as the gleaming ghost of a dragon appeared in front of her. Its hide was a deep gold to Joy's dusky rose color. Its mouth moved and Louise felt ripples of something move across her skin. But she heard nothing—only the wind rushing over the hilltop.

"Providence!" Gracie whispered with surprise.

Joy waved both paws at the ghost and launched into a tirade in some language that Louise had never heard before. The baby dragon threw in hand gestures she had obviously learned off the streets of New York and a butt wiggle.

There was loud rush of wind and a second dragon appeared, this one blood red and smaller. Smaller being relative—it looked nearly fifteen feet long from whiskered nose to crocodile-like spiked tail. Its eyebrows lifted with surprise at the sight of Joy and Louise. When it leaned in to press a paw to Louise's chest (scaring her by its sheer size), Joy smacked its paw away.

"Mine!" Joy plastered herself to the side of Louise's head.

"This is Impatience." Gracie whispered an introduction. "He's—he's—helpful."

Joy renewed her tirade. Louise guessed that the baby dragon had summoned the dragons to ask for their help. Louise wasn't sure it would actually work; Joy was being extremely rude.

The conversation came to a sudden halt as all three dragons turned to eye Gracie.

The tengu woman looked surprised and then nodded, replying in their flowing language.

Crow Boy landed silently beside Louise and knelt down in respect to Providence. He listened for a moment and his eyes widened and he gave Gracie a worried look.

"What's going on?" Louise whispered. "The oni are coming! We don't have time to stand around and talk!"

Conversation stopped again as everyone focused on her.

Louise squeaked in surprise. "What?"

Providence pointed a long clawed finger at her and then flicked it up, toward the gossamer.

Crow Boy bowed his head low and rose, scooping up Louise.

"Hey!" Louise cried as Joy leapt to Gracie's shoulder. "Wait! Are they going to move the babies?"

"Yes, they are." Crow Boy vaulted upwards, unfurling his great black wings. "We must be ready to leave as soon as they do."

Louise glanced back down at Gracie and gasped. The tengu woman blazed as if crafted from light. "What are they doing to her?"

"She agreed to be the babies' surrogate mother."

"She said she couldn't."

"They are making it so she can. Joy needed Providence's permission to use his dream crow."

A mote of light wafted from where the broken *nactka* sat to the gathering of dragons. It merged with Gracie.

Louise went limp in Crow Boy's arms as he winged upwards. It was done. For better or worse, the babies were on their way to becoming real.

46: ROCK-A-BYE BABY, ON A TREETOP

"I still say it's a little creepy," Jillian said sleepily.

Open warfare between the elves and oni had spilled into the streets of Pittsburgh. The tengu had allied with Alexander, hence the reference to "Tinker *domi*." Hours before the twins had stolen the gossamer, however, Alexander had gone into hiding. Until Alexander resurfaced, the tengu wanted to keep the girls and the babies safely hidden. So the twins were living with Gracie at the tengus' secret village.

Gracie had a little house, two hundred feet up a massive old ironwood tree. It was charming until the twins realized it had no Internet and its meager power came from a mix of tiny windmills and solar panels. There was no refrigerator or television or even electric lights.

After dark, they were only permitted elf shines that drifted about the room like fireflies. Enchanting, unless you actually wanted to see something. There wasn't much that they could do after dusk except talk and sleep.

Not that Louise really minded: the enforced rest was healing. Jillian stopped hiding behind masks and stated hard truths in her own voice.

And yes, their siblings' eggs were a little creepy.

They had been in the tengu village only a day before Gracie started to lay the four eggs. The eggs were a beautiful shade of sky blue with black speckles. They were also surprisingly large for having come out of petite Gracie Wong. Not that the twins *saw* the actual laying. They had been busy exploring the tengu village. While the twins delighted in the countless wide-scattered tree houses, the aerial gardens, and the cunningly hidden subterranean community baths and bakeries, Gracie laid the eggs, one at a time. They'd return from their explorations to find another egg had been added to the blanket-lined, temperature-controlled, nesting box until there were four.

And Louise was fine with that arrangement. She'd seen her own birth enough times—thanks to the video their parents had made—to know that the event was probably stressfully painful and icky. The twins really weren't up to experiencing that four times with a total stranger.

"How can we know it's really"—Jillian yawned deeply—"them?"

"It's them." Louise touched each lightly. "This is Green. This is Red. This is Nikola. And this is Chuck."

"Are you sure?"

"Yes, I'm sure." Completely. Totally. It was an amazing, wonderful feeling.

Jillian lay back on the floor beside the nesting box. "We should get a marker and write their initials on them. Little smiley faces. Except Chuck. She gets fangs or something."

"I wonder if they'll remember anything," Louise said.

"I hope they don't. I hope they forget it all. If nothing else, I think Chuck would be mad to find out that she can't pick her gender."

Louise laughed.

Joy appeared at the edge of the nesting box, a fabric bag clutched in her front paws. "Cookies!"

"What kind?" Louise took the bag and untied it. "Oh, awesome, rugelach!"

Jillian took one and tasted it. "Oh! These are super awesome rugelach."

They were probably the best ones Louise had ever tasted, pure buttery bliss in one mouthful.

"Nom, nom, nom." Joy stuffed one into her mouth. That she only took one meant that Miao the baker had probably given her several dozen in addition to the bag for the twins.

Jillian took three more, trying to make sure Joy didn't eat them all. "Why in the world are the tengu making Jewish cookies?"

"Because Miao learned to bake in Brooklyn." And Miao was super nice to them because they were Joy's Chosen and Tinker *domi*'s little sisters and the dream crow's foster children. And Louise had mentioned that rugelach were her favorite cookies. Obviously Miao was trying to make Louise happy.

After the indifference of Ming's staff, the small act of kindness was cathartic. It made Louise glad that the room was so dim, so Jillian wouldn't see the tears rolling down her cheeks. Jillian wouldn't understand that Louise now felt safe enough to cry.

Joy licked clean her paws and climbed in with the eggs to sleep. In a matter of minutes, she was stretched out on her back, front paws on her full belly, gently snoring.

Even though it was stiflingly hot next to the nesting box, the twins lay bracketing it and ate rugelach and whispered about nothing more important than what they would name their baby sisters. The elf shines drifted through the darkness like fireflies as the night wind gently rocked the house.